NEW YORK TIMES BESTSELLING AUTHOR
JULIA KENT

Love You Again

(Love You, Maine, Book 2)
by Julia Kent

Luke Luview has given up on love. Finally ready to let go of his late wife's clothes, the grieving small-town police officer and single dad thinks he's hearing things when he opens the charity box door. Who knocks from the *inside* of a donation bin?

The raccoon he assumes is in there turns out to be way prettier – and very familiar. Rescuing the first girl he ever kissed means life has dealt him a wild card with Kylie Hood, his late wife's best friend who left town suddenly fifteen years ago under a cloud of scandal.

When Kylie shows up at his house the next morning with a thank you gift and a dazzling smile just as his nanny quits on the spot, he is stuck.

And this time, Kylie rescues *him*.

Kylie Hood will never depend on a man again. Dumped by her boyfriend and fired by his parents from her children's programming job at their ski resort in rural Maine, she hits rock bottom while throwing out her ex's clothes — along with her phone and car keys.

Being rescued by Luke Luview, of all people, is a gift and a curse. The boy she once loved is now all grown up, everything her ex wasn't – and absolutely off limits.

Accepting his offer to be his temporary nanny while she job searches in New York City, Kylie falls hard for his sweet daughter, and even harder for Luke. A clause in her employment contract means they can't fraternize, but fate has other plans, and forbidden fruit is twice as sweet.

As the town she left reluctantly years ago accepts her more and more, and Luke makes it clear he wants a second chance with her in their close-knit community, Kylie has to decide: an exciting new career in Manhattan on her own, or an instant family and a sense of belonging in her small hometown?

And as Luke wrestles with the pain of being left behind by his wife's accidental death, he has to balance his responsibilities to his daughter with his own needs. Needs he's ignored for far too long.

Needs only Kylie can meet.

But not if she leaves.

Can Luke and Kylie rekindle their first love and find a new future together in a place where love conquers all?

If you're looking for a fun read about first kisses and second chances, featuring a hot single-dad police officer and his accidental nanny, set in a small town in New England, with a golden retriever named Jester, a heroine whose dream in life is to run a fairy camp, and a hero who wants to build a place where everyone belongs—then this is your book.

Grab a cup of coffee or tea, and maybe some edible glitter, and get your happy meter ready as you read the second book in the Love You, Maine, series—where love isn't just a feeling... it's a way of life.

Standalone
   Slow burn
   Single dad widower
   Nanny/police officer
   Second chance
   ... and a golden retriever named Jester

Chapter One

Kylie

It was the last time she ever had to deal with him.

At least, that's what she told herself.

"What am I doing?" she muttered. White puffs of condensation punctuated her words, the ice-cold night crisp and clear. Returning to western Maine after years of living in Indiana and New York had been a stark reminder of what *real* cold was like.

No snow tonight, at least, which made this easier.

Kylie could use a little *easier* in her life.

The black plastic trash bags mocked her, all six piled up in a mess in her hatchback. Her ex-boyfriend, Perry, had spent the last three months avoiding all her demands to come get his stuff, and it was finally time to act.

Being dumped in August by the guy she'd been in love with for seven years, and lived with for three, had been bad enough. Worse had been the way he'd done it: by phone.

From Thailand.

What was supposed to be a two-month work trip for him had turned into a meet cute that Kylie would find unbearably adorable if it had been anyone but her own *boyfriend*. The call

1

from Thailand had been unexpected, unbelievable, and life-altering.

"I–I know it sounds crazy, Ky, but Systina and I are–well, we're soulmates. Real ones. I can't explain it any more than that. Sometimes fate comes along and hits you like a lightning bolt, and this is one of those times. I have clarity now about who I am and how the rest of my life needs to be, and I'm so sorry. I really am."

Perry had sounded more excited dumping her than he ever had when he'd claimed to love her.

The call had lasted 7 minutes, 13 seconds.

Her phone said so.

Six years ended in 7 minutes, 13 seconds.

Poof.

Never once had Perry uttered the words *break up*. He just blathered on about soulmates, and Systina, and how she was Swedish royalty with a Nepalese father, and that they'd met at a youth hostel jazz performance, and how Kylie needed to help him close his bank accounts in the U.S., ship his various and sundry personal items to him in Thailand, and basically become his executive assistant, wrapping up his life with her in a neat little bow so he could go out into the big, wide world with his true lightning-bolt soulmate and leave her behind.

The sad part? Kylie had done it. Most of it, anyway.

Until the rage kicked in.

On autopilot, she'd felt a deep sense of ethical responsibility to not lash out and be unreasonable. To show she was a more evolved adult than Perry. For three months, she had collected his vital records from his desk and couriered them to him in Thailand. She'd shipped items to his sister in California, no small feat from their tiny town in Maine. Jo at the post office in Fixby Hills gave her sad, puppy dog eyes every time Kylie came in with yet another box or thick, padded envelope to ship.

And the gossip mill got another half hour of filler for the day.

Sometime in late October, though, she snapped out of it. She bagged up the rest of Perry's crap and called him and his sister with a single message:

"Come get the rest of your stuff. You have one month. Then I'm donating it to charity."

No reply from either.

Here it was, exactly one month and one day since that message. As a courtesy, she'd sent one final warning yesterday.

No reply.

Exorcising Perry from her physical life was a much-needed rite, one she'd prefer to perform with a sage stick, wine, and her sister, Wendy, but this was a decent substitute on Thanksgiving Day.

She was grateful to be done with Perry.

Tossing a hatchback's worth of his junk into a charity donation bin would be a great way to lose fifty pounds or so.

She patted her thighs.

Who was she kidding? After this, she'd go back to her apartment, eat the rest of the pumpkin pie she'd had for Thanksgiving dinner, cry, then watch *Elf*.

And laugh.

The thought made her smile as she reached for the first bag, an overstuffed monstrosity that puffed when she grabbed it, the scent of Perry's aftershave wafting up. Three months ago, she'd have sobbed, but now?

Now, she just saw red.

Deke's Service Station and Breakfast Diner was deserted but it would be bustling early with the five a.m. construction crowd, guys coming in for a fill-up, pack of ciggies, and some coffee from the counter. Maybe a nice fresh donut, or a packaged bear claw pastry. Perhaps a full breakfast if they had time, eggs and hash browns or pancakes all served with ruthless efficiency and wisecracks that only come from one local to another.

This time of night, though, it was creepily quiet, the new moon shining down like it was trying to protect her.

From what? Humiliation?

Too late.

Clutching the first big bag, she reached up for the donation bin's handle, a two-foot-wide bar that you pulled down to reveal an opening that the bags could be tossed into. It reminded her of returning library books, though she hated having that pleasant experience tainted by Perry and his whole "finding himself" experience in Thailand.

Oh, sure. He found himself, all right.

Found himself inside Systina the Wundersoulmate. Perry had never been an introspective guy, so she knew *exactly* what part of him he found "deep" inside Systina.

"Cathartic," she whispered. "This is going to be so cathartic."

As Kylie stood, holding the bar with one hand, the bag in the other, she pondered for a moment, then acted. Wedging her left elbow into the pull-down door to hold it open, she heaved the bag up to the door, hands on the broad side of it, and shoved.

Hard.

"FREE!" she called out. "I'm FREE OF YOU, PERRY!"

Except she pushed with a little too much force, a little too much gusto. Her car keys and phone apparently decided they, too, would be free.

In abject horror, Kylie watched them disappear into the steel container and tumble five feet down, swallowed by the dark, empty space. Her breath formed a white billow of anxiety as she screamed one word.

Like FREE, it started with the letter F.

Chapter Two

Luke

It was just a coat.

At least, that's what he told himself.

"You sure about this?" his sister Colleen asked yet again, her question making him grind his teeth. Thanksgiving dinner had been anything but traditional, the cartons of Chinese takeout still on the table.

No multi-generational gathering. No sprawling extended family. No football.

No turkey, no pumpkin pie, no mashed potatoes, no green bean casserole. No cranberry anything.

And especially no heart-shaped cakes.

His late wife, Amber, had died on Thanksgiving Day two years ago, and anything that reminded him of the holiday made his stomach turn.

General Tso's chicken and stir-fried rice, though, didn't.

Plus, it was his six-year-old daughter's favorite.

"Yes. Quit asking. You trying to undermine me?" he grunted at his sis, trying but failing to terminate the topic.

"I'm not." Colleen gave him a sad smile. The two of them

looked alike, just like their dad. Blond, blue eyes, dimpled cheeks, and ears they could wiggle without moving another muscle. Not that Colleen did that anymore, but she could when they were kids.

Their brothers, Dennis and Kell, looked like their mom. Dark hair, deep gray eyes with corners that turned down, laugh lines pushed up by apple cheeks when they smiled.

But Luke got the same-shaped eyes as his mom. Ah, family. A big genetic roll of the dice.

"Good. I've made up my mind. That bag haunts me."

"I think you're right. Two years, Luke."

"I know." He shrugged into his jacket, peeking out the window. Cold, clear, and even better, no snow. That would make this easier.

He needed easy.

"And you've wanted to do this for so long."

"Yep."

"And you really don't want to talk about it."

"Nope."

"DADDDDEEEEE!" Harriet launched herself into his arms, her face smeared with orange sauce. His little girl looked so much like her mother it pained him sometimes to watch her. "I want to go with you!"

"Can't, honey."

"You have to work? Have to go catch bad guys again?"

Harriet had learned recently in school what police officers do, and had connected the dots.

"Sometimes I catch bad guys, but I do a lot of other work, honey. Most of what I do is help good people."

"How do you know if they're good or bad?" she asked.

Colleen caught his eye and gave a nonverbal cue that asked that same question.

"They have a secret tattoo on the back of their neck that tells you," he said, pulling on one of his daughter's dark braids, the ends curly.

"They do?" Harriet immediately touched the back of hers. "Where is mine?"

Luke bent down and kissed that spot. "There. I just put one on you."

"A good one, right?"

"The good one was already there, sweetie."

"You were born with it!" Colleen chimed in, beginning to clean up their ever-so-fancy holiday meal. Oatmeal butterscotch cookies waited for dessert, but Luke's stomach was having none of that.

He had a job to do before he could come home and enjoy anything.

And the job didn't involve bad guys.

If only.

"How long will you be gone? Aunt Colleen says we're watching that funny movie with the big green man."

"*Elf*?"

"Yeah! The one we watched last week."

"You already saw it?"

"I want maple syrup on my s'getti next time, Daddy."

"Oh, you definitely already watched it." He bent down and planted a kiss on the top of her dark, curly head, the dark hair soft and wispy, but so much like Amber's. His own wavy blond hair, clipped close from a haircut two days ago, didn't show at all in his only child.

Harriet was one hundred percent her mother's daughter. Every day, it was like looking at a miniature Amber.

Which was a mixed blessing. The pain and the beauty mixed together—some days more pain, some days more beauty—made him feel oh, so human.

"Hate to say it, Luke, but I've got to be at work in ninety minutes. That enough time?" Colleen called out from the kitchen, the sound of efficient movement punctuating her words. His big sister had always been embedded in their lives, but even more so since Amber's passing. She practically lived with him and Harriet.

Actually *had* for two months after his wife's sudden death. All the way through that first horrific Christmas. His younger brother, Kell, and parents took plenty of shifts, too, but Colleen had stepped right in, taking over.

"More than enough time."

"You sure you–" Colleen bit her lips, clipping her own words. Already in scrubs for her nursing shift at the local emergency room, she held a crochet hook and a half-finished afghan square, a blend of the standard red, white, and pink that permeated everything in Luview, Maine. For the last few weeks, she'd been trying to teach Harriet.

Emphasis on *try*.

Harriet was more interested in baking than fiber arts.

He cut his sister a glare at the truncated question. It was sharper than he intended, but he couldn't help himself. Rolling his shoulders, he softened the look, then sighed.

"I am. I know it's irrational."

"Feelings usually are."

He made a disgruntled noise in the back of his throat, the kind he used to wrangle drunks at Bilbee's Tavern after closing, when they refused to call for a ride and badgered poor Edina at the bar to give them their keys.

Or a ride.

And not the kind you take in a car.

"That sound doesn't work on me," Colleen said with a snort.

Dang.

"Works fine on Spud."

"Spud is a seventy-eight-year-old Vietnam vet in love with a bottle."

"Your point?"

"You need different techniques when you're helping *good* people." She smacked his arm and he couldn't help but laugh. Being a small-town police officer meant creating lots of emotional walls to do the most basic elements of his job.

Being a daddy to a sweet, loving little girl who wanted nothing more than her mommy every waking moment meant those walls had to come up and down in ways that were dizzying.

Shifting from one emotional state to another took a level of effort that drained him.

Earlier today, they'd visited Amber's grave, Harriet's tears harder to manage than his own. When she'd asked Luke whether she could ever be good enough to get Mommy to come back, he'd damn near lost his mind. How do you answer that?

You don't. He just held her and told her how much her mother loved her.

Driving around the center of his hometown, the touristy Luview, Maine–aka Love You, Maine–the town where every day is Valentine's Day–had been an exercise in restraint. The last thing he needed was to be love bombed by romantic love when all he felt was the absence of it.

Living in a heart-shaped world was nearly impossible when your own heart had been ripped out by a cruel twist of fate.

Rituals completed, they'd come home, watched TV with Colleen, and ordered takeout. His sister wouldn't leave them on this day; his brother Kell was in L.A. with his girlfriend, Rachel, visiting her family. Their older brother was stationed in Germany, a FaceTime away, with Mom and Dad. They'd decided to visit Dennis when cheap plane tickets became available.

They'd been his rock two years ago, always there whenever he needed them.

And he'd needed them, all right.

Everyone knew Luke didn't want to celebrate Thanksgiving anyhow, so it was better this way.

"The only good people I'm going to meet on this errand are stray dogs and squirrels," he announced as he reached for the small bag, working hard not to look at it. Amber's special red poncho, the rest of her outfit, and the clothes he'd been wearing the day she died were inside.

He was going to donate them. Wanted to burn them, but it felt wrong somehow. Donation made more sense. Let someone in the world benefit.

Pain was easier to bear if it had a function. A purpose.

The plan was simple: drive half an hour away to an old gas station in Fixby Hills, where no one would see him. The donation bin there was for some charity that would take the items down to Manchester, New Hampshire.

He'd never see the coat again.

Which was the entire point of this strange exercise.

"Don't use your grumpy sound on the animals," Colleen teased.

He harrumphed loudly.

They shared a laugh.

And then Luke walked out to his personal vehicle, a black Jeep parked next to his pink police car, and marveled at the clear night, his breath a silent white message that rose up and disappeared into the ether, as if it didn't quite make it to heaven.

"Amber," he murmured before climbing in. "I'm doing the best I can. But this is so, so hard."

He climbed in. Started the engine. Pressed his lips together.

And backed out of his driveway, determined.

Determined to unstick himself from this place where he couldn't move forward.

He was stuck. Stuck by grief. Stuck by circumstance.

And it was time to set part of him free.

Chapter Three

Kylie

That didn't happen.
That did not happen.
This wasn't real.
This couldn't be happening.

The words looped through her mind, but no matter how intently she thought them, reality didn't change.

Standing on tiptoe, Kylie pulled the handle down again and peered into the bin, eyes straining. The bright moon behind her caught the glint of metal from the carabiner clip of her keychain, and a little sliver of her phone's glass face. The screen was still on, the glow of her open Candy Crush app mocking her, the light just enough to illuminate her keychain.

On top of black plastic trash bags, a good five feet down and a million miles away, her keys and phone smiled up at her as if to say, *"How you doing?"*

"I CANNOT BELIEVE THIS!!" she screamed, letting the door slam shut with a thud that echoed in the dark night. Something in the woods, about twenty feet away, skittered.

She froze in place, body tingling with fear.

Taking stock of her surroundings, she gathered her coat tight around her, pulling her long, loose hair out from its confines at the neckline around the hood. She was shivering as much from fear as cold, heart racing so fast it surely made her blood boil enough to shake off the chill.

The sound of her breath in her ears was a kind of torture. The truth was sinking in second by second, her eyes going wide, the cold making her corneas sting, her ears ring, and her feet go numb.

Not from the temperature, either.

"I'm stuck," she whispered, breath warming her nose, which instantly chilled again when she inhaled. "Stuck! What was I thinking?" she groaned, running through the last few minutes in her mind. Holding the keys and phone in her hand was second nature. It was how she made sure she didn't lock them in the car.

And she hadn't.

Hah.

Looking at the country road, she listened for the sound of a passing car. None had come by in the ten minutes she'd been here. That had been the point, right?

It was late on Thanksgiving evening. No one was driving anywhere. People were beached whales, eating their third piece of homemade pumpkin pie in a state of extreme self-loathing. Drive somewhere? Not in a food coma.

Privacy. She'd wanted *privacy*.

"I've got plenty of privacy," she muttered, starting to pace. "I'm all alone. Just what I wanted, huh? Thanks, Perry!"

Think, think, think.

How could she get herself out of this?

She took a few steps back from the bin and found herself next to the driver's side door. With a trembling hand, she lifted the car door handle. It opened.

Whew! She could climb in and stay warm, which she did.

And promptly realized there was no way to use the heater.

Her sister had chided her for years for not having an emergency kit in her car, so now she had one. It was for broken car parts, flat tires, getting stuck in snowstorms.

Not for being stupid. If some company made a kit for that, they'd earn billions.

"THIS IS ALL PERRY'S FAULT!" Kylie shouted, banging the steering wheel, the tears hitting her fast and ugly. It was true. If he hadn't been such a jerk, if he hadn't dumped her for a woman whose name was a freaking poetry format spelled wrong, if he had figured out how to get his stuff, if he'd just been a decent human being and loved her back, she wouldn't have accidentally thrown her car keys and phone into a donation drop bin and been stranded in the cold on Thanksgiving night in the middle of nowhere.

This was *definitely* Perry's fault.

But even he couldn't save her.

Not that the rat bastard would. The guy wouldn't even bother to rescue his old concert t-shirts, much less his ex-girlfriend.

Heart thumping like a djembe drum in expert hands, she took deep breaths, working hard to calm herself. "You're safe," she lied into the night, hoping the words would reach a piece of her she couldn't easily access. "You have a car. No one can get you."

Locking the doors was easy, even without keys. She was at a service station with a breakfast diner attached. It would open in nine or ten hours.

Her shoulders relaxed a centimeter. She was safe.

It might be a cold night, but she wouldn't be mauled by a bear.

The thought made her laugh, then start to cry, the seconds ticking by in that unique way loneliness marks time. For the next five minutes, she cried.

And cried.

And cried so hard, it was as if her tear ducts thought that if they worked hard enough, she could conjure her car keys and phone.

Alas, she wasn't capable of that kind of magic.

"If fairies are real, now's the time to show yourself," she said aloud to no one, everyone, opening her swollen eyes slowly in case, well...

You never know, right?

Cold silence and the scent of her own humid breath against the shock of cold was all she got.

She was stuck.

Really stuck.

Her sister, Wendy, was back at their apartment, finishing her packing. On Saturday, Wendy was all wrapped up with Maine. She'd moved in with Kylie after Perry dumped her and stayed longer than the planned month, but her paperwork had finally come through. She was going to work as an au pair for a wealthy family in the South of France.

"Paris at Christmas," was all she muttered these days, starry-eyed. "You should become an au pair, too, Kylie!"

Wendy was eight years younger, fresh out of community college and ready to travel.

But Kylie wanted roots, not wings.

"Ha," she huffed into the night. "I want to set down roots somewhere? Guess I just did. I am *sooooo* stuck."

Cold seeped into the tips of her toes the way only a frigid night in northern New England really can. Born and raised here, she'd left at fifteen, when The Divorce happened.

And yes, she thought of it with capitals. Their parents had split in the most angry, bitter way possible, her mom announcing the day after their last day at summer camp the August before her sophomore year of high school that they were moving.

To Indiana.

When she'd met Perry seven years ago, in their final year of college, it had been fate. Or so she'd thought. Because Perry's family ran a chain of successful ski resorts, and one of them was 45 minutes away from where she'd grown up, in Luview, Maine. The place where love wasn't just a feeling.

It was an industry.

Luview, Maine–cutely pronounced Love You–turned love into a vacation destination, and romance into an income stream. While that sounded cynical, it was true. Founded in the late nineteenth century by Abram and Adelaide Luview, a couple who went for a swim in the local hot springs and fell in love, over time the legend spread. By the early twenty-first century, there was no part of Love You, Maine that didn't involve hearts, love, or the colors red, white, and pink.

Including the pink police cars. Fire engines were already red.

Love You Coffee had heart-shaped mugs and nothing they served was round or square. If you wanted a bagel, it was a heart. Cupcake? A heart.

Plates? Take a wild guess.

Almost every restaurant was tied into the theme, and so was nearly every flower shop, antique store, movie theater, and more. Home to the world's largest romance novel bookstore, Love You, Maine, was a place to find love, fall in love, or fall in love again.

And it was Kylie's hometown.

Perry's family, though... they didn't buy into any of it. His family's company, Nordicbeth Resorts, which ran a number of ski areas, was a behemoth in northern New England. Tiny Love You was just an afterthought to a corporation like that.

Last year, they'd hired her to manage children's programming for their resorts. Perry hated the idea of moving up here. He loved life in New York City, where they'd gone to college, but a hefty promotion for him and a full-time, on-site job working with kids for her was a perfect step forward in their life together.

Until Systina the Ubershag crossed Perry's path.

Six months ago, they'd moved here. Busy with life and work that first month, she hadn't bothered to go to her old hometown. Then Perry went on his trip to Thailand.

And never came back.

Too humiliated to do anything but work or stay home, she'd lived in a rut until three weeks ago.

When she was downsized.

Yeah, *downsized*.

Which meant she'd essentially been fired.

She knew this was all his fault. Perry never did like loose ends.

And speaking of those...

Turning around, she grabbed one of the bags from the back of the hatchback and hauled it forward, doing the same with the other four until she was surrounded by Perry's old crap.

It kept her warm. His clothes were more affectionate and loving than he ever was.

The thought made her cry harder, the plastic heating up as she breathed against it, until condensation chilled her cheek.

She couldn't see the time because she had no phone and couldn't turn on the car.

And her feet were starting to get so cold, soon she wouldn't feel them.

Headlights flashed in her rearview mirror, forcing her to shove the bags off her and open the door, her body tumbling out like a pretzel on its side, one hand pressed to the ground so she didn't land on her knee. Scrambling to her feet, she slammed the car door shut and ran to the road, waving wildly.

"HELP! STOP! HELP!" she screamed, but the car was already gone, turning right onto another road so far away, she couldn't see it from here.

Shivering, she jogged back to her car and reached for the handle.

It didn't budge.

Rattling it hard, she willed it to open.

And then she saw that one of the bags had rolled against the door's locking mechanism. The weight of Perry's unclaimed crap must have pressed the lock button. His battery toothbrush poked through the plastic trash bag, spinning away.

Mocking her.

"AHHHHHHHHHHHHHHHHHHHH!" she screamed, primal and feral, horrified and outright livid. Adrenaline rushed through her, warming her body through sheer will and fury alone, but that wouldn't last long.

And late November in the mountains of Maine meant she had to find warmth.

The wall of glass surrounding the office at Deke's Service Station and Breakfast Diner looked vulnerable. Scanning the ground, she found some cinder blocks dotting the snow-covered ground on either side of the donation box.

One throw and the glass would shatter. The building had to be warmer than out here. Plus, she'd set off an alarm and the police would come.

And then she'd be rescued.

Or... booked and charged with a crime, her mug shot all over the local news, Perry's parents aghast, her arrest permanently on her record, banning her from ever working with children again.

Wait. No. Bad plan.

Bad, bad plan.

Bending down, she looked under the car. It would shield her from the wind, but nothing else.

And a determined animal could gnaw on her leg easily.

The road itself wasn't an option. The nearest house was easily a few miles away, which meant walking on a snow-covered road in late November in Maine, in the dark. Either a band of coyotes would get her, or a plow truck would clip her before she'd reach civilization.

Hmm. What about a friendly coyote? A loner. They were warm, right? Maybe she could befriend one and snuggle with it under the car.

Good grief. Now she'd really lost it.

She had no choice.

Turning slowly, she eyed the donation box. Of average height and maybe slightly-above-average weight, she could do it.

"I have to climb in," she choked out, her only witnesses a few squirrels in the woods.

At least, she *hoped* those were squirrels she heard.

Fisher cats were mean little buggers. Foxes weren't fun, either, and a pack of coyotes or wolves could even kill if they wanted to.

She was unarmed, unprotected, and increasingly unhinged.

Think, think, think, she told herself, staring at the lever for the steel bin. It was chest height on her. When she'd pulled into the parking lot, she'd parked near the donation box but not right in front of it, so she had to find a way to get herself up about two feet, balance her body, and climb in.

Climb in.

Hysterical laughter poured out of her, the sound wobbly as she shivered, her ribs tightening as her muscles contracted and tried to keep her warm.

"Ew. What if there's an animal in there?" she said aloud, because why not talk to herself at this point?

She was a stupid crazy lady who threw her keys and phone in a charity bin.

"I'll climb in, find my keys and phone, stack the stuff inside in a big pile, climb up it, and wiggle back out. That's the plan, Kylie."

Eyeing the box, she wondered if she was too short to climb out. What if there wasn't as much stuff in there as she'd thought? What if the door worked in a weird way and you could get in but couldn't get out? Strategy demanded that she think these things through, even as her calves turned into slabs of frozen meat worthy of display at the local butcher shop.

Fate wasn't handing her any real choices, was it?

Over by the gas station's air pump, she spotted more concrete cinder blocks, a few broken but four or five intact. By the time she stacked four cinder blocks in a pile that was frighteningly unstable but sturdy enough to do the job, her fingers were bright red. She knew she'd have burning pain later as they warmed, but she'd left her gloves at home, a terrible decision that brought a heaping dose of shame for a woman born and raised in New England.

Standing on top of the pile, she grabbed the handle, pulled down, and stared into the abyss.

The abyss looked back.

"Hello?" she called into the space, as if a troll lurked inside, waiting to ask her the password.

Nothing replied.

Ears perked, she listened for scuffling noises that might indicate feral inhabitants.

Again, nothing.

A sliver of moonlight shone from behind her, illuminating the curve of the carabiner clip on her keychain. She knew her phone must be nearby, hidden among a few small boxes, loose clothing of all description, loads of white kitchen-size trash bags, some re-used department store bags, overstuffed black utility bags, and what looked like a very broken plastic tricycle.

Her nose was cold, but not so cold that it was numb to the odor.

Oh, man.

Kylie had lived in New York City. She had wandered down back alleys after nightclub trips where she had some instant regrets and some that stretched on for days, but nothing compared to the smell in there.

It smelled like her own foolishness.

"There has to be another way," she murmured, but deep in her heart, she knew there wasn't.

Wendy was back at the apartment, half an hour away, sitting on a beanbag chair, triple-checking her flight from Manchester to New York City to Paris and working hard to bring her checked bag down to the 23 kilogram weight limit. How many scarves did she really need?

A new round of frigid shivering made Kylie envy all those scarves, which she would put to good use if she had them.

Suddenly, the yowls of a pack of fighting dogs cut through the relative quiet of the woods behind the gas station. Yipping and howling, the noise assumed a condensed quality, like someone took twenty dogs and crammed them into five.

Some of them sounded like they were in pain.

And close.

Too close.

"Coyotes? Foxes? Wolves?" she gasped, looking up at the sky as if chastising God. "Really? This isn't bad enough?"

The dog sounds died down, then ratcheted up again, louder.

Closer.

Standing on tiptoes, she faltered, palm scraping against a metal edge, hard enough to nearly pierce her skin. She wobbled because she couldn't feel her toes. They were *that* cold. If she didn't do something soon, she wouldn't even have the choice to climb in the bin.

Better do it now, while she could.

Just like that, she went from one choice to none.

Cold metal cut into her ribs as she leaned in and assessed the situation, the delicate balance of the levered door making her see the folly of her balance. If she went in face down, head first, and the door closed on her, she could cut herself off at the knees. When it was pulled down, the metal door formed a shelf, wide enough for three large trash bags. Turning around carefully, she used her hands to boost herself up so that she was sitting on the door, legs dangling in front of her. Then she pulled her legs up and curled herself like a kid hiding in a kitchen cabinet during hide-and-seek.

How would she tip herself in?

Unable to look inside, she had to rely on memory. She tried to imagine soft bags of clothing donations in there, ready to break her fall, soft and welcoming, like a mother's arms should be.

"AAAAOOOoooooooooo!" howled the pack, scaring her so abruptly that she pitched to the left, her shoulder pushing hard, and down she went. The loud clang of the door slamming shut was buried by pure panic as she tipped in, falling and landing in a *whuff!* of stale dryer sheets, faint mildew, moth balls, and something rotten.

It was pitch dark.

Hip screaming from the fall, she closed her eyes and took a couple of shallow breaths, rot assaulting her senses. Aside from the hip, she'd banged up her right shoulder, and a stinging sensation ran along the small of her back, where she'd scratched against something.

Good thing she'd gotten that tetanus booster two years ago.

But she was in, and she was warmer, and her hand brushed against something that jingled.

"KEYS!" she shouted, pawing for them, wishing her hand had touched her phone first. That, unlike her key ring, had a flashlight. Fingertips brushing against metal that clinked, she grabbed the keys and–

Huh.

Not keys.

"HANDCUFFS?" she gasped, feeling in the dark, a feather-like material making her drop the handcuffs instantly. They clinked against something. Instinct made her search, and thank goodness, because she found her phone.

Lumbering up on her knees, phone clutched in her hand, she swiped up, then hit the flashlight icon.

"LIGHT!" Her breath was a hot, humid cluster of air that made her feel warmer.

But illuminating the inside of this metal box didn't help matters much.

It was as scary and stinky as she'd worried. Her landing had ripped open black and white trash bags, the half-broken, smelly donations a testament to the carelessness of the average person.

Because they didn't care. Not one bit.

"Wendy, please answer," she whispered as she went to her contacts, hit the name Wendy, and—

Call failed.

"What?"

She tried again.

Call failed.

And that's when she saw the two most feared words on the planet:

No and *Signal*.

Right there, in the upper corner of her phone where the cell data bars belonged.

"No *signal?*" she screamed. "NO SIGNAL???"

Holding the phone up, she knee-walked to one corner of the bin.

No Signal.

The next corner—

No Signal.

The third?

Same.

The fourth was an exercise in futility, but she was a masochist and tried anyhow, the two words mocking her.

Standing on tiptoes, she managed to push the hinged door open a couple of inches. Maybe, if she held the phone up high, she could—

No.

Just... no signal.

Slumping to the center of the box, she muttered one profanity after another, until she sounded like a chicken.

"I had a signal in the car!" Looking at the wall, her high school physics raced through her mind. Was the metal blocking the signal? Had she accidentally put herself in a Faraday cage?

That wouldn't be a problem when she got outside. Just had to find her keys, climb back out, and she'd be fine.

The keys weren't hard to locate once she had the flashlight, and as she clutched both in her hands, she swore she'd never let them go, ever, again.

Superglue would be used if needed.

Climbing up a mound of bags, she reached for the top edge of the metal door.

Too short.

Panic hit hard as she looked around, the evidence clear. Eight plastic bags, one of them full of Perry's belongings, two small cardboard boxes, and three brown paper bags stuffed with plastic stuff were it.

And the donation bin was eight feet high.

Of all the luck to climb in when the bin was relatively empty. Why hadn't she thrown all of Perry's useless belongings in first, then lost her keys and phone?

If she'd done that, the bags couldn't have locked her out of her car.

There you had it: another way this was all Perry's fault.

Piling everything into the tallest tower possible, she reached on tippy toe, barely able to push the door open an inch. It was easier on the outside because there was a handle to pull down.

Losing her footing, she felt backwards, shoulder slamming into the cold, hard metal side, her head narrowly escaping a bang.

In the distance, the coyotes howled again, perhaps fueled by her noises, or maybe just mating once more.

Joining in their screams, Kylie howled, too.

But the sound just echoed back on her.

She was stuck.

And it was entirely her fault.

Chapter Four

Luke

Deke's Service Station was rusting from the inside out.

Not the cars parked all around, though, half of them waiting for repair, the other half just waiting.

Maybe for a meteor to hit.

The place was a little bit of everything up here in the mountains: gas station, convenience store, diner, coffee shop, auto repair, and in a pinch, Deke could officiate at a wedding and notarize a mortgage refi.

Small town life meant being a Jack of All Trades.

Luke was a police officer, occasionally worked security for big events in Manchester, was on staff at the summer camp before it closed two years ago, and acted as a ref for soccer tournaments in a pinch. A fourteen-week bartending course in college gave him that skill, too, and after EMT certification, he'd even gotten his phlebotomist's certificate to help with Red Cross blood banks.

He could do everything but cheat death.

Give him enough time, and he might succeed.

But not soon enough for his late wife.

The bag next to him on the front seat of his car held exactly sixteen articles of clothing: two pairs of socks, two pairs of underwear, two shirts, two pairs of pants, two pairs of shoes, one standard-issue red leather Luview police officer's jacket, and a big, red, fleece-lined rain poncho. Amber had worn that poncho for years, loving to go on long walks in the rain, one of the many quirks he'd adored about her.

Until it, and a gentle old man having a heart attack at the worst possible moment ever, had led to her death.

All sixteen articles of clothing had been on Luke's or Amber's body the day he'd found her.

By accident.

Training Jude DiPalma that day had meant driving him around the county, pointing out the basics, the new cop as green as a freshly cut maple tree. Twenty-one then and unable to grow a mustache, Jude needed to be cut, chopped, stacked, and seasoned before he could be unleashed on the citizens of Cambridge County, Maine.

And Jude got one hell of a first-day crisis.

In the form of Luke's dead wife.

The shock of red laying in a ditch was bad enough, freakishly beautiful against the fresh white snow, but some piece of Luke knew, before his mind could even form the thought, that it was Amber. Thanksgiving Day had been a rainy one, and the car smashed into the tree next to her let off a terrible sound, like a dying loon, as the horn malfunctioned.

The sound was so loud, it cut through time.

"Just feel it," he muttered aloud in the present. The words were forced and halting but he said them anyhow, just like he trudged through whatever life threw his way. It was who he was, steady, reliable, and unflinchingly grounded in reality.

Until reality cracked in two.

The grief specialist he and Harriet saw for months after the accident told him that experiencing emotions in the moment was how to get through the mourning, stressing that then-four-year-old Harriet would be confused.

"Children are masters at feeling emotions in the present. They haven't learned to tamp them down yet. Let her express what she needs to and just be there with her. It's enough to hold her. You don't have to have all the answers. Your presence and love are the answer," Maura Kirkendaal had stressed. She was still a constant in their lives, though he'd left counseling a year ago.

Harriet really was a pro at processing her emotions.

Luke? Not so much.

A white puff of air filled the space between him and the steering wheel, and he realized he'd sighed. How long had he been sitting here, mind and memory in the past? Shoving his hands into gloves, he opened the rear door, grabbed the white plastic bag, and made his way to the front of the bin.

Determined, focused, and grim: That was Luke Luview these days. A bad match for a town that existed to make people feel good about love.

Living in Love You, Maine–heck, *being* a Luview–was never harder than when you had a broken heart.

Time to let go of some of the pain.

"AAAAAAoooooooooo," called out a band of coyotes in the distance, making Luke jolt. His personal weapon was at home. He didn't carry it in the glove compartment or on his body when he was off duty, but as the coyote population grew in the area, maybe he should.

A few feet from the donation bin's front, he looked at the lever to pull down, squeezing the bag slightly. A whiff of Amber's perfume caught his nose, so faint he almost imagined it.

Colleen had washed all the clothes a few weeks ago, so he knew he imagined Amber's scent. Didn't matter. He'd take the illusion. That was how much he hurt.

A skitter inside the box made him frown.

Damn animals. They got in those bins all the time. He felt sorry for the poor sap who emptied these metal boxes, carting all the goods to the warehouse in Manchester where they cleaned and sorted, getting it all ready for the second-hand retail stores.

Just do this, he thought, swallowing hard as the coyotes mated in the distance. The sound was violent and creepy, but for whatever reason, it felt fitting.

Throwing the tangible reminders of that terrible day into the donation box felt dangerous, too.

"I love you, Amber," he murmured. "But I have to let you go.

25

Have to let that day go. Harriet needs a daddy who isn't tied down by grief. Just because I'm doing this doesn't mean I love you any less, though."

Tears pricked his eyes. "Why is this so hard? Because it's hard," he said with a huff. "That's what you would say if you were here. You'd hug me and comfort me and tell me feelings are meant to be felt or they'd be called something else. You'd have all the right words. I don't have any. I just have a big hole in my life, Amber. And you're never going to fill it. Colleen says I can't feel guilty for moving on. I don't. But I sure do feel weird."

And then he reached for the handle, pulled it down, and threw the bag in while calling out loudly, "I love you."

To his utter shock, she replied from the darkness of the box, "I'm in here!"

Chapter Five

Kylie

"I'm in here!"

The words came out with no rhyme or reason. "Help!" seemed too extreme to spring on someone, even if it was what she needed most. But the warning that a human was inside the bin seemed smart.

"Amber?" a man's voice shouted, sharp and urgent.

"What? No! My name is Kylie. KY-LEE!" she screamed, as if enunciating would help.

Silence.

Too much silence.

"HELLO? DON'T LEAVE! HELP!"

"What are you doing in there?" the guy shouted, louder this time.

"Oh! Oh! Thank you!! Someone *is* there. Help! Help me!" Banging on the side of the box, as if that would help, she hit hard enough to groan, her knuckles ringing in pain.

"Cut that out! You'll hurt yourself."

A loud, grumbly groan was unmistakable, the sound setting

off all the anger inside that she had suppressed for the last three months.

And then the hinged door creaked open, cold air blowing in. A head appeared, eyes dark in the shadows.

"What did you say your name is?" he asked sharply, as if he expected compliance.

"Kylie."

"How long have you been living in there?"

Living?

"I just got stuck! Maybe a half hour ago?"

"You know these aren't good places to sleep."

"Why would I want to sleep in here?"

Silence.

Bang bang bang

The hard knock to her left made her jump.

"Anyone else in there with you?"

"What?"

"Are you in there with a man?"

"Why would I be in here with a man?"

"Or a woman?"

"WHAT?"

"Ma'am, I am not one to judge, but plenty of people use these donation bins for less than legal reasons, so I have to ask: Are you in there with a john?"

"Who is John?" she squeaked.

He cleared his throat with meaning. "A john. You know. A paying customer."

Horror washed over Kylie as she realized what he was implying.

No. Not implying.

Outright *saying*.

"YOU THINK I AM A PROSTITUTE?" she bellowed, mustering every ounce of diaphragmatic energy to unleash whatever demons resided inside her vocal cords.

"I'm not judging, ma'am."

"Yes, you are!"

"No, ma'am. Just assessing the situation. Gathering facts. Determining my course of action. Bins like this are a lot cheaper than motels, and none of the bed and breakfasts in Luview will rent by the hour, so..."

He let out the kind of sigh that took Kylie's anger from a ten to a fourteen.

"You *are* judging! Don't you sigh like that at me!"

"Like what?"

"Like I'm a problem!"

Silence.

"Well, Kylie... you said your name is Kylie?"

"Yes."

A chuckle floated through the open door as she looked up, trying to see his face. "You *are* a problem. You're stuck inside a donation bin. By definition, that's a problem."

"Excuse me?"

"You. Are. A. Problem," he said slowly.

Loudly.

"HEY!"

"Truth hurts."

She threw a donated high-heeled shoe at his face. Guy had quick reflexes. It missed.

"CUT THAT OUT! I'm a police officer. I could charge you for assaulting an officer."

"You're a jerk!"

Hold on.

Police?

"And you're trespassing."

"*Trespassing?* I fell in! How can I be trespassing?"

"You could be arrested for stealing."

"Stealing *what?* Banana hooks and old food dehydrators? Come on." She squinted, looking up at his shadowed face. "And if you're really a police officer, show me a badge."

"I don't have one on me."

"HAH! Then you're lying."

Suddenly, she was glad she was stuck in here, safe from him.

Wait.

If the guy wanted to, he could climb in with her. So much for safety.

"Not lying." He paused. "What's your last name, Kylie?"

"Tell me your name first."

"Luke. Luke Luview."

She damn near swallowed her tongue.

A tongue he'd touched once.

With his own.

"Luke? *The* Luke?"

A robust chuckle filled the air. "Don't know that I've ever been called *the* Luke before. Have we met?"

A sharp inhale made her nostrils nearly freeze shut.

He didn't remember.

For some reason, that made her even more furious.

"My name is Kylie Hood. Do you need ID? It's in my car. I am not a PROSTITUTE!"

"Kylie—wait. Kylie *Hood?*" Half his head came through just as she shone her flashlight right in his face, making him wince.

It really was him.

Luke Luview.

The first boy she'd ever kissed.

"Um, hi." Waving like an idiot, she smiled.

"'Um, hi?' The first time I've seen you in fifteen years, you're hiding in a donation box and looking up at me like a rabid raccoon and your first words are '*Um, hi?*'"

"My first words, technically, were 'I'm in here!'" she said primly.

"Don't get pedantic."

"Don't get all domineering!"

"I'm a law enforcement officer. It's in my job description."

She sniffed. "If you're going to play that game, then being pedantic is in *my* job description. I'm a licensed teacher!"

"For someone who is entrusted with our vulnerable youth, you're not instilling much confidence."

"HEY!"

"How the hell did you get in there, Kylie?"

"I was bored, Luke. Thought I'd find something to do around here other than tapping maples and tipping cows."

"You succeeded."

He peered in, shielding his eyes. Luke's face was broader and stronger than the last time she saw him, the beginnings of five o'clock scruff on his cheeks and chin. Same bright blue eyes, same blond, wavy hair, though it was cut with a military-like precision that aligned with his claims of being a police officer.

Luke Luview was a *cop*.

All she could see of him was his head and an arm, but she suspected the rest was just as fine.

"Could you help me get out of here?" she begged.

"Of course. What'd you think I'd do? Leave you to rot?"

Her only answer was a series of loud laughs that bordered on hysterical crying, but somehow, she reined that in.

"Let me call the station. They'll send someone out to help."

"NO!"

Confusion radiated back at her from his voice, the tilt of his head. "You... don't want help?"

"Can't you just do it? Without letting anyone know? It's embarrassing enough, but you know how Luview is. I'll be a laughingstock for the next three months. Especially if Nadine Khouri still lives here. She was the biggest gossip in town when I was a kid."

Amusement filled his voice. "Still is. And I work with her every day at the station."

Kylie gasped. Right. Every town had its tongue-wagging supergossip, and Nadine was it. Kylie had forgotten that Nadine worked as administrative support at the police station, the best job *ever* for knowing all the dirt in a tiny town.

"That's right," was all Kylie could mutter.

"Why would you care? You don't live here." He frowned. "Don't you live in Indiana? How did you get in here?"

"I teleported. Touched the wrong standing stone and *poof!* I was in here."

"Hah." His smile was gracious and genuine, showing those Luview dimples. "You always were funny."

"I was?"

"You were. And creative. Geez, Kylie. This is..."

"Weird."

"Yep."

31

This time, his groan didn't sound like he was being annoyed at Kylie. It sounded like he was fighting with himself.

"I should put this on the official record, but I can get you out myself."

"How? I'm too short to make it up to the door."

"I'll get you out the side door."

"THERE'S A SIDE DOOR?"

That rumbling laugh sent goosebumps across her cold skin.

"Yeah. It's padlocked from the outside, though. Have to go home and get my bolt cutters from my work car."

"Oh."

"I'm thirty minutes away, so it'll be an hour. You'll have to wait it out here. You have food? Water?"

"Sure, Luke. I packed a picnic basket and everything. Enjoying my merlot and sheep's milk gouda from the Netherlands in here."

She got silence in response, the top door slamming shut.

Dang. Should have kept her sarcasm to herself. Now she'd gone and done it.

The door creaked open again.

"Incoming!"

A granola bar thwacked her between the eyes. Reflexively, she ducked, a bottled water plunking on the bagged donations to her right.

Luke's head appeared in the opening again. "That should hold you until I can get back."

Then he shut the door.

Her stomach roared in appreciation, but her body was hit with pure panic, like anxiety turned to buckshot.

"Don't leave me!" She banged on the wall. Her vision narrowed, heartbeat in her ears, sense of impending doom overtaking her.

Oh, no.

Not a panic attack. Even Perry leaving her hadn't triggered one of these.

"I have to leave. Can't get you out without tools," he shouted, the sound muffled, growing weaker by the second as her ears began to ring.

"Help," she whispered, knowing he couldn't hear her.

Breathe, she told herself.

You're not dying.

You're not.

It just feels like you are.

"Kylie?" he knocked gently.

She wanted to answer, but her lungs and vocal cords seemed to have relocated to another planet.

"Kylie." Luke's voice changed, firm and commanding. "Say something."

I can't, she thought, opening and closing her mouth like a fish, her breath erratic.

The pull-down door opened, Luke's flashlight shining in.

"What's wrong?"

She shook her head.

"Panic attack?"

She nodded.

His tone changed instantly. "Can you stand up?"

She shook her head.

"Stand up, Kylie."

She shook her head again. Didn't he hear her?

Wait. How could he hear her? She couldn't speak.

"I said, *stand up.*"

Something about his voice felt like an order she couldn't disobey. She stood, legs like overcooked calamari.

"Reach one hand up for mine," he commanded.

His bare hand was inside the box. Doing as told, she felt his warm grasp calm her instantly. It didn't neutralize the panic, but took it down a notch.

Any relief was better than none.

Normally, she'd be humiliated beyond belief to have someone witness her panic attack, but she was already so embarrassed, she really couldn't go a whole lot lower.

"Lots of people have these attacks," he assured her. "You'll be fine. It's normal to freak out. Want me to breathe with you?"

She squeezed his hand, grateful for the touch.

"No," she croaked out. A long, shuddering breath came next, her shoulders starting to drop a little. "No."

"I'm here. Not leaving until you're fine. I'm *here*, Kylie. You're safe with me. You're safe. You're always safe with me."

The trembling began then, a telltale sign the panic attack was ending. Long ago, a doctor explained why this happened, something about hormones and adrenaline, cortisol and enzymes, but she was a human development major, not an expert on biochemistry.

She just recognized it as a stage. A positive one.

A sign that this betrayal of the body and mind would end.

"Your hands are icicles." He squeezed, gently but over and over, trying to help get blood flowing, she knew. "Are you in danger of hypothermia?"

"I'm warm," she finally said, teeth rattling. "It's stress. Panic. Not t-t-emperature." Talking was like walking through a landmine field, only words and thoughts were the dangerous explosives.

"You're good. We've got all the time in the world. Not leaving until you're ready."

And yet, the sooner he left, the sooner he could get her out of here.

Too bad her stupid autonomic nervous system didn't understand rational, linear thought.

His hand, though. Warm and caring, the skin of his fingers worn and thick. This was the hand of a man who did hard work. It anchored her to the world, made her feel less fear, connected her to someone who cared. He cared with his touch. Luke made her feel seen.

Other than Wendy, who cared about her, anyhow?

Mom, a little. Dad, less.

Perry?

No. He was the reason she was here.

As her mind wandered, Luke squeezing her hand with a compassionate, steady, determined rhythm, she did one final shake, like a dog walking out of a lake.

She was centered again. Shaky, but centered.

"Go," she said, his hand jolting as if startled.

"What? No. You need me."

"I do," she said, the verbal intimacy accentuated by the warm touch of his hand. Her skin throbbed with something deeper than simple desire.

Though there was plenty of that.

"I do, but I need to be freed more."

He squeezed her hand once, hard. "You sure?"

She wavered for a split second.

"Yes."

And let go of his hand.

The loss chilled her.

Luke stood in the shadows, flashlight pointed considerately to the side, illuminating but not blinding her. He sighed.

Then one corner of his mouth crooked up in an amused and–dare she think it?

Sexy as all get out smile.

"But Kylie, before I go–you have to tell me what happened."

"I feel so stupid."

"It *is* pretty stupid," he said in agreement, making her grind her teeth.

"Luke."

"Come on, Ky." Her nickname coming from this grown man's rumbling baritone made her blood race. "It's objectively stupid that you're trapped in a charity donation box."

"Yes," she admitted, finally starting to laugh. "And it's all my boyfriend's fault."

"Boyfriend?"

"Ex. *Ex*-boyfriend."

"He put you in here? Are you injured?" The change in Luke's tone was extraordinary, suddenly furious. Murderous, even. Perry better watch out. Good thing that jerk was thousands of miles away, for his own sake. "Why didn't you say so?"

"No! No. He's in Thailand, deep in Systina."

"Systina? Is that... a province? A city?"

"His soulmate. True love."

"You're not making sense, Kylie. Did you bang your head when you fell in there?"

"That would have been merciful. I'll take being unconscious over having to explain myself."

"Look. Before I drive away and leave you in a metal box with a granola bar, a bottle of water, and a pile of other people's discards, I need to know that you're uninjured and safe. I promise I'll be back, but I won't leave you if you need immediate assistance. I really should call a county sheriff's deputy to come and–"

"NO! PLEASE!" The thought of Perry's family hearing about this was unbearable. "I'm fine. Just humiliated."

"Awww, Kylie. It'll make a good story to tell your kids someday." He paused. "You have kids?"

"No. You?"

"I do. One. She's six."

"That's amazing." Kylie sighed. "I heard you married Amber McFarland."

Silence.

"Luke?"

"Yeah. I did." Something in his voice made her go guarded.

"Nice."

"I'll go now. The sooner I leave, the sooner I can get you out of there."

The coyotes in the woods invaded the quiet, their howls making Kylie's heart race.

Or maybe that was Luke.

"I'm fine," she assured him. "Eighty-nine percent battery life on my phone, a granola bar, and a bottle of water. I can burrow in the bags of clothes for warmth. What more could a girl ask for? This is a budget spa night for me. Just throw me some cucumber slices and a hot washcloth and I'm in heaven."

"You have really low expectations, Kylie."

A flash of Perry filled her mind.

"Oh, Luke. You have no idea."

The glow of the flashlight illuminated his eyes just enough to catch the deep concern in them.

"I'm coming back for you. Promise. You're fine in here."

"I know."

"I know you know. Just making sure you *know*." The emphasis on that last word, how it made his voice go soft and deep, blanketed her with warmth.

"Thank you," she whispered.

But he didn't hear her, the bang of the steel door his response.

And with that, she heard a car engine turn on, tires on gravel, as Luke Luview, the one who got away, got away again.

But this time, he was coming back.

And he would save her.

Chapter Six

Luke

The first girl he ever kissed was stuck inside a charity donation box and he just called her a prostitute.

Yet another horrible Thanksgiving for the record books.

Kylie Hood. What on earth was *Kylie Hood* doing back in town?

And stuck like a homeless person inside one of those containers?

Luke had twenty-seven minutes before he made it home to Harriet, the night clear, the drive simple, so he let his mind wander.

Wander back fifteen years.

To Kylie, him, a pier on Lake Wannacanhopa, and a kiss.

The best kiss ever.

Now, Amber and Luke had plenty of kisses that were extraordinary and that should have knocked that kiss with Kylie out of first place, but there's nothing like your first kiss.

Nothing.

It's the one that wires you forever, neurons firing, burning memories into flesh and bone.

And his flesh was responding to Kylie with a heat he found uncomfortably thrilling.

Protocol said he should call a deputy and have them drive over to Deke's, rescue Kylie, and file a proper report with the sheriff's office. All kinds of liability issues were at play in this situation, but the way she pleaded for privacy tugged on Luke's heartstrings.

He got it. Small towns could be vicious when you made a mistake.

But why was she *here*? And what the hell was her ex-boyfriend up to, causing her to get stuck like that? Whoever he was, he was a dead man.

Not literally. He couldn't run around killing people, of course. But he could make life hard for the guy, if he was the reason why poor Kylie was trapped in there.

The drive home flew by as his mind and heart took him back all those years, to a simpler stage of life, when the world revolved around Lake Wannacanhopa and the daily rhythm of summer camp in the mountains. Polar Bear Plunges and morning songs, art time and No Talent shows, canoe rides and wilderness hikes.

Signing out rowboats and kayaks and playing tennis and horseshoes.

Every summer since he was ten and Kylie was eight, they'd spent ten glorious weeks together.

Seven years of fun.

And then one day, she disappeared.

"Disappeared" wasn't exactly true, but it's how it felt to a naïve seventeen-year-old boy who'd just had his first real kiss. Kylie's hastily scribbled letter, received three days after her mom moved them to Indiana, had broken his heart.

Still had the finger-worn letter and envelope somewhere in a box in his closet.

They'd stayed in touch for a few months, but MySpace friends didn't cut it. When Facebook became more popular, he'd never been able to find her. She stopped answering emails.

And that had been that.

Until a half hour ago, when Kylie Hood looked up at him from the dark, like a ghost from his past, and smiled in relief at the sight of him. Plenty of people expressed relief when he appeared to dig a car out of a ditch, transport a non-verbal stroke patient to the hospital, help get a woman in labor to the maternity ward (though he hadn't actually delivered a baby, at least not yet), jump a dead battery, or break up a rare bar brawl, but finding a human being trapped in a donation box was a first for him.

And it was *Kylie*.

"What kind of day is this?" he muttered as he made the turn onto the long county road that took him home. Cars were clustered in driveways and along the roadside in front of some houses, the big holiday still going strong in almost every home but his. Two years and four hours ago, Amber had decided to go for a walk in the rain.

And he'd never been able to stomach turkey again.

"Colleen is never going to believe this," he continued under his breath, pressing the accelerator a little out of his comfort zone for driving his own personal car. Time was of the essence. Kylie put on a brave front, but it was cold, and he knew it wasn't comfortable in there.

Speaking of uncomfortable, he had a body and heart going haywire, nerves twanging louder and louder as he got closer to home.

Kylie lived around here now? And he didn't know? He warmed at the memory of her. They'd been kids, fifteen and seventeen, when he'd taken the chance and gone for that kiss. Crossing the line from his own body to hers was like a polar bear plunge, only the stakes were higher.

She'd kissed him right back.

No icy shock there. No, sir. The surprise had been how soft her mouth was against his, how her hands went to the nape of his neck, fingers twisting in his shaggy, overgrown, end-of-summer waves.

Just the memory set his senses on fire.

Time seemed to have treated her well, though under the circumstances, it'd been hard to see her. Didn't need to, though. He could feel her goodness, hear her sweet disposition in her voice, even through the panic.

Kylie Hood always had a sharp wit with a gentle smile attached, and a laugh that washed away all the negativity in the world.

His phone buzzed on the dash and he glanced quickly.

Colleen.

Have to be at my shift in forty minutes. I hate to rush you, but you know, the text read.

Yeah. He knew.

Colleen was a nurse. Luke was a police officer. Dennis was in the army, working a job he couldn't talk about, and Kell worked with their parents, helping to run the family tree business while expanding his own crazy hand-pulled poison ivy company. The four Luview kids were a study in complementary skills.

Perfect for the family compound they were all buying together.

Twenty minutes later, he pulled into his own driveway, killed the engine, and looked at the big picture window, the glow of light illuminating his life. Watching like this was a ritual of sorts; the half a minute he spent out here clearing his mind before turning his attention fully to his daughter was a needed transition.

Some days, he really did work with bad guys. No man needed to bring that kind of energy back home to a sensitive little girl. Harriet already knew more than she should about how cruel the world could be.

And she'd learned it at the tender age of four.

Luke climbed out of the car, the tip of his nose turning cold in the short walk between the car and house.

Kylie must be freezing.

He quickened his step.

"Hey! *Whew!*" Colleen called out. "Just in time." Her expression softened. "You okay?"

"Yep. Thanks." He didn't want to process his feelings, especially because Kylie's appearance had complicated those. "Harriet, how about we go on an errand?"

Colleen's eyebrow quirked. "Errand? On Thanksgiving?"

Uh oh.

Should have waited until she was gone to bring it up.

"I was at Deke's and saw a stray. Figured I'd go and see if I could help get it out of the cold," he said, the words not technically a lie.

"Why not call Mel?" Mel Chassi ran a local animal sanctuary and had a heart that bled dog food.

"I can handle it." He cut Colleen a glance. "Besides, I need to keep busy."

Her guard dropped. Perfect response.

Also true.

"SURE!" Always up for an adventure, Harriet was already wriggling into her coat, stepping into her boots as well. "Can we get a candy bar at Deke's?"

"It's closed, honey."

Harriet pouted. "Okay. I'll still go, but it won't be as much fun."

Colleen was in her coat, purse on her shoulder, keys in hand.

"Talk to you tomorrow?"

"Right."

She shook her head. "You're allowed to have feelings, Luke."

"Who says I don't?"

Harriet lunged at Colleen's midsection, giving her a huge, fierce hug. "See you on Tuesday, right?"

"What's happening on Tuesday?" Luke asked.

"Library trip. Special sand-art project I signed us up for."

Harriet peeled herself off her aunt and opened the door for her.

"You're late for work, Aunt Colleen!" Harriet informed her, using some of Luke's mannerisms as she exuded authority. "It's disrespectful to be late."

His sister disappeared into the cold night, the air holding her laughter.

Meanwhile, Luke grabbed bolt cutters, his daughter, and went on a rescue mission.

Chapter Seven

Kylie

People donated the weirdest stuff.

And they were remarkably comfortable with leaving their name attached to their items.

Increasingly cold, Kylie found that burying herself between two plastic trash bags wasn't keeping her warm enough, so she carefully untied two of the larger trash bags, hoping to find blankets.

Instead, she got two extremes: the broken mundane and the horrifyingly bizarre.

It would never occur to her to throw a broken item into a donation bin. That's what trash cans are for.

"Maybe it broke when they threw it in here?" she muttered, the sound of her own voice calming her as she stared at the child's toy oven, plastic door ripped off and missing. If she pawed around enough, she'd likely find it, but why bother?

A towel, shredded as if a tiger had mauled it, rolled out of a bag.

Smelled like a tiger mauled it, too.

Most of the cloth items she found were wool sweaters shrunk

to doll size, stained sheets that looked like they were last used at a crime scene, and loads of plastic pieces of toys.

The horrifyingly bizarre items made Kylie feel like she lived in a parallel universe.

"*Amish Vampires From Space,*" she read aloud as she lifted a paperback from a bag, turning the book over in her hands. "How do you suck blood in a vacuum? And what do vampires do about flying near the sun? Wouldn't they die? And Amish people can't drive spaceships, so who pilots them?"

She was chattering nervously, wondering how long it would take Luke to free her. Seeing her breath with her words showed her that it really was getting colder.

A teeny, tiny little sleeping bag with a big zipper around the edges, a soft shade of pink but faded around the top, made her smile. This was for a baby in a carriage on cold days. Her frozen feet begged to go in it, so she lifted her boots and stuffed them inside.

And then realized the thing was full of cat hair.

Extraordinary amounts of cat hair.

And Kylie was allergic.

In a panic, she ripped her feet out of the thing, flinging it to the far corner, which only stirred up more hair and dander. Everything in the box was now coated with it. Sneeze after sneeze made her lose her wits, her hands covered in cat cooties.

Don't rub your eyes, she reminded herself.

Suddenly less interested in exploring, she took a few slow, deep breaths and found the water bottle Luke gave her. Flushing out her system would help with the cat allergy. Fortunately, she wasn't highly allergic, just a mild case of the sneezes and swollen eyes if she wasn't careful.

Which she wasn't.

Not in here, sadly.

A bright red poncho, over in the corner opposite where the baby-sleeping-bag-of-sneezing-doom had been, beckoned. Of course it was red. So were half the items in this donation box.

That's how it worked when you lived near the small town of Love You, Maine, where every day is Valentine's Day. You couldn't spit without hitting something red, white, or pink.

Victorian B&Bs were painted ladies in the trifecta of colors. Store signs and crosswalks were red, white, and pink. Police cars, municipal trucks, curtains, children's clothing, baseball uniforms, you name it.

You'd better love red, white, and pink.

When Kylie had moved abruptly to Indiana, she'd been shocked by all the different colors the kids wore to high school. Kelly green! Purple! Mustard yellow! Plenty of people rebelled in Love You, but they mostly just wore black.

Indiana was a whole 'nother world, in more ways than one.

She reached for the poncho, surprised by how big it was. A thick Gore-Tex material on one side and sherpa fleece on the other, it was perfect. Centering her head in the poncho hole, she pulled it on, the hood comfortable though severely torn at one seam, her body enveloped by warmth immediately.

Or at least, something more than sub-zero cold.

"That's better," she said, looking at her phone.

Fifty-seven percent charge left. And according to the clock, Luke had been gone for thirty-seven minutes. She was burning through her battery keeping the flashlight on, but she didn't care. The only thing worse than being trapped in this bin would be being trapped in this bin in the pitch dark.

The water bottle Luke had thrown to her beckoned. The icy liquid made her shiver, but she was two-thirds through it before she halted, bottle tipped up, coyotes howling again.

Better save some.

What if Luke ran out of gas on the way home? What if he got in a car accident? What if he decided not to help her?

That last one was stupid. Of course he would.

Despair threatened to take over, flickering at the dark edges of her mind. She adjusted herself on top of one of the unopened trash bags and felt a lump along the side of the poncho.

A scarf.

Ragged and holey, it was baby soft. Cashmere? Kylie wasn't sure. Held together with stitches and sheer luck, the beige thing looked like moths had had their own Thanksgiving feast on it. She could see why the owner of the poncho had put it in this tiny little zippered pocket.

And forgotten about it.

On impulse, Kylie shoved it in her back pants pocket, a faint waft of perfume tickling her already overstimulated nose.

"*Achoo! Achoo!*" Her skin began to get that slightly itchy, slightly swollen feeling that followed cat exposure, making Kylie groan. Her nose would fill up soon. Could this get any worse?

And then her bladder said, "Hold my beer."

The women in Kylie's family were famous for their thimble bladder, as her Grandma Hood always called it. Kylie looked at the phone again.

Forty-four minutes.

What had Luke said? He was a half hour away?

She could hold it.

Plink!

Plink!

Plink!

The sounds came faster and faster, until a deluge of sleet turned the metal box into a calypso drum.

One with a waterfall attached.

And that's when Kylie began to weep softly.

While sneezing loudly.

And crossing her legs.

"COME ON!" she screamed, her voice caught in the box, bouncing back louder and sharper in her ears than she liked. The throbbing pressure in her pelvis was doubly cruel. It was a reminder that she had nowhere to pee, and also that the last time her nether regions got this much stimulation was...

Too long ago.

Hearing the sleet made her think of rain, and rain was water, and the sound of water always made her need to pee. Always. There was no way she'd drop trou in this charity box and go on the donated clothes, but if Luke didn't hurry back, she was going to start pawing through the bags in hopes of finding a kid's potty.

Her flashlight glinted off the near-empty water bottle.

Curses. She'd done this to herself.

But maybe it was Luke's fault. A little.

For taking care of her.

Chapter Eight

Luke

"We're gonna go help a good guy, right?" Harriet loved riding in his work car. Loved it a little too much, eyes eager and a bit too excited. Luke saw that look in the journalists who did ride-alongs, or the high school kids in Civil Air Patrol who were on their way to the military.

They were ready to fight evil and win. But evil was a little more nuanced than that.

"Right."

"What if a bad guy comes along?"

Luke didn't like this turn of conversation.

"No bad guys out there on Thanksgiving, honey."

"But a bad guy killed Mommy."

No matter how many times he tried to explain that the man driving the car that hit Amber while she was out for a walk wasn't a bad man—he was a wonderful, kind man who had a heart attack at the wheel and lost control—Harriet still called him "the bad guy."

Which, in a six-year-old's mind, made perfect sense.

"He wasn't a bad guy, sweetie. Something bad happened to him, too."

"He died, like Mommy."

"Yes."

"Are they together?" This was always Harriet's question whenever the subject came up, and Luke never had an answer. Who knew? Was the afterlife like one big summer festival on the town common, where people mingled and chattered and bought hand-crafted goat's milk soap while eating pink kettle corn and watching a local cover band play Beatles songs as kids wandered around holding heart-shaped red balloons and grew stickier by the minute munching on candied apples?

Harriet informed him one night, about a year ago, that Mommy's angel wings were really itchy. He'd just nodded and kissed her forehead.

Then gone into the hallway and banged his own forehead against the wallboard, softly and with meaning.

"I don't know if they're together, Harriet."

"Yes, you do."

This was a first.

"What did you say, honey?"

"You *do* know." The pout that greeted him in the rearview mirror told him this wasn't going to be like the other conversations on this topic.

His little girl was leveling up.

"I do?"

"You know everything, Daddy. And I know why you won't tell me."

"Why not?"

"Because Mommy isn't in heaven."

His stomach clenched. "Who told you that?"

"Jace Morgenstern." A classmate. Kindergarteners were way more advanced–and meaner–than he remembered from his time at Luview Elementary.

Nothing like living in a town your ancestors founded. Not only were half the buildings and streets named after your family, most of your cousins filled the town. The dating pool had been slim pickings.

Speaking of dating—he wondered how cold Kylie was right now.

And his foot pressed the gas pedal a little harder.

Icy drops began to bounce on the windshield, and he backed off again on the accelerator. He could only imagine what it sounded like in that steel box she was trapped in.

Calypso music took over the background of his mind.

"Where does Jace think your mommy is?"

"He thinks she's a spy! A secret spy who had to run away to go get bad guys. Jace says Mommy isn't in heaven because she's alive, Daddy!" Harriet squinted at him in the rearview mirror. "And I think you know it."

Speechless.

His own daughter rendered him *speechless*.

"Harriet, honey," he started, unsure what to say next.

"Jace thinks you're a spy, too."

"Me?"

"Yes."

"Why?"

"Because spies are really good with guns and I told him you have a gun."

"Jace thinks he knows a lot about me and Mommy," he said slowly.

"Jace wants a daddy who is a cop."

Luke knew that Jace's dad was a line cook at Mario's Diner, two towns over. Lyle Morgenstern had a hair-trigger temper and, unfortunately, a strong dislike for following the law.

"Why?"

"Because he thinks cops are cool."

"Sounds like Jace has a big imagination."

"Are you really a spy?"

"No."

"What about Mommy?" From the way Harriet asked, Luke knew she was overly attached to this easy idea. Easy because, for a six-year-old kid, it *was* easy. Made more sense than the messy truth.

"Mommy was a bookkeeper, sweetie. For the hospital."

"Not a spy?"

49

"No. Not a spy. She liked numbers and she was good with them."

"Like me! I get hundreds on my math worksheets."

"You inherited her math ability."

"Hair it?" Harriet played with one of her long curls.

"Inherit. It means you got it from her."

"What did I get from you?"

Your interrogation skills, he thought but didn't say aloud.

"The shape of my eyes."

"Round?"

He couldn't help but laugh.

"No, honey. The way my eyes turn down a little at the outer corners."

"Like a sad puppy dog?"

This was a first.

"Where did you hear that?"

"Gamma. She says when Mommy died, you looked like a sad puppy dog all the time. Do I look like a sad dog with my eyes?" She reached up to touch them with the pads of her fingers.

"No, no. You look like a happy puppy."

"Arf! Arf!" she barked. Half of raising kids was just rolling with the punches and entering their made-up world.

"Woof! Woof!" he countered, deep like a German Shepherd.

Pressing a button on the dash, the Disney princess movie soundtrack came on, practically forcing Harriet to start humming and singing along, dropping the very uncomfortable subject that Luke would do anything to avoid.

Including listening to "Let It Go" ten thousand times in a row.

What the hell was Jace Morgenstern filling Harriet's head with? Kids could come up with crazy ideas, but he suspected Jace's father had been the source of some of that.

Because Lyle Morgenstern hated Luke.

Occupational hazard: People don't like it when you arrest and jail them.

Who knew?

Oh, right.

Luke.

Luke knew.

Working in law enforcement in rural Maine was more about community policing and roadside support than arrests, convictions, and violence. Sure, there was some of that, but it was mostly just plain helping people.

Serve and protect, not chase and subdue.

And right now, he was serving and protecting Kylie Hood.

The thought made his pulse step up the beat a bit, worry flooding him. Luckily, the sleet had stopped quickly, but he worried a little about road conditions. He needed to get to Kylie as fast as possible, but without sliding into a ditch on the way.

"Daddy! Are we going too fast?"

"No, sweetie. I'm a very careful driver."

"Because going too fast is against the law!"

"We're not. We're going to help someone."

"Who?"

"A..."

"Look! A deer!"

The glow of eyes in headlights made Luke reflexively slow down, though the doe was at least a hundred feet away and motionless. In Maine, you learned really early as a driver not to take chances with wildlife big enough to shatter your windshield if you hit it.

The only consolation for motorists hitting and killing deer was that they got to keep the venison.

"I see her."

"She's so pretty–oh! Another one!"

Crisis averted. Harriet loved nature, just like her mom and dad. Luke wouldn't live anywhere else. He'd seen enough of the world, getting a study-abroad scholarship in Italy in college, Amber joining him. They'd spent six months in Rome, using their weekends and breaks to travel everywhere.

And he liked being a tourist.

But had no desire to live anywhere but here in Luview, Maine.

"Why do their eyes glow like that?"

"Because the headlights shine on them."

"But the headlights shine on trees and they don't glow."

Luke blinked a few times, dredging through his rudimentary understanding of science, reflective surfaces, and eye biology.

"I don't know why."

"You do!"

"Uh, Harriet, I–"

"Maybe they're part fairy."

"Sure. Let's go with that." He'd learned not to argue or correct when he didn't know the actual facts.

"If deers are part fairy, what else is? Are unicorns a kind of fairy?"

"They could be."

Five minutes away. He could talk about fairies for five more minutes before using the bolt cutters to release Kylie.

And then what?

"What else could be? If light shines on things and they glow, is that a clue?"

"Mmmm," he said, noncommittal.

"Daddy!"

"I guess, sweetheart."

"I wish I glowed in the light."

His eyes caught her gaze in the rearview mirror, top right tooth missing, rosebud lips stretched in a trusting, joyful grin.

"You do," he assured her, heart swelling. "If anyone glows in the light, it's you."

Chapter Nine

Kylie

Her phone battery was down to thirty-one percent when she heard the roar of an engine, then the slow, steady thrum of one slowing down. It sounded very close to the donation bin. Then it stopped. She could hear two car doors open, then close.

"Kylie?" Luke shouted from outside, muffled but *here*. He kept his promise. He came back. Not that she *really* doubted it, but...

She knocked on the metal wall. "Still here!"

"You okay?"

"Other than being cold and needing to pee, yes!"

"Daddy? Who's that?"

Daddy?

Bang bang bang

To her right, Luke knocked on the wall.

"Kylie? There's a door here. It's padlocked. I'm using the bolt cutters to snip it, then I'll open it. Move away, just in case."

She scooched to the side.

"How do you know how to get me out?"

"I do this all the time."

"Women with jerk ex-boyfriends who leave their junk in their houses accidentally get stuck in these donation bins frequently?"

"No. Homeless people do, though."

"Homeless people?"

"Sure. They climb in on purpose. It's warm and safe in there, at least compared to the streets."

"And prostitutes, of course," she said loudly. Keeping the acid out of her voice wasn't possible.

"What's a prostitute?" The little girl was suddenly in the pull-down door, face and shoulders visible in silhouette, eager dark eyes coming into view as she came toward Kylie, arms outstretched as she began to slowly slide into the bin with her.

She looked exactly like Amber McFarland when they were six, the past slamming into Kylie's heart like a meteor crashing to Earth.

Dark, wispy curls. Pert nose and deep brown eyes. The funny little crinkle in the space at the bridge of her nose that every McFarland had. Amber was an only child, but she had cousins and her dad, and they all had that genetic quirk.

And then Kylie remembered. That's right.

Luke had *married* Amber.

"Harriet! Get down from there. Get off the car!" Kylie heard something heavy drop to the ground, and suddenly the girl, shining excited eyes on Kylie's, squealed.

"Daddy! My ankles are ticklish! Let me go!"

"Harriet, get out of there." Luke's voice was protective, firm, and tight.

And accustomed to being in command.

"You're hurting me, Daddy!" Kylie saw how Harriet's ribs were jammed against the lip of the bin's opening and reached up, standing on the mound of bags, steadying the little girl by holding her under the shoulders. She was too far down for Luke to pull her back up, but he was trying.

Luke paused, voice tight with anger and concern.

"I can't believe you did this, Harriet. You climbed on the hood of the car! You–"

"Let me go! I want to play with the nice trash lady!"

"Luke, you're pulling her ribs up. They're caught on the edge of the slot. I've got her," Kylie called out. "You can let her go. She's fine with me."

A grunt. A loud sigh. "You sure?"

"Sure."

The full weight of her came down, Kylie's flashlight already turned face down on a bag, but the *whuff* of their landing on top of the trash bags made the already dark bin even darker.

Giggles echoed everywhere.

Infectious giggles.

"I'm cutting the lock now!" Luke bellowed outside as Kylie scrambled to locate her phone in the near-total darkness.

Harriet gasped. "This is fun! Like having your own playhouse. Who are you? Do you live in here? It's so cold and dark. What do you eat? Where do you go to the bathroom? Are you a spy?"

Peppered by Luke's daughter's questions, Kylie couldn't help but smile and giggle at the same time.

"Let me find my flashlight, sweetie."

"My name is Harriet. But Daddy calls me sweetie. Do you know my daddy?"

Ignoring that question, Kylie rolled on her side, the wide poncho caught on her knees, half choking her. She reached down to free herself and her fingers brushed against glass.

Aha. The phone.

Turning it over, she swiped up and pressed the flashlight icon as Luke called out, "Almost there."

An enormous gasp, ageless with wonder, filled the air as light illuminated her and Harriet.

The little girl looked Kylie up and down, then threw her arms around her neck, screaming, "MOMMY!"

Chapter Ten

Luke

"MOMMY!"

Harriet's shrill scream sent something primal racing through him, a shock of tingling nerves giving him the extra bit of strength to clip the damn bolt, unloop the padlock, and pry open the slightly bent door.

Inside the bin, he found Kylie covered in Amber's old red poncho, with Harriet in her arms, screaming "Mommy! Mommy!" over and over again, a helpless look in Kylie's eyes.

She held his daughter steadfastly, stroking her dark curls with a maternal touch.

It wasn't Amber. His connection to reality was strong enough not to go where Harriet had gone.

But damn if his heart didn't do a two-step on triple speed at the sight before him.

"Wait." Harriet pulled back and put her little palms on either side of Kylie's face, squeezing until Kylie looked like a pufferfish. "You're not Mommy. You're the trash lady. Why are you wearing Mommy's poncho?"

Kylie looked at him for an answer.

Heck if he had one.

When in doubt, act.

"Hey, kiddo. Get out of there. Kylie needs some space and air."

"Who's Kylie?"

"Be. I'b Kydee," Kylie said, face still smooshed. The confused look on Harriet's face changed to sheer delight.

"Say it again!"

Luke crouched down and hooked one arm around his kid's waist, backing out of the musty bin with her wiggling in his arms.

"Come on. Let Kylie out."

The air in there was humid and a bit off, mustiness mingled with dirty plastic and the mixed scent of loads of people's discards.

"Thank you," Kylie said with so much gratitude in her voice as she shined the flashlight toward the small door, following him. As soon as he was out of the bin, Harriet got loose, stepping back to watch Kylie's exit.

Out in the air, she held up her car keys in one hand, phone in the other, and before he knew it, she was hugging him, hot breath on his chest.

"You're a godsend."

"No, he's not. He's a police officer," Harriet chirped, making Kylie laugh, her soft body against him stirring up pieces of himself he hadn't let loose in two years.

His arms, held aloft in surprise, wrapped around her waist. The red poncho crossed all the wires between his heart, mind, and body, the last whiff of Amber in the cloth mixing with his memory of kissing Kylie fifteen years ago on that lake pier.

"Thank you so much, Luke," she whispered breathlessly, waving to Harriet. "I appreciate your keeping this a secret."

"You don't look like a dog."

Luke and Kylie looked down to see Harriet tapping her thigh, clearly confused, pointing at Kylie.

"Excuse me?"

"Daddy said you were a dog."

Cold air entered the space between his body and Kylie's.

That was the quickest end to a hug he'd ever experienced.

"*Excuse me?*" This time, the words were pointed.

Pointed at him.

"I told her we were rescuing a stray. She made the leap." Palms up, he surrendered. "I never called you a dog." He couldn't help but look her over. "And I never would."

"Then what are you? A witch who lives in dumpsters?"

"Harriet," he admonished.

Pressing her finger to her lips, she looked at Harriet, who mimicked the gesture.

"It's a secret."

Kylie bent toward her, little finger hooked. Harriet knew how to pinkie swear, eyes solemn as she did it.

"I'll keep your secret, trash lady witch."

Luke watched as Kylie laughed, then winced.

"You injured?" he asked.

"Only my bladder." Self-deprecating laughter made him tilt his head, wondering what that meant, until he got it and smiled back, shooing her off with both hands.

"Go. I'll clean up here. Get home. Get a shower and a good, stiff drink."

"I owe you, Luke. Thank you so, so much."

"Don't owe me a thing."

"You rescued me from this ridiculous situation. I have to return the favor somehow."

One corner of his mouth went up as Harriet scampered into the car, clearly escaping the biting cold.

He pointed to the red poncho.

"Take that off and throw it back in the donation bin."

"This?"

"Yeah."

"Why?"

His arms crossed over his chest involuntarily, heart pounding against one wrist. "I'm asking for a favor."

As she pulled up, peeling herself out of the huge blanket-like piece of clothing, her cute little body stretched up, curves on display in the moonlight. For a split second, he remembered he was a man, and not just a dad or a law enforcement officer.

A man.

With needs.

"Sure," Kylie said, balling up Amber's poncho, tossing it back in through the side door he'd just forced open. "Done. But that's not enough."

"Not enough for what?"

"I still owe you."

"DADDDEEEEE! I'm cold! And Jester needs to go for his piddle."

"Jester?"

"Our dog."

"Piddle?" she asked Luke, who rolled his eyes as he closed the side door, giving the padlock a measured look, the pieces broken by the bolt cutters.

He shrugged, then turned to her and explained. "That's what my mom calls it when you take the dog out to do its business."

Kylie winced again. "Speaking of piddling..." Waving as she trotted off to her car, she turned away, keying into her car.

An overstuffed black trash bag rolled out onto the ground.

Grabbing it, she hauled it back to the bin, Luke politely pulling the handle down.

"Where are your keys and phone?" he asked, laughing.

She patted her back pocket. "Safely in here."

Their eyes met, his filled with tempered amusement, hers so emotional, so overwhelmed. He wanted to help her to be calmer. More focused. Wanted her to really look at him and appreciate the moment, as weird as it was.

But she couldn't.

And he respected that.

"Goodbye, Perry," she muttered with a frustrated anger that made Luke want to find the guy himself and have a few words.

In two trips, she rid herself of the infernal Perry, at least in physical form, and scrambled into her car.

Then she stepped out of it, and threw herself into his arms. The unexpected shock of a woman's soft, curvy body made electricity run through him, the chill disappearing as Kylie hugged him, her arms around his neck, his encircling her waist. Their thick coats meant they barely touched, and yet the connection was electric.

"Thank you," she whispered in his ear, her lips so close, his body responding in ways he hadn't felt in years.

"You're very welcome," he said as his arms tightened just as she let go.

And ran back to her car.

The engine started up easily and she backed out of the spot by Deke's station building, then drove to the end of the parking lot, smoothly turning away from his town.

He watched until the red tail lights were gone.

And then the coyotes howled until he climbed into the cruiser and played "Let It Go" all the way home.

Chapter Eleven

Kylie

Her sister Wendy watched with the same expression of wide-eyed awe she had when she was little as Kylie combed out her long blonde ringlets, the wet hair warm against her still-chilled skin. The gas stove was keeping her feet and shins warm but the rest of her was still desperately cold.

"I can't believe you did that."

"I know, right? Who throws their keys and phone in a stupid donation bin?"

"Not that! I mean that you let him get away!"

"Huh?"

"Kylie! You've talked about Luke Luview for *years!* He's 'the one who got away,'" she added, using finger quotes.

"Oh, stop."

"*Pfft.* Please. I'm not the one who needs to stop. You wouldn't shut up about him for two years after we moved."

"You were little. How would you know that?"

"Because I lived with you. I might have been seven when we moved but my ears still worked just fine. Remember how Mom banned you from speaking his name in the car?"

"I–"

"And now he rescued you! That's so romantic."

"I was in the equivalent of a garbage bin, Wendy. It was anything but romantic."

"You have to thank him."

"I already did!"

"You know what I mean." Wendy waggled her eyebrows.

"Wen! No! Not like that."

"I thought you said he was cute."

"He was! Is! But..."

"But what?"

"First of all, I'm not asking a cop out on a date after he rescued me from the most humiliating experience of my life."

"That was not the most humiliating experience of your life."

"Of course it was!"

"No. Choosing Perry definitely ranks higher."

"Hey!"

"I never liked him. And he proved me right."

"I know. And he sure did. This is all Perry's fault."

"Yep."

"And second of all, Luke's married. To Amber McFarland."

"Who?"

"You were too young to remember her."

"I don't remember life in Luview the way you do."

"I wish you did. It was so wonderful."

Wendy just shrugged.

"Okay. So the hot cop is married. You still have to go see Mr. Out-of-the-Box and thank him. Personally. Bring your pile-on brownies. Cops love baked goods."

"That's a stereotype."

"Doesn't mean it's not true."

"He has a six-year-old daughter. Sweet little spunky kid."

"Then you need to give her the full fairy treatment."

"Ooooo."

"Muffins and everything!"

"I haven't made sparkle muffins in forever."

"I know. Not since Perry left you."

All the tension that had finally left Kylie's body came roaring back, her efforts to relax completely useless. "Thanks for the reminder."

"Oh, Ky, I didn't mean to do that to you! I just meant some stress baking might be good for you."

"I stress baked plenty after Perry dumped me."

Wendy patted her belly. "I know."

Kylie lifted her gaze from her hands to Wendy, then back. "I could make it a two-fer. A send-off basket for you, and a thank you basket for Luke and Harriet."

And Amber, she thought.

"You're giving me a full fairy-treatment basket? SQUEEEE!" Wendy screamed. "I would have moved out sooner if I knew I'd get that!"

Unexpected tears rushed to Kylie's eyes.

As of Saturday at six a.m., Kylie really would be alone.

One hundred percent.

No boyfriend.

No sister.

No job.

No one.

For years, since her dad cheated on her mother and, in a fit of shame, her mom packed everything up in a single day and moved them to Indiana, Wendy and Kylie had been told over and over and over that you couldn't trust anyone, and especially not love.

"Make sure you always have a career," was their mother's mantra. She'd been able to find clerical work as they settled into their grandparents' house, and their dad was forced to pay child support and some limited alimony, but it was clear something broke inside her mother.

Something that never quite healed.

Kylie knew all too well from observing it, from being a victim of it, that when you relied on other people, relaxed, and gave in, they could betray you.

Independence was *crucial*.

And she'd made a huge mistake in over-relying on Perry's world when she moved here. Having her own job hadn't mattered, had it? He'd made a single phone call and *poof!* It disappeared.

It disappeared because his parents decided she was just a number. Something for human resources to handle. A tiny problem someone else could fix.

And now her mom was right. She was alone. No boyfriend. No job.

And soon, no Wendy.

Wendy stood up, oblivious to Kylie's emotional turmoil, and rummaged through the somewhat bare cupboards. Wendy had been eating down her food, but the baking supplies were still in full force.

"Plenty of edible glitter. Natural food dyes. Powdered sugar. You're good, Ky. You can do it, make this guy fall in love with you via fairy muffins."

"Stop! He's married."

"If we'd stayed here when we were kids, bet he would have married you."

"And if wishes were horses, I'd have a stable full. How about a counter full of fairy muffins instead?"

"Mmm. Now you're talking." Wendy wandered down the short hall to the small den where she'd been living these last few months. Fortunately, Perry had agreed to send his share of the rent through the end of the lease, so that was covered.

Which was great and all–he might have been "kind" to do that–but he clearly was also the reason she got fired from his parents' chain of resorts, so what Perry giveth, Perry taketh away.

Fairy muffins were Kylie's silly invention, something she'd thrown together her freshman year of college while working at a summer camp in Indiana. Edible glitter had just become a thing, and between brightly colored frosting, the glitter, and a few secret ingredients that made her muffins *sing*, including wings made of spun sugar and little marzipan fairy figurines, her creations had become legend.

"Do we have marzipan?" she muttered to herself, combing through the increasingly empty cabinets. She was moving out in three months, the lease she'd signed with Perry last year coming to the end of its twelve-month term soon.

So much had changed in under a year.

Scratch that.

So much had changed in the last *four hours*.

Unlike Wendy, who retrieved ingredients as she went along, Kylie liked to line up all her ducks in a neat little ingredient row before getting started.

Flour. Baking powder. Sugar. Butter. Salt. Vanilla. As she assembled everything on the counter, the recipe she created years ago thoroughly memorized, she let herself think about Luke's embrace, his strong grip telling her, wordlessly, that he would keep her safe.

That he had saved her.

Fifteen years, half a continent, and what seemed like a lifetime had passed since she'd seen him last. Yet there he was, her knight in shining armor, just when she needed him most.

The opposite of Perry.

"Snake," she hissed as she creamed butter and sugar together, imagining she was whipping his head to pudding.

The rhythm and flow of baking took her out of her thoughts, making the world nothing but grains, fats, sugars, and... glitter.

By the time she popped the two muffin tins in the oven, Wendy was back, yawning, holding up two sundresses.

"Which one is more likely to help me land a hot, rich French guy who will propose within a week and whisk me off to his chateau in Monaco, where I'll live like a queen?"

Kylie pointed to a yellow dress with roses all over it.

"And the one that gets me laid more?"

"Oh, the red spaghetti strap one. Definitely."

Unable to decide, Wendy finally said, "I'll squeeze them both in."

"You have no room in that cargo container you call a suitcase."

"I can leave my deodorant here."

"Just don't leave your birth control!"

"If I did, it's not like you'd use it."

"Hey!"

"Hey right back, Ky. You're not dating," she said reproachfully.

Leave it to a twenty-two-year-old sister to find five months of celibacy a bigger sin than edible glitter.

"I told you, he's married!"

"Who? Oh, Luke?" A sly grin made Wendy look older. "You *are* thinking about him, aren't you? Knew it."

"Of course I am."

"You're no fun–can't tease you when you admit stuff."

"Sorry to disappoint."

"What did he smell like?"

"Smell?"

"You said you hugged him."

"He smelled like married."

Married to her old friend Amber.

A rush of excitement shot through her, warmth following as she realized she could see Amber again. Yes, some piece of her was still attracted to Luke, but Kylie had to tamp it down.

Hard.

Because he was married, for goodness sake.

That didn't mean she couldn't reach out and reconnect with her old best friend, though. She and Amber had been so close when they were young, and surely Luke would tell her all about finding her in the metal bin.

If nothing else, little Harriet would natter on about Kylie the Trash Witch.

"Ha ha. I'm not suggesting you make him break vows. Just curious."

"Why?"

"You haven't touched a guy in five months."

"You keep mentioning that," Kylie said through gritted teeth. "And besides, I didn't smell much other than the musty, rotten odor of the inside of that donation bin and humanity's careless depravity."

Wendy's giggles got the better of her. "I still can't believe you climbed in like that."

"What was I supposed to do? You weren't picking up my tele-pathic cry for help."

"Sorry. My new earbuds blocked the signal."

They smirked at each other.

"I'm going to miss you," Kylie blurted out. "You were always such a pain-in-the-butt little sister, but having you live here these last few months really helped me."

Tears filled Wendy's eyes. "Mom told me I was crazy to come out here. Said you were silly, too, moving back to Maine."

"Mom's idea of how the world should work doesn't exactly align with mine," Kylie said tactfully.

"Hah! How do you think she feels about me going to France?"

"I know how she feels. Our monthly phone calls are nothing but 'Wendy's too young' and 'You need to talk some sense into her' and 'What's that backwater town like now?'"

"She hates Maine because it reminds her of her marriage falling apart."

"That was Dad's fault," Kylie said tightly. They weren't talking about it openly, but there it was. The real reason Mom gave them twenty-four hours' notice that they were moving when they were eight and fifteen: Dad had cheated on her during a business trip to Chicago.

And had said something at the local watering hole while he was drunk. Once you said a word at Bilbee's Tavern, there was no taking it back.

She was humiliated. Small-town gossip is like lighter fluid on a bonfire when it comes to affairs.

And when you live in a place where love itself is a product, you're damaged goods when your own love breaks in two.

So they moved to Indiana to live with Grandma and Grandpa until she could "get on her feet." Three years later, just as Kylie was leaving for college, Mom found her feet.

Six feet, in fact, when she married their stepfather, Tom.

Until Perry did almost the exact same thing to Kylie on his Thailand adventure, she had hated her mother for the move. And until five months ago, that resentment had been at the center of her relationship with her mother.

Now, she knew.

Knew that humiliation was like an outside layer of skin forced on you.

"I know it was Dad's fault," Wendy said. "I don't remember it all like you do, Ky, but I get it. He's, well... he's Dad." Their father lived in Belize now, with the woman he cheated on their mother with. Kylie couldn't quite bring herself to refer to Pauline as her stepmother, but *stepmonster* worked just fine. Their dad had a condo in South Carolina and a place in Belize, and considered himself retired at the age of fifty-three.

Pauline came from money, some sort of old shipping fortune.

"I know. Dad is Dad and that's life."

"You going to Myrtle Beach for Christmas?"

"Without you there? Heck no."

Wendy snorted. "I hope to be in Germany for the Christmas markets. Or Paris on New Year's Eve, watching it light up."

"You realize being an au pair is work, right? Forty to fifty hours a week of watching actual children. It's not just a way to see Europe."

"Duh."

Kylie grabbed the butter, powdered sugar, edible glitter, vanilla, and some cream and got to work on the frosting, the mixer soon chugging along, doing its job.

"France has everything you could ever want," Kylie said wistfully.

"No."

Surprise made her look up to find Wendy's eyes filled with tears again.

"France doesn't have your fairy muffins."

Another hug, more crying, and soon the room smelled like golden sweetness.

But tasted like bittersweet goodbyes.

Chapter Twelve

Luke

Jester smiled at Luke as he whipped him with a cat o' nine tails. The golden retriever wore a black leather motorcycle club jacket with an insignia that looked like a grimy goat eating a human heart.

At least, that's what Luke's half-asleep, still-dreaming brain tried to tell him.

Being licked awake was the norm in Luke's household, but he'd have enjoyed it a hell of a lot more if it were a different kind of mammal.

Preferably one he'd just rescued from a donation bin.

"All right, all right," he muttered as Jester leaped up on the bed, knowing it wasn't allowed. Luke thumped him gently on the butt and the dog jumped down, smiling up at Luke, tail wagging like a metronome–if it were set for "Flight of the Bumblebee."

Luke's bare foot hit the cold floor, the other foot protesting as he squinted to find his slippers. Living in northern New England meant they were a necessity, like running water or heat.

So were his glasses, until he could put in his contacts.

Jester whined, a friendly sound of pleading as his owner

ineptly searched the room. Glasses were on the nightstand on Amber's side of the bed, and his slippers, well...

He found one.

"You," he said to Jester, growling. He waved his right slipper in front of the dog. "Find."

Jester's rear end faded down the hallway. Back in seconds, he gripped the left slipper in his mouth, dropping it obediently at Luke's feet.

It was suspiciously chewed.

Beggars couldn't be choosers in the Maine cold. At least the dog only mauled the sole, he thought, as he put the thing on and went into the kitchen to make coffee.

The day stretched before him, Black Friday some kind of existential punishment every year. The outlet malls were a good forty minutes away, but the injuries and general mayhem weren't confined to Conway, New Hampshire. Plenty of smaller businesses had huge Black Friday sales these days, and the worst part was the roadside calls.

People who got up at two a.m. to drive to Conway, got their cheap stuff, had lunch, then hit slick back roads weren't necessarily the best drivers on black ice. Luke anticipated a day of blown tires and lots of cars in ditches.

Nadine, the station admin, would have a neat, tidy spreadsheet of all the local stores running Black Friday sales, too.

As he walked into the kitchen, he found Harriet in front of the television, watching some kids' cartoon, stuffing her face with cookies that he thought he'd hidden carefully.

His daughter's rule-breaking tendency was testing his law enforcement abilities.

"Harriet?"

"Hi, Daddy!" Guileless, she jumped up and gave his waist a hug.

"You're not allowed to have cookies for breakfast. You know that."

"But I'm allowed to have applesauce for breakfast."

The *non sequitur* before he'd had a single drop of coffee was a bit much.

"Huh?"

"Aunt Colleen said these are applesauce cookies. Applesauce is healthy." The missing tooth in her smile only added to her charm.

"But I told you last night that the cookies were being put away and they're for dessert only."

Her little face screwed up in concentration, just like Amber's had. "Oh. Right. I forgot."

Holding his palm out flat, he parented non-verbally.

Harriet ran over to the bag of cookies, brought them back, and put them in his hand. They were still ice cold.

"And quit ruining my good hiding spots," he muttered, realizing she'd had to search the freezer and look under the cauliflower–which she hated–to find these.

Tossing a filter, grounds, and water into the coffee machine, he got it percolating as Harriet, bless her, opened the back door for Jester to go out and do his business. The backyard held a foot and a half of snow, all from last week's three storms, but Luke had taken his beast of a snow blower and plowed an elaborate maze back there, more for the dog's benefit than Harriet's.

The coffee machine gurgled, sputtering at the end, the sound a trigger for Luke's hand to automatically open the cupboard, grab a mug, and pour. Squeals of pure joy made him look out the window, finding his dog and his kid running along the paths, Harriet in jammies and slippers.

You could always spot a born-and-raised Mainer in winter by their lack of outerwear.

And their paradoxical deep respect for being prepared for the cold.

Harriet was in kindergarten now, the local school still doing half days for the little ones. After Amber had died, her life insurance money and the Social Security check he received for Harriet had been enough to hire a nanny.

Harriet had clung to him like Velcro for that first year, and there was no way she was going to handle any new change, including kindergarten. Putting her in day care wasn't going to cut it; she needed to be in her own home with a caregiver. With a summer birthday, and Amber's death, it made sense to hold her back a bit. Instead, he kept her in her familiar preschool.

His mom had taken on the Herculean task of becoming Harriet's caregiver after Luke's bereavement leave, vacation, and family leave time was up, but she had her limits. Colleen and Kell helped out, and his dad stepped in sometimes, but they all had their own lives.

Last year, he'd hired Nicole, a nineteen-year-old with stars in her eyes and actress ambitions, but a bank account that forced her to face reality.

She was great with Harriet, but not the most organized thinker.

And, as he looked around his disheveled house, piles of clean laundry still sitting in baskets he plucked their clothes out of, LEGO toys a bruised-foot minefield, and picture books scattered like a tornado hit a library, he sourly realized she wasn't completing the "light-housekeeping-duties" part of her job.

Then again, neither was he.

"DADDY!" Harriet and Jester reappeared, the dog's paws covered in snow that would soon melt on the hardwood floors and carpet, another reason for perpetual slipper wearing. No one wanted soggy socks slipped into winter boots.

"Yes?"

"What am I doing with Nicole today?"

His phone buzzed. *Reminder: meeting with chief.*

He had thirty-eight minutes to shower, shave, and head out the door.

"Not sure," he said, drinking more coffee. "Sweetie, you watch TV. I'm going to shower real quick."

"K." Already sucked into some show involving a panda and a talking pillow, Harriet ignored him.

Jester, too.

His shower, shave, and dress routine was interrupted by the groan-worthy realization that his red uniform shirt was a wrinkled mess. Hair still wet but face shaved, he wandered out into the living room in his red uniform pants and white t-shirt and found it.

The iron and ironing board were still in the corner from Wednesday, when he'd done the exact same damn thing.

Turning the iron on, he shook it. Good. Enough water in there for a steam press and he'd be fine.

Ding dong!

The doorbell instantly made Jester bark, Harriet squeak, and Luke's skin tingle in surprise.

Who could that be?

His family didn't bother knocking. Delivery guys left stuff at the door. Their town was so small and rural that no one went door to door selling anything or trying to convert you.

But neighbors did plenty of stopping by on the fly, so this could be anyone from old Mrs. Petrinelli from down the street needing someone to restart her wireless router to Annabeth Khouri with a box of baked goods and a smile that said "date me."

Harriet jumped up and beat Luke to the door, opening it as he protested.

Before them stood Kylie Hood, looking ten thousand times better than last night, if that were possible.

And she was holding an enormous gift basket that practically glowed.

"Hi!" she said brightly, a little nervous in a way that made him smother a smile. "I, uh, hope you don't mind. I looked up your address and didn't know how to call you, and I wanted to thank you."

"CUPCAKES!" Harriet shrieked. "With GLITTER!"

Kylie bent down at the knees to talk to his little girl at eye level, a gesture he had grown to appreciate in adults. It signaled to him that Kylie viewed his daughter as a full human being, worthy of respect.

"Yes! This is a fairy basket," she said, then stood again and thrust it at Luke, who instinctively reached forward. Their fingers brushed against each other as he did, the *zing* from physical contact with Kylie a pleasant surprise.

"Fairy basket?"

"Everything in here is fairy inspired."

"Are you a fairy? I thought you were a trash witch," Harriet asked, touching Kylie's arm with her fingertip, pressing lightly over and over as if testing the merchandise.

Luke cleared his throat and gave Kylie a raised-eyebrow look. "She is not a trash witch."

Kylie laughed it off, but Luke wondered what the difference was in his child's strange little imagination.

"First of all," he said, mind scattered but suddenly unable to focus on anything but Kylie, "you didn't have to do this."

"I know I didn't. I wanted to. I can't repay you enough for helping me. But fairy muffins are a start."

He walked to the table and shoved aside a pile of markers, glitter pens, and a huge drawing tablet to make room for the basket. "Thank you."

"You're welcome." She just stood there, looking around.

Harriet pawed at the cellophane. "I want a fairy muffin!"

"You already had cookies for breakfast, kiddo."

"Strict dad," Kylie joked, and he rolled his eyes.

"She got into them before I was up."

"Hah!"

A look passed between them, one that made him smile even more as they connected.

Man, he'd missed her.

Yet he hadn't thought of her in a long time.

Why was she suddenly in his life again?

Out of the corner of his eye, he saw Harriet emerge from the kitchen, scissors in hand.

"What are you doing?"

"Opening the gift! If it's a gift, you have to try it, right?"

This was a battle he didn't want to have.

"Fine," he said with a long sigh. "*One* muffin."

Kylie stepped forward and gave his arm a nudge. "Pushover."

He put his hands on his hips, skin buzzing from that contact. "When it comes to her, yes."

Kylie stepped close to him and whispered. "I made a dozen. That way there's plenty for all of you."

"All of us?"

"Sure! You, Harriet, and Amber. I heard you guys got married." Kylie looked around the living room. "Is she at work?"

His heart sank.

His body tensed.

And grief hit him like a wave, almost knocking him off his feet.

Eyes darting to Harriet, he checked to see if she'd heard Kylie's comment. Based on the way his daughter was biting her lower lip and cutting open the basket with fierce determination, she hadn't.

Whew.

A frown on Kylie's face bought him time, the words in his mouth but not quite in order. Before he could reply, his phone rang.

He muttered a curse and jogged to it. Nicole. The nanny. Probably calling with some ridiculous excuse for being late.

"Hi," he said tersely into the phone before she could say a word. "Not today. Have to be on time. Big meeting at work."

And then he walked right past Kylie into his bedroom because waves always pull you out from shore.

Especially the big ones you didn't see coming.

Chapter Thirteen

Kylie

Whoa. That had gone from friendly to foul in two seconds flat.

What had she said to upset him so much?

"Trash witch lady? I mean, fairy lady? Could you help me?"

"My name is Kylie."

"Oh! I have a Kylie in my class. She can't drink cow's milk. She has to bring her own every day and it smells like oil."

"Is she allergic to cow's milk?"

"'Lergic. Yeah. We can't bring ice cream for birthday treats because Kylie can't eat it, but that's okay. Daddy brought cherry popsicles instead for my birthday!"

"He did? How old are you?"

"Six."

"Are you in first grade?"

"Kindergarten, silly! Except my birthday is a summer birthday, so in preschool we got to celebrate it on our half birthday. I think it's the same in kindergarten, too."

Harriet was struggling to cut the cellophane, a task Kylie took care of fast. She slid the tiny face painting kit from the basket and watched Harriet hone in on the biggest, glitteriest muffin.

"What's... this?"

"It's a cupcake."

Harriet screwed her face up in confusion. "I've never seen a cupcake like this. Are they cupcakes or muffins?"

"Does it matter?"

"Why are they circles?"

"Circles?" Now Kylie was confused.

"The shape is wrong!" Studying the pastry like it was radioactive material from an alien spaceship, the little girl with dark brown curls and bright eyes that turned down at the corners spun the muffin around in her hand. "I've never eaten a circle like this."

And then it hit Kylie. Right. This was Love You, Maine.

Where everything that *could be* heart-shaped *was*, almost as a requirement.

"People who don't live in Luview eat cupcakes and muffins like this, sweetie. Circle cupcakes. Everything isn't a heart."

"It's not?"

The hearty laugh that poured out of Kylie made her awkwardness disappear. Years ago, when they'd fled to Indiana, part of the sensation of disruption she'd experienced had been a very unique form of culture shock. When you live in a tourist town known for Love with a capital L, you don't realize that heart-shaped everything isn't normal.

Or that people wear colors other than red, pink, and white.

Or that the rest of the world doesn't dye their animals pink for public festivals and holidays. Doesn't have more picturesque proposal sites than bathrooms. Doesn't have a justice of the peace convention and a romance novel cover-model workshop the way other towns have business conferences for lawyers, insurance salespeople, and software developers.

Love You, Maine, was like growing up in Disney World and not knowing that the rest of the world didn't live the same way.

Kylie knew better.

Harriet didn't.

"Most people eat round muffins. Round cookies. Round– "

"WAFFLES?" Harriet squealed. "Like the ones Daddy buys from the store sometimes? I know about those."

"Yep."

Harriet's eyes shifted to the fairy basket, suspicion coloring her expression.

"They taste the same, right? Those cupcakes?" She pointed to one.

"Muffins with frosting."

"That's a cupcake!"

"Well, sort of. They're morning glory muffins."

"With pineapple and carrots? That's Daddy's favorite! Whenever we go to Greta's, he always gets one. Sometimes she gives him one for free!"

Greta.

There was only one Greta who made morning glory muffins, and it was Greta Mitteracht from Love You Bakery, the town pastry shop, café, and gossip hole.

There was a blast from the past. How many loaded brownies had she shared with Amber, Luke, Kell, Moore, Layla, and Brewer when they were kids?

"Does Greta still serve loaded brownies?"

Harriet shrugged. "When we go in there, Wolf helps us."

Wolf was Wolfgang Mitteracht, Greta's son, champion basketball player. He was in Dennis Luview's class, so much older than Kylie, and every girl's first crush.

"Wolf runs the place now?"

Harriet took a huge bite out of her muffin, nose streaking with glitter. "Mmmm hmm. YUM!"

While she chomped away, Kylie looked around. This was Amber and Luke's house, huh? Messier than she would have expected, but then again, she wasn't exactly pristine in her housekeeping habits, either.

Still. For a guy who was in law enforcement, and what she remembered about Amber being super organized when they were kids, this was a little weird.

"Where's your mommy? At work?"

Harriet's eyes went sad, her throat moving as she swallowed a mouthful of muffin. She sniffled.

Uh, oh, Kylie thought, gut tightening. She'd just stepped into some kind of emotional minefield. But before Harriet could reply, they turned toward the sound of a bison stuck in a whirlpool.

Or, at least, a very angry Luke.

Heavy footsteps and an increasingly loud voice from the other room made it clear Luke's conversation wasn't pleasant. Was he fighting with Amber? Were they divorcing? What could make this sweet child's face go so somber?

"You can't do this to her!" Luke said loudly into the phone, and Kylie jumped. "I know I can be a jerk sometimes, but why punish her?"

Silence.

Then:

"So you're leaving? Just like that? Because you met a guy at *trivia night* at Bilbee's and he's from Boston and–*what?*"

Oh, no. Kylie didn't want to hear this. Amber was leaving Luke? Cheating on him and dumping him over the phone? The Amber McFarland she remembered growing up with was absolutely, positively *not* the type to do that.

People change, though.

Sometimes suddenly.

Painfully.

And then there was her own ex, who did it *stupidly*.

"He's an *agent?* He says he can help you get *acting* work in *L.A.?* This just goes from bad to worse."

Kylie felt a sharp tug on the hem of her shirt. She looked down to find a very serious Harriet looking back up.

"My mommy isn't here," Harriet said sadly. Kylie's protective instincts toward small children kicked in.

Amber was in the middle of breaking up with Luke and leaving her marriage so she could become an actress in Hollywood?

Suddenly, her experience with Perry didn't seem so bad. At least she hadn't been dumped with a kid, too.

Poor Luke.

"I see she isn't!" Kylie replied, realizing she needed to change the subject and erase some of Harriet's pain. "I brought a fairy face painting kit. Do you want me to paint one on your cheek?"

"YES!"

As if Kylie expected any other answer.

Moving to a chair, she settled the little girl in place and began painting in light arcs, careful to let Harriet chew as she devoured the muffin. If Luke's comment about cookies for breakfast were true, Kylie felt bad for whoever was spending the next few hours with her.

The kid was going to be zooming on pure sugar. At least the muffins had nuts for protein.

A door opened down the hallway and *thump thump thump* came the happy sound of a big, very loud dog bounding along, until suddenly, Kylie's hand slipped on Harriet's face, painting a purple lightning bolt, and a big mess of butterscotch-colored fur crowded her crotch.

"JESTER! DOWN!" Luke bellowed, on the dog's heels, grabbing his collar with one strong, taut hand, phone still in the other. "Sorry," he muttered to Kylie, pulling the dog to the back door, where he sent the beast outside.

"What happened to my face?" Harriet asked.

"I drew a super cool purple lightning bolt. Your fairy power is strong," Kylie lied, making the best of it all.

"YAY!! What's my fairy name?"

Kylie leaned forward and whispered in her ear. "Shocky."

"Shocky? Ooo, I like that!"

"Look," she heard Luke say into the phone, from down the hall. "How much money to stay? Just to come back today. We don't have to think about the future. Just now."

Dude was desperate. She was embarrassed on his behalf.

"I know I owe you but think of Harriet. If you just disappear, you'll break her heart." His words were certainly shredding Kylie's. What kind of relationship did he and Amber have if he had to beg her to stay with her own child? And offer her money to come back for just a day?

"Three weeks? You just want to run off with some guy for *three weeks* and *maybe* come back and see her?"

Kylie focused on the lines on the wings of the butterfly she drew along the edge of the little girl's face, her heart twisting, tears threatening. Never one to hide her emotions easily, she was starting to get that sense of urgency and pain she developed when other people were in emotional crisis around her.

Call it emotion, tension, stress, vibration, whatever–she felt it with her whole body, heart, and soul.

And now here she was in Amber McFarland's house as the woman was dumping her husband and daughter for a sham agent the day after her husband rescued Kylie from a donation bin.

When did life get this bizarre?

"Can I see?" Harriet begged, prompting Kylie to pull the small mirror from the kit, grateful she didn't have to interrupt Luke in any way.

"Sure. Here you go." She held up the mirror.

"OH! It's perfect! Better than anyone else can do it."

"I'm sure your mommy can paint your face better than I can," she assured Harriet, who gave her another one of those strange, sad looks.

And just like that, Kylie was angry. Furious, even. Who the hell did Amber think she was, ruining Luke and Harriet like this? When you became a wife and mother, you had a responsibility to do your best by the people who loved you.

How dare she?

"My mommy never paints my face like this," Harriet said sadly.

"She doesn't?" Righteous indignation grew inside Kylie.

"No. I don't see her anymore."

"FINE!" Luke bellowed. "I'll mail your stuff and you're done. You're making a big mistake and I'm disappointed in you. Can't believe I have to pick up the pieces, but now I'm late for work and it's your fault. You need to be more responsible."

The distinct sound of a man punching a wall came through, loud and clear.

Then heavy breathing, filled with rage.

"You don't see your mommy?" Kylie asked Harriet, her attention split between wanting to help Luke and needing to keep his child occupied, to shield her from whatever mess her parents were in the middle of. "I'm so sorry."

"That's what everyone says."

"They do?" Oh, no. The whole town must know about Luke and Amber's marriage disintegrating. This was exactly what her own mother had been afraid of.

The searing shame of having your private dirty laundry exposed.

"Yeah."

"I'm sure you'll see her again, though."

Harriet gave her a deeply confused, slightly disgusted look. "No. I won't. I can't."

"You can't?"

A bedroom door opened, Luke walking down the hall, phone in hand, marching for... an ironing board? Hands deft and quick, he began steam pressing what looked like a typical red Love You police uniform shirt, eyes wild.

He completely ignored Kylie, but she could feel his embarrassment.

"Need help?"

A snort was his answer.

Head down, he worked on his task, and said, "Now is not the best time for us to catch up. I really appreciate the, uh, fairy basket." The last two words came out slow, halting. "But I'm experiencing a sudden mess and I need to figure it all out."

"I couldn't help but overhear."

Mouth stretching in disgust, he grimaced, wholly adult, suddenly mature and struggling. She could see the teen in him from years ago, but also appreciate how different he was now, bigger and more worldly.

Carrying so many burdens.

"I'm sorry Amber's doing this to you."

Jerking up with shock, he moved the iron and before she could shout a warning, his fingertip brushed against the edge, making him yelp.

"Damn it!" he shouted, sucking on his finger.

Harriet pulled on the hem of Kylie's shirt. She looked down as Luke moved the iron so it didn't burn his shirt, then looked at Kylie like she was crazy.

"Kylie?"

"Yes?"

"Mommy can't do *anything* here."

"She can't?" Harriet's scowl pierced Kylie's heart.

"No."

"Why not?"

"Because Mommy's in heaven."

Chapter Fourteen

Luke

His six-year-old had more clarity than he did.

"Heaven?" Kylie choked out, genuine shock filling her face in a way that broke something in him, sinking him even deeper into grief. When people learned about Amber's death, it always made him relive it a little.

Assuming Kylie already knew about it was a form of denial.

Looking to Luke for confirmation, Kylie caught his gaze, tears forming in her beautiful green eyes.

He nodded. Once.

"Oh, dear God, Luke." Her hand flew to her mouth. "I had no idea."

"I'm figuring that out just now." Regret flooded his veins. So caught up in the mess with his babysitter, who was quitting with no notice, he hadn't thought about how to bring Kylie up to speed on his life.

Then again, why would he?

She was a blip from his past, intersecting with his present for a fleetingly weird moment.

"Amber... how?"

"Car accident. I really thought you knew."

"No."

A million questions flew through him. Why had Kylie disappeared on social media? Why had her letters stopped coming? No emails, nothing back after she'd moved. It was like she cut Luview, Maine, out of her life forever when she left, and now suddenly she was back?

Stuck in a donation box at Deke's?

And now in his home, absorbing the truth.

She walked up to him, close, and whispered, "I feel so insensitive. I kept asking Harriet about her mom."

"It's okay."

"It's not." She gripped his bare forearm with an intensity that was half apologetic, half determined, and one hundred percent Kylie. "It's *not*. I should have been more delicate."

"Can't beat yourself up for what you don't know."

Kylie swallowed hard.

But she would. He could tell. It was Harriet's tender feelings that Kylie was upset about, more than what she "should" have done, and that made Luke connect with her all the more.

Kylie leaned closer. "Then if that wasn't a fight with Amber, who the heck was that on the phone?"

"The nanny. Nicole. She just quit." Their whispered, confidential conversation gave him a thrill he wasn't expecting, the closeness intoxicating.

"Quit?"

"Yep. Naïve, nineteen-year-old kid who thinks she'll be an actress someday. Said she's on the road with this guy already, headed to Boston. And I have to be at work in–" he looked at the wall clock, "–twenty-two minutes."

Pressed shirt required.

Ironing was the only thing he could do, but his finger still hurt from the burn. Ignoring the pain, he began pressing the shirt again.

"Oh, dear."

"Right. My mom and dad are in Germany visiting Dennis, my sister's working at the hospital, Kell's in Los Angeles, and Jester isn't exactly a licensed day care provider."

As if on cue, Jester whined from the other side of the back door, nose pressed against the glass. Harriet got up and let him in while Luke finished ironing, then commanded, "Jester, SIT."

The dog did.

"Thank you. Didn't need his nose in my crotch again," Kylie joked.

"Sorry about that. He knows better." *So do I*, he thought, blinking hard at the intrusion.

What the heck was wrong with him?

"He's a dog. It's how they are." She looked around the house, taking it all in, measuring something he couldn't figure out. Shrugging into his now-unwrinkled uniform shirt, he buttoned up and began to undo his pants button to tuck in.

Hold up there, bud. No need for an audience.

Instead, he walked into the bedroom and straightened himself up, including straightening something that was making his pants a tighter fit. His body was responding to Kylie in ways he hadn't experienced in a long, long time.

And it felt *good*.

Would feel much better if he didn't have a busy work day, a meeting with a grumpy boss, a six-year-old who needed to be watched, and twenty minutes to find a solution.

By the time he walked back into the living room, Kylie was petting a very happy Jester, Harriet was munching on a small plate of cheese and apple slices, and the first girl he'd ever kissed gave him an evaluative look that made him do a double take.

"I'll stay with her," Kylie chirped. Yeah, *chirped*. She sounded like a freaking bluebird of happiness.

He stared at her. "You'll *what*?"

"I'll stay with her."

"No. Thanks, but no way. You're a stranger."

"I'm Red Cross certified in CPR and first aid. I have a master's degree in education and am a licensed teacher. And I'm not a stranger." A blush formed on the tips of her ears as she looked up at him in a way that made Luke remember the past, a pier, a pretty girl, and a perfect moon.

He recalled that blushing-ear quirk from years ago. Kylie

hadn't changed one bit. The taste of her cinnamon gum from that kiss on the pier at camp made his mouth water.

"No. You're not a stranger. But...Harriet doesn't know you. And you're not exactly trustworthy."

"Excuse me?"

"You got stuck in a charity donation box on Thanksgiving night, Kylie. I have a right to question the executive functioning skills of someone who does that."

"It was an accident! And you've got it all backwards, Luke. The fact that you found me in that donation box is a testament to my resourcefulness! Not a reason to question my abilities."

His phone beeped with a reminder that he had to leave right now for work, to make it to the meeting with the chief on time.

"How so?" Crossing his arms over his chest, his forearm scraped against the bottom of his badge.

This felt exactly like those moments when people tried to talk themselves out of speeding tickets.

After being caught doing 92 in a 55 zone.

"I could have frozen to death. I found the safest way to stay warm and went for it."

"You locked yourself out of your car after throwing your keys and phone in that bin. You literally had no other option. A rabid raccoon would have instinctively done the same thing."

Her eye roll forced him to suppress a grin. "I could have walked to the nearest house."

"That would have been a four-mile walk."

"My point exactly! I made the most logical choice." The grin on her face made it clear she thought she was winning this... whatever.

Whatever this conversation was.

Mentally scanning through his options, he realized the babysitter pickings really were slim.

Mom and Dad, and Kell were away.

Colleen was at work.

Kell was in L.A. with his girlfriend, Rachel, visiting her family for Thanksgiving.

Annabeth was always up for whatever Luke wanted, but he

knew asking her to watch Harriet would be misinterpreted. He wasn't looking for a wife.

He just needed someone to keep his kid safe for a workday.

And Luke had already taken yesterday's holiday off.

Today was Black Friday. That meant arrests over people fighting to get the newest television or gaming system at a discount. Cars in ditches because of tired drivers.

Disgruntled neighbors arguing over the outcome of football games or the leaves blown into their yards.

And Colleen's hospital was about to have the Black Friday injury bump. Sleep-deprived consumers and packaged goods from overseas that used zip-ties requiring wire cutters to release products didn't play well together.

His neighbor down the street, Mrs. Petrinelli, was good in a pinch, but she was in her 80s and couldn't watch Harriet for the eight (fine... *ten*) hours he needed.

Kylie Hood was his best option.

Kylie Hood was his *only* option.

"I want Kylie!" Harriet piped up, using that tone Luke knew all too well.

Because she sounded just like Amber when she used it.

"See? Your child has great judgment."

"Daddy interviews nannies before he hires them," Harriet announced, reaching for a green glitter pen, uncapping it, and sniffing. "Don't you need to interview Kylie?"

His phone buzzed. Another reminder. He had ten minutes to get to that meeting, and the drive was eight of those.

"One day," he muttered.

"Ask her a question, Daddy! You asked Nicole a lot of questions."

"Sweetie," he said, bending down. "Nicole's not coming back. She just quit."

"Quit? Like, stopped?"

"Yes. Stopped being your nanny."

"You told me quitting is bad! Like when I wanted to quit ballet."

"It *is* bad." Quitting was more nuanced than that, of course. This was the parenting a six-year-old version.

"So Nicole is bad?"

Luke was taken aback. "Well, I–"

"Go arrest her, Daddy!"

"Arrest her?"

"You arrest bad guys! If Nicole was bad, she needs to be arrested."

Suppressing his inner groan was becoming an art form. He shuddered to imagine what arguments with Harriet would be like when she hit the teen years.

But part of him was quite proud. His kid wasn't a doormat. And in a world where people would take advantage of each other with breathtaking, infuriating sociopathy at times, as he knew all too well from his job, he'd rather raise a headstrong daughter than one who was too "good."

"You do have handcuffs if you need them," Kylie pointed out, looking at his belt.

While he knew what she meant, the words out of her mouth made his blood heat up in ways that most certainly weren't appropriate.

"Hah," he grunted, turning away, willing his body to get itself under control.

"I mean it, Luke. This is how I make it up to you. You did me a huge favor last night. Now I can even the score."

Of all the appeals she could make, this one would work, because she was right. Also, it was the way things operated here in small-town Maine. Everyone helped each other, but you also wanted to give others a chance to help. Sometimes to save face, but mostly to balance it all out. No one took more than they gave and felt good about it.

Not if they had a moral core.

"Fine," he ground out. "Just for today. You deadbolt the house when you're inside. Go anywhere you want that has sidewalks."

"Sidewalks?"

"Sidewalks," he said firmly. "Don't break that rule."

"Okay." Questions swirled in those pretty eyes, but he didn't have time to answer them.

"Can I drive her places?"

"Yes. There's an extra car seat in the closet here. At least Nicole didn't take it home with her before she bailed."

"I know how to install them, so we're good."

"Just don't lose your keys and phone while you're out with her."

Kylie stuck her tongue out at him. Harriet giggled and did the same.

Quickly, he scribbled the house keypad code down on a piece of paper, along with his cellphone, work number, Colleen's number, and–

"What's your number?" he asked, pulling out his phone.

She recited it. He texted her. It pinged.

"Good. Now we'll never lose track of each other."

The words were out of his mouth before he realized what he'd just said.

Kylie looked stricken.

Duty called, though, and his boss needed someone to yell at, so with a quick kiss on Harriet's head and a hurried thank you, he was halfway out the door before Kylie rushed up to him.

"Luke!" She handed him a muffin.

"Thanks!" With a wave, he jogged to his car, climbed in, started it, and took a bite.

He groaned in sheer pleasure.

Backing out of the driveway, he wolfed the muffin down, dismayed to realize he had glitter on his thigh, streaking his red uniform pants.

Life could turn on a dime, couldn't it? he thought to himself, marveling at the last twelve hours.

Wondering when his life had turned into a soap opera.

Minus the sex.

Chapter Fifteen

Kylie

Luview, Maine, had barely changed in fifteen years.

Yet in other ways, it was an alien landscape.

Luke and Harriet lived in one of the older parts of town, in a rare small subdivision that was a little bit like the Midwestern town in Indiana where Kylie had moved at fifteen. Luview wasn't a suburb by any stretch of the imagination, but in this part of town there were about thirty houses, all small ranches, clustered together on three side streets within walking distance of the town center.

Luke and Harriet–and at some point, Amber with them– lived in one.

When Kylie lived here as a kid, they had a cottage near one of the lakes, where the summer people lived until thirty years ago, when owners began winterizing cottages. Theirs had been a rambling place. The original one-bedroom cottage had a huge wrap-around screened porch, a place for endless sleepovers with friends and late-night fun. The addition had two more bedrooms, a much-needed second bath, and a large recreation room where Kylie's dad had installed his prized pool table. Mark

91

Hood had bought the place from his father, and when he died, they'd inherited quite a bit of money.

The inheritance had come in the year before he cheated on her mother.

And was long gone by the time Kylie reached college age.

Life here in Luview had been idyllic, sweet and perfect, and Kylie's heart began to pump faster as she walked along Clannaugh, mind filling in the map of the town. How quickly it all poured in, filling in like a paint-by-numbers canvas, all of it red, white, pink, and green.

For the trees and grass.

None of that was present now, as snow covered everything, but when she closed her eyes, she saw it all, just like she had while living in Indiana, crying her eyes out that first year, hating the move.

Suppressing the memories that made her ache had been a coping mechanism, especially when Luke had suddenly stopped replying to emails, blocked her on the one social media account she had back then, and just... disappeared.

Like her job at Nordicbeth.

Poof!

Harriet had begged to walk to the library, so Kylie bundled her up, leashed Jester, and decided this would be a great way to explore the town, kill some time, get some exercise, and give the dog a way to burn off some energy. Luke lived three blocks from the library, so, worst case, they could turn back in ten minutes and be fine.

Thanksgiving weekend in Love You, Maine, was a relatively quiet time. February was the worst, the streets crowded, everything painted in red like the sky opened up and bled on the town. June was nothing but a blur of brides and grooms, pink-dyed animals and everything wedding. Bridezillas dominated back when Kylie lived here and before she'd even heard the term, and the locals stayed far away–unless they ran a wedding-related business.

Which was, come to think of it... pretty much everyone in Love You, Maine. If you weren't a wedding planner or a dress shop, you provided flowers, food, officiants, event space – everyone was connected on some level to weddings and love.

So the non-love-related holidays were a rare treat, townsfolk out and about, people happy and relaxed, cherishing their time off. Black Friday meant there was more activity than usual on the roads, but the library should be quiet.

And Kylie was looking for quiet.

Because the last thing she wanted was to expose herself to town gossip yet again. Her mother's last-minute upheaval fifteen years ago had scarred her, but she viewed it through a different lens now.

A lens that involved licking her own wounds after being burned by love.

Jaded and *Love You* didn't go together.

Ever.

"Hello, Nicole! Oh!" said an old woman, waving from the porch of a house a few doors down from Luke's. "You're not Nicole!" The woman squinted, instantly suspicious, gaze going to Jester and Harriet.

Harriet elbowed her on the hip. "That's Mrs. Petrinelli. She's super nice and she gives me hot chocolate when I build a snowman in her front yard. Jester gets cheese from her for a treat, but don't tell Daddy."

"Why not?"

"He doesn't want Jester to get spoiled."

"Hi there!" Kylie called out. She knew from experience that the best way to handle small-town suspicion was to be as friendly as possible, and to establish your street cred fast. "I'm Kylie Hood! We used to live here in Luview years ago!"

"Mark Hood's daughter?" Her eyebrows shot up.

Uh oh.

Kylie forgot how bad her dad's scandal had been.

Not only had he been loud about it in Bilbee's, he'd gone on to enumerate all the ways Kylie's mom was... deficient.

In bed.

"Yes, ma'am!" she said brightly, faking it.

"You poor thing. Your mother ran out of town with her tail between her legs, didn't she? If you ask me, *he's* the one who should have been ashamed." Kylie could hear her judgmental sniff all the way down there on the sidewalk.

She suddenly really, *really* liked Mrs. Petrinelli.

"Thank you," was all Kylie could think to say, some piece of her fifteen-year-old self ready to cry with relief.

"Heard he married that hussy and they live down south." The way she said *down south* might as well have been the words *in hell.*

"Yes, they do."

"What are you doing with Harriet and Jester?"

"Helping out. Luke's nanny just quit on him."

Oops.

Mistake #1: In small towns, every detail about every person was fodder for gossip. The whole town would know before Luke arrived at work.

Mrs. Petrinelli stepped off her porch, her thin frame encased in an enormous down coat, sharp brown eyes buried in wrinkles, most of her eyelashes gone but all her wits intact. "Nicole quit?"

"Yes, ma'am."

"I knew it. That girl was a silly little dingbat."

"Dingbat," Harriet repeated, giggling.

"Why on earth didn't Luke ask me to babysit sweet little Harriet?"

This wasn't a rhetorical question; Kylie had to tread carefully here. Luke was in for a tongue lashing from a town institution if Kylie didn't answer this just right.

"Luke helped me out and I was returning the favor."

That did it.

"Oh." Mrs. Petrinelli nodded with approval, mouth tightening as her eyebrows shot up. "And do you have experience with children?"

"I do. I taught for a while. Have my teaching license. I managed children's programming for Nordicbeth, too."

Mistake #2: giving the woman any details about herself that could connect her to Perry and her own mess.

"I see. Good place, even if the owners are a bit full of themselves." *Sniff.*

Jester saved her, pulling hard on the leash as a squirrel darted across the sidewalk a hundred feet ahead.

"Gotta go, ma'am. Nice to meet you!"

"You're a local! I've met you before! My name is Anne, not Ma'am!" Mrs. Petrinelli protested, but Kylie took her chance to escape.

Pretending Jester was pulling harder than he really was, Kylie left with only two mistakes under her belt.

And for the next nine minutes, she just walked with a happy dog, a chattering kid, and a balmy thirty-four-degree Maine winter day.

Then it hit her: Would the library be open the day after Thanksgiving?

Oh, well. No matter what, the walk was good for the three of them.

The library was a small brick building—bright red, of course—with two big window seats on either side, fire engine red shutters and door, and a foyer she hoped was dog friendly. The heart-shaped sign said Luview Library, with a silhouette of a young girl reading a book on a swing.

And a big sign taped to the glass door said, OPEN TODAY.

A blast of heat from an ancient grid radiator seemed gratuitous, given the above-freezing day, but she welcomed it nonetheless.

And sure enough, there was a place to tie Jester's leash, and a bowl with water in it nearby.

She texted Luke quickly:

At the library. How do I check books out for Harriet? Library card?

He responded immediately.

It's a tiny town, big city girl. Harriet IS the library card.

She couldn't help but laugh.

"What's so funny?" Harriet asked as Kylie opened the main door for her.

Kylie bopped her on the nose with her finger. "You."

Giggles brought them into the library, where time really had stood still. The oak shelves rose up as if climbing to touch the ceiling, smaller, angled shelves dominating the periodicals section.

Thin light-gray carpeting covered the floors, old and worn, dirty by the main doors. Practical boot mats were conspicuously placed near the entrance.

The rustle of newspapers being read transported her back in time, each large page whispering as someone with gray or white hair flipped to a new section.

Computer monitors in a long, raised row on a counter were flat screen, the only reminder of the present. No music. No noise louder than quiet voices discussing the location of books.

Luview, Maine, had the best library in the world. That's how it had felt as a child, at least.

And Kylie's sigh felt like finding a new way to breathe and thrive.

"Oh, my goodness. That can't be Kylie Hood, can it?" gasped the librarian behind the desk, a woman with gray hair, eyeglasses on the same red beaded chain Kylie remembered, and who, as she walked out from behind the desk, moved with a noticeable limp.

"Mrs. Chen?" Excitement got the best of her and soon she was hugging the old woman, who was an older, grayer version of one of her favorite people in town. For years, Kylie used the library the way most kids used their computers, killing time with books instead of video games or social media.

She'd read every single novel in the children's section before they'd moved.

"Kylie! I haven't seen you in years! Look at you, all grown up. My, my, my. What brings you back?" Kind, smart eyes met hers.

Guilt flooded Kylie's veins. She'd been living so close this last year, but hadn't visited. Why not?

She knew why, but couldn't deal with that right now. Her reason was busy soulmating halfway across the world.

Emphasis on the *mating* part.

"I'm—I—"

Her stumbling made Mrs. Chen immediately cut her off. "No need to explain. I shouldn't pry. It's just good to see you, and that's enough! How long are you in town? I'd love to have coffee or tea and chat." She winked. "Or even a cocktail, now that you're of age."

"Mrs. Chen!"

The older woman chuckled. "Call me Dotty. We're adults."

She'd always been Mrs. Chen in Kylie's mind, but out of politeness she replied, "Of course, Dotty."

Boy, did that feel weird.

"Kylie's my nanny today!" Harriet piped up, making Mrs. Chen's eyebrows fly over the rim of her glasses.

"What happened to Nicole?" Before Kylie or Harriet could explain, she cut them off. "Let me guess. She met the man of her dreams and is going to Hollywood to be a star."

"How did you know?"

"Because the gossip mill is ahead of you by about thirty minutes. You know how small towns are."

Kylie's cheeks went warm.

She did.

And she was grateful to Luke for not blabbing about her donation box mishap.

"Mrs. Chen! Kylie is a trash fairy."

Bending down slightly, but not at the knee, Mrs. Chen gave Harriet a confused look. "Kylie is a what?"

"A fairy baker," Kylie said a little too loudly. The sound echoed through the high-ceilinged building, enough to make one of the librarians at the desk say "*Shhh.*"

"Yeah! A fairy baker. Only she doesn't bake the fairies, because then they would be dead. Like Mommy," Harriet replied, oblivious to the impact her words had on Mrs. Chen and Kylie, who both winced.

Kylie gave Mrs. Chen–*Dotty*–an amused look and explained. "I bake fairy muffins."

"Did Kylie the fairy baker do this beautiful butterfly on your cheek?" Dotty stroked Harriet's temple with a feather-soft caress. "And lightning on the other!"

"Yep! She's really good."

"I'll bet she is."

Harriet scampered off to the children's section, three books in her arms before Kylie could wave to Dotty and catch up. As they browsed, she inhaled deeply, the Luview Library's scent forever ingrained in her olfactory pathways.

Old books and woodsmoke.

Down in the basement, the little wood stove that warmed the place when the power went out was used weekly by a knitting group. Or, at least, she assumed it still was. Fifteen years ago, yes.

Now? Who knew?

"Kylie? Can you hold these?" Harriet plunked a stack of seven or eight books in her arms, and seemed ready to go back for more.

"Wait a minute! You need a limit. My arms are strong but not *that* strong, and we still have more walking to do."

Harriet squeezed Kylie's biceps. "Yours aren't as big as Daddy's."

A blast of internal heat made Kylie lose focus as she pictured those arms, the ones she'd just seen as he ironed in his short-sleeve t-shirt. "Right."

"Okay. Only eight."

Kylie hefted the weight, making a decision. "Two more."

Harriet grinned and ran off, easily finding more stories to add to the pile.

Checkout was electronic now, and they must have had Harriet's library card in the computer system, because soon Dotty was sliding the stack across the counter with a grin.

"Here you go. Need a bag?"

"Thank you!"

Dotty pulled out an obviously re-used paper shopping bag with handles from a small basket. "Remind Luke to bring his extras in next time he's here with Harriet."

"Sure will."

Dotty's hand covered hers, a gentle squeeze making Kylie feel important. "I mean it about getting together, Kylie. I've always wondered about you."

Tears threatened to overcome her.

She squeezed back.

"Thank you. You, too." Kylie let go and scribbled her phone number on a piece of scrap paper, handing it to Dotty. "There. Now we're in touch."

"My day is all the better for it."

Out in the foyer, Jester saw them through the glass doors and woofed lightly.

"You're being summoned," Dotty said with a laugh, waving them off, turning to answer a ringing phone.

The bag of books was harder to manage than she'd expected, Jester's eager pull on the leash requiring all her attention to stay balanced.

"Kylie?" Harriet said shyly.

"Hmmm?"

"Can we just go back to the house and read?"

Kylie squinted one eye, mugging at her.

"You don't just want to read, do you?"

Harriet's eyes flew open.

Hah. Caught.

"How about this? We'll go home, Jester can run around in the backyard, and I'll read all these books to you."

"ALL of them?"

"Yes. Then we'll have lunch, and after *that*, you can have another fairy muffin."

"And then we'll build snow forts!"

"Deal."

Harriet hugged her and they turned back toward the house, waving at Mrs. Petrinelli as they walked quickly past.

At the front door, she pulled out the piece of paper Luke had given her, his steady hand the same as when they were kids. Back then, he'd talked about being an architect, and his penmanship was like something you'd find on a house blueprint.

What made him become a police officer?

The code was easy and soon they were inside, Jester whining at his food bowl, Harriet using the bathroom, and Kylie surveying the house.

This would not do.

The general state of messiness in the house made more sense now that she knew Amber was gone, and Luke was a single dad. A single-dad widower, with a full-time job, no less. Raising Harriet alone had to be hard.

The Luview family helped him, though. She remembered Dean and Deanna Luview as warm, kind people, running the area's big tree service company. All four Luview kids had worked for their mom and dad at some point, and over the years, plenty of high schoolers had worked stacking wood that the Luviews sold by the cord.

Kylie, like lots of other local kids, took a part-time, seasonal job at Love You Chocolate as soon as she turned fourteen. February always turned the town into a giant festival, with thousands of tourists pouring in, and the red foil heart chocolates famously sold by the company were a popular item.

But she'd only had that seasonal job for one year. Not the four or five she'd always assumed.

For certain, the Luviews would have rallied around Luke today, but they weren't around. He'd said they were in Germany visiting Dennis, which meant he must live there. And Kell was in Los Angeles? Hmm. Of all the people in Luview, Kell was the last person she'd imagine ever leaving. Such a hometown guy.

For as much as the town looked the same, so much really had changed after all.

Shaking herself out of her own thoughts, she looked at the living room again and sighed.

"Any nanny worth her paycheck would have done better than this, though," she said under her breath as she walked into the kitchen and looked at the fridge. At least it was mostly full. Looked like Luke had been sensible and shopped before the big holiday rush.

Finding her phone, Kylie opened up her trusty organization app and began voice dictation, a satisfying checklist forming before her eyes. Using some drag-and-drop fingertip techniques, within twenty minutes she had the rest of her day planned.

"Harriet," she said, the little girl looking up from the television, "want to help me with a special project?"

"Sure!"

"We're going to surprise your daddy."

"He doesn't like surprises."

"I promise he'll like this one."

"Okay. What is it?"

Telling her they were about to clean up would be the fastest way to get Harriet to turn into a whimpering mess. She had to make it fun. A game.

An adventure.

"Fairies," she whispered, "like to hide in dark places."

"Right!"

"And they really like to hide in corners."

Harriet looked at one and blinked rapidly.

"And under the beds and couches."

A wary eye went to the easy chair in front of the television. "Are they here?"

"We can make them come out."

"We can?"

Kylie nodded. If Harriet thought it was her own idea to straighten up, she'd be on board.

Jester made a snuffly sound, clearly taking a nap.

"I know!" Harriet whispered. "If we look everywhere and make less dark places, we can make them come out."

"Oooo, I love it." Kylie pulled out her app. Harriet looked over her shoulder.

"What's that?"

"My organizing app."

"I see my name on it."

"You can read?"

"A little. My name and Jester and Amber and Luke. And my address, 14 Clannaugh Lane, Luview, Maine."

"That's great!"

"What's the app say?"

"It says you should start by pulling out anything you find under the couch and chairs and putting it away. The fairies will only come out if there's nothing to hide behind."

"OKAY!"

Kylie quietly pressed the checkbox next to "Convince Harriet."

For the next two hours, they happily tidied to Taylor Swift songs, occasionally stopping to lip sync the extra cool lyrics. Kylie made sure they both stayed hydrated, and at lunchtime, she made sandwiches, carrot sticks, and pulled out the coveted muffins.

"Those fairies are really, really good at hiding," Harriet said sadly. "We cleaned so good and didn't find any!"

Faking a sympathetic pout, Kylie said in commiseration, "Sometimes the fairies outsmart us."

"They sure do!"

Kylie winked. "We just have to try again tomorrow."

Harriet's yawn made Kylie squint one eye at her and ask, "Do you need a power nap?"

That stopped a protest short. "What's a power nap?"

"It's what the fairies do. You sleep, but you sleep extra intensely. You use less time and wake up with extra energy!"

"I want that! But can I do it on the couch?" Another yawn.

"Sure."

Jester hopped up on the couch and snuggled in with Harriet, making Kylie pause.

"Is he allowed on the couch?"

"Daddy says no, but Aunt Colleen says yes."

"Hmm."

Kylie let it slide. It was just for one day, and she wanted the poor child to have fun. She was remarkably flexible for a little kid, and Kylie didn't have to be a hammer dropper here.

The dog stayed.

And soon, Harriet was sound asleep.

Quickly, Kylie grabbed some dollhouse furniture from one of Harriet's toy sets and arranged it in the corner, sprinkled a little glitter on top, and smiled to herself, imagining the little girl waking up to the fairy magic.

This must be a taste of what parents went through with Santa and the tooth fairy.

And Kylie ate it *allllll* up.

Leaving teaching had been a tough choice, but Perry had convinced her it was a "dead-end" career. Working in children's programming would be better. She had to admit, once she'd gotten into the new field, he'd been right about one thing:

While teaching absolutely was *not* a dead end, creating curricula and shaping frameworks for delivering important concepts to children via fun entertainment turned out to be her jam.

Which was why being fired from a job she loved sucked so much.

Her phone buzzed. She checked and found a text from Luke.

I forgot some paperwork. You guys home? I don't want to scare you by suddenly appearing.

It's your own house! she wrote back, walking into the bathroom and surveying her features.

Did she have a brush in her purse? And a lipstick?

Just being cautious, didn't want to surprise you.

Are you checking up on me? Making sure I'm doing the job right?

All she got was a thumbs up icon in response, then he stopped texting.

Setting her phone on the counter, she quietly walked back into the living room, where Jester was sleeping like he was Harriet's twin. Her purse was easy to grab and bring into the bathroom.

Score! Her brush was in there, and some tinted lip gloss, and a hair tie.

Brushing her long blonde hair into a low ponytail was easy. Calming her nerves wasn't. As she left the bathroom, setting her purse on the dining table, the front door made four muted beeps. It clicked open and Luke walked in, a vision in red.

Red leather work jacket included.

"Wow," she whispered, holding her finger over her lips, pointing to the napping child and dog.

Luke's eyebrows went up. "What was the 'wow' for?"

"I forgot how all the cops in town look like red Twizzlers."

"Not true. Some of us look more like red heart candies. Rusty's putting on a gut."

"Who is Rusty?"

"New guy. Sleeps around." Luke gave her side eye. "Stay away from him."

She didn't know whether to laugh, be offended, or be grateful.

"I can't believe you got her to nap," he said, coming close so his voice didn't wake Harriet. A whiff of aftershave hit her, mixed with a very masculine scent. She wanted to close her eyes and take a deep inhale, but held back.

"It was easy."

"Don't sell yourself short. You have a skill."

"Thanks."

Luke smiled at her, then walked down the hall to the room with the big bed she knew must be his.

His and Amber's, before.

He walked out holding a small folder. "Chief's mad I didn't file some paperwork on time."

"Are you in big trouble?"

"No. Just missed something that turned out to be more important than I originally thought. It's my fault."

"You say that so calmly."

He shrugged. "I'm human. I make mistakes. If I'm going to make them, I'd rather do it with paperwork than out in the field, or with my little girl."

"You really work hard to be a good dad."

"It's my most important job. Even being a police officer comes second."

"As it should. Priorities."

He looked surprised. "Exactly. I take crap for it sometimes."

"You do?"

"Some of the other guys at the station. They think I'm too focused on Harriet. That I should just let Mom, Dad, Colleen, and Kell watch her more."

"She needs you."

"She needs a mom," he said softly, face tender and open. As their shared gaze lengthened, making Kylie's throat tighten and her heart race, he seemed to pull in, shut down a bit.

Wiggling the folder, he gave her a polite nod. "Looks like you have it under control. See you when I'm off work."

"Okay."

"Thanks, Kylie. I really appreciate it."

"It's my pleasure," she said, touching his arm. "Really. And it's nice to have a conversation that's not through a steel door."

Laughing, he walked out the door, clearly trying to keep his voice down. As he walked down the sidewalk to his pink cruiser, Kylie let herself snicker. No matter how attractive he was, the guy her sister called "Hot Cop" was dressed in black work boots, red pants, a short red leather jacket, and wore a red police officer's hat.

He looked like he fell upside down in a vat of fruit punch.

"Ah, Love You," she murmured. "So much love, so much to laugh at."

Turning her attention back to the living room, she viewed it through new eyes.

Doing housework without a six-year-old to manage was a lot easier, and an hour later, Kylie was done with everything but sweeping in the living room, kitchen, half bath off the foyer, and the foyer itself. Cleaning the bedrooms and bathrooms felt intrusive, so she didn't go that far.

But the piles of clean clothes and towels in the laundry basket had to be folded neatly, sorted, and put in each bedroom.

Her eyes stopped on a framed picture of Amber, Luke, and Harriet a number of years ago, Harriet a toddler in a snowsuit, sitting on a sled. Amber wore a hat, but her signature dark curls spilled out from under it, long and matted with snow.

It was clear she and Luke had just been in an epic snow battle, but Harriet was pristine.

Another photo, this one at an amusement park in what was clearly Florida, was a selfie. All three were grinning, Luke eating a chocolate-coated ice cream bar, Harriet wearing a character hat.

Amber was glowing.

Radiant, even.

Kylie picked up the picture, focusing more on Amber than anyone else. They'd been good buddies for a long time, and while it had hurt when Luke had blocked her on social media, stopped sending her letters, and her emails to him had bounced, it really stung when Amber faded quickly from her life.

They were fifteen back then, though. Time and experience helped her to see it was just... being fifteen.

In fact, if Amber were alive, they'd be hugging and catching up, Luke teasing her about getting caught in the donation bin while promising to hold the secret.

Amber *wasn't* alive, though.

All the shadows and questions from the past would never be answered.

With no idea how long Harriet would nap, she took another look around and decided helping Luke with dinner was next.

There was a crockpot, and all the ingredients to make a fine chili and pop-the-can biscuits, with a small head of lettuce she could turn into a simple salad for him and Harriet.

But first–*coffee*.

She'd earned it.

Settling someone else's home to rights felt good. When you organized your own home, you were one hundred percent responsible for every item out of place, and the cascade of decisions that had to be made, often attached to procrastination, shame, and other foibles, could be paralyzing.

That's why it took Kylie longer than it should have to get rid of Perry's crap.

And look how *that* turned out.

"Yeah," she chuckled, low and quiet, eyes combing the clean living room.

Luke's living room.

Single-dad, still-hot Luke.

"Look how that turned out."

Chapter Sixteen

Luke

Word had traveled fast.

So fast, Nadine had verbally assaulted him before he could take off his hat.

"Nicole quit? And Kylie Hood is back in town? You're a regular *National Enquirer* disguised as a man, Luke," she cracked as he froze in place, arm stuck in front of the coat rack, his mind still processing what she said. Nadine was a town treasure, part of the station since before he'd been a gleam in his father's eye, and she was somewhere in her seventies.

With zero plans to retire anytime soon.

Sharp as a tack, with wild orange hair she had done twice a week in a faithful bouffant down at her daughter's salon, and a wiry, thin face that showed all she'd weathered, those chocolate brown eyes were the kicker.

They knew everything.

Of course she knew already. *Of course.*

"Why don't you tell me all about my life, Nadine? Seems like you know more than I do."

"Hah! You have a go at running this police station without knowing what everyone's up to. I couldn't avoid it if I tried."

One of the big town gossips, Nadine was anything *but* avoiding the scuttle.

"Got a big meeting with Chief Anderssen, Nadine. If you want to spill the tea, I don't have time."

She snorted. "As if you'd ever gossip with me, Luke. You're tight as a drum."

"Good to know."

And then it began.

All day, he'd suffered at work.

First, the teasing, the questions, the prying into his personal life.

Second, the dressing down from the chief about a case that had gone sideways.

But then the unexpected had happened: Chief of Police Dawson Anderssen had told Luke he was retiring in two years.

And he wanted Luke to be the next police chief.

"Sir," he'd demurred, secretly pleased but also half sick to his stomach from overwhelm. "I'm honored. But I'm not sure I'm the right candidate."

"If I pick you, you are."

Dawson always had a way of being blunt.

And certain.

A towering giant of a man, he was half as wide as he was tall, imposing and solid. Anyone trying to cross him would think twice.

Luke didn't have that kind of physical presence, though he was tall and strong enough. At just a titch over six feet and two hundred pounds of muscle and bone, he did just fine in the power department.

But Dawson had a wisdom and gravitas Luke admired.

Before Amber died, Luke thought he had it in him, too.

Now, though...

The stone-cold certainty about making decisions was there. The intuitive ability to take control or restore order was absolutely present. But leading the town's law enforcement, given how his life had cracked apart out of the blue—that was daunting.

"You're young. I'll give you that. But you've seen your share of hardship, Luke. And you've been damn good at your job since the day you were hired, nine years ago. Someone has to succeed me. You're better than anyone else."

The other deputies were going to turn green when they heard about this.

He was about to have a lot of frenemies.

"I need some time, Dawson."

"Of course. You got a lot on your plate with Harriet. You also have time. Two more years, Luke. She'll be well into second grade and what happened to Amber years more behind you."

That last sentence damn near did him in.

He knew what his boss meant.

How it felt was a whole different matter.

Before he was required to speak, Nadine walked in and interrupted them, complaining about some county environmental code they needed to enforce.

Stunned, but with dignity intact and pride throttling nice and high, Luke had retreated.

And spent the day doing grunt work.

Now, he hurried up his own walkway, punching in the code to unlock the deadbolt and pleased to find Kylie had engaged it.

Nicole "forgot" all the time, a bad habit Luke couldn't stand. Yes, they lived in the middle of nowhere, but danger was random.

He knew that all too well.

He opened the door...

And entered into paradise.

The tantalizing odor of garlic, tomato, oregano, and cumin assaulted his nose, making his stomach growl. Every square inch of his floor not covered by furniture was... visible.

He could *see* the hardwood floor and carpet.

The throw pillows on the couches were in the right place, plumped and arranged by color. Quilts were folded neatly over the back of the couch and recliner chair. The dining table was set.

With actual placemats.

The lazy Susan in the middle of it was wiped down, with salt, pepper, a napkin holder with real napkins, and the vinegar and oil he preferred on salad in the cruets.

He blinked.

Wrong house?

Nope. It was his.

Jester rested in his dog bed, tail thumping twice as Luke walked in the door, eyes meeting his with a wide awe that seemed to say, *Can you believe this? We hit the jackpot.*

Then the dog jumped up, lunged at Luke, and nearly licked him to death.

"Hi, Daddy!" Tackled by fifty pounds of solid progeny that made Jester back off, he found his heart lifted by the sight of a happy kid, an engaged Kylie, and–*this.*

A happy home.

One deep inhale and whatever was in the crockpot had him half crazed. His mom and Colleen cooked for them when they could. He could do the basics, and rode a mean grill in the summer, but this was bliss.

Pure bliss.

For once, he didn't have to come home, take one look around, and feel guilty.

That was worth more than anyone could understand.

He turned to Kylie, gratitude on the tip of his tongue, but the thank you he expected to say wasn't what came out of his mouth.

Instead, be blurted out:

"You're hired."

"What?"

"Hired. You want a job? I follow all employment laws. You'll get a salary, health insurance, paid time off, and I pay all the Social Security taxes."

"Hired for what?"

"To be Harriet's nanny."

Chin dropping, eyebrows raised, mouth open in shock, Kylie gaped at him.

"Nanny?" she gasped.

Then she began laughing hysterically.

Harriet gave them quizzical looks and he knew he needed to manage this situation, *fast.* Emotion had gotten the better of him, but he wasn't wrong.

She was perfect. Exactly what he and Harriet needed.

And he was desperate.

Desperate for more of *this*.

"Let me back up. I guess you already have a job?" No use in hiding his disappointment, which he let leach into his voice.

"Actually, no. Just got fired."

"Fired?"

"My ex's family owned the resort."

"Resort?"

She sighed. Loudly. "I used to work for Nordicbeth Resorts as children's programming director."

"Nordicbeth Resorts?"

"Yes."

"Who was your ex? Tim?"

Tim was Perry's brother.

"No. Perry."

Luke couldn't help himself, making a derogatory noise. "That priggish little... that pompous ass? Really? *Him?*"

"Hey, now–"

"I can see why you dumped him. You deserve way better than that. Glad you got away from him."

Kylie didn't say a word. Discomfort covered her expression, though.

"He got you fired? Did you–were you bad at your job?"

"No! I was great! I'm working on lining up interviews for new jobs."

"Perfect! You have a new job now. You're hired."

"Luke."

"Mmm?"

"I can't."

"Why not?" He named a figure. She didn't seem impressed. He couldn't afford more and, for this town, he paid well.

Plus, she seemed to get along really well with Harriet. Job enjoyment had to count for something.

"I'm only here for three more months, until my lease is up. Perry says he'll pay his half of the rent until then. And my sister leaves town tomorrow."

"Then you're all alone?" he asked, suddenly touched by her

isolation. If Luke understood anything, it was the deep pain of loneliness.

"I'm fine."

"You'd be finer spending your days with the best little kid *ever*."

She was softening, but she was also a mature adult who knew this wasn't as simple as he was making it out to be.

"You need a job. I need a nanny. Harriet needs a stable grownup she can rely on."

"Luke, I–"

"Please." The word came out with more intensity than he intended, his heart caught up in an imagined future where everything was just a little bit easier. Where he didn't have to worry every minute. Where life was orderly, organized, calm.

Where he could *breathe*.

And where those sweet Kylie eyes looked at him five days a week, above that gorgeous smile.

"Three months," she said slowly. "I'm here for three months."

"I'll take it. A trial period."

"I can promise you that, but nothing more. I'm applying for jobs in New York and if the right one comes along early…" Gaze drifting to Harriet, the crease between her eyes, at the bridge of her nose, tightened with concern. Kylie was a deeply moral person, he knew.

She didn't want to hurt Harriet.

And that, more than anything, was exactly why he wanted to hire her.

Well–among other reasons.

"Three months it is, then," he agreed, holding out his hand for a shake, ignoring the New York part. He'd process that later.

As her palm slid against his, the pad of his thumb caressed the soft skin on the back of her hand.

She closed her eyes and sighed for a brief second.

Did she feel it, too?

"But," she said, withdrawing her hand, "I have conditions."

"Name them."

"Your salary and benefits are fine. I want complete freedom to do fun stuff with Harriet."

"Done." He held up one finger. "Let me print out the contract I had with Nicole. You can read through it and we can sign it right now."

Harriet chose that exact moment to join the discussion, positioning herself between the two of them as he went to the desk in his bedroom. "Kylie's my new nanny?"

"I am!"

"YAY! Now I can have fairy muffins every day!"

"We can add that in the contract," he heard Kylie shout from down the hall as he clicked through his computer files, finding the old contract Nicole signed. A few changes of dates and names and he printed it.

Three pages.

Long enough to be professional, short enough for Kylie to read on the spot.

When he brought the document back to her, she began scanning quickly, nodding as he stood, one hand on his hip, one scratching the top of Jester's head, his nose filled with the delightful scents of her cooking.

Dinner was already done. He could feed Harriet and have some actual time for himself tonight.

Time... remember free time? He smiled at the thought.

On page three, Kylie looked up, ear tips turning red.

"Something wrong?"

"Number 14, Part A."

"What's that?"

"No fraternization policy."

Oh, man. He'd forgotten about that. In an abundance of caution, he'd had his lawyer add a section making it clear, in this legal employment contract, that he and his nanny could not have a romantic relationship.

Ever.

His lawyer called it the Don't Bang Your Nanny clause.

As a law enforcement officer, he wanted to take no chances.

And that meant destroying any chance he had with Kylie now.

Surprise at her reaction turned to amusement inside him, and then desire, a flicker turning into a flame. Was she questioning it because she was attracted to him?

The feeling was mutual.

"Is that a problem?" he asked, taking a step closer, his voice going low and soft. Kylie's lashes fluttered as her eyes turned up at him, heat building between them.

"Of course not," she insisted, taking a step back, though the way her throat trembled when she swallowed said otherwise. "A smart, clear directive. We know where things stand."

"We do."

"You have a pen?"

Pulling one from his front shirt pocket–the very same pen he'd used to write eleven speeding tickets today as Black Friday shoppers spent more time celebrating their scores and less minding their speedometers–he handed it to her with a flourish, their fingers brushing against each other, electricity flying fast and free.

She signed. She smiled.

He cheered inside.

Because for the next three months, Kylie Hood would be in his home five days a week, cooking, cleaning, and nurturing Harriet, making his life so much easier.

But Number 14, Part A of that contract? And the way she looked at him with those doe eyes?

That made everything harder.

Everything.

Harder.

Chapter Seventeen

Kylie

"Hood?"

The woman at the small hostess stand with a scarred wood surface patted two plastic-covered paper bags filled with takeout cartons. Kylie approached the cash register and, when prompted, slid her credit card in, chip first.

"Thank you," she said, but the woman was busy, already on her phone, scribbling an order while ringing Kylie out. The scent of ginger, garlic, and spiced beef made her mouth water.

Just outside of the town line, there was an Asian fusion restaurant, and Kylie was exploiting every opportunity to order from Mountain Dragon. There was nothing like this here in town when she was a kid.

"Kylie?"

At the sound of her name, she whipped around to find Luke's sister, Colleen, giving her a crooked smile and a look Kylie knew all too well.

Small-town once-over.

Between Mrs. Petrinelli and Mrs. Chen, the rumor mill had

surely completed a full circuit by now. No secret survived even a whiff of public exposure.

"Hi, Colleen!" Kylie reached for her takeout bags, the moist heat a welcome sensorial change from the spike of fear in her.

"Haven't seen you in years! Luke told me about today. You're Harriet's new nanny?"

Not about last night, I hope, Kylie thought but didn't say. Colleen's face would show it if he'd blabbed.

Clearly, he'd kept the secret about the donation bin.

Colleen was reserved and hard to read, unlike her mother, who had always been a very open, welcoming woman. Kylie didn't perceive Colleen's demeanor as negative.

More like very, very guarded.

"Just helping out."

"Three months, huh?"

"Luke really filled you in, I see."

"We're a close family. If my shifts at the hospital didn't overlap all the time with Luke's, I'd babysit her myself."

Kylie could read between the lines. That was code for: *You're watching precious cargo. Don't you dare harm a hair on my niece's head.*

Or a single vessel in her heart.

"I'm sure Harriet would much prefer you over me. I'll do my absolute best, though. She's a sweetie who deserves that."

"Right. Glad you understand." Colleen's smile widened.

Kylie had passed some unspoken test.

"What're you getting?"

"Bi bim bap."

Disgust twisted Colleen's smile. "You and Luke with the gooey egg yolk."

"Yum!"

"Gross! I'll stick to my egg rolls and orange chicken."

"Those are great, too."

"Are you always so flexible?"

Kylie shrugged. "I just like to try new things."

Colleen's eyes narrowed as if to say, *My brother better not be one of them.*

An image of Number 14, Part A popped like a photo being taken, the image flash-frozen in her mind.

"Luview?" The woman at the register, her name tag impossible to read, pointed to a small bag. Looked like Colleen was eating alone tonight.

Two people behind her snickered. Being descendants of the town's founder meant Luke and his siblings, along with his many cousins in town, were ever aware of their last name.

Colleen grabbed her small bag. "Gotta go. See you around, Kylie!"

And with that, the unexpected interrogation was over.

The long drive back to her apartment gave her time for her mind to wander, retrieving as many memories of Colleen as she could. Years ago, she'd spent nearly every waking moment tracing the fine emotional outlines of her years in Luview, as if doing so would permanently etch them inside her, as if to say, *This was real.*

This is me.

Indiana wasn't bad. It just wasn't *here*.

Transferring as a rising sophomore from a state most people in the Midwest thought was populated mostly by moose didn't help, either. Unlike Luview, in Rio (pronounced RYE-oh), Indiana, she had no history.

And history mattered.

Fortunately, Kylie had an easy connection with little kids. With loads of church camps and after-school programs nearby, she'd quickly become the go-to teen girl for any program involving childcare and fun.

Little kids didn't judge you.

Little kids didn't have pecking orders (or, at least, different ones).

Little kids knew how to live in the moment.

And, best of all, they knew how to feel unadulterated joy and share in it with you.

When a camp director made an offhand comment about majoring in education and human development during the summer between Kylie's junior and senior years of high school, she had a sudden sense of how her life could be. The structure of it all fell into place. A teaching degree, but not just to be in a classroom.

To be with *kids*.

To walk the journey of life together with small people who were authentic.

Life here in Luview always held a place inside her nothing else could fill. After her mom forced them to leave so quickly, she'd begged for a social media account to connect with friends, quickly requesting them. Not allowed to have a cellphone until she was sixteen, she'd done the best she could with email, her one social media account, and good old-fashioned snail mail.

And for the first month, Luke had messaged her every day. Sent three letters in envelopes she wore to silk with her fingers. They had two phone calls.

Then... silence.

And then worse.

Because he'd blocked her on social media.

And her final email to him bounced back, undeliverable.

For some reason she never understood, but that broke her teenage heart, he'd cut her out.

Kylie sniffed in the silent car, startled by the sound. The turn into the driveway of her apartment, one of four in a carved-up old house, was made by reflex. Memory Lane wasn't just a road in your mind and heart.

It required careful navigation. Lots of curves and speed bumps, and sometimes, it washed out.

Leaving you with nowhere to go.

One long set of stairs led up to the small apartment over a two-car garage. The door was unlocked and Wendy opened it as Kylie fumbled.

"Here," she said, taking one of the bags from Kylie's left arm, the bicep aching.

Bi bim bap was light, but the ramen soup was the opposite.

Quickly, they settled in for dinner, both eager and hungry. Kylie shed her venture into the past, wholly focused on the precious few hours left with her sister.

"We never had any good Korean food like this in Indiana," Wendy said between moans of culinary delight.

"That's because we didn't have *any* Korean food in Rio, Indiana," Kylie corrected her sister, who was currently bingeing on bi bim bap, breaking the yolk on her fried egg and mixing the goo into her rice, beef, and vegetable mixture. Of all the ways this region of Maine had changed since Kylie last lived here, it was culinary variety that was greatest.

And most appreciated.

"How did I live for so long without eating this?" Wendy groaned as she savored each bite, making Kylie smile.

"Because we lived in Rio," Kylie emphasized, pronouncing it like the locals did. "Do they have good Korean food in France?" she teased.

"If they don't, I'll suffer. Poor me, eating from French bakeries, shopping for produce at the markets, getting gourmet cheese from the fromageries...."

"Poor you. Right."

They laughed and chatted through the rest of dinner, until Kylie pulled out her secret weapon.

"Chocolate gummy worm bombs? No way!" Wendy squealed with delight.

"Complete with crushed Oreos in the center."

"Kylie!" Wendy began to cry, dabbing at her lower lids with her fingertip.

"Why are you upset?"

"Because I'm leaving you! I'm leaving everything! I'm going to a foreign country where I barely speak the language, moving in with strangers, and watching their kids all day. What was I thinking? I'm insane!"

Waterworks ensued.

It was about time.

Wendy was always the first to volunteer for an adventure, eager to try something new, something exciting–and often the guinea pig who acted first, thought later.

Here came the delayed thoughts and feelings.

In triplicate.

"You're going to do great," Kylie soothed, rubbing her sister's back, trying to calm her down. "I really admire you."

That stopped Wendy's tears in their tracks. "You do?"

"Of course."

"I can't believe you just said that. Why would you admire me? You're so much more accomplished. You have a master's degree. You've lived and worked in New York City. I'm some podunk girl with a two-year degree who is nothing but an imposter going off to France!"

"Stop it! You're way more than that, Wendy. You're young and free and full of life. The Durand family is lucky to have you! You'll teach their kids English and be a steady, stable presence for them, and you'll get to live immersed in another culture. And get paid for it!"

"I–I–I hope you're right."

Kylie handed her a takeout napkin. It was the closest thing to a tissue they had, other than toilet paper.

"You're just having last-minute jitters. It's normal."

Wendy wiped her eyes. "Remind me to ask you to be my maid of honor at my wedding. You're good at this."

"Pay my plane ticket to France for the wedding. I hope you meet your Prince Charming there."

"I'll settle for a guy with two last names, a hot bod, and a strong accent. Everything sounds dirtier in French."

Wendy was back to normal.

Crisis averted.

As her sister devoured the rest of her food, Kylie was not far behind her. Soon she was slicing the special dessert and they were exploding from gluttony.

If something had to make you explode, there were worse ways to go.

Wendy groaned. "I'm going to get on that plane bloated and it's all your fault."

"Guilty as charged. But we can't leave any. That would be wasteful." Kylie forced herself to take another bite.

"I've gone past self-loathing into some state I didn't know existed."

"Oh, so I see Perry's dumped you, too?"

Her bitter laugh filled the air.

"At least you have a job for the next three months now," Wendy said with a wink. "With Hot Cop."

"Stop calling him that. And it's in my employment contract–no fraternizing."

"He just put that in there to protect himself. No scandals."

"It's smart. Makes me respect him even more."

"Oh, I can tell how much you want to 'respect' him," Wendy said, using finger quotes. "You'd 'respect' him all night long if you could. Naked. In bed. Cops have handcuffs, right?"

For that, Wendy earned an arm smack.

"Hey! Now that you know he's not married, he's fair game."

"No, he's not! He's my boss now. And it's perfect. I get to play with Harriet and get paid to do it, all while job hunting before my lease is up. Something's finally going right."

A big yawn from Wendy was contagious, Kylie's body stretching as she let it do its job. "Don't you need to go to bed?"

Wendy looked at the clock. "It's not like I'll really sleep, but yes. My ride is scheduled for five a.m." It was almost eleven already.

Kylie was exhausted.

Next to the door, Wendy's luggage and her carry-on were neatly stacked. She knew her sister would get up at four, shower, eat, and leave at five.

That would be it.

Another yawn. They hugged, then went to sleep, Kylie's alarm set for half past four.

As she faded off to sleep, all she could see was Luke's face.

And Number 14, Part A of that contract.

* * *

As scheduled, Kylie's alarm went off at 4:30.

Coffee didn't seem appropriate when she planned to go right back to bed, so she made herself some lemon tea while Wendy finished showering, the sound of the hair dryer going off making Kylie's stomach tighten.

As kids, she and Wendy had never been super close, given the eight-year difference in age. But her willingness to come on the spur of the moment and move in with Kylie after Perry was such a jerk meant so much.

And gave them this precious time together.

Soon enough, Wendy came out of the bathroom, zipping her toiletry bag and tucking it into her suitcase, which protested at the seams.

All that was left of Wendy in the tiny apartment was... nothing, actually.

Kylie owned everything that remained and it wasn't much.

A bed. A nightstand. A couch. An end table. A small kitchen table and two chairs. Perry (or, more accurately, Perry's sister) had taken the television and stand, so she'd gotten rid of cable. Streaming from her laptop was enough.

Life shrank when people left you.

Two headlights appeared, the driver flicking them off, running lights on, looming with the reminder of the pending transition.

Minutes.

She had *minutes*.

Stomach tightening, she remembered the day after she kissed Luke at summer camp, how her mother's eyes were raw and red, suitcases already packed. Mom was a wreck, raging against her father, and the abrupt move was sold to her and Wendy as a "trip" to see Grandma and Grandpa for a few weeks.

The lie was the part Kylie couldn't forgive.

Because they never came back.

"Well," Wendy said, spooling a scarf around her neck, coming out of the hallway with her coat already on. "This is it!"

"This is it."

Voice going high and reedy with emotion, Wendy declared, "I'm going to hug you once, then go. I can't drag this out."

"I know."

The hug was tight. Kylie felt her blood drain then surge, like high tide.

Wendy smiled a shaky but determined smile, then turned away, grabbing her large suitcase and her carry-on and waving good-bye.

Kylie waved into the dark from the front window, until she was gone.

A sick feeling, the kind you get from waking before your

body's ready, washed over her. Bed beckoning, she went to crawl into it, but stopped. Instead, she headed for the small desk in the corner of her bedroom.

In the left drawer, she found what she was looking for.

Three letters.

Postmarked fifteen years ago, all addressed to Grandma and Grandpa's house in Rio, Indiana, in Luke's flat architect's hand.

Seeing her name in his hand made her cry.

For years, she'd dreamed about coming home, but never—not once—did it involve seeing Luke for the first time while trapped in a donation bin.

Or becoming his nanny.

Or being wholly alone.

That's what life just gave her, all in the span of a day and a half.

You can yearn for something. Squeeze every drop of hope from the sky and try to marinate your wish in it, until the flavor and scent are so ripe, you almost manifest it.

Almost.

But not quite.

As Kylie drifted off to sleep, letting herself indulge in a heaping dose of self-pity, she smiled in the end because, this life?

It might not be what she wanted.

But she had a feeling it was what she needed.

Chapter Eighteen

Luke

The melon options were getting better and better at the grocery store.

"Hi!" Kylie said, clearly surprised to run into him and Harriet in the produce section of Kendrill's Market, the one and only real grocery store in town. Their signature red plastic basket, shaped like a—what else?—heart, was hanging from her ski-jacket-covered forearm. It was Sunday, after church, and he marveled at her presence.

Two and a half days ago, he found her in that donation box.

A day and a half ago, he hired her to be his nanny.

Colleen ran into her at Mountain Dragon last night, getting takeout.

And now...

Luke stood in front of the cantaloupes, thumb pressing the dot on the end, the way his mom had taught him.

Ripe. Perfect. Ready to devour and enjoy.

"Hi, yourself," he said with a smile as he put the fruit in his shopping cart, Harriet standing on tiptoe to peek into Kylie's basket. Strawberries, yogurt, half and half, powdered sugar, and assorted herbs were all he saw.

"Where's the glitter?" Harriet demanded, frowning. "We need more for muffins."

Kylie saluted her. "Yes, ma'am."

"Daddy, I'm going to the bakery to get the free kid's cookie. Last time, you said I could go alone. I want to do it again."

"No problem."

"And every time, from now on!" she added emphatically as she disappeared toward that side of the store. The place was small, and everyone in town knew her.

He wasn't worried.

"She is definitely the boss," Luke grumbled, earning a hearty laugh from Kylie.

Which triggered his own.

A tingling began in his quads, creeping up his back, filling out the base of the neck, feeding into his eyes. Peripheral vision widening, he was all too aware of why this feeling was spreading over him.

It was the primitive sense of being watched.

Because in Love You, Maine, gossip was a kind of currency.

And he and Kylie were the latest gold rush. Bitcoin had nothing on the volatility of rumors and scandal involving potential romance.

"Hey there, Luke," called out Ed Khouri, the head butcher. Actually, the *only* butcher. There wasn't any need for more in a town so small. Even during tourist season, when the town's numbers swelled by a factor of ten, butchers weren't in high demand.

Luke nodded, Ed's eyes lighting up with innuendo. Great. Ed was married to Nadine down at the station. In his mid-seventies, he was still strong as an ox, though their grandson Mark was being trained in the family business, too. Ed had worked at Kendrill's for Luke's entire life. The store might not be his, but the meat counter certainly was.

"I see you eat healthy," Luke commented, peering in Kylie's basket, ignoring Ed.

Her eyes drifted to his shopping cart, which currently held a two-pack of WD-40, two enormous blocks of toilet paper, a three-pack of duct tape, a cantaloupe, and a pair of pantyhose.

Kylie cleared her throat. "I don't think I want to know how you eat."

He cringed. "I can explain everything."

"Pantyhose?"

"They're a great makeshift wattle."

"Waddle?"

"W-a-t-t-l-e. I'll fill it with mulch and use it to divert a drainage problem in the back yard."

"Clever."

"Thank you."

"And the rest?"

"Well..."

"You have fun with your pantyhose, lubrication, and that nice round handful," she cracked, eyeing the melon, which she plucked out of his hand and sniffed. She put it back on the display, picked up another, sniffed it, and handed it over to him.

"What was wrong with the other one?"

"Slightly underripe."

"You know the difference?"

"My mom taught me."

"My mom taught me to press my thumb in the spot on the end. If it's soft, but not too soft, it's perfect and ripe."

"I guess we have different skill sets for produce, then. Complementary, but different."

"Exactly how it should be."

Her eyes flared slightly, and he wondered how she took that.

"How is your mom? And your dad? I meant to ask, but things got kind of busy yesterday."

"Mom and Dad are the same. Running the tree business. Dad wanted Dennis to take over, but he's staying in the army."

"That's right! He'd been in the army for years when I left town."

Luke nodded. "And Kell is in L.A."

"He lives there?"

"God, no!" The way that came out made him hurry to

explain, laughing a bit. "Kell's here to stay. His girlfriend, Rachel, is from L.A."

"I always thought Kell would end up marrying a local."

"So did we. But he went to UMass ag school, got his certified arborist credentials, spent a year in D.C. doing environmental policy, and came home."

"Did he meet Rachel in D.C.?"

Luke hesitated, trying to condense the story into a few sentences. Instead, he smiled.

"It's a long story, but a good one. Happy to tell it over coffee sometime."

"Sure!" She looked uncertain. "I didn't mean to pry."

"You're not. You're just asking about people you remember. That's called being curious and caring, Kylie."

"Thanks."

If it weren't for all the eyes on them, Luke would step closer, bring her in for a hug, then take her out for coffee and catch up. And he was close to doing that, but then:

"DADDDEEEEEE!!!"

Harriet came running back to him, clutching two big apples.

"*Shhh*," he said, trying to get his little girl to stop the shrieks that peeled paint.

"Sorry!" she said, chest heaving from exertion. "They don't do cookies anymore!" She pouted. "It's a fruit basket, but you get two. They had my favorite!"

"Your favorite?" Kylie asked.

"Honeycrisp!"

"Good to know."

The moment was lost, Kylie now shifting from adult mode to kid mode, the connection fraying between them.

"Harriet eats a ton of cantaloupe. I need another one, and these melons won't squeeze themselves," he joked, then felt like an idiot the second the words were out.

Kylie picked up another from the display, smelled the end, then handed it to him.

"Bye, guys. See you tonight."

The tips of Kylie's ears turned bright red and she walked slowly away, giving him a fine view of her assets.

She'd grown into a luscious woman.

One with a smart mouth, too.

Back in high school, she was a sweet, unassuming—but smart—young woman. He'd liked how easy it felt to spend time with her. Being with her meant no one pressured him to be Luke, the captain of the baseball team. Luke, expected to work for his dad's tree service. Luke, honors student.

Luke, descendant of Abram Luview, town founder.

With Kylie, he could be free and easy, who he was at the core and nothing more.

Because that was enough with her.

Was it enough now?

The damn clause in the contract they'd signed on Friday reared up, smacking him upside the head.

No.

No.

He couldn't think about her that way.

Harriet needed her more than he did.

At least, that's what he told himself.

He and Harriet finished shopping, the back of the car filled with two weeks' worth of groceries, save a few milk and bread runs. Since Amber died, this was how he operated: an economy of time, always.

Had to be super-efficient or he couldn't hold all the pieces together.

Harriet had wheedled some cocoa peanut butter cereal out of him and two extra bags of butterscotch chips for homemade cookies.

Fair enough.

But the edible sparkles got eyebrows raised when he checked out. No sign of Kylie there, either. Given her single status, he assumed shopping trips were shorter for her.

This Sunday was different, with his parents in Germany. Normally, if he wasn't working, they headed to church in the morning, Harriet eager to peel off and join the kids in Sunday School. Luke was grateful for an hour where she was entertained and he sat in a pew, just a passive listener, soaking in something meaningful that he didn't have to act on.

Thinking was overrated.

Especially for a guy who was a doer for a living.

Luke worked the night shift tonight, so Kylie was coming over at ten p.m. He appreciated her flexibility. Nicole had groused at the occasional weird shift, but Kylie took it in stride when he mentioned it, cracking a joke about getting paid to read and sleep.

"Harriet? Honey? Can you be a helper and grab these two bags?" he asked her as they unloaded the trunk. Part of parenting, his mom had told him, was letting go of doing things the most efficient way. You had to learn to let your child gain skills and abilities, which in turn gave them self-confidence and competency.

Even if it took ten times longer to do a simple task.

At six, Harriet could carry two bags.

"Are they light ones?"

"Here."

"It's too heavy, Daddy!"

"You're a strong kid."

"I can't do it! It's too hard."

"You can do hard things."

That was the phrase the child therapist had suggested he use to give Harriet more resilience.

You can do hard things.

During the worst of moments, he'd used it plenty on himself, too.

As they reached the front door, he keyed in the code and opened it, Jester immediately at his knees. Harriet knew better than to dump the bags at the doorway, and with great sighing fanfare, plunked them on the dining table.

Luke did the same, then gave her a fist bump.

"Good job. Now let's get the rest."

"There's *more*?"

Five minutes and two more trips later, Harriet put the dry goods away while Luke played fridge Tetris to fit everything in. He liked having a full fridge. It cut down on short runs to the store, which were hard to do with a little kid.

He started to make himself a cup of coffee, but Harriet

bounded up to him and said sweetly, "When can we FaceTime Gamma and Gampa?"

He looked at the clock. Noon. Which meant seven p.m. in Germany.

Except they were on some river cruise for the next couple of days.

"We can't tonight, but in a few days."

She pouted.

"I'm bored."

"I can tell."

"When's Kylie coming over?"

The mention of her name made him smile.

"Ten o'clock."

"But I'll be in bed!"

"Yes. You can play with her before school tomorrow."

"That's no fun!"

"You like fun, don't you?"

"Duh, Daddy!"

"Hey! Where'd you learn that?"

"It's what Jace Morgenstern says all the time. 'Duh!'"

He didn't want to talk about the Morgensterns.

All the food in his cupboards, fridge, and freezer mocked him, but he decided on the fly to take the easy way.

"How would you like to go to Greta's for lunch?" Love You Bakery was the official name of the local café, but everyone in town just called it Greta's, after the owner and founder.

Harriet squealed with glee.

"It's their rush time, kiddo. We might have to wait in line for a long time."

"Can we eat at the counter?"

"Only if there's room."

"I can be patient and wait."

Hah. Right. He knew her definition of patience was three seconds, but he also knew he had ten hours with her ahead of him, and if he did something fun like this, it would make the day better.

Plus, who wanted to turn down a hot Love You Bakery brunch?

"We'll go to Greta's on one condition," he announced.

"What's a condition?"

Requests for word definitions were becoming increasingly complex, he'd noticed, always marveling at how Harriet seemed to just grow on her own.

"It's a stipulation," he replied, realizing that didn't help. "A rule."

"What's your rule for going to Greta's?"

"We have to walk."

"That's not a rule! That's fun!"

It was too cold to bring Jester and make him sit outside while they ate brunch, so he gave the old boy some fresh water and food, and soon he and Harriet were on their way, walking hand in hand. As they reached Mrs. Petrinelli's house, he braced himself.

She would be offended by Kylie being Nicole's replacement.

"Luke! Luke!" Waving hard, she came onto the porch, coat clearly thrown on in haste, half open as she squeezed it together. "How are you?"

"Doing great. You?"

"I see you have a new nanny."

"We do."

"She's Mark Hood's daughter. Poor dear."

The mention of Kylie's dad's name took him back. *Way* back. The Hood family had been part of Luview since Mark Hood's dad bought a summer home long ago. It's where Kylie and her family lived fifteen years ago, after the summer cottage had been fully winterized and expanded.

Kylie was a townie because she'd been born and raised here, but long-time townsfolk considered Mark an outsider because he'd taken over his father's vacation home.

But everyone still knew all their business.

And Mark Hood had cheated on Kylie's mom. Talked about it openly at Bilbee's Tavern. That's why they'd moved so fast.

"Kylie's a grown woman with a life of her own, Mrs. Petrinelli," he reminded her, hoping to head off gossip but knowing the gesture was futile.

Had to try anyway.

"I see you've noticed she's a grown woman."

Did the old lady just *wink* at him?

"We're headed to Greta's and don't want to miss getting a seat. Need anything from there?" he called out as they kept walking.

"No, but thank you! I already got my apple fritter and my Sunday newspaper." She waved back and went inside, her daily dose of town dirt like drinking a cup of morning coffee.

As he and Harriet made their way to Main Street, it hit him: This was life now.

Everyone would ask about Kylie.

He had to accept it. Reality couldn't be wished away.

Not that he wished *her* away. Just the busybody intrusion.

"Can I get a chocolate chip waffle? And bacon?" Harriet asked as they reached Greta's, which occupied an old, three-story house, now converted into a café.

The outside was done in painted lady style, a perfect combo of white, pink, and red, with hearts carved out of all the trim, the shingled sections of the siding cut into heart shapes, too.

Love You Bakery looked like Cupid puked all over it.

The third floor was an apartment, but the first and second floors held the kitchen, hostess area, and dining areas. Each room was painted in bright colors, with comfortable recliners in corners for people to sit and sip coffee.

Sundays were busy. Every seat was taken, and about ten people waited in the foyer.

Which was a light crowd.

In February, the lines were half a block long.

"Luke!" Wolf, Greta's son, gave him a hearty greeting, a nod for Harriet enough to make her wave back. A beefy guy with short hair and two gray stripes running down his beard at the chin, he hummed to himself as he worked the hostess station, jotting down names without asking.

Party of two, Luke and Harriet.

As always.

"Hey, Wolf. What's the wait?"

He looked at the counter. "Got two seats if you want 'em, but first I have to check with Joe." He turned to someone Luke didn't recognize, a rarity in Luview, though Greta's was well enough known that out-of-towners came for Sunday brunch.

"Hey Joe—you still want to wait for a table?"

Joe looked to be about ninety, with a wife not much younger, both smiling.

Joe patted his cane. "No counter. Bones too fragile. Go on and give it to them." Friendly smiles were exchanged, and soon Harriet and Luke had their heart-shaped, red-vinyl-covered counter stools, right near the noisy cash register, but seats were seats on a Sunday at Greta's. Maple and sage filled his nose.

"Same as always?" Marni asked from behind the counter, slapping two waters, a cup of coffee, and a kid's orange juice in front of them. Every glass and mug was a heart. Most people drank from the point.

"Chocolate chip waffle and bacon, please!" Harriet peeped, reaching for the cup of ragtag crayons next to the sugar dispenser, beginning to draw on her placemat. Greta and Wolf included all 64 crayon colors in their choices, unlike Love You Coffee, which took the town's colors to the extreme: only red, white, and pink crayons for kids.

All of Harriet's drawings done there had pink skies and red lawns.

"I'll have an everything omelet this time," Luke said. "Rye toast."

Marni was Wolf's daughter, sixteen and whip smart, with an eyebrow piercing that went up as she questioned his choice.

"You always get the Western omelet."

"I'm exploring life. Taking risks. Living on the edge."

"Old people are so weird." With a sniff, she walked into the kitchen.

If Luke was old, what was Greta?

Speaking of whom...

"Lukey!" The old woman still had a trace of her German accent, enough to notice but not so much that she was hard to understand. She was somewhere north of seventy and knew everyone in town.

Greta was the only person in Luview who could get away with calling him Lukey. Even his mom wasn't allowed.

Anymore.

Luke stood, bending down to give her a hug. As people grew older here, he noticed, they became more affectionate. Women hugged more. Men shook hands and clapped backs. Grounding yourself in others might be a function of age? He'd find out soon enough.

If he were lucky enough to grow old.

"Heard you lost your nanny to Hollywood."

"Yeah."

"But got a new one already." Greta winked. "Your old flame."

Oh, no.

"Not an old flame, Greta. An old friend from high school."

"Don't try to snow me. I hear everything. You and Kylie Hood are the talk of the town."

"Then the town must be as boring as people over in Conway say, because I'm not interesting."

"Says who? You must be blind to how many women are interested in you, Luke."

"Are you flirting with me?"

"If I am, will it get me anywhere?"

"Tutti! Cut it out. Leave the poor guy alone," Wolf shouted from the grill through the pickup window.

Greta called back something in German that made Wolf wave his spatula at her in mock anger, but the guy grinned as he went back to the grill.

Half the customers laughed, though Luke was unsettled to see more than a few women nodding in agreement with Greta.

It's not like he didn't know some women found him attractive.

He just wasn't interested.

"Speak of the devil... I mean, nanny," Greta purred, mouth curling into a delighted smile as Luke watched her write the gossip in her mind in real time. Following her gaze, his heart leapt at the sight of Kylie walking up to the pastry counter and pointing to a loaded brownie. It was cut in the shape of a heart, with pink cream cheese frosting lining the edges.

She held up two fingers and Marni grabbed them with wax paper and put them in a white bakery bag.

"KYLIE!" Greta bellowed. If Luke had any hope of a quiet brunch with his daughter, it all died with that one word.

Phones came out. Women glared. People huddled. Men grinned.

And Harriet squealed.

Embarrassment radiated from Kylie as she accepted the bakery bag from Marni, her other hand busy paying with her card in a swipe machine. It was clear she wasn't accustomed to being the center of attention in a crowd.

Though he was certain she was used to plenty of admiring gazes. Something feral in him rose up as he noticed how many men were noticing her.

Too many.

"Hi?" she said back to Greta, voice going up like a question.

"What took you so long to come back?" Greta demanded.

The visible draining of tension in Kylie's shoulders filled Luke with a warm sense of appreciation, and a dawning realization. She didn't feel like she belonged here.

But he could tell she wanted to.

"Born and raised here," he declared, voice meant to carry.

A few nods, some raised eyebrows, and still plenty of attention. Folks were enjoying the spectacle, sizing up the situation as if he and Kylie were an episode of a reality television show.

Love You, Widower Single Dad Edition.

Before Kylie could muster up something to say, she glanced out the window, did a double take, and pointed.

A woman in a long, beige down parka, New England Patriots knitted hat, and reflective sunglasses walked past, an animal on a leash before her.

But it wasn't a dog.

"Is that a pig? No. Wait. A *boar?* A–what on earth is she walking?" Kylie wondered aloud.

"Capybara." Luke couldn't believe he was saying it, but...

"Sappy what?"

"Capybara." He laughed, standing up to talk to her. "We're all used to Mel walking weird things around town."

The change in conversation seemed to make people look away. Unlike Kylie, they were used to Mel's antics.

"Wait 'til next August when the summer people leave and she has to clean up their abandoned-pet messes. All sorts of animals end up on leashes. And then there are the pink bunnies at Easter..."

"Mel?"

"Mel Chassi? Remember her?"

"The woman who managed the horses at camp?"

"You *do* remember her. Yep. She runs an animal sanctuary now. Great place to kennel your dog, too, if you go out of town. The kennel helps fund the sanctuary."

"Good for her."

"It's right next to the place we're buying."

"You're moving?"

The casual way they spoke about different town topics really made people lose interest. Maybe being boring really was the best way to live your own life, without prying eyes.

If so, his goal was to be a real snoozer.

"We are."

"Luke! Your food! Remember food?" Wolf shouted, plopping his omelet and Harriet's waffle and bacon in front of their seats, the strips of pig mercifully straight. Out-of-towners got theirs twisted into a heart.

You knew you were a local when Wolf didn't bother.

Harriet had lost interest in their conversation and was coloring away happily, abandoning the drawing to grab a pitcher of maple syrup and begin pouring with abandon. A covert look up at Luke made it clear she was about to have a waffle floating in a lake of the sweet stuff.

"You might want to rescue that poor waffle from drowning," Kylie joked, but she wasn't–not really. She was on at ten tonight, and they both knew what sugared-up kids were like.

"Want to sit with us?" he asked, knowing he was feeding the gossip flames, but not caring.

A slightly wild, anxious look crossed Kylie's face as their eyes met. She held up her bag. "Thanks, but I'm headed home. Been up early. My sister left at the crack of dawn, and I need a nap before work."

"See you tonight, then," he said with a smile.

Eyebrows climbed into the rafters.

As Kylie departed and Luke sat down again, Greta came over, but his eyes were on a part of Kylie's body that definitely fit in here.

Her heart-shaped–

"Tonight?" Greta asked, insinuation in her voice. "Kylie's coming over tonight?"

"I work the night shift, Greta. I need a babysitter."

"Mmm hmm. And she spends the night?"

"Yes."

"In your bed?"

That stopped him short. The idea of Kylie in his bed was… tantalizing.

And uncomfortable.

Like this conversation.

"What you're implying is never going to happen," he said softly. "Legally, I mean. She's my employee. There's a clause in her employment contract that says there's to be no fraternization between me and the nanny."

Greta gasped. "Why would you ever have such a thing?"

"To protect us both."

"Huh."

"So we can't date, Greta," he whispered. "But please–this is confidential. I'd hate for anyone to find out."

"Of course. I won't tell!" Chiding eyes met his. "You know me. I'm as tight as a sealed drum when it comes to secrets."

"Right."

He also knew that was a lie. They both did.

"She only has to cover night shifts until Mom and Dad get back."

"I hope they're having fun in my home country. I am so jealous."

"Weren't you there last summer?"

She gave a sad smile. "For my sister's funeral."

"I'm sorry, I didn't realize."

"Eh. I don't want to talk about death. I want to talk about new beginnings."

Wolf grabbed a long piece of chalk and began erasing the big blackboard behind the counter. The door opened and Dotty Chen, the town librarian, walked in, smiled at Luke, and looked back behind her, outside.

"Didn't I just see Kylie in here?" she asked him as she looked at the bakery case, half paying attention to the food but more interested in his business.

"I give it two weeks," he heard Wolf say to someone, but his attention was focused on his food. Harriet was dripping syrup all over the front of her pink turtleneck.

"One."

"A month."

What were they talking about?

Out of the corner of his eye, he saw Greta whisper something in Dotty's ear. The librarian fiddled with her glasses, then replied quietly, but just loud enough that Luke could hear.

"Forbidden love is one of the most enduring stories in literature. And it always ends with the couple getting together."

Her eyes cut over to Luke.

"Put me down for five dollars on New Year's Eve. December 31."

That's when he realized Wolf had drawn a betting pool on the blackboard. A grid with what looked like – *no*.

Ninety squares?

And he knew *exactly* what–or *who*–they were betting on.

"You know it's illegal to run a lottery that isn't sanctioned by the state!" he called out to Wolf, who gave him a slick grin.

"At the rate we're going, you'll have to arrest half the town."

"Don't tempt me."

To the sounds of snickers and guffaws, he ate the rest of his omelet, used his toast to mop up some of Harriet's syrup, and finished his coffee.

And wondered what the odds really were.

As he and Harriet stood at the register to pay, horns began to honk outside, mayhem setting off his radar. Tossing a tip on the counter, he sprinted outside to find Mel running after the capybara, which was making a mad jog for freedom.

Why couldn't the town lay bets on *that*?

Chapter Nineteen

Kylie

No offense to Luke, but his couch felt like Kylie was sleeping on a bed of rocks mixed in with a stuffed animal collection.

One where the animals had lots of hooves and horns.

Harriet had been sound asleep when she arrived at 9:45 p.m. A few short sentences were all Luke said to her as he left, the conversation cordial but efficient. She worked for him now.

That's how bosses were with employees.

Right?

Light peeked through the living room curtains as she cracked one eye open and shut it abruptly. How could it be sunrise already? She hadn't slept a wink.

Until midnight, she'd cleaned and cooked and done laundry, a neatly folded basket of which sat on the floor in front of the washer and dryer in the hallway closet. Too respectful to go into Luke's bedroom, she'd left it there, planning to ask what, exactly, "light housekeeping" meant to him. It was just towels, sheets, and three pairs of what appeared to be jersey-knit pajama bottoms of his.

Did he want her to do all his and Harriet's laundry as part of the job? Would she learn whether he was a boxers or briefs kind of guy?

Boxer briefs?

Or... commando?

That thought made her sit up in frustration. Great. Now she was thinking about Luke's... you know.

With a body like his, all compact muscle and long bones, it had to be boxer briefs.

Or nothing at all.

A noise down the hallway made her ears perk, but Jester didn't move an inch, sound asleep in his dog bed, so she wasn't worried about safety.

Harriet might wake up and wonder where her daddy was, though.

Kylie stood and stretched, staying silent through a long, blood-beating yawn.

Tiptoeing down the hall, she had her head down and didn't see him until she felt him, all broad shoulders, bare skin, and rock-hard muscle.

"Oof!" burst out as she crashed into Luke, who was standing in front of the laundry closet.

First, she noticed dampness, along with a radiant heat and musk that made her senses go wild.

Second, she realized she had one hand flat on his bare, broad chest.

Third, as she looked up, his mouth was inches from hers, Luke's eyes burning with surprise and--

Oh, yes.

Lust.

"I am so sorry!" she gasped, stumbling backwards, calves hitting the laundry basket. She lost her balance and grabbed onto his arm.

"I can't--I--" he started, but at the last instant she righted herself, and that's when she realized he was wearing a towel.

And nothing *but* a towel.

Fresh from the shower, he smelled like summer rain and lime, his hair wet and tousled, one hand clenching the ends of the towel around his waist like he was saving its life.

Luke was naked.

Big, thickly muscled, and hot as hell.

"So big!" Frozen, hand still on his chest, she knew she should move away and break contact, but something primal said *Touch*.

Touch touch touch.

Touch him.

Touch him everywhere.

Hold on.

So big.

Did she just say *So big?*

No no no no no.

Number 14, Part A of the contract, she reminded herself.

Don't Bang the Boss.

"Kylie?"

"Mmm?" Words failed her.

Her fingers, on the other hand, were not failing in any way, shape, or form. In fact, they were doing quite well for themselves.

And speaking of forms, Luke's was, well...

So big.

"What are you doing with those fingers, Kylie?" he asked softly, snapping her out of her trance, making her freeze.

"I, uh..."

"You're killing me," he murmured, but, honorable guy that he was, the man took a step back.

Ending physical contact.

"Oh!" she let out, the sound punctuating the tension between them. Heat was pouring off her in waves, and she saw her ferocious, deep need reflected back at her in Luke's gaze.

And suddenly, her crotch was the center of attention.

"JESTER!" Luke snapped at the dog, who inserted himself between them, nose in the most inconvenient place possible. It's like the dog could smell her desire.

Could he really?

Properly chastened, Jester went back into the living room, the interlude just enough to clear Kylie's head.

"I don't even know what to say." She giggled a little, nervously, at the end. "I didn't realize you were home."

"Got here ten minutes ago. You didn't answer when I whispered your name. Figured I'd take a quick shower while you were still here and Harriet wasn't up yet."

"Pecs," she said, her mouth apparently busy saying whatever her gaze fell on.

"Excuse me?"

"Expect! I wasn't expecting you home so early."

"Yeah. The bad guys all seemed to take a night off." He grinned at her. "Couldn't find my pajama bottoms."

"They're in that basket."

"You don't need to do my laundry," he said, frowning a little.

"They were in with the sheets and towels. I didn't go into your bedroom," she said quickly. "I wasn't sure what you meant by light housekeeping."

"Nicole was supposed to just do Harriet's clothes."

"Supposed to?"

"She didn't do it half the time."

"Well, I'm not Nicole."

"You most certainly are not."

Her eyes had been combing over *his* body, but now she found herself the object of a once-over, a slow, steady smolder that made her nearly burst into flame when his eyes finally met hers. Luke took a step toward her, the attraction magnetic and impossible to deny, the urge to kiss him more like instinct than want.

Kylie couldn't *not* kiss him.

Number 14, Part A be damned.

And then:

"Daddy!" Her curly head a mop of tangles, sleepy Harriet woke up at the sight of Luke, her arms going around his waist at the hip. He pivoted, bending down so she could move the hug to his neck.

Giving Kylie an ample eyeful of thick, muscular thigh.

And, she suspected, if the hallway weren't so shadowed, even more.

"Hey, kiddo."

"Kylie's still putting me on the bus, right?"

"Um, sure."

"Good!" Letting go, Harriet ran down the hall, Jester's tail thumping when she appeared.

The television clicked on.

Kylie thumbed toward the living room. "I'm just going to get her some breakfast and put her on the bus."

"Great. Thanks. I have a call I need to make to the sheriff, so I'd appreciate it."

"Might want to get dressed, too."

He looked down at himself and laughed. "Yeah. That."

As Luke turned away, Kylie held her breath, finally exhaling when she reached the kitchen.

Yeah. That.

That had been swoon-worthy.

Given this was her first early morning shift on the job, Kylie had to wing it. When asked, Harriet explained helpfully that she liked simple O cereal in chocolate milk.

The trick failed.

"You can't eat sugar all the time, sweetie. How about some apple slices and cheese, too?"

"Yum!"

Luke had written out a set of basic instructions in case he wasn't home in time for the bus, so Kylie followed them, assembling Harriet's lunch.

Weird.

"Dried seaweed strips?" Kylie searched the cupboards, finding foil-wrapped packages, clearly purchased in bulk. She added one to the pink lunchbox.

"Cheese stick." That was easy.

"Two clementines." A bowl overflowing with the little orange fruit, Honeycrisp apples, kiwis, and pears made that easy, too.

"Pine nuts."

Hold on. *Pine nuts?* The kind you use to make pesto?

Sure enough, a small container of them was in the cupboard, by the spices.

"Harriet? How many pine nuts do you get in your lunch?"

"Lots!"

That was helpful.

Kylie shook a few tablespoons into a zip bag and hoped that was good enough.

"Two deli pickles."

A jar of large pickles, half empty, sat on a shelf in the fridge.

And, finally...

Hold on.

The list didn't really mean what she was reading, did it?

A peanut butter sandwich with hemp seeds, banana slices, and crushed sweet potato chips *in* the sandwich?

Luke's handwriting was crystal clear.

Her cognitive dissonance was the problem.

"Harriet? Honey? Do you eat a peanut butter sandwich with hemp seeds, bananas, and crushed sweet potato chips in it?"

Not adding, *"Really?"* was an exercise in restraint.

"Mmm hmmm." The kid was distracted by cartoons, but added, "It was Mommy's favorite."

Hand reaching for the bread, Kylie froze. It suddenly made more sense, and Kylie assembled the sandwich with a small wave of grief she wasn't expecting.

Along with a heaping dose of guilt.

This was Amber's child. Amber's husband. Amber's house.

And Kylie had no right to be attracted to Luke like a slobbering teen.

Lunch for Harriet neatly assembled, she rounded up her school backpack, boots, coat, mittens, and snow pants, a glance at the clock telling her she had seven minutes before the bus came.

Luke's voice, low and calm, floated down the hallway from his bedroom. That work call must be going well. Kylie felt good to be keeping things humming along with Harriet so Luke could do his job.

Protecting Luview, Maine, was important.

Also, she was charmed. Luke was undeniably hot. Touching him, looking at him, feeling his innate sexy goodness–these were pretty amazing job perks.

"You okay?" His sudden appearance jerked her out of her own head and made her squeak in surprise, the bag of sweet potato chips nearly toppling over and spilling. Lightning-fast reflexes meant he saved it, but only by brushing his arm against her breast and ribs, sending sparks flying along her skin.

"Fine. Thanks," she said, busying herself with the task of making the strange sandwich.

"It's a different kind of sandwich. Like tasting new things?" he asked in a way that made her mind wander to less innocent places.

"Sure!"

His phone buzzed before he could say another word. "Shoot. Work. Gotta go."

"When do you sleep?"

"When she's at school. Only have to do the night shift here and there. I'll nap when you leave, then get her off the bus, run some errands, and later get a full night's sleep tonight."

"That sounds hard."

Luke looked around the house, which was spotless. "It was harder before you appeared, Magic Trash Fairy."

"Hey!" She punched his arm. It didn't move.

So much muscle.

So big.

Laughing, he left the room, already on the phone before he shut his bedroom door.

"Harriet! Time to get ready for the bus."

Wrestling a little kid into snow pants, boots, coat, mittens, hat, and anchoring a backpack on their back was a northern New England Olympic nannying sport, and Kylie's old muscle memory kicked in. It's not as if there weren't plenty of snow in Indiana, but this part of Maine was extra.

Extra *everything*.

Including a hot cop she'd like to do something extra with.

She'd slept in her clothes, not having a specific plan for how to handle nannying overnight, so it was easy to put on her own boots and outerwear. Harriet stood by the door, watching.

Kylie's hand was on the doorknob when Harriet said, "You're forgetting Jester."

"Jester?"

At the mention of his name, the golden retriever leaped over to them, tail going nuts, head under Kylie's gloved hand.

"Daddy and Aunt Colleen and Uncle Kell and Nicole and Mrs. Petrinelli and Gamma and Gampa take him with us to the bus stop."

"Oh! Sure." Kylie grabbed the leash from the hook next to

the door and hooked him on as she considered Harriet's words. It took a village to keep this household functioning.

And with that, they were off.

Luke's instructions for finding the bus stop were easy enough: stop sign at the corner of Clannaugh and Main. A cluster of kids in basically the same outerwear as Harriet were all standing there when they arrived, their mothers looking curiously at Kylie.

"Nicole's really gone, huh?" one of them asked, not bothering to raise her sunglasses, which were mirrored and reminded Kylie of the evil-queen stepmother in *Snow White*.

"Hi," Kylie said, dodging the question. "I'm Kylie."

"We know who you are, hon," she said in *that* tone.

The tone Kylie hated.

Even Jester stopped wagging his tail.

"You know, sweetie," Mirror Mirror on the Wall said, bending down at the waist, hovering over Harriet. "I keep telling your daddy I'm happy to come over and help make life easier for him."

The purr in her voice made Kylie's hackles raise.

Ah. Now the tone made more sense.

This one wanted Luke.

"I guess Luke didn't need you," Kylie replied before she had the sense to shut her mouth. It was out there, though; her years in New York had given her a thicker skin than most folks realized.

"Excuse me?" Mirror raised her glasses, revealing a perfectly made-up face, Instagram-ideal lashes, and a sneer that could peel paint.

"Did you apply to be Luke's nanny?" Kylie challenged, playing dumb.

"She applied to be Luke's *something*," another mom cracked, earning titters from the two others and a nasty, head-whipping glare from Mirror.

All four women were older than Kylie, somewhere between five and ten years older, so she didn't try to pattern match and retrieve old memories from years ago. This group was virgin territory, and first encounters meant something in a small town.

She was no one here. Someone who left and came back, but didn't have a role.

Her identity now depended entirely on Harriet and Luke.

The bus rumbled along and stopped, pneumatic doors wheezing as they opened and the kids climbed on. Harriet ran to the first step, turned around, and waved to Kylie.

She returned the wave, smile plastered on her face, holding Jester back from running onto the fun bus full of kids.

Mirror stomped off to a running SUV not more than thirty feet from the bus stop and drove away. Kylie waited until the bus door closed to begin her walk back.

One of the moms stopped her, hand extended. They shook through thick gloves.

"You don't remember me, but I'm Izzy Chassi."

"Izzy? I remember an Izzy who used to babysit me, but your last name was different."

She smiled. "Right. Maiden name was Morgenstern. I married a Chassi."

Kylie laughed with recognition. "You always let us eat the entire huge bag of chips and the two-liter bottle of soda Mom and Dad left for you to snack on, and you never told them where it really went."

Izzy laughed, shaking her head, long beach curls poking out from under a thick wool cap. Her face had no makeup, eye lashes short, face gaunt.

"I did that for every family I babysat for. Never liked that kind of junk food anyway. I'm more of an ice-cream-and-brownie-binge kind of gal. Welcome back!"

"Thanks."

"You've made quite a splash."

"Guess so."

"Don't mind Mindy."

"Mindy?"

"The bi-otch back there."

Kylie snorted. "Glad I'm not the only one who thought that."

"She's divorced. Been hitting on Luke for a long time. He's clearly not interested."

Yay, Luke, for having taste! she thought, but couldn't say.

"Better get used to that, though."

"What?"

"A little unsolicited advice: There are no fewer than six women in town who are vying for the position of the next Mrs. Luke Luview. You've become a complication."

"Me? Because I'm Harriet's nanny?"

"No. No one was threatened by Nicole. But they all know about you. Some of them remember how you kissed him at camp right before you left."

Flabbergasted, Kylie felt faint. "They *what*?"

"It's stupid, right? We left that kind of stuff behind in middle school, except–some of us didn't. Welcome back to Luview, Kylie. Nothing in the past ever stays there."

Izzy's phone dinged with a text.

"Shoot. Work issue. Gotta go."

And with that, she broke out into a jog, leaving Kylie with a dog eager to chase a squirrel that just crossed the road, and a nagging sense that nothing about Luke was what it seemed.

One thing, though, was for sure:

She wasn't about to eat any apples offered by Mindy.

Chapter Twenty

Luke

It wasn't often Luke got a call to handle large animals, but when he did, there were two people he could rely on: Darren Duarte and Mel Chassi.

Both of whom hated each other's guts.

But they had one major thing in common, other than being each other's ex: They loved animals to the core of their beings.

Darren was the town veterinarian, and Luke was in his office before they headed out for lunch, the doc stocking pharmaceutical packages and organizing a cabinet while Luke availed himself of some crappy overcooked coffee from the machine. Darren was a decade older, so their friendship had formed fairly late, about five years ago, and Luke liked their conversations.

Talking about something other than his kid was nice sometimes.

"Kylie Hood, huh? Man. Haven't heard that name in years. I hear she has a smoking hot bod and a smile that lights up the town."

"Cut it out, Darren."

"What? I can't pay her a compliment?"

"Not when it comes from your pants."

"Speaking of pants..." Darren looked down at his work khakis, which were currently crusted with a mud-like substance that Luke suspected was not mud. "That pony really didn't like being in a Ford Fiesta."

"Who the hell crams a horse inside a hatchback?"

It was a rhetorical question.

They both knew.

"Old man Bevenili doesn't spend a dime without making it scream. You know that. Didn't want to pay the vet transport fee."

"Crazy."

"To you and me? Sure. To a guy who is eighty-nine and living only on his Social Security check and whatever the farm brings in? Makes sense. Most of the work I do for him is barter."

"What does he produce that you want?" Luke asked, incredulous.

"For one thing, Bevenili's land has some of the best mushrooms around."

"That's your hobby!"

"Sure is. And he makes it easy. I'm set for life as long as he and his ponies stay alive and I can go on the hunt."

Around here, the mushroom people were some of the weirdest characters in the area. Mycologist rhymed with psychologist, which was what most of them needed. Luke was sure most of them were good, well-balanced, emotionally healthy humans.

Those weren't the ones he ran into in the woods.

"Good for you. Have fun. I'll just buy my boring white cap mushrooms at Kendrill's Market, like everyone else."

"You have no idea what you're missing."

"Accidental poisoning, fisher cat bites, wild boars—you're right, Darren. I'm really depriving myself."

"Let's get back to Kylie Hood. You like her?"

"Of course. Wouldn't have hired her if I didn't."

"You *like* her?" His tone took a prurient turn.

"Cut it out, Darren," Luke warned.

"Can't bang your nanny, dude. Everyone knows that."

"Hey!"

"What? Just because you don't like the answer doesn't mean it's not true."

"Not that. Don't be so disrespectful about Kylie."

"What was disrespectful?"

"Bang."

"You want me to use a different word? How about fu–"

Luke shut him up with a well-timed water bottle to the head. Too bad Darren had great reflexes from years of avoiding horse kicks.

Their phones buzzed like mad, in unison, and they both went instantly serious.

And both muttered a curse.

"Giraffe accident at Murphy's Curve," Luke read, rubbing one eye because there was no way his phone actually said that.

"Mine says the same thing."

Murphy's Curve was less than five minutes from the veterinary hospital.

"Let's go–must be bad if we're both called at the same time." Darren grabbed a huge medical bag and ran outside, climbing into his pickup truck. Luke got in his cruiser and turned on the siren and lights, because *hey*.

Wasn't every day you had a giraffe accident. If anything called for flashing lights, it was *this*.

Four and a half minutes later, they pulled up to Murphy's Curve, the name a bit misleading. Yes, it was a curve. Yes, the Murphy farm was here, where it had been in continuous operation since 1730.

But it was the bridge you drove under that epitomized Murphy's Curve.

Every year, at least three or four truck drivers made the grave mistake of thinking the warning sign that screamed "10 feet, 2 inches!" couldn't be right.

Normally, it was the top of a moving van or a bread truck that was stuck in the stone arch of the ancient bridge.

But this time?

It was a giraffe's head.

A dark green SUV that had seen better days was parked smack in the middle of the right lane, its hood under the tunnel, the hatch still in the sun. A giraffe's neck and head stuck out of the open sunroof on the vehicle, the poor thing looking half drunk way up high, its head mercifully *not* stuck, but resting against the top of the arch.

"Oh, no. Not her," Darren moaned as Luke got out of his car and began to assess the situation. Mel Chassi was arguing with Potter Barnes, a deputy with the sheriff's office. Potter was nice enough but not exactly blessed in the spatial reasoning department, and it was clear he was intimidated by Mel.

Which made him about average, because most people were.

Mel wasn't particularly big or tall, and she didn't have bucketloads of charisma, but what she lacked in those departments, she made up for in intensity. Eight years older than Luke, she was fiercely protective of animals. *All* animals.

Except for humans.

And right now, her giraffe was preventing her from driving under the Murphy's Curve bridge, its head pressing up on the arch, making Luke wonder if it were literally stuck.

And how in the heck that had happened.

"Oh, goody. More cops," Mel said as he walked over, looking up.

"Here to help, Mel. You know how we work."

Deprecating snorts he was used to, but Mel elevated it to an art. "In that case, maybe you can help Potter here understand that what I need is a veterinary chiropractor, so poor Needle can get back to the sanctuary."

"Needle?" Darren looked up at the distressed animal, who seemed frozen in place, the top of its head scraping the bottom of the arch.

"You here to help or make fun of names?" Mel challenged.

"How did this happen?" Luke inquired, ready for a doozy of a story.

"One of those exotic animal collectors," Mel said, as if she had a rotten oyster in her mouth. "Some jerk near Farmington. Abandoned all of them when his prized tiger got loose. I offered to watch Needle here until someone from a ranch down in Florida can get up here."

"So this poor thing has never even been to your place yet?"

Darren asked, righteous anger on the animal's part making Luke warm up on the inside. His buddy could be gruff, but he was also moral to the core.

"Right. She's traumatized. And I've been driving nice and slow the entire way, but..."

"From Farmington? That's an hour on back roads!"

"Closer to two going as slow as I have."

"No trailer?"

"Hitch broke."

"So you came in an SUV to get a giraffe!"

"In my defense, Needle is a baby."

Luke, Darren, and Potter all craned their necks up to look at Needle.

"I don't know anything about giraffes, but that doesn't seem like a baby," Potter said contemplatively.

"I was given all my information from a very nice, distraught humane society volunteer. Once I got there, I couldn't do anything but put the poor thing in my SUV and drive. And for the record, she *is* a baby. Poor thing is still nursing. Estimated to be about a week or two old. No mother giraffe at the 'collector's' compound. No way could I fit a full-sized giraffe in an SUV!"

"How much does she weigh?" Luke asked.

"About two hundred and fifty pounds."

Potter let out a low whistle.

"How, exactly, did you get her in there?" Darren asked.

"We sedated her."

"A properly trained vet did that, I hope."

"Yes."

"Then why didn't he accompany you? Or why not call me?"

"*She* was a bit busy managing the three baby elephants and a very sick mama."

"Good grief!" Luke couldn't help but interject. "Elephants?"

"These 'collectors' have no decency. They abuse and neglect the animals, then sell them to people."

"Rachel's dad collects exotic animals," Luke mused aloud. "Kell mentioned it to me."

"Really? My opinion of him just dropped."

"I'm sure they don't abuse their animals."

"Well, poor Needle here definitely wasn't treated well. And I'm probably going back for more rescues."

"No elephants!" Darren boomed, earning a withering look from Mel.

"If I have to, I will. You know how I work. Get them safe and stable first, then find someone who knows how to help them."

Darren huffed. "Oh, I know all too well. You have a huge heart. Too huge. You act like there are no limits to how much you can do, and -- "

"Are you going to give me a lecture like you did when we were married, or are you going to help poor Needle here?"

"I can manage both at the same time."

"And that's why I didn't call you when I was informed of the mess in Farmington," she said with an angry sigh.

Luke was about to intervene and calm all the ruffled feathers when Darren shook his head, looked up at Needle, and declared: "All you need is some muscle relaxers and she'll fold like a snipped rope." Reaching into his bag, he pulled out a syringe.

"Don't you dare," Mel growled.

"You want my help, or not?"

"*Not.* Not if that's the only solution."

Needle began making weird sounds, breathing hard and sputtering.

Darren frowned. "She's in distress. We need to hurry."

"No muscle relaxers! The cranio person's almost here."

"The what?"

Mel sighed, exasperated. "The vet chiro is out of town, so I called in a cranio-sacral specialist."

"For a giraffe? You and your woo."

"It's not woo! She'll be able to get Needle to relax the fascia enough to bend. Poor thing's been sedated once already."

"I can get her to relax that with one jab." Darren walked over to Needle, touching her gently, making calming noises. Mel seemed to relax as she recognized the compassion in her ex.

"No drugs! Needle's a slow acetylator."

"Huh?" Luke asked, wondering if that was something like an elevator.

"Uh-SEE-til-ay-tor," Mel said slowly. "It means drugs don't clear her system quickly."

"She's going into some kind of respiratory distress right now, Mel." Darren's voice was concerned. He peered inside the SUV. "And she just ruined your backseat upholstery. Good thing it's vinyl. Why aren't you using your pickup?"

"It's in the shop! Deke's taking forever to fix it."

Darren just grunted.

"Broken trailer hitch. Broken pickup. Too many animals. You're spread too thin, Mel."

"Lecturing me again, Darren. Are you going to help, or flap your jaw?"

Needle's chest began to suck in and blow out fast, the skin between her ribs looking funny. Luke's college science courses were a vague memory, but even he could tell something was wrong.

"That's it. I have an obligation," Darren muttered, removing the cap from the syringe. "What's her weight again? Two fifty?"

"You can't do this!"

"Give me the weight or I estimate, and we know how fraught that can be."

"Darren, no!"

"Mel. *Mel*. This isn't up for debate."

"Yes, two fifty!" Mel said in a panic. "But *please!*"

"Luke! Potter! Get ready to catch her head," Darren announced.

"EXCUSE ME, SIR?" Potter screamed from the other side of the car.

"Don't be so dramatic," Mel said, her finger in Darren's face. "Needle's small and young. She'll just collapse onto the car, and we can catch her before she hits, but you're a cruel SOB to do this to her, Darren."

"I'd be a lot more cruel if I let her suffer."

Swiftly, he jabbed the giraffe and stood back, waiting, arms outstretched. All four humans instinctively took places around the SUV, spread equally out, ready to catch.

But to Luke's surprise, the giraffe slow relaxed her body,

folding inside the vehicle's interior, curling in like a tired dog, her head coming down to rest on the SUV's roof.

It was simple, surprisingly elegant, and an enormous relief.

And just then, Luke heard a familiar voice.

"Luke?"

Across the road, on the sidewalk, Kylie and Harriet waved just as Needle's eyes rolled back and her head began to droop, sliding to the right of the roof.

Harriet launched herself toward the road, screaming "Daddy!" just as his ears picked up the sound of a car coming around the bend, still out of sight but oh, God, *no*.

"NO!" he screamed.

Luke reacted before his mind could process what he saw.

One step. Two. Harriet was taking off in a full-throttle run, and he imagined what was about to happen, everything precious to him taken out in a split second yet again as the car sped forward, his mind's eye creating a horror film of Harriet being struck and thrown, his helplessness blinding him, instinct making him sprint.

His daughter was about to die the same way her mother had.

Except – that's not what *actually* happened.

Kylie grabbed the loop on top of Harriet's backpack and pulled hard, yanking her back before she could even get both feet in the road.

But even that was too much.

Without thought, he suddenly found himself on their side of the road, bent down to hug Harriet and hiss in her ear, "Don't you *ever, ever* do that again. What do I say about sidewalks?"

"Stay on them, Daddy." Harriet began to sob, her body trembling in his arms, her tiny voice small and fearful. "I'm sorry!"

"Luke," Kylie said, her voice nothing but confusion and admonishment. "You're scaring her."

"Good. She *should* be scared. Damn right."

Darren was behind him suddenly, his steady, calm presence pissing Luke off.

"Luke," he said slowly. "She's fine."

"And YOU," Luke shouted, getting right up in Kylie's grill,

rage wiping away all pretense of politeness. "You need to do your job better. What did I tell *you* about sidewalks?"

Shock turned Kylie's eyes into double moons, but she didn't flinch.

Didn't take a step back.

To his surprise, she moved toward him, lower lids rising as her eyes narrowed.

Darren put his hand on Luke's shoulder and said, "Hey. Buddy. It's okay. What happened to Amber didn't happen to Harriet. Apples and oranges, man. Apples and oranges."

Kylie's brows went down as her gaze cut from Luke to Darren behind him. An old, rusted pickup truck rumbled slowly past Mel's SUV with Needle slumped over on the roof, Potter and Mel doing their best to hold the giraffe's head up.

Luke just blinked at Darren's words.

His friend was talking to him like he was a combat vet experiencing a flashback.

How did Luke know?

Because that was how *he'd* been trained to handle that kind of situation.

"Thank you," he said, the words coming out like taffy, gratitude washing over him as he looked at Kylie, but bent down for a gentler, less frantic hug from Harriet. "Darren's right. I lost my temper. You did nothing wrong."

"I grabbed her backpack and pulled her to safety," Kylie said in a mystified voice. "I hope I didn't hurt her."

"You didn't!" Harriet chirped. "But Daddy yelled. He yelled HARD!"

"I'm sorry, sweetie." His mouth felt fuzzy, eyes dry, brain spinning. He had to get out of there. Needed space.

Needed silence.

Needed to be alone.

"Potter's got a handle on this, Luke," Darren urged, hand still on his shoulder, eyes filled with worry. "Why don't you head back to work and let Mel and me take it from here?"

Mel's son, Jeff, was pulling up with a horse trailer, Mel nattering at him about how he should have been back at the sanctuary long ago in the first place, and how this mess wouldn't have happened... but her words turned to nothing but a vocal blur.

"You sure?"

"Positive."

Another car took the corner, slowing down when the driver saw the mess with Needle, and Luke's heart finally stopped trying to claw its way out of his chest. Sweat soaked his armpits and neck, his body in full battle mode. Still breathing hard, he willed himself to self-regulate.

The car. Harriet running. Amber in her red poncho against the snow, the angle of her extremities making it evident before he even touched her that her death had been instantaneous–all of it flooded him.

The body does, indeed, keep score. Every muscle, every cell, had stored away what he'd experienced.

And called it forth in a split second.

Luke looked at Kylie, taking deep breaths. Synchronizing hers with his rhythm, he felt her calm witness to his emotional reaction and appreciated it more than she could imagine.

"Hey," she said, touching his arm. "What was that about? She was always safe."

"I see that now. In the moment, I didn't. And Amber..."

"Amber?"

Trying to explain it all set his heart jumping again, a visceral pull to go silent making it impossible to talk.

"I'll...Kylie, I need some space. Need to calm down. Can we talk later?"

"Of course."

"Thanks." He started to turn away.

"Luke?" Kylie asked, sounding unsure. "Should we go home or head to the park like I'd planned?"

"Park," he said quickly. "Just stay on the sidewalks."

Her hand went to his forearm, the touch soft and caring. "Of course. Always."

Always was a funny word.

Because Luke knew all too well that people thought it meant forever.

And he knew that nothing did.

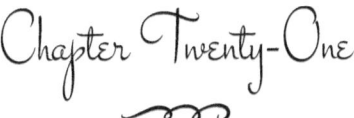

Chapter Twenty-One

Kylie

"Help!" Wendy's internet was laggy, but good enough. There were rolling hills behind her, green and lush, with rows and rows of grapevines making Kylie jealous. Her sister had been gone for three weeks now, and this was the first time the internet connection had been strong enough for a serious video call. Everything else had been texts, pictures, and a few quick phone calls, but mostly silence.

Wendy was living her best life.

And Kylie couldn't be happier for her.

"Are you under a pergola? And is that a stone fence behind you?"

"YES!" Wendy squealed into the camera, except the lag cut it in half, making her look like it was a bad edit. "This place is magical. The parents are super chill. Not sure if they like me or not, but they give me lots of freedom as long as I keep Jean-Marc and Estelle happy. They love to ride bikes, so my quads are already getting bigger and stronger. I'll have one fine ass by the time I come home."

Wendy's chatter was so good to hear.

"Tell me more!"

"The food, Kylie—I had no idea fruits and vegetables could taste like this! I don't know what they do that's so different, but every bite is like eating the best food in a super-expensive restaurant. I'm eating way more fruit than I normally would because the berries are so delicious!"

"Go back to the flight. Tell me everything from the last time I saw you. I want to feel like I'm there, too."

"You'll come over in June, right? If we can get you a cheap enough ticket? I'm making enough money. I can help with it."

"Yes! If we can swing it." Kylie hated taking a paycheck from Luke every week, even if it was direct-deposited, without fanfare. It felt weird to get paid to play with Harriet and fall for him at the same time.

Hold up. Fall for him?

No.

No no no.

Number 14, Part A. New York. Job applications. Two and a half months left on her lease. She was absolutely, positively, not falling in love with Luke Luview.

Friends? Sure.

Falling for Harriet? Of course.

Kylie was bonding with her, and it broke her heart to know she'd be leaving soon, but that's how working with children often rolled out. You were a temporary person in their life. Even when Kylie taught in the classroom, it worked that way. The kids were hers for nine months, and then... they weren't.

Nannying for Harriet was just a shorter version of being a classroom teacher.

At least, that's what she told herself.

Wendy's words were a welcome balm, rolling off her as her little sister excitedly described arriving at the Paris airport, how the Durands—Miriam and Jacques—had sent a driver to pick her up. They were wealthy but not indulgent, and from Wendy's description, Kylie could tell they might be hands off and not give Wendy quite as much guidance as she'd like, but her sister was in good hands.

There were worse things in life than being given a little too much freedom.

"–and they want to go to Berlin at Christmas, Kylie! Miriam has an aunt who lives there and the Christmas markets are one of her favorite holiday activities, so I'm getting paid *and* they're covering all my travel expenses. This job is the best!"

"Your nanny job is way more exciting than mine. I just make peanut butter sandwiches with bananas, hemp seeds, and crushed sweet potato chips. You get Paris."

"You make *what?*"

Kylie laughed. "Never mind."

Wendy giggled. "I never would have guessed we'd have the same job!"

Ouch. Shouldn't have smarted, but it did. Wendy was eight years younger and living in France.

Kylie was stuck in Maine with a lease, hadn't heard back from any of the jobs she'd applied for in New York, and was an emotional mess about Luke.

"Kylie? I didn't hurt your feelings, did I?"

"What?"

"It's just–you know. You have a master's degree and way more experience than me. It's not like I was comparing us and saying I'm your equal. I just thought it was funny we're both nannies at the same time!" Wendy's voice tended to go higher and higher when she was nervous, and at the rate she was going, Kylie would need a special noise detector to catch her decibel level.

"I'm not offended! Just thinking."

"About Luke?"

Caught.

"Yes."

"I knew it! Are you two shagging?"

"WHAT?"

"Shagging. It's a British term for having sex."

"You're learning lots of new terms, aren't you?"

"Yep! I can swear in French like you wouldn't believe."

"I'll bet."

"You didn't answer my question, Ky."

"No. We're not sleeping together," she said firmly. "There's a clause in my employment contract that says we can't."

"Contracts can be renegotiated."

"My heart isn't a line item in a contract, Wendy."

"Oof. Sorry. You're right. It's that bad?"

"YAAASSSSS," Kylie groaned. "It is. I'm hopeless. He's really, really hot when he's wearing only a towel…"

"A towel!"

"…fresh out of the shower."

"You've been holding out on me!"

"Nothing happened. We haven't even kissed. But there's definitely something there."

"He was your first love."

"I know. But what he did fifteen years ago still hurts. Ghosting on me like that."

"You should ask him."

"I'd rather catch a fainting giraffe's head."

"That's a really weird thing to say."

"Not in Love You, Maine."

Tap tap tap

Kylie screamed, the sound of someone knocking on her front door so unexpected, she had an adrenaline surge of surprise.

"Kylie?"

That was Luke's voice on the other side of the front door.

"Kylie?" Wendy asked, voice filled with concern. "What just happened?"

"Someone's at my door."

"Food?"

"No."

"What kind of person just spontaneously appears at your door?"

"It's Maine, Wendy. That's how it works here. It's Luke."

"Luke? He's at your apartment? Now?"

"Yes! I don't know why."

"*Brown chicken, brown cow* is why."

"Huh?"

"Say it fast a few times. Never mind. Go! Get your groove on!"

"I need to get a bra on before I do that!"

"Why bother? Sounds like he'll be taking it off you soon."

"HEY!"

"Love you," Wendy said hurriedly. "Go get 'em."

Call ended.

With no time to get dressed beyond her sweatpants, loose hoodie, and heart-shaped red slippers, Kylie grabbed the doorknob and pressed her palm against her chest, holding all the emotions behind her fingers.

Like that worked.

As she opened the door, the distinct scent of Korean food–spiced beef and yummy aromatic rice–scrambled her senses. Luke wore a cap, a thin down coat, jeans, and boots.

And he held a Mountain Dragon bag.

"Peace offering?" He held the bag aloft. It was printed with green dragons on the outside, all breathing–yep.

Hearts.

"For what?"

"For yelling at you."

"You're the first boss who's ever apologized for that, much less brought me takeout!"

"I'm not your normal boss."

"No kidding."

"Can I come in and we can talk?" Pleading puppy dog eyes met hers, and she melted.

"Sure," she agreed, desperate for more than just talk, but she'd take what she could get.

"Nice place," he said as he entered and looked around.

"You're a good liar."

"Not lying! It's nice." Luke set the food on her tiny dining table and pulled off his hat, then coat, the stretch of his flannel-covered arms making her flush with the memory of his bare skin.

"It's... a place."

"Two more months, right?"

"Just about. A little more."

She reached for his coat and his smile pulled the outer corners of his eyes down in that deep, compassionate way. He was so smart, but not showy about it. Luke was good to the core, honorable and true, and that made this all the more difficult.

Number 14, Part A.

Two and a half months.

"Any luck with your job search?" he asked as she went into the tiny kitchen and found plates, forks, and napkins.

"Not yet. Seventeen applications. I even applied for a coordinator's job with a children's programming channel."

A low whistle was his reply. "Wow. That's the big leagues."

"The job I'm trying for is a glorified gopher, but it's the biggest kid's programming channel in the world, so...."

"Is it what you really want?"

She was reaching for a small container of food. "I wouldn't apply if it weren't."

"Can I be blunt?"

No conversation ever took a turn for the better when those words were spoken. Suddenly, her appetite disappeared.

"Of course."

"I really wish you would stay here in Maine."

Well, now.

The universe just proved her wrong.

"You do?"

"Harriet adores you."

And you? she wanted to ask, but the words got stuck in her throat.

"I adore her right back," Kylie finally managed, giving him a genuine smile. "You have raised a sweet, loving little girl who views the world with so much trust."

He blinked, slow and steady, face immobile, and Kylie wondered if she'd said the wrong thing.

"That means a lot to me." Luke's words sounded like gravel. "I want her to trust. I want her not to be damaged by losing her mother like that."

"You've succeeded."

"Wasn't all me. My mom, Dad, Colleen, and Kell all helped. Mrs. Petrinelli, too. Half the damn town came out to help me."

"Love You, Maine, is special. A town full of nothing but love."

"It is." His stomach growled.

"Shall we eat and then talk?"

"Sounds good."

The silence lasted two minutes, overshadowed by the extraordinary taste of the food. She was halfway through her bowl before she pulled back and gave him a quizzical look.

"Wait a minute. How did you know I like bi bim bap?"

"Colleen told me."

"How did she know?"

"She was there when you picked your food up one day."

"That was three weeks ago! Right when I started working for you."

He shrugged, but there was something in his eyes that told her this drop-in visit wasn't just an apology. More was brewing between them, and he was weakening her resolve.

Not that it was very strong to begin with.

"Please thank Colleen next time you see her."

"I will when I get home."

"Home? She's there?"

"How do you think I'm visiting you? Harriet has to have someone there, remember? Even if she thinks the iPad, a cell-phone, and Jester are babysitter enough."

"If you left Harriet and Jester by themselves in the house, all the junk food would be eaten in thirty minutes and your walls would be decorated in glitter gel pen art."

"Have you been spying on my house? Because that happened a year ago, one morning when I tried to sleep in. Why do you think the foyer's a different color than the hallway?"

Their shared laughter cut the tension.

But then again, the sexual tension building between them wasn't the kind Kylie wanted less of.

On his last bite, Luke finished and stood. "Trash can?"

"Under the sink. How can you eat all that in one sitting?"

He patted his flat stomach. "Metabolism."

She put the lid on her half-eaten bowl and patted the top. "Saving room for lemon bars."

"Lemon bars? You didn't mention anything about dessert!"

"I wasn't expecting you to show up like a knight in shining sriracha sauce."

Luke pulled the hem of his shirt up, exposing half an eight-pack of abs. "Hurry up and metabolize," he ordered his stomach. "Kylie's got lemon bars. Do they have glitter in them, too?" he asked as she tried not to drool.

Instead, she poured them both glasses of water and pointed to the couch.

"Glitter free."

"Whew."

"Not a fan of my edible glitter?"

"Not a fan of being teased at the station non-stop for looking like a fortune teller."

Palm up, she extended her flat hand. "Want to predict my future?"

The touch of his hot hand holding hers sent instant sparks across her skin. With a feather-light touch, his fingertip stroked the lines of her palm, his head bent down, staring intently. Lightning rippled through her, hot and sharp, the taste of a kiss from fifteen years ago instantly on her tongue again.

"I see a glittery future with many fairy muffins, a girl with dark, curly hair, and a dog's nose in your crotch."

While his words were funny, the look in his eyes when he stared at her wasn't. Swallowing hard, she stayed in place, his finger stroking back and forth now, igniting fire in all the right places on her body.

If he took one step forward, she would break her contract.

And, maybe, her heart.

So Kylie smiled and pulled her hand out of his grasp. "Lemon bars!" she exclaimed as Luke let out a long, slow breath, his hand going to the back of his neck, stretching.

"Sure. Sounds good." His voice was full of something she couldn't quite name, but there was no way he felt what she felt.

Right?

Because if he did, if he was as attracted to her as she was to him, then this was getting dangerous.

Fast.

The lemon bars would, at a minimum, keep their hands and

mouths busy doing something other than what she *wanted* to do with her hands and her mouth.

Not to mention his hands.

His mouth.

"Mmmmmmm," he groaned as he took his first bite, closing his eyes, savoring Kylie's creation. "What is in this?"

"Ground vanilla bean on top. A dash of cayenne."

"Pepper?"

Pleased with her invention, and thrilled he noticed the unique flavor, she couldn't help herself. She had to talk about it. "Yep! It cuts through the sweetness of the vanilla and adds a new layer on top of the citrus."

"Sure does." His eyebrows knitted as he thought. "Cinnamon?"

"Yes! And a dash of anise."

"That's a lot of layers."

"I enjoy complexity."

"I can see that." Luke smiled. "I like it in food. Not so much in people."

"Then we're twins." She offered him a fist bump. He returned it with a laugh.

"I only do that with Harriet."

"Fist bumps aren't just for kids."

He peered at her, then took another lemon bar and ate quietly. Kylie was close to bursting, so she nibbled hers slowly.

Besides, the complexity she was enjoying right now wasn't on her tongue.

Or at least, not yet.

Stop it, she chided herself in her mind, cursing the little sexually charged devil that lived in her subconscious. That voice just laughed maniacally and shoved an image of Luke in a towel in front of her mind's eye.

And then without the towel.

"This is nice," Luke said, cutting her thoughts short.

Thank goodness.

"It is?"

"I don't spend time alone with adults other than at work or with my family, or maybe helping someone with a home or yard project. Can't remember the last time I sat alone and had a one-on-one conversation about something other than work, Harriet, or sports."

She held up the lemon bar. "I'll talk about baking and fairies any time."

"What's the deal with the fairies? I've never met a grown-up who's obsessed with them. You weren't when you lived here."

"No. I wasn't. It's because of a summer job I had in college. Fairy camp."

"Fairy *camp*? You were a camp counselor to fairies?" A teasing glint filled his eyes. "You do realize fairies aren't real?"

"*I* know they aren't, but kids are different. The thin line between real and fantasy isn't as stark as it is for grown-ups. I love creating a fantasy world. We built a week-long curriculum where we wove folklore, fantasy, and practical skills."

"Practical skills? With *fairies?*"

"Sure! Like fairy tracking."

"Tracking?"

"We teach kids how to track animals when they learn to hunt, right? Or to stay safe in the woods? So for fairy camp, we taught them to track fairies."

"What kind of signs and marks do fairies leave?"

"Really small ones."

Luke cracked up.

"Every camper was given a magnifying lens to look for details."

He made a face that said he was impressed. "You used fairies to trick the kids into learning actual, real lessons."

"'Tricked' is a harsh word, but yes."

"That's hard core."

"It works on Harriet."

"It does?"

"I convinced her that the messier a room is, the more places the fairies have to hide. So you're more likely to see a fairy if the house is clean."

His jaw dropped. "That's why she keeps saying we have to pick up?"

Joy spiked through her. "She does?"

He turned toward her on the couch, relaxing suddenly. "Yes! I thought she was just going through some phase, but now I see there's more to it. You devious little nanny, you!"

"Devious? No! I'm leveraging her imagination to teach her a real-world skill."

"Right. You tricked her."

Unable to help herself, she gave him a playful smack on the arm. He grabbed her hand, holding it as they laughed, but the air between them changed. Deepened.

Blazed.

This time, Luke was the one who broke away, standing. "More water?" he asked, pointing to Kylie's empty glass.

She nodded.

As he filled their glasses, she took long, slow breaths. What was happening? Was he here to initiate something? Was this a booty call and she was too clueless to see it?

Or was Luke really just being a friend?

She could use a new friend.

She could *definitely* use a new friend with benefits.

But Number 14, Part A loomed large.

Don't bang your boss, Kylie.

"Here," he said, startling her out of her thoughts as he handed her the glass, then sat down. This time, he sat a bit further away from her on the couch. The moment seemed to have passed, but there was no question that there had been a moment.

Moments.

And there would be more coming, too.

Should she say something? Confront it head on?

"You know, Kylie, the last time I had this much fun just talking to someone was with Amber."

Hoo boy.

Luke just took this in a totally new direction.

"I'm so sorry."

"Thanks. Everyone says that."

"Sorry. I don't want to sound like everyone. You clearly loved her. *Love* her," she added quickly.

"I do. Did. All of it. But it's been two years." His eyes met hers. "I'm lonely. Colleen and Mom have been yammering at me for a long time that I should own up to that. Now I can."

"Now?"

A long, sultry silence spread between them.

Until Kylie ruined it by saying, "Loads of women in town would like to make you less lonely."

He leaned in. "They would?"

"Mindy Maasten made that clear at the bus stop last week."

He snorted. "Mindy? Nope. Never."

"She seems nice," Kylie said, sarcasm giving her words a sharp bite.

Luke's eyebrows shot up. "Didn't know you had some mean girl in you."

"Only when someone else starts it."

"You've tapped into your anger, then?"

"After what Perry did to me? Hell, yes."

His laugh wasn't quite all there, a troubled look filling his face.

"I can't even be angry."

She was confused. "About Mindy? Or Perry?"

"About Amber."

"Of course you can."

"No, Kylie, that's the problem–I can't." Pain walked across his face like it owned the landscape. "Do you know how Amber died?"

"No."

"That explains it, then. I thought you knew. No offense, but how could you move back here and not Google?"

"You really want to know?"

"I wouldn't have asked if I didn't."

"At first, it was because Perry hates the town. He thinks it's over-the-top, cheesy, schlocky–pick a negative word, and Perry felt it."

"Hmm. Lots of people think that, but once they're here, they change their mind. Like Kell's girlfriend, Rachel."

"You know that, and I know that, but his family definitely seems immune to Love You's charms."

"I see them here, having dinner, occasionally shopping at the jewelry store or visiting the wealth management office."

"They'll come here. And Nordicbeth certainly benefits from all the tourists the town brings to the area. But Perry hates it here. When we moved back, I was busy with my new job, new life with him, and after a while, I started to feel like it would be too painful to go into Luview. I don't really fit in."

"You do. You were born here."

"I was. But we left and Mom never brought us back. Dad didn't bother. And by the time I was old enough to come myself, I didn't have friends here anymore, so…"

Self-consciousness kicked in, his eyes so open and focused on her. He had been talking about Amber and the conversation took this turn, and now she was close to telling him the real reason why she didn't come visit her hometown, even living so close:

Because there was no place for her, anywhere. She didn't want to be the "new person" in a town where she should have been a townie all along. There was no place where she really fit in. Avoiding rejection was easier.

Instead, she said, "And then, after Perry dumped me, I wasn't exactly interested in coming back with my tail between my legs."

He grimaced. "Ouch. Yeah. I can see that."

"Luke." She covered the back of his hand with her palm. "How *did* Amber die?"

"Car accident."

"Was she driving?"

"No. She was walking on the side of the road and a car hit her."

"Oh, no." Shock hit her, hard. "That's why you were so upset about Harriet at Murphy's Curve."

"Yes."

"Oh, Luke."

A long, slow, deep breath came out of him, echoing in his throat like it was calling into the past. "Amber liked to take long walks. It was Thanksgiving, so there wasn't much traffic. Big shoulder, plenty of room. And she wore that crazy red poncho."

"Red poncho?"

"The one you put on in the donation box."

"That was *hers?*"

"Yep. I–that night, I was donating what she and I were wearing the day she died."

"Luke, I'm–"

"Can you let me finish the story? It's not the kind that's easy to tell with lots of interruptions."

"Of course. And you don't have to tell it if you don't want–"

His fingers pressed against her lips, eyes searching, filled with a combination of attraction and grief, and she wanted to wash away all of the misery he carried in him.

"Let me finish."

She nodded.

"The guy who hit her had a heart attack at the wheel. They say he was dead before his head hit the steering wheel. He lost control of the car, but his weight pushed on the accelerator. Amber couldn't even jump out of the way in time, he was going so fast. She was dead instantly."

"I'm so sorry." Garbled sounds came out of her, because Luke's hand still covered her mouth, but she didn't care. The impulse to say something, to connect, to be with him in feeling was too great.

"Thank you. But do you see why I can't be mad?" Plaintive pain came through in his voice, his hand dropping from her mouth, her hand squeezing his, hard.

"So much pain."

"That's an understatement. The driver was a local, too."

"Oh, no! Who?"

"The town clerk. Stan Petrinelli."

"Mrs. Petrinelli's husband?" Kylie gasped. "She–she lives down the street from you! Babysits for you! She's–oh, wow."

He nodded, jaw tight but moving, his attempt to control his emotions achingly difficult to watch. All she wanted was to make his hurt go away.

"Yes. Anne carries a lot of misplaced guilt about it. Not her fault, for goodness sake. Stan had been to a cardiologist. Went faithfully. Took medication for some condition. No one knows why, but that was the exact moment his heart just... gave out." His voice cracked. "And ripped mine out of my chest."

"Oh, Luke." She squeezed his hands, feeling helpless.

"Wasn't the driver's fault. Wasn't Amber's fault. Suddenly, the town had two people to grieve." He dipped his head and whispered softly, "Only it was really three."

"Three?"

Another long sigh, then he looked up at her, eyes shining, as he gripped her hand. "Amber was pregnant."

Kylie was speechless.

"We were about to announce the pregnancy that afternoon at our Thanksgiving celebration with family."

Full-throated pain filled her, eyes overflowing with tears that spilled onto her cheeks before the first gasp escaped her. Squeezing his hand, she reached for him by instinct, to hold this man who had experienced too much tragedy.

Too much to bear alone.

They breathed together, her arms around his shoulders, his wrapped about her waist, the contact nothing more than comfort, a recognition of his pain. Luke's pain was hers, too, in this moment. So much lost. So much he and Harriet could never get back.

So much loneliness.

His body loosened in her embrace, Luke's hot breath on her neck smelling like lemon and vanilla, her own body melting into his arms. Sharing this space together, they just breathed, as if being present for each other were enough.

Because it was.

Luke took the first step to break the hug, pulling back but stopping her as Kylie tried to untangle herself fully. His hands went up the side of her arms, resting on her shoulders, then cupped her jaw, tips of his fingers sliding behind her ears, their eyes locked.

The second kiss Luke and Kylie ever shared wasn't one she ever expected, but it was one the universe sent to them, inspired by the past, by grief, by shared longing, by serendipity. His lips were warm and strong, the rasp of his inhale intense as he deepened his attention, chest against chest, his hands buried in her hair now, tongue against hers, the heat of their mouths melting everything else away.

"Kylie," he murmured against her mouth, then kissed her again, as if he had to name this to believe it. Her hands wandered the broad muscle of his back, mind repeating his name over and over until the words changed from *Luke Luke Luke* to *Oh Oh Oh.*

Oh, yes.

Oh, please.

Oh, *more.*

He pulled back, forehead touching hers, breath ragged as his hands dropped to clasp hers, their panting filling the air with warmth, with sweet citrus, with the unmistakable energy of two people on the cusp of something new.

Something wonderful.

Or a terrible mistake.

"I'm sorry," he said slowly, pulling back to look her in the eye. Luke wasn't a man who shied away from owning his own actions, or emotions. "That was–"

"Amazing," she jumped in with a sad smile. "But not allowed."

"Number 14, Part A," they said in unison, the moment snapping clean in half, her nervousness taking over as she shifted away from him.

Luke stood abruptly, but reached down to lift another lemon bar from the plate, take a huge bite, and give her a chipmunk-cheek grin. Turning away, he put on his coat and hat and walked to the door.

"Thank you for everything, Kylie," he said, body taut with a coiled, repressed energy that made her want to strip naked and beg him to stay.

"I–"

"I'm leaving now. Not because I want to leave. What I want to do, very much, is stay. I want to stay and carry you into the bedroom. I want to undress you and watch you as I undress. I want to see the desire I just felt in your kiss. I want to spend hours making love with you, then hours more just being with you. I want lemon bars and goofy movies in bed, then I want to make pancakes and bacon for you in the morning while we make love some more, share the newspaper, just... be. But I won't do any of that. I want a lot of things life won't let me have, Kylie. And right now, unfortunately, you're one of them."

Stomach sinking, heart soaring, his words touched a place inside her that wanted nothing more than to be seen. Observed. Adored and known, accepted and embraced. He was more than she'd ever hoped for, the taste of him on her tongue, her heart ready to leap into his arms.

Perry never gave her anything close to what Luke had just offered, and she'd been with him for seven years. How could a handful of weeks and a single kiss from Luke feel like it was so much more?

"No one's ever said anything like that to me," she replied, the words lacking, but as she stood before him, stunned and excited, they were true.

Too true.

For years she'd settled for Perry, knowing it wasn't quite right, never quite enough, but the best she deserved.

And now, Luke was here, offering more. Telling her she deserved more. The closed-off guy who shouldered so many responsibilities had just opened up to her, and what a confession.

Luke was a forever guy. The kind you settled down with, your life planned out before you start. Being with him was no mystery. The entire blueprint of their forever filled in her mind's eye as they breathed together, his hand on her doorknob, his eyes at war.

Fighting himself. She felt it, too, a battle inside, warring priorities always defaulting to responsibility. Luke was no fling, and Kylie was no fool.

She couldn't hurt him or Harriet just because she was lonely.

Something more held him back, too. He was saying life wouldn't let him have her. Whatever that meant, his message was clear:

No sex. Even if they both wanted each other desperately.

Respect filled her, along with a thousand searching questions she wanted to ask him, not to pin him down or convince him to sleep with her, but to understand.

And to make him feel understood.

Instead, she took the emotionally safer route.

"Don't bang your boss," she blurted aloud, using humor to break the tension, taking the coward's way out.

Luke's entire demeanor startled, like a knight in shining armor being shoved to the right a foot by an unseen force. He opened her front door, a blistering wind shoving a blast of cold air on her, for which she was suddenly grateful.

Then one corner of Luke's mouth went up in a luscious, extraordinary grin as he left her with the parting words:

"Don't bang your nanny."

Her heart slammed in her chest as he left, but he turned back to add:

"No matter how much you want to."

Chapter Twenty-Two

Luke

"That was fast," Colleen said with a leer only a big sister could master. "Been so long, you went off like Coke poured over Pop Rocks?"

"*Shhhh*," he shushed her, giving her a vicious glare. "Harriet might hear you."

"She's asleep."

"I wasn't gone that long."

"Poor kid was tired. So the date was a bomb?"

"Wasn't a date."

"You were only there for two hours."

"So? Who named you my hover sister?"

"Uh, me. I did. Two years ago."

"You're fired."

"WOO HOO! Master gave Dobby a sock!"

"Shut up."

"Kylie shot you down? Huh. Guess I lose in the betting pool."

"You placed a bet?" Luke knew all about the stupid betting pool Wolf over at Greta's had going.

"Sure. Why not?"

"You have insider knowledge?"

"Made it even better odds."

"My love life isn't something other people should make money from. That's skating close to porn."

"Ew! Gross, Luke!"

He let out a tense laugh and made his way to the fridge for a beer. The sight of the bottle in his hand made Colleen peer at him.

"Of all the people who should understand, sis, you should get it. Your love life is the talk of the town."

"I have no love life because of all the gossip!"

"Third-Date Colleen isn't the best nickname, huh?"

"Shut up. It's just superstition. Is it my fault every guy I've dated has ended up in my emergency room after the third date?"

"Yes."

She threw a kitchen towel at him. Jester jumped up, snatched it in his teeth, and made off for his dog bed like he'd killed a bird in mid-air, eyes cutting over to Luke in triumph.

See? I protected you, a mere human, from certain death, those eyes said. *Give me a treat.*

"It's not my fault, but everyone in town thinks it is, so that's all I get to be. Third-Date Colleen."

"I'm Poor Luke the Young Widower, shortened to just Poor Luke. I'll trade you."

"You changed the subject from your pathetic love life to *my* pathetic love life, bro. Tell me what happened with Kylie."

He let out a sigh that rattled his back teeth, opened the beer, and chugged about half in one long sequence of gulps. Doing something that shocked his body felt good. His throat ached from the cold, the chill of the bottle against his fingers making him feel alive. While he'd wanted to engage his limbs in a very different set of activities tonight, all of them naked with Kylie, he hadn't.

Why?

She'd been ready. Eager. Willing. Choosing to end things before they got out of hand made him look like a gentleman, following his stupid contract.

But the woman wasn't dumb. She knew he was halting for other reasons.

Reasons he barely understood himself.

As he downed his beer, Colleen looked a bit worried.

"Bad enough to need a drink?"

"Something like that."

"Did you or did you not sleep with her?"

"No."

"But something happened."

"Not talking about this. Thanks for watching Harriet. Sorry you lost your bet."

"Luke." Her voice softened, and so did his emotional armor. "Talk to me."

"Look. I'm a man. A man who spent the last two years pretending not to have needs. And now Kylie Hood comes into town, full of fairy magic and order and lightness, and I'm being stupid. I'm just turning toward the familiar. Whatever I'm feeling is all about comfort, about the past. It's just nostalgia. None of it's real. Kylie's leaving town in two months *and* she's my nanny. Nothing can happen between us."

"Something *did* happen!"

"Thanks for listening, sis."

She caught his forearm, the one not holding his beer.

"Luke. Mom and I have spent a lot of time encouraging you to get on with your life. If you think you can find happiness with Kylie, go for it."

"I'm not going to hurt Harriet by banging the nanny."

"You sound like Darren."

"Darren's a smart guy. A doctor, you know."

"Darren's about as qualified to hand out relationship advice as I am to teach a monkey how to skateboard."

"Pretty sure that's Mel's next project."

"You're changing the subject again."

"Sure am."

"You don't have to feel guilty for moving on."

"You're right, I've heard that from you or Mom about a thousand times."

"Moving on doesn't mean you love Amber and the baby any less."

Ka-boom.

There it was.

Rubbing his eye, his fingers moved to his brow, where he had the beginnings of a tension headache. All the good feelings with Kylie, especially with her in his arms and that smoking hot kiss, were tangled up with this festering pool of emotions.

Emotions he avoided for a reason.

"I told Kylie about the baby."

"Wow. I mean... *wow.* You really are falling for her if you're getting that intimate."

"I told you we didn't sleep together."

"I said intimate. Not physical. You showed her a piece of your heart only the close family knows about."

"Yeah."

"Which means you want her to be close to you, too."

"Yes."

"You're a grown-up, Luke. You're a leader. A protector. You're a strong man with a good heart. Harriet couldn't have a better father. But you deserve something for yourself, too. Maybe that's Kylie."

"She works for me."

"Then fire her."

"Harriet would kill me in my sleep with a single LEGO."

His sister burst into giggles. "That's true."

The beer was taking the slightest edge off, blurring a few harsh lines, which allowed him to let a small wall down. "Colleen, I don't know what to do. I went to her apartment with takeout to apologize for yelling at her and ended up kissing her."

Colleen's grin stretched wide. Luke was pretty sure he saw betting grid dollar signs in them.

"Then I freaked out and left. I told her I can't bang the nanny."

"You did *not* say that!"

He leveled her with a flat look.

"You did say that. Geez, Luke, you need lessons on how to woo a woman."

"I need lessons on how not to be attracted to her."

Raucous laughter poured out of her. "Hah! Good luck with that."

"I don't know what to do," he confessed, plopping into his recliner. Jester came up to him, nuzzling his elbow, demanding head scratches.

"You know what you want to do."

"Yeah, sure, but being an adult means you don't run off half cocked and do whatever your impulses tell you to do."

She snickered. He rolled his eyes.

"No one can tell you what to do, but Luke—the fact that you're conflicted is a sign."

"How so?"

"When Mindy Maasten came on to you like a bulldozer, you weren't conflicted. Your answer was a clear no."

"Right."

"And when Annabeth Kouri decided to stop by every Sunday before church for ten weeks in a row, you weren't conflicted."

"She kept inviting me to Mass. I'm not Catholic."

"That's not the point!"

"You're saying the fact that I don't know how to handle my feelings for Kylie is a sign that I should go for it, because I have any feelings at all?"

Colleen touched the tip of her nose with one finger and pointed at him with another.

"Bingo."

"This is complicated."

"Nah. Banging your nanny is pretty simple."

He grabbed a throw pillow and tossed it at her. Before it hit, Jester leaped into the air and caught it with his teeth.

"Good boy," she said as Jester loped over to Luke, dropped the pillow in his lap, and panted as if to say, *More playing catch, please!*

"Get out of my house, you evil sister," he said, pointing to the door.

She blew him a kiss.

"Just wait another week before you sleep with her."

"Excuse me?"

"Another week. Mama wants that $450 prize pot. I need new tires for my car."

He tossed the pillow again, pleasing the dog. Colleen's laughter mocked him, fading away as she went out the door.

Leaving him alone with his own thoughts, a light buzz, a dog eager for more pillow catch, and a raging hard-on.

Tossing the pillow a few times for Jester was something he could do, so he did, until the dog dropped the game and settled down in his bed.

What the hell had he just done at Kylie's? Dumped his heart out on her lap, talked about his dead wife, told her about the pregnancy–something only his close family knew–and then...

Kissed her?

"Regular Romeo, aren't you? Kiss a woman after talking about your wife and baby dying," he muttered, eyeing his empty beer bottle, tempted to have a second but knowing he'd regret it in the morning. Besides, he was the only responsible adult in the house, no matter how much he wished Jester could fill that role sometimes.

One drink limit.

Replaying that kiss didn't help matters, scrambling his brain and blood until he was throbbing so hard, he felt like an electric bass. What on earth had made him lose his restraint and cross that line?

Kylie.

That's what.

That's *who*.

Now he had overshared, kissed her, and she was coming tomorrow morning as usual to take care of Harriet.

Could he have made a bigger mess of things?

Oh. Right.

His last words to her were, "Don't bang your nanny."

So yes. Yes, he could.

"Ah, geez," he groaned, body itching to do something, hit something, smash something–anything to get the antsy sense of unsettled feelings out of his system.

Jester stood and nosed the back door, Luke obliging him by sliding the glass door open. A glint of moonlight in the back yard fell on a pile of large rounds from a tree job his dad and Kell had performed. They were seasoned and would be easy to split, then stack. That gave him an option:

Chop wood.

Like everyone in their area, he had a wood stove, and chopping wood was in his blood. If he grabbed gloves and an ax, could he divert enough blood into his arms and away from his other wood?

But laziness won, and he turned to the kitchen instead to drink a huge glass of water and think while Jester systematically defiled each one of the paths he'd plowed outside. The dog seemed determined to turn every inch of snow yellow.

He decided to check email.

Deleting all the spam was easy, if annoying. Then he had an email from Harriet's kindergarten teacher, asking for a standard conference. Email from Mom and Dad, chronicling their time in Germany. Something from the real estate agent about the purchase of Camp Wannacanhopa.

A notice that the closing had been scheduled for Thursday, and asking him to confirm.

Joy filled him, along with a healthy dose of pride. The old camp had been empty for two years, needing too much work to be of interest to folks who wanted it operational quickly, and too remote to be of interest to most developers. Other than a close call earlier in the year when the huge chocolatier Kell's now-girlfriend worked for wanted to buy it and turn it into a theme park, a deal that had gone south, thankfully, buying the camp had been relatively easy.

With some careful work and help from his family, he'd been able to swing the mortgage.

In four days, he'd be the proud owner of 151 acres, a lodge with a dining hall, a director's house, an office, and numerous smaller outbuildings. His very own sanctuary.

Of course, it would be shared with his family, but he was the one who technically bought it, because he'd used Amber's lump-sum life insurance policy as part of the enormous down payment.

Life was about to change. But this time, it would change because *he* initiated it. Not because life threw him a curveball.

And speaking of curveballs—an email from Amber's mom.

Dear Luke, it read. *Tally and I won't be up north for the holidays, as you know, but we'd love to have you and Harriet come here for February break. I know we talked about it last time we were on the phone, but I wanted to confirm so you could ask for the time off. Fortunately, it's after Valentine's Day. Tally's legs are getting weaker and it's harder to travel.*

Tallman McFarland, aka Tally, was his father-in-law. Amber's dad was a late-in-life father, but still only in his early seventies. Amber was their only child. An autoimmune disorder was progressively eating away at him, and Luke took great pains to make sure Harriet saw Amber's parents as much as possible, which meant flying to Florida twice a year. Marilyn and Tally had already moved away before Amber's accident, drawn to warmer weather and easier winters for Tally's condition.

Calling them on Thanksgiving two years ago had been one of the hardest tasks of his life, second only to telling Harriet her mommy wasn't coming back.

The beer made his fingers fly on the keyboard, answering Marilyn with a strong affirmative. Luke genuinely enjoyed his visits with them, and their joy in Harriet was infectious. Tally played a mean game of pool when his legs worked all right. When they didn't, Luke sat with the two of them on the beach by their condo, filling them in on Luview town gossip as they sipped Tally's newest whisky. Harriet loved collecting shells and running after the seabirds at the water's edge.

A dull dread shot through him.

Right now, *he* was the main subject of Luview town gossip. His love life.

Oh, geez.

Whining outside the door told him Jester was done spraying his territory, so he let the beast in. More whining as Jester made it clear the king demanded to be fed.

For a guy who was supposed to be in charge, Luke was doing everyone else's bidding more often than not. And now he was fodder for the crowd at Greta's, his every move being scrutinized by people with nothing better to do than gawk.

Another layer of moving on from Amber would be telling Marilyn and Tally he had a new romantic interest.

"But I don't," he said firmly, spooking Jester, who looked at him like he was nuts.

Which was about right.

A yawn surprised him, but then again, it had been a long, hard–but good–day. A flash of that kiss slammed through him, like the crack of a baseball against a bat in that split second when you knew you'd hit a home run.

Luke turned out the lights, crawled into bed, and prepared for a crappy night's sleep.

Which was entirely his fault.

Sheet tent and all.

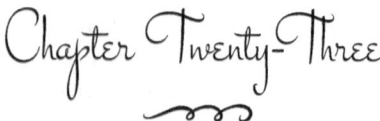

Chapter Twenty-Three

Kylie

His handwriting always made her smile.

Each stroke was bold and complete, confident and artistic, the perfect blend of someone who knew what they were doing but didn't spend more time than needed in communicating a message. Luke's notes were works of art, so memorable, she could picture the words in her mind as if she were eidetic.

But she wasn't.

She had a photographic memory for only one thing: Luke Luview.

Disappointment filled Kylie as she entered the house the day after her encounter with Luke, finding it empty. Of course Luke wasn't here. Her job was to take care of his child so he could work. Luke had put Harriet on the bus that morning, and he'd likely been gone for hours. The bus would drop her off in fifteen minutes.

Jester jumped up and gave her a respectful side hug; he was quickly learning to heed her commands.

"You'll always be here for me, won't you, Jester?"

The dog's eyebrows lifted, mouth opening in a toothy grin,

tongue lolling as she hit the right spot on the top of his head. If only human beings were as easy to please.

Keeping an eye out for the bus, Kylie took a few minutes to make a pot of coffee and quickly load dishes into the dishwasher. Because she came five days a week now, housekeeping was easier and easier. Almost too easy, in some ways. Luke seemed to be good at keeping the place clean once he had a system to follow, and Kylie imposed a system.

They were turning into a well-oiled machine.

An image of a well-oiled, shirtless Luke hit her mind.

And suddenly, her heart.

Among other places on her body.

"Stop it," she muttered to herself, the memory of their kiss yesterday pouring through her, heating her skin. The house smelled like spiced beef and fresh soap, the scent stronger as she picked up a few stray clothes and wandered down the hall to the hamper next to the washing machine.

A deep breath didn't help matters. Her nose was searching for his scent.

Searching for *him*.

"Number 14, Part A," she said in a mocking voice, making fun of herself, the contract, and the way they both knew it was farce. And yet–something had to hold them back, right?

Being together would be a mistake.

A mistake they couldn't walk back.

Harriet's heart mattered. It was too risky to give in to a hormone-induced need to blow off some steam and relive a nostalgic teen moment as two consenting adults. That wasn't a good enough reason to sleep with Luke.

Not that she needed any reasons to sleep with the man. Those were in abundant supply.

What she didn't possess, though, was an ounce of common sense.

An unfamiliar basket was on the dining table, a cheery red collection with green and white ribbon sat on the dining table. Christmas was coming, and Kylie had been wracking her brain to choose the perfect gift for Harriet.

Looked like someone was already in the holiday gift-giving spirit.

Inside the basket, a series of opened bakery boxes made Kylie's mouth water. Donut holes. Macaron cookies. Rugelach. Someone had assembled a lovely assortment of tasty pastries, all of them heart-shaped, of course.

A card lay on the table, staring up at her, begging for a quick snoop.

Loopy, feminine handwriting in red ink on the pink card stock was barely visible from the side. A wave of jealousy hit her, hard and fast, her fingers snatching the bi-fold stationery before she could stop herself.

"My offer stands, any time. I have plenty more sweetness whenever you want it, Luke. XOXO Annabeth."

Annabeth?

It was an unusual name. Kylie remembered Annabeth Khouri, who was older than Luke, closer to Colleen in age. She had to be thirty-five or so now. If Kylie's memory was right, her mom was the police department secretary and her dad was the butcher at Kendrill's Market.

When they were teenagers, Annabeth had long, perfectly coiffed, curly brown hair, big eyes, elegant brows, and flawless skin.

Then there were the claws. Annabeth's were sharp.

Were Annabeth and Luke an item?

"No," she gasped, more upset than she had any right to be. "Luke wouldn't do that."

Do what?

Kiss her if he were sleeping with someone else.

Deep in her bones, she knew that much was true. Whatever Annabeth was up to, Luke wasn't part of it.

Examining the pastries, she instantly knew.

"Hah! Amateur. Didn't even bake your own 'sweets,'" she said triumphantly to no one except Jester, who quirked his head and studied her.

On impulse, she grabbed a rugelach, snapped a piece off, and tossed it as an offering to the dog, popping the rest in her mouth.

Yum. Greta's never disappointed.

"But my lemon bars are even better."

Right when she was leaving this morning, she'd grabbed the container of lemon bars from her kitchen on a whim. The memory of Luke's lemon-flavored kiss made her knees weak and her head a bit floaty, but as she stared at Annabeth's basket of predatory pastry, she realized she could kill two birds with one stone.

Give Harriet a fun outing to visit Daddy at work, and deliver some yummy lemon bars to the station.

Homemade lemon bars.

Ones she could still taste in his kiss.

The clock struck half past noon and she jolted, the bus coming any minute. Shrugging into her coat, she pulled on her boots, grabbed the plastic container, and hurried out the door before Jester could beg for the leash.

Mid-December in northern New England had two settings: Booger-Freezing Cold and Shiver.

Just... *shiver*.

She was born and raised here, and Indiana wasn't exactly tropical, but her body was still adjusting to the sheer crispness of the cold. Razor sharp, it scraped against any patch of bare skin like it wanted you to bleed.

Walking briskly, she willed her blood to warm her up, mentally calculating whether Harriet could handle the walk into town in weather this cold.

Probably. When Kylie was six, it was never too cold for an adventure. She assumed Harriet was the same.

As she approached the bus stop, she saw a new woman there, dressed in skinny jeans and a perfectly coordinated red ski jacket, boots, scarf, and hat. Instagram perfect.

The woman was a walking color palette of perfection.

Izzy Chassi was there, and Kylie's tension dropped at her friendly wave. But the mommy in mirrored sunglasses was there, too, head huddled with the new mom.

Uh oh.

"Hi!" Kylie said brightly, going out of her way to make eye contact.

"Hi, Kylie!" Izzy said, looking at the other women. "Mindy,

you remember Kylie, right?" she said to the mirrored sunglass woman, giving Kylie a name.

"Oh, yes."

"Annabeth? Remember Kylie? Kylie Hood? She's moved back and watches Harriet now."

Kylie's heart stopped.

Something slithered in the space between them, Annabeth's eyes narrowing under the rim of her slouching toque, the fold of fabric in sync with the curl of her coat collar.

How could someone be so aligned?

"I–I guess?" Annabeth's careful, snotty answer would have made Kylie's stomach drop ten years ago, but years of living in New York City had taught her something about people:

The meaner they are, the less secure they are, too.

"I remember you!" Kylie said, holding her gaze, chin up and shoulders straight. "Cheerleader, right? Good to see you. Love the hat."

Annabeth's hand moved up instinctively, touching it with a studied flourish. "Thank you. I got it in Boston."

"Good for you!"

It was clear that Annabeth didn't know what to do with Kylie's reaction.

"What's in the container?" Izzy asked Kylie, eyebrows up, Mindy giving Annabeth laser-eyed nonverbal signals that Kylie interpreted as *Help me put the new girl in her place.*

"Lemon bars." Kylie peeled the lid off and held the container out. "Want one?"

Izzy plucked a small one. Mindy abandoned her locked look with Annabeth and went for it.

Never underestimate the power of sweet lemon to diffuse a social mess.

Annabeth sneered. "I'm good, thanks."

"Mmmmm," Mindy and Izzy groaned in unison. "These are amazing."

"Thanks!" Kylie looked around. The morning kindergarteners were the only kids on the bus at noon, and normally it was her, Izzy, Mindy, and a grandmother, Sally Bentini. "Where's Sally?"

"Robbie's got the flu."

"Aww. Poor kid."

"You have to give me the recipe for those," Mindy said, eyeing Kylie's container like she wanted another one. "If you cook like that, I'll bet Luke loves having you around." Her eyes cut nervously to Annabeth, as if she'd made a mistake.

A scowl greeted her.

"I'm the one who loves being around. Watching Harriet is a blast."

Annabeth made a decidedly unladylike noise. "It's great that being a nanny completes you. I'm just here picking up Carla's kid to help out, and that's more than enough kid time for me."

Kylie smiled, buying herself a few seconds, struggling to find the right reply. She opened the container and offered more to Mindy, but held Annabeth's sharp look as Mindy smiled and took another.

Ready.

"It is, isn't it?" she replied to Annabeth, whose sneer remained intact.

Aim.

"Hmmm," Annabeth murmured, giving Mindy a knowing smile.

Fire.

"Harriet's amazing, and I love reconnecting with Luke, you know? Such a nice guy."

Annabeth's face turned a furious red as Izzy tried to suppress a snicker.

Just then, the bus pulled up, the pneumatic wheeze of the doors shutting out other sounds.

Then squeals from Harriet.

"KYLIE!" she squealed. "Where's Jester?"

"I left him home, honey. We need to walk into town and visit your daddy!"

"YAY! Are those lemon bars? You brought Daddy's favorite!"

Mindy and Izzy looked at Kylie with strange expressions, but Annabeth's was crystal clear:

Total contempt.

"Yes. You think he'll like them?"

"He told me this morning that you gave him some when he visited you last night at your apartment."

Oh, no.

No no no.

Gossip in small towns starts with a whisper and ends with a bang.

And speaking of banging, the rumor mill was about to conclude that Kylie and Luke were doing plenty of it.

Annabeth's eyes turned murderous, while Mindy gave Kylie a look of newfound appreciation that said she'd underestimated her.

Izzy looked like she wanted to high-five Kylie.

"Bye, guys!" Kylie said hastily, skedaddling toward town with Harriet, her brain exploding into confetti as she tried to process what had just happened. By the time she and Harriet reached the station, half the town would know what Harriet just said.

Should she warn Luke?

For the next ten minutes, she and Harriet walked fast along the streets downtown, Harriet chattering away about the kindergarten class pet, a hamster named Munchalicious.

Kylie didn't want to know the origins of *that* name.

Christmas had definitely come to town. The edge of the shopping district was obvious, with fresh-cut greenery and red, white, and silver decorations everywhere, and the occasional splash of metallic pink thrown in for good measure. Holiday lights were on, even in daylight, the effect cheerful and warm. Kylie felt the glow of nostalgia for a holiday experience she'd never had as an adult.

Small-town New England Christmases couldn't be beat.

Especially the ones in her imagination.

Hallmark movies were popular for a reason. Everyone wanted to feel like they fit in somewhere, and that sense was always stronger around holidays with family.

Family of origin, or family of choice. Didn't matter.

We all just want to be part of something special, where we're accepted for who we are—no matter what.

"The Christmas parade is this weekend!" Harriet said,

pointing to a poster. "Gampa's helping Santa and he's going to be in the parade."

The mention of Luke's dad made Kylie jolt a bit. That's right. His parents were coming home from Germany any day now.

"He is?"

"Yes! Santa's too busy making presents to come to the parade, so Gampa wears a costume and pretends to be him so everyone can be happy. Gampa says he's secret friends with Santa and he already told him what I want."

"What do you want?"

"A new mommy."

Kylie stopped dead in her tracks, heart in her throat.

"A what?" she choked out.

"A new mommy," Harriet said, unfazed. "I asked for one last Christmas, too, but Santa brought me a tablet computer instead."

What was Kylie supposed to say to *that?*

"I always ask for my real mommy, too, but Daddy explained that when someone dies, they never come back."

Pulse racing erratically, she took Harriet's outstretched hand in hers, glove to mitten, as they reached the station.

The police station was attached to town hall, a boring red brick building with white pillars and glass double doors at the entry. It looked like a highway rest area, but with bigger antenna towers.

The pink cruisers, however, were not boring. Years ago, someone had the bright idea of making sure none of the police vehicles had blue lights on them. Only red and white.

Until it was pointed out that they had to have blue lights, by law. Teeth were gnashed, concessions made, but the bottom line was that Luke and his fellow police officers drove around town looking like a box of candy hearts. The pink and white ones, with a splash of red-hot cinnamon thrown in for good measure.

As she opened the front door, the distinctive scent of bleach, burning rubber, and old burritos mixed with microwave popcorn made her smile.

Every police station had a similar scent.

"NADINE!" Harriet screeched, winding her way down the hall, her little feet having memorized the trek long ago. Kylie was struck by how at home Harriet felt here, grounded and accepted. Her assumption that she had a right to be here was hard-wired into her DNA.

A wave of sadness washed over her. Would Kylie ever find that again?

"Hey there, sweetheart." Nadine slid the jar of lollipops to the edge of her desk. "Take two."

"Two?"

Nadine winked at Harriet, long, fake eyelashes framing eyes that alternated between open and loving (toward Harriet), and suspicious and cunning (toward Kylie). "Don't tell your daddy. It'll be our secret."

Harriet went somber. "Daddy says grown-ups never, ever need to have secrets with little kids. Now I *have* to tell Daddy you said that!"

"I'm right here. You're terrible at subterfuge, Nadine," rumbled a voice that sent *zing*s through Kylie's blood. Luke appeared, a vision in red like his fellow police officers, grinning at all of them. He ruffled Harriet's hair. "And good girl."

Harriet beamed.

"I wasn't exactly trying to *hide* it from you," Nadine defended herself. Luke rolled his eyes, focusing his happy attention on Kylie.

Who couldn't help but grin back.

Luke in uniform was quite the strong character, his long-sleeved red shirt tucked into red pants, flat stomach bisected by a black belt. Law enforcement officers from other towns made fun of Love You, Maine's uniforms, and the fact that speeding tickets and parking citations were written on heart-shaped paper just added to the mockery.

While Kylie could do without the weird uniform, Luke could wear a brown paper bag and she'd still find him attractive.

Or... no paper bag at all.

His eyes drifted to the container in her hand, then he groaned. "You did not bring those evil temptations with you."

"I think *she's* the evil temptation," Nadine muttered under her breath, soft enough for plausible deniability but loud enough to make sure Kylie heard.

Then she remembered.

Nadine was Annabeth's *mother*.

Nadine Khouri was one of Luview's institutions, a former PTA president, chair of the Friends of the Library, and wedding coordinator for the local Congregational church, to name just a few of her activities. There wasn't a piece of gossip Nadine didn't know, and the woman had the memory of an elephant.

An immortal elephant.

"Lemon bar?" Kylie offered her sweetly, extending the container with the lid pulled off.

Unlike her daughter, Nadine partook quickly, and with her first bite, Kylie had her hooked.

"Mmmm. What's in these?" the older woman asked, eyes rolling in ecstasy.

"Angel's tears and devil's blood," Luke joked, winking at Kylie.

The comment was loud enough to bring two more people to Nadine's desk.

"If being good at baking is a dark art, then guilty as charged," Kylie half joked.

"These lemon bars are good enough to put someone under a spell," Nadine added, gaze pinging between her and Luke, her smile widening.

Funny enough, so did Luke's.

Chapter Twenty-Four

Luke

Luke couldn't help it.

She made him grin like a kiss-drunk teen on a moonlit pier at summer camp.

And it was one o'clock in the afternoon at work, sun shining outside on a crisp, cold day, so he had no excuse.

"What're you doing here?" he asked Kylie as Harriet death-gripped his leg and giggled, making Luke monster-walk her over to Nadine's desk, where she began double-fisting lollipops from the jar the admin always kept on her desk.

"I couldn't possibly eat all of these myself," Kylie said, patting her hips, making his blood go from a simmer to a boil in two seconds flat. Those hugs they'd shared had curves his hands needed to study.

Had studied, in his dreams.

Frustrating dreams.

"So I thought I'd bring the extras around when Harriet and I went for a walk."

"Thank you," Nadine said sincerely as she finished the last bite of what Luke knew would not be her one and only cookie.

"Give me one of those," Rusty Drummond demanded, sneaking between Luke and Kylie with a wink sent her way. "I've heard plenty about these fairy muffins you make. Are these leprechaun lemon bars? What's next–gnome brownies?"

A nice-enough guy, Rusty was from Augusta and new to Luview. "New" meant he'd been with the force for about five years, and until the moment he winked at Kylie, he and Luke had gotten on just fine.

Suddenly, Luke was ready to throttle him.

The guy was known around town by the single women as "BCR."

Booty Call Rusty.

A polite laugh from Kylie set him at ease, her glance at Luke endearing–and clear–as she replied, "Nothing special. Just made with love."

Her eyes caught his in that moment, and Luke's breath halted in his chest.

"Homemade is the best," Nadine said to Kylie with a wicked grin his way.

"Don't you think? Store bought is never quite as good," Kylie agreed.

Nadine's nod seemed to please Kylie. Luke's radar pinged. There was subtext here, and he couldn't quite read her. Kylie was genuine and sweet, but there was an edge to her that he knew came from an innate intelligence, a way she read people that was different from his own. Pattern matching was his superpower, an intuitive sense that made him a great cop, and right now, the pattern he was studying was her.

What was going on?

"I love that painting behind you, Nadine. The light is perfect." Kylie's words made Nadine puff up with pride.

"Thank you. I painted it myself."

"Really? You have an eye for composition."

Nadine looked like she was considering adopting Kylie. Boy, had he underestimated his old first kiss, his new nanny, his–whatever Kylie was to him these days.

A charmer, that one.

"You know your art terms," Nadine replied.

Kylie shrugged. "A little. I took some art appreciation work-shops at museums in New York."

Suspicion fell like a veil over Nadine's face. "New York?"

"I lived there for nine years. College, then grad school, and a little after that."

"You went to graduate school for art?"

"Oh, no! I can't paint anything more complicated than a stick figure. I just went to museums on the weekends for fun."

Tension released from Nadine's shoulders. "Oh. Nice."

The older woman evidently had no idea how to handle a hometown girl who'd left, lived in the heart of metropolitan sophistication in the U.S., and come back to become a nanny.

A nanny with an *eye*.

Luke felt the two halves of Kylie, sharp and distinct, through Nadine's watchful gaze. On the one hand, she was born and raised in Luview, which meant she belonged. Raised here until the age of fifteen, being part of the town was her birthright. No one had to explain how Luview worked.

Wasn't her fault her mom skedaddled at the first whiff of scandal.

On the other hand, that was fifteen years ago. The Kylie Hood who returned wasn't the sweet Maine girl she'd been. She was a sophisticated New York City woman who had urban expe-rience, a city sense of morality, and worse, the thick skin of a survivor.

Of course Nadine Khouri didn't know how to handle her.

Because people like Kylie weren't supposed to exist here.

That's what Luke found so damned appealing, the combina-tion of the familiar and the new. Kylie was both, and he couldn't pull away. Every day, he fell just a little more for her, and that was bad.

And not just because of Number 14, Part A, either.

Because this wasn't just lust. If it were primal attraction, he could fight it.

This was more.

"Hey, bro." Luke, Nadine, Rusty, and Kylie looked up to find his younger brother, Kell, standing there, sweating like a pig, brown hair half standing on end and half plastered to the side of his head. A thick brown beard, neatly trimmed and shining, covered his face. He wore a lined flannel shirt, snow boots, jeans, and worn leather gloves, which he peeled off as he reached for a paper coffee cup.

Then he did a double take.

"*Kylie?*" His voice cracked a little, like he was going through puberty.

Hearing her name out of his brother's mouth would have made him growl if he didn't know how happy Kell was now. His little bro was in a committed relationship with Rachel, now the town's director of business development.

"Yes?" Nervous laughter made her even more appealing. "Sorry, do I know you?"

"Kell Luview."

Her jaw dropped. "Kell? *Little Kell?*"

Those words were an oxymoron as she looked straight up– and Kylie was 5'5". Luke's brother had four inches of height and a good fifty pounds of pure muscle on him.

There was a reason they called him Bunyan.

Nadine giggled. "No one's called him little since he was fifteen and had his big growth spurt!"

"He was fourteen when I left Luview! Only a year younger than me, but at that age, it seems like more," Kylie retorted, but with an affectionate grin. "Anyway, you were little compared to this!"

She let herself be swallowed by Kell's tree-trunk arms. Luke couldn't help but join in the smile, remembering those long days on the lake the summer before Kylie left. He was a counselor at the camp, and Kell would tag along with his group of friends half the time.

Kylie had been a junior counselor that summer, working with the little ones, while Kell was in no-man's-land, too old to be part of the kiddie crowd and just a little too young for the teens to accept him.

"I'm an adult now," Kell laughed as he set her down.

"You might have grown, but I'm not so sure about the adult part," Luke joked. He knew Kell had a huge crush on Kylie when they were younger, which was amusing then.

Now? Not so much.

Easy, boy, he told himself. *Kell's head over heels in love with Rachel. Where is all this protective jealousy coming from?*

Never felt any of this with Amber, the voice continued.

Luke let out a snort, meant as a response to his stupid inner voice, but everyone thought he was teasing Kell, who shot him a glare.

"I run my own business and manage to get dressed every day, Luke," Kell shot back, eyes on his brother. "And in something other than red and pink."

"Hey!" Rusty and Nadine snapped.

Kell smirked. It was an old joke.

"What do you do?" Kylie asked Kell.

"Poison ivy puller."

"Huh?"

"I pull poison ivy."

"That's a job?"

"Sure is. In the off season, I climb trees. I work with Dad at the tree service."

"People get paid to climb trees for a living? How did I not know this? Where do I sign up?" she joked.

"He's being obtuse," Luke cut in. "Kell's a tree guy. The poison ivy's a side gig. He's slowly taking over from Dad."

"So you're working with your parents at Luview Tree. That's great!"

Kell nodded. "Yes and no. I help with the tree stuff, but the poison ivy's taken off."

"How do you pull poison ivy for a living?"

"Very carefully," Luke, Rusty, Nadine, and Kell all said together, the joke ancient.

"You looking for a job?" Kell asked, eyes sparking with mirth. "Bet I pay way better than Luke."

"You're sniping my nanny?"

Kylie winced when Luke said the word *nanny*.

Oh, no. Something in her eyes reflected pain, which she clearly struggled to hide. Already, she was more than a nanny to him, but in public, he couldn't say that.

Seconds ticked by as Kylie looked at Kell, mulling over his words.

"Do you have a cute six-year-old I get to spend time with all day long?"

"*I'm* cute, but I'm definitely not six," Kell shot back with a grin flirtatious enough to make Luke's fists curl involuntarily.

If it weren't for Rachel, he'd be dead lumberjack meat.

"Hah. I think Luke told me you have a girlfriend, right?"

"Yes, Rachel." His face transformed when he said her name, calming Luke's strange inner beast. "We just got back from visiting her family in L.A."

"How'd that go?" Luke asked. "Meeting the parents for the first time..."

"I've met Portia before. Remember? We all have."

"Porsche?" Kylie asked. "Like the car?"

"Portia Starman," Nadine interrupted, excited. "The television star–she's Rachel's mother!"

Kylie turned to Kell. "You're dating the daughter of a TV star?"

"It's a long story."

"And Luke said you met her in D.C.?"

"I worked there for a year. We were both fellows at an environmental think tank."

"Fancy! Good for you!"

He shrugged. "Eh. City life didn't agree with me."

"So she gave up L.A. and D.C. for you?"

Nadine let out a sound of judgment so strong, Luke thought immediately of Judge Judy.

"Rachel," Nadine said pointedly, "still has a few things to learn about living here."

Kylie reared back. "That sounds ominous."

"She's nice." Nadine's condescending sniff made Luke wonder how long it would take for *some* locals to truly accept outsiders. "But she is crazy about her electric trolley idea."

"Trolley?" Kylie asked. "Like I remember from Old Orchard Beach?"

Right answer. Nadine beamed at her, reaching to touch her shoulder, turning to Kell.

"See? That's the difference between a hometown girl and an outsider. Kylie knew instantly about the OOB trolley. Rachel didn't."

"Nadine," Kell said patiently, but Luke felt the undercurrent of annoyance. "Rachel loves this town. She moved here."

"She's only been here for nine months, Kell."

"And in those nine months, she's accomplished so much."

"Like those stupid parking machines?" Nadine snapped back. While the adults were distracted, Harriet took the opportunity to sneak a lemon bar. Because he had no desire to have a sugared-up kid all night, he took the lid to the container and closed the lemon bars up tight.

Also? He wanted some for later in the day for himself.

"Parking meters?" Kylie asked innocently, eliciting groans from all the staff sitting at the desks around them.

"Sore spot," he hissed, loud enough for Nadine to hear.

"Not everyone has a smartphone!" Nadine shouted. "She had all the parking meters replaced with those machines!"

Kell cut her off. "The town has a parking problem. Rachel set up parking apps for the areas furthest from the center of town, so you can pay with your phone."

"Sure," Kylie said. "They're all over New York and Boston."

Nadine's sniff made it clear Kylie wasn't earning herself any points with that comment.

"After listening to the public," Kell said pointedly, "she made sure the meters downtown offer both options. Coin and parking app. And revenue has shot up."

"The meters near my daughter's hair salon are app only!" Nadine complained.

"Annabeth's clientele figured it out just fine," Luke said. Kylie's eyes flared when he said Annabeth's name.

There it was again, a strange sense that something was off.

"What're you here for, again?" Luke challenged Kell. Rusty covered his mouth to hide a grin. Was he being that obvious?

"Tree," Kell said simply. "Blocking Old Core Road. Got most of it out of the way, but you told me to have an officer check the road when I finished, so here I am."

"You couldn't have called?"

Kell winked at Kylie, popped the lid off the container, and stole another lemon bar. "Then I'd have missed out on all the sweet stuff."

"Come on." Luke grabbed his keys and hat. "I'll go check out the mess you made and finish clearing it."

"Grumpy McGrumperson," Nadine said under her breath, but not quietly enough.

Ruffling Harriet's curls, he gave Kylie a polite smile, put on his hat, grabbed his coat, and walked out to his car, Kell on his heels.

His brother let out a low whistle.

"That bad?" he said to Luke.

"Huh?"

"Haven't seen you this mad about me talking to someone you like since, well," Kell paused. "Never."

"Shut up."

"We aren't kids. You can't make me." Kell's hearty laugh was a reminder of their size difference now.

Luke's little brother was anything but.

"I have handcuffs and I know how to use them."

"That'll come in handy with Kylie."

Kell's words were teasing and light, but they triggered something primal in Luke, who got in Kell's face, hand tight on his elbow.

"Don't."

"Whoa, bro. I've got Rachel. You know that. Just having fun. Kylie didn't seem to mind. Geez, Luke. Man. It's cool. I'm–I'm not after her. I wouldn't do that."

"Good." Tension poured out of him as he let go of Kell's rock-hard arm. It was like trying to dig your fingers into a brick.

"You realize plenty of other guys will be soon. Rusty was giving her the eye."

"If he likes his eyeballs, he'd better stop."

"Listen to you! You turn into a damn caveman around her. I never saw you like this around..."

Kell stopped before he said Amber's name.

Words jumbled inside him, none of them quite right, so Luke stomped to his cruiser, slammed the door shut, turned on the engine, shoved it into reverse–and realized he had no idea where on Old Core Road Kell was going.

One punch of his steering wheel and Kell magically pulled in front of him, his big six-wheel work truck emblazoned with the logo for Luview Tree Service.

Old Core Road was close to a big logging area. The curves were dangerous in winter, so Luke drove with caution. Kell took him just past the turn for the country road that went to the camp they were buying. A tug of desire–the other kind, not the kind attached to Kylie–surged in him.

His camp. His land. His compound.

Their dream.

Amber had floated the idea first, when rumors spread that Camp Wannacanhopa was being sold. He'd just come home from work after a motorcycle rally outside Luview, his brain tired from too many tricked-out bikes without mufflers, the sound turning into a buzz in his head.

"Luke!" she'd gushed. "The camp's for sale!"

"The what?"

"The camp!" Amber's eyes had been shining like distant stars, bright and beautiful. "Trish at work told me. The Louis family is finally selling."

"Hmm."

His answer made her shoot him a sad grin. "I wish we could buy it."

A snort was the most he could muster. "Win the lottery and we'll talk. Some developer will buy it and put ski condos on it."

"Oh, I hope not! We have so many great memories there."

That had softened him. Sliding his arm around her shoulders, he'd given her a kiss on the cheek. The memory was as fresh now, two and a half years later, as if it were yesterday.

"We do."

"Wouldn't it be wonderful to live there?"

"It's a camp, Amber. You're a bookkeeper and I'm a police officer. What would we do with a camp?"

"All that land! And the lake. The lodge. The outbuildings. Imagine raising Harriet there! And our other babies."

"Other babies?" His hand had slid to her belly, her lips on his suddenly, the kiss a promise of a nice end to a long day.

Her laughter was infectious. "A girl can dream, right?"

A girl can dream.

Soon, Amber's dream would be a reality.

Because Luke was buying the camp, after all. The Louis family hadn't put it on the market back when Amber was still alive, though. They'd changed their minds, and Amber had let the idea go.

Not that they had the money then. No winning lottery tickets.

And now? He hadn't won the lottery. The thought turned his stomach, less than it used to, but it still pulled.

Although Amber worked at the small local hospital, it was part of a large network, and she was always the type to maximize her benefits. She had paid a little extra out of every paycheck for the maximum death benefit. Her dad's autoimmune illness and decline had been part of it, Amber insisting they look at long-term care insurance as well. They were young, she reasoned, so the premiums were low. Luke, like Amber, maxxed out his life insurance.

When she'd insisted, he'd told her he'd go along with it to make her happy, but knew they'd never need it.

How wrong he'd been.

Amber's life insurance money had come in not long before the Louis family finally listed the property, and when it came on the market, his mom had been the one to point out the life insurance payout. The owners agreed to sell it to him for less than a big corporate offer.

It was a deal he couldn't refuse.

They'd all go in on it together. By the time his mom had finished calling Kell, Den, and Colleen, and talking to their dad, it felt inevitable. A family compound. Everyone would sell their homes or give up their leases, his parents and Kell would move the business, and they'd consolidate.

Coordinate.

Work together as a team to care for three generations.

When you're part of a team, you don't flirt with other team

members' love interests, he reminded himself as Kell slowed down before a scattering of sawdust in the road.

"What's wrong with me?" he muttered as he pulled over, put the car in park, and got out to look. Kell was head over heels in love with Rachel. He hadn't been flirting.

Booty Call Rusty, though—he needed to have a talk with *him*.

Jealousy was Luke's problem, and he was as green as poison ivy from it.

"Hey, Grumpy. You look like I squatted on the hood of your car and defiled it."

"Don't laugh. Rusty had that happen to him when he worked in Augusta."

Kell made a face. "That's why I'll never live in a big city again."

"Augusta's not a big city," Luke said, laughing as Kell kicked a large chunk of bark out of the road. "And besides, we know why you hate cities."

Kell's eyes went troubled, then cleared fast, like a quick rain cloud. "Yeah. But now Rachel lives here and it's all good."

Years ago, he'd gone off to D.C. fresh out of agriculture school, determined to help fight for forest management and eco-friendly systems.

He fell in love.

He fought the good fight.

And she broke his heart.

Rachel changed all that, fortunately.

Luke clapped him on the shoulder. "I'm glad you're so stuck on her."

"Ha ha." Kell and Rachel met again when she came to Love You, Maine, to secure a big multinational deal for the local chocolate company. Her car broke down and he tried to fix a hose with superglue. Rachel grabbed his hand at the wrong moment... and the rest was history.

They were stuck with each other now, in a different way.

Deeply in love.

"This looks good," Luke told him, kicking another small branch out of the way.

"Thanks. You don't."

"Don't what?"

"Look good. You're rattled. Is it Kylie?"

No use in pretending.

"I–yes."

"You love her?"

"What?"

"You sleep with her yet?"

"No."

"You knew how to answer *that* question. Now answer the first one."

"How can I be in love with someone who's only been in my life again for three weeks?"

"That's not an answer."

Luke huffed.

"Or is it?" Kell shot back, eyebrows up.

An old pickup truck, loaded with a couple of cords of wood, rumbled on by. Pete Heller waved as he drove past, mercifully not stopping to chat. The wind whipped Luke's hat brim up as Pete moved beyond them, Kell offering an arm up in greeting.

"Let's go to the camp," Kell called out as Luke held his hat on his head.

"Huh?"

"Camp!"

Luke nodded, climbing into his cruiser without another word, the road welcome after the conversation. Kell had a way about him, quietly self-assured, easy with a grin but hard to get close to. All four kids in the family were doers, moving through time and space every day to earn a paycheck. Kell was a tree guy, Luke a police officer, Colleen a nurse, and Dennis, well...

No one knew exactly what he did in the Special Forces, but he sure did move.

For Kell to bring up squishy emotions like love meant that Luke was a goner. It must be written all over his face. Being the subject of town gossip was bad enough, but he could roll his eyes and mock the busybodies.

His own brother? The one who walled himself off and deflected when the subject got too serious? Once he started talking about feelings, it must be bad.

"Bad," Luke muttered, fishing in the console for a piece of gum. A pack of all-natural chicle-based crap Colleen insisted he try was all he could find. There was a picture of a fennel bulb on the box.

Who eats fennel-flavored gum?

His sister. That's who.

"Looks like hamster food," he said to himself as he shook three little pieces out and popped them in his mouth, surprised by the pleasant flavor. It reminded him of the seed and candy mixture he had once at Love You India, a local restaurant.

Maybe Colleen was on to something.

Every time he made the turn onto the long dirt road leading up to the camp, he grinned, a breath of pride filling his lungs. Familiarity only made it better. Knowing he was about to own the very place where so many memories were made for him and his family and friends gave Luke a burst of adrenaline that stretched across time.

And then the inevitable tug of guilt kicked in.

Because he couldn't have afforded it without Amber's life insurance money.

Kell's work truck ate the road like it was nothing, Luke's cruiser steady and strong behind him, until they came to a stop at the main office building. Turning the camp into a personal home base was a project he relished. Mom and Dad had already laid claim to three of the smaller cabins, one to live in, one for Mom's sewing, one for Dad's woodworking.

Luke and Harriet got the main lodge. Colleen staked out the old camp director's house, and Kell planned to build his own place.

Dennis? Who knew? He lived in Germany for now, but when he came back to Luview, Maine, he'd always have a home.

There was a comfort in numbers, in teamwork, in having a place for the family that would never change. In the aftermath of Amber's death, he'd needed this. Clung to it. Nurtured the idea and ushered it through from dream to reality.

Now it was here.

Amber wasn't, but Kylie was.

And that complicated things.

The two men got out of their respective vehicles, Kell bending down to drag a thick pine branch that had fallen from one of the tall soldiers in the center of the circular driveway. Twelve tall pines, planted carefully in a circle that formed a perimeter around a flagpole, now dwarfed Old Glory.

Or at least, the pole. No flag was flying right now, but it would be again.

Soon.

"Gotta say, I thought you were crazy when you told us your idea," Kell said in a voice filled with reproach and happiness, a combo Luke struggled to reconcile. "But damn, this place is good. We're going to have a fine life here."

"Yep."

Kell's steady gaze unnerved him. "Are you bringing Kylie?"

"Bringing her where?" His heart sped up at the thought.

"Here."

"She's been here."

"Duh. I know that. I meant... here." Kell spread his arms. "Into your new life."

"I told you, I can't."

"You know what, Luke? Maybe I kept my mouth a little too shut after Amber died."

Luke shut his own mouth.

"You're crazy. You know that? Crazy to buy the camp, maybe. Crazy not to date any of the women pouring all over you. But you're craziest for keeping Kylie at arm's length. You two were meant to be together."

"Excuse me?"

"Cut it out, Luke. Quit playing dumb."

"Not playing anything."

"You couldn't stop talking about her when she disappeared. Then suddenly, you did, because you were dating Amber. I know you loved Amber. Love her still. But there was always something special about Kylie, too. You can have both, you know."

"Both?"

"You can love Amber for who she was, and also love Kylie for who she is. If you don't do that, you're a dumbass."

"Hey!"

Kell shrugged. "Truth hurts." He kicked a stick out of the path. "You bringing her to Christmas?"

Christmas. Right. That was soon.

"She's probably going back to Indiana to visit her mom. Or to South Carolina with her dad."

"For a guy who isn't dating her, you know a lot about her life."

"She's my nanny. I have to know her situation."

"She's more than your nanny, dude. Stop ignoring fate."

"Fate? When did you get all gushy like that? She's only been back for a few weeks, and now you want to turn her into my soulmate?" Ignoring his thumping heart was impossible.

"Not gushy. Just pointing out the obvious. She's in your life for a reason. How did you two meet again? Never heard that story."

Uh oh. He'd promised not to tell anyone the truth about Kylie getting stuck in the donation bin.

"Ran into her at Deke's."

"Randomly? She was visiting?"

"She moved here last year. Her boyfriend was one of Nordicbeth sons."

"Which one?"

"Perry."

"That jerk?"

"Yeah."

Kell made a face. "He was supposed to be in charge of a big tree project we did there a couple years ago. Insisted on all kinds of work that wasn't in the contract. He wasn't even a facilities guy. Threw his weight around, went on about being vice president, asked us to violate OSHA laws. It was a mess. Dad had to privately talk to Perry's dad and it got ugly."

"You lost Nordicbeth business?"

"Nope. But Perry never ran a tree job again. Man, I can't imagine her with him. What a strange couple."

"I don't know much about it. She said they moved up here from New York last year. She worked in children's programming at Nordicbeth. Perry went on some trip to Thailand, started sleeping with someone there, and dumped her by phone."

"What an asshole!"

"Right. Then he got her fired from her job."

"Double asshole!"

"She's licking her wounds, for sure."

"And she never came to Luview to see people?"

"She was embarrassed. Between what happened with her dad
– "

"Not her fault."

"Plus, Perry dumped her. You know."

"Ouch."

"Right. Last place you want to go after being dumped is the love capital of the world."

"No kidding. Man, I didn't know all that. Now you *have* to bring her to Christmas."

"I do?"

Luke's phone buzzed. So did Kell's.

"Car in a ditch on Route 33," Luke muttered.

"Tree branch sheared off a gutter and left a two-foot hole in the roof at a Fryeburg apartment complex," Kell announced, the two shaking their heads at each other as if to say, *Can you believe this?*

Before Luke could climb in his car, Kell shouted, "INVITE HER, DUMBASS!" Gravel sprayed as he took off down the dirt road, stones kicking up like they were judging him.

Christmas, huh?

That wouldn't violate Number 14, Part A, would it? It's not like inviting her to a family gathering was the same as sleeping with her.

Not even close.

He sighed and followed Kell.

And then there was the mistletoe...

Chapter Twenty-Five

Kylie

The last two weeks had gone by in a blur.

A blur of avoiding Luke, trying not to hear the whispers around town, and applying for jobs.

Jobs that weren't panning out.

Low-grade panic was setting in, and she wondered if conflict were inevitable. Would she ever be one of those people who knew themselves so well that they never experienced this internal mess? If she stayed here, asked to be Harriet's permanent nanny, settled into a new apartment in Luview and let her life take root in the place where she spent the first fifteen years of her life, would that be so... bad?

The ambitious piece of her said *yes*. Yes, it would. She hadn't fought so hard in New York, and later at Nordicbeth Resorts, to establish herself in children's programming, to just leave it all behind.

And then there was the nasty fact that the voice telling her all of the above was Perry's, the sneer in it making her insides twist into a knot. Meeting him in college had been a breath of fresh air, his casual confidence and devil-may-care approach to life so unlike anyone she'd ever known.

He had a mean streak, yes, but she'd slowly come to believe him when he said you had to be a jerk to get ahead in life. Not that she'd taken on that character trait. More that she'd been caught up in his confidence, his willingness to help her to find greater career success, and his sharp-eyed view of her talents.

"You're smart," he'd always said. "Teaching is a waste, but it gives you credentials for the corporate world if you're really into working with children. Lots of money in the children's market. That's why my parents focus so much of their marketing on kids. It reels the adults in, and they have the wallets."

Perry's cynicism came with a lot of love bombing, of course. She never would have stayed so long if it hadn't.

But he had an on/off switch, and when he'd dumped her, he'd really turned it off. Blocked her calls. Never answered her emails. Used his sister as a go-between.

It was as if she'd never existed.

How do you spend all those years loving someone and then cut them out of your life like a fingersnap?

It was maddening. Kylie felt so bereft. So discarded.

So abandoned.

Now she was torn. Ambition had replaced connection for so long, but now that she was in her happy place, could she give up all the dreams she'd painstakingly built for herself?

It just felt like she was avoiding the truth.

And the truth was, she was falling even harder for Luke Luview, and being his nanny meant giving in to desire.

Should desire override her entire life?

If Wendy were here, her answer would be immediate: "Yes."

And then there was today's date: December 18.

Kylie was feeling the pressure.

Christmas was coming. Her mom was sending terse emails and texts, asking whether Kylie was coming to Indiana. Postponing her answer was an exercise in avoidance.

If she stayed, she'd eat takeout or frozen dinners and watch television all day, which would be a first.

But if she went to Indiana, there'd be no Wendy to buffer her from her mom and stepdad.

Tough choices.

And it wasn't like her dad and stepmother ever–*ever*–invited her to visit for any holiday.

Being alone felt like a blessing and a curse. Grown-ups dealt with whatever life gave them, adapting and shifting to the circumstances. Maybe spending the holiday alone would be good for her. Help with personal growth. Let her stretch her independence wings.

Or maybe she'd just cry all day and squirt maple syrup straight in her mouth while eating candy-cane Oreos and watching *It's a Wonderful Life*.

"I'm hopeless," she muttered as a text came through on her phone. Wendy, at the Christmas market in Berlin, grinning.

A second picture: Wendy with a tall blond guy with dazzling blue eyes, his arm around her, squeezing her elbow.

This is Johann. Met him two days ago. We have so much in common and it turns out he lives in Paris! I thought I'd find a hot French guy but instead I met a hot German!

The next text was a picture of Wendy with two dark-haired kids, both clutching ice skates and looking impatient.

Wendy was living her best life.

Kylie was contemplating mainlining maple syrup and having a Christmas sobfest.

Love it, she texted back. *I'm so happy for you!*

And she was. Truly.

What're you doing for Christmas? Wendy texted back. *Indiana?*

Not sure, Kylie replied.

Stay there. Maine is prettier. Tell Mom you have to work. Nannying is like that. She'll back off.

Wendy was right. Their stepdad would probably be relieved to have a holiday where he had their mom to himself.

And Kylie would be relieved not to go back and be judged.

I'll figure it out, she texted Wendy, realizing she needed to go into town to pick up Harriet's Christmas gift, a fairy cape she'd had custom made by Labrecque's, the dry cleaner and tailor shop in town.

Love you! Wendy wrote back, with a row of laughing emojis. When you're from Luview, Maine, "Love You" becomes its own circular joke.

Luview, too, Kylie shot back, then grabbed her coat. She'd better get moving. Parking would be a pain. Wherever there were stores, the week before Christmas was always busy, and downtown Luview was no exception.

Side streets like Clannaugh, where Luke and Harriet lived, were the natural choice for out-of-the-way parking, so Kylie carefully slid her car into a street spot at the corner of Clannaugh and Main, not feeling one lick of guilt. All of the parking meters in Luview were covered in red plastic bags printed with white images of a gift box and the words "Free Parking–Our Gift to You!"

Hah. Even crusty old Nadine couldn't complain about *that*.

Crowds were bustling, happy and busy, the sidewalks perfectly cleared of snow, the weather a luxurious thirty-one degrees on December 18. Perfect.

As she opened the door to the tailor shop, "Hark! The Herald Angels Sing" played in soothing instrumental tones over the local radio station, WLUV. Labrecque's was the only dry cleaner and tailor shop in town, and a place that time forgot. It was a service business, so it didn't get as much foot traffic as retail shops, but it still had to fit into the love themes of the town.

Except for wedding seasons. Then it was all alterations, all the time.

If she'd stayed here for high school, Kylie would have had her prom dress altered here. Mrs. Labrecque carried dyeable shoes, the only footwear you could buy here, and prided herself on producing perfect matches for any material.

Instead, Kylie had gone to the senior prom in Rio, Indiana, with Bryan Abrams, a perfectly fine guy who had done the obligatory dancing with her, kissed her once on the lips, and quietly faded away.

When she learned he was living in Chicago with his boyfriend, she hadn't exactly been shocked.

"Kylie?" Judy Labrecque looked like a middle school girls' track coach, always wearing fitted golf pants, new cross-trainers, and with the flat, smooth musculature of someone who did Pilates and triathlons for fun. Other than some salted-gray hairs that poked out of her short, curly hair, you'd guess she was ten years younger than sixty-one.

Labrecque's had been in her family for three generations, and her dedication to excellence reflected that.

"Hey, Judy. How's it going?"

"Your cape is ready, and it's perfect," Judy said in that clipped way she had, her economy of words and emotion so natural to her, it didn't feel off. Just... perfect.

Like their sewing.

"Wonderful!" Kylie watched as Judy pulled the garment from the large white box she'd stored it in. Harriet was going to be so happy. A swirl of chiffon layers and glittery ribbon, the cape was meant to make her feel like Tinkerbell, a fae creation of cloth that would transport the little girl into a pretend place where she could embody pure joy.

As childhood should be.

Someone walked in from outside, the cold rush of air shaking her out of the spell the gorgeous little cape had put on her.

"You're all paid up, Kylie," Judy said with a grin. "Can't wait to see Harriet in this."

"I'm sure you'll *only* see Harriet in this. Forever. She's never going to take it off."

"Have fun at bathtime, then."

With a laugh, Kylie departed, and Judy turned to help a white-haired woman Kylie didn't know, talking about taking in a wool suit. Outside, people were everywhere, but the sidewalks were orderly. The town was decorated so beautifully, she couldn't help but pause for a moment, take a deep breath, and sigh.

Relax.

Be.

Love You, Maine, was a vision. The picturesque New England town really was perfection at Christmas, though the place was known for Valentine's Day. Snow covered the rolling hills. The streets were filled with kids and Santas with big red pots, collecting money for charity. Merchants offered spiced hot cider inside stores, the coffee shops and restaurants busy.

Greta's was selling green heart cookies with red bows and silver dragées like the world would end if every dozen weren't sold.

Love You, Maine, made you feel included, embraced, validated.

Like you were part of something gentle and kind.

Sure, it was overly commercial at times, and profit might dominate the town's push to be all about love, 24/7/365.

But something genuine made people come back, and it wasn't just the famous hot springs.

A dip in the water, even fingertips, at the same time as someone you desired would bring you together, the old legend said. As a townie, she'd been taught the magic of it in childhood. Then, like the Tooth Fairy, the Easter Bunny, and Santa Claus, as she aged, the disappointing truth came out.

For kids raised in Luview, the idea that anyone would magically love you after a plunge in the hot springs was laughable.

But it didn't stop people from trying.

High school kids went for a swim after dances, the breakups and new relationships forming always a swirl of too much for her. She'd only been here for her freshman year, anyhow.

She noticed an antiques store, the kind she'd never go into if she didn't happen to be strolling by. Love You Again, the sign said. Her memory tried to place it, finally realizing this used to be a watch repair shop.

Even in Love You, things change.

What caught her eye was a small wooden giraffe on a wicker table, the neck crooked. It reminded her of Needle getting stuck under the bridge, of the day Luke yelled at her, of a time when she didn't understand.

Didn't know how Amber had died.

She smiled, feeling guilty, the mix of grief and humor weird even for her. Would Luke find the crooked-neck giraffe as amusing as she did?

The price tag said seventeen dollars. Heck, why not buy it and decide later?

A young girl with braces and a huge grin was wrapping the giraffe in tissue, chattering away about Greta's peppermint brownies, when the shop's door opened. The sleigh bells hanging from the knob jingled, fitting perfectly with the mood.

"Buying me a present?" asked a familiar, happy voice.

Kylie turned to find Luke standing there, wearing a ski jacket, jeans, boots, and a red knit hat. Out of uniform, he cut a fine form.

In uniform, too. Luke was hot, period, and the teenage clerk's reaction–flushed cheeks, a bigger grin, an averted gaze–made it clear Kylie wasn't his only fan.

"Well," she replied, grateful the giraffe was in the paper bag already, "I might be." Warmth filled her, the kind no heater can manufacture. All her uncertainty about job hunting, her future, her ambitions, melted away around him.

Why fight this?

What if she could just let it happen?

"Hmmm." He picked up an object, pale off-white in color, that had a rounded peak with curved slopes and six little holes carved into the center of the peak. "What's this, Alexis?"

The girl's eyes went wide with horror.

"Um, that?"

"Yes," Luke asked patiently, turning it over in his hand. "Is it ivory?"

"Mmm hmm."

"Elephant?"

"Yes." Her eyes cut to the back of the store. "Let me get Grandpa. He can, uh, explain it better."

Kylie thought it looked a lot like a woman's breast, but said nothing.

Luke frowned at the teenager. "But you know what it is?" He turned it over, peak down, like a cup. "Is it, like, an old valet? For change and cufflinks? It holds something?" Cradling it in his palm, Luke held it like he was cupping a breast.

Suddenly, Kylie's cheeks were aflame, too.

"Hiya, Luke. I see you found the nipple shield," said a bald man, tall and slender, moving into the room quickly, carrying an old clown doll so creepy that Kylie nearly wet her pants. "Did Alexis explain what it is?"

"Nipple shield?" Luke sputtered.

"Breast," Kylie said simply, earning her a look from everyone as Luke carefully put the item back where he found it. "It's for breastfeeding."

"Oh," Luke said in a low, clipped tone, setting it down carefully, as if it might give him a disease.

"Excuse me?" the man said to her, then smiled. "Kylie Hood?"

"Yes."

"John Mangus."

"Mangus. Like Angus Mangus's dad?" Angus's real name wasn't Angus—it was Steve—but with a last name like that, he'd reinvented himself in kindergarten and it stuck.

"The same. Heard you were back in town."

"Hi!"

"And Luke, you're amazing. You come into my store and immediately find a breast to fondle."

Luke gave him a flat look. John burst out laughing.

"On that note," Luke said loudly, taking Kylie's elbow in a gentlemanly gesture, "we'll take our leave. Good to see you, John."

"And you!" he called back as Luke ushered her to the sidewalk. For a moment, Kylie felt a rush of joy that invaded every cell of her being. One week 'til Christmas, and she had a gift for Harriet and now one for Luke. She was walking down the street in Love You, Maine, with a man she'd kissed and who insisted on carrying the larger package for her, holiday music melodious and fun as they strolled.

"Luke!" a woman's voice called out, and Kylie tensed. Suddenly selfish, she wanted Luke to herself.

"Rachel!"

Emotions pivoting on a dime, Kylie turned to find a smiling woman with long, dark hair in curls around her shoulders, wearing a white hat with a huge faux-fur pompom, a red wool coat, and boots no self-respecting Mainer would ever wear.

"Is this the famous Kylie?" she asked, holding out her hand to shake. Kylie accepted the offer, gloved hands performing the ritual.

"I should say the same," Kylie replied, laughing. "I've heard so much about you! How was L.A.?"

"Sunny, warm, and sunny. Did I mention the warm part?"

"Your first full winter here, Rachel," Luke said. "It's the hardest one."

"They get easier after this?" she asked.

"No," Kylie and Luke replied simultaneously, and laughed. Rachel's eyes flashed, but Kylie saw the speculation behind them.

"What are you two up to? Christmas shopping, I assume?"

Luke looked at Kylie. "She got Harriet something special."

Rachel's brow went up. "Anything I need to know? This will be my first Christmas with the family, too. We got her something from her list. The one Deanna gave Kell."

"There's a list?" Kylie gasped.

Luke rubbed her back lightly, in a calming gesture. "Whatever you got her will be perfect."

"You're from here, right?" Rachel asked. "So you know all about the businesses in town?"

"I haven't been back in fifteen years. A lot is the same, but there's plenty of change, too."

Rachel squinted, as if thinking. "I'd love to pick your brain, Kylie."

"You would?"

"I'm the director of business development and planning for the town, but I'm an outsider. I can see Luview through fresh eyes, but you have a unique perspective. Your memory is frozen in time, fifteen years ago. Your perception could help me understand how changes affect residents. Can we have coffee sometime? Maybe after Christmas?"

"Of course! At Greta's?"

"Have you been to Love You Coffee?"

"There's a coffee shop other than Greta's now?"

"Luke!" Rachel admonished him. "You haven't exposed Kylie to the sheer caffeinated love bomb of a Love You Coffee latte?"

"Are they calling your creation the Love Bomb, Rachel?" he joked.

"No, but what a great idea!"

"What's your special latte?" Kylie asked. For someone who'd only lived here for nine months, Rachel sure seemed to fit in already.

Maybe Kylie could be accepted here, more than she ever expected.

"Half almond milk, half two percent, double shot, with a teaspoon of ground organic Madagascar vanilla."

"That sounds amazing."

Rachel shot Luke a look. He groaned.

"She wants us to get coffee, Kylie. You're killing me."

"No time?" Rachel asked.

"I had three cups at home already," he said.

"Kylie? How about it? Ten minutes out of your day, meet Reef and Skylar, and have the best coffee you've had in ages."

"The last good coffee I had was at Greta's."

Rachel leaned in and whispered, "Don't tell Wolf or Greta I said this, because I'll deny it, but Reef has them beat."

Luke pretended to be mortified. "Like, wow," he said in an imitation of one of the teens from *Mean Girls*. "Rachel, like, just dissed Greta's!"

"With a tease like that, how can I say no?" Kylie said, looking at Luke.

Luke smirked. "So all I have to do is tease you to get you to say yes to things?"

Rachel gave them a look, palms going up. "I'm not touching that comment with a ten-foot pole, but come on. Let's get coffees."

"I'll pass, but Kylie can get a Love Bomb."

The three of them walked down the street, the coffee shop within a two-minute walk.

As they approached, Kylie asked, "How hard was it giving up the city?"

Luke's sharp look put her on guard.

"Hard," Rachel admitted as Luke moved ahead of them to get the coffee shop door, opening it and gesturing them in ahead of him. "I miss good food."

"The Food Alchemist has good food," Luke argued as they stood behind three people in line.

"Sure," Rachel agreed. "But in L.A. you have endless choices. Here, we have The Food Alchemist, Love You India, Mountain Dragon, Bilbee's, and Greta's."

"Hey, now. Deke's has a breakfast diner," he said. "We're making progress."

Rachel laughed. "You lived in New York for years, right?" she said to Kylie. "You get it."

"I do." An intense look from Luke caught her off guard again. Was she imagining it, or was he upset whenever cities were mentioned?

It was their turn. A man Kylie had never seen before, pierced and tattooed, with both braids and locs, took their order.

"Hey, Reef," Rachel said. "Two of my drinks."

Reef looked at Kylie, then Luke. "February 23," he muttered.

Luke let out a grunt that turned into a growl.

Rachel snorted.

Kylie looked around at the coffee shop, the decor rivaling anything she'd find back in New York. It was clean, spare, and simple, but with comfortable chairs and tables everywhere, designed to be a place to sit and sip, talk and connect.

But unlike anyplace in New York, the mugs were all red, shaped like hearts.

"Here," Reef said. "Charge to your account?" He looked at Rachel, who nodded, as Kylie and Luke both pulled out cash.

"I got it," Luke insisted, handing him a twenty.

"Luke!" Rachel protested.

His head shake made it clear he was buying, and that was that.

"Thank you," the women said to him in unison. They all moved away from the counter to a tall table designed for standing around, and Rachel urged Kylie to take a sip.

She did.

"Yum," she said sincerely, then as the drink hit her, she added, "This is delicious."

"Told you!" She thumbed toward Luke. "Mr. Sourpuss here doesn't like it."

"A man can't have preferences?"

Rachel's phone buzzed. A look of alarm covered her face as she checked it.

"Oh, no! I forgot about a meeting with a new business owner, someone starting a dog cake company." She squeezed Kylie's shoulder and waved to Luke as she left. "Nice meeting you. I know I'll see you again soon!"

And she was gone.

"Welcome to Rachel," Luke said as he nodded toward the door. Kylie followed.

"She seems great."

"You two have a lot in common."

"Because we both lived in cities?"

"You're both involved with Luview men." he said softly in her ear.

All she could do was drink more coffee and smile. This was definitely heating up, and she wasn't fighting it. When was the last time she felt so comfortable? So included? So accepted? It had been so long.

Too long.

As they strolled, she marveled at the charming downtown scene.

"Pinch me," she said.

His eyes drifted to her behind. "Is that a serious invitation?"

"Not there!"

A devilish grin made her appreciate the more passionate side of Luke Luview. Buttoned up in public, as a police officer had to be, he definitely had a wilder side underneath.

Would it come out in bed?

"Why'd you ask me to pinch you, then?"

"This is so beautiful. I'd forgotten how fun Christmas in Maine could be."

"That's right. You weren't here last year, were you?"

"No. We moved here March first. That's why my lease is up February 28."

At the mention of her lease, his face went tense, jaw clenching. Luke turned to her, stopping on the walk, face serious.

"Kylie, can I show you something?"

"Umm..."

"How much time do you have?"

"It's my day off."

"I don't want to intrude on your personal life."

She couldn't help but snort, leaning in. "Should have thought of that before you kissed me."

"Trust me. I did."

"Is that what you want to... show me? Something..."

"Hah! No. Not that. I want to take you to a special place where we can talk."

Talk.

Was talk a euphemism for...? Her face must have been puzzled, because he clarified:

"I'm not trying to sleep with you. Not today, at least."

"Where do you want to go?"

"It's a surprise."

Dotty Chen walked past them, arms pulled down by full bags. As she opened the coffee shop door, Wolf passed her, hurrying out with a large stack of to-go cups, apparently borrowed from Love You Coffee in one of the many help-your-neighbor-out exchanges Kylie found so endearing here.

"You have to wait! I have all my money on New Year's Eve," Dotty whispered to Kylie.

"You what?"

"The betting pool! You two can't make it official until December 31. I need new gutters." The wink was what did Kylie in.

Yanking Luke's arm, she pulled him away.

"Where are we going?" she demanded.

"Away from people who place bets on us."

* * *

"No way," she gasped. As they turned off the main road, memories poured over her, the drive up the old dirt road unmistakable.

"Way."

"The camp? This time of year?"

He paused the Jeep in front of the old sign.

"It's not a camp anymore."

"It's not? What is it?"

"My new home."

"You bought Camp Wannacanhopa?"

"Me, Mom and Dad, Colleen, Den, and Kell."

"You're all going to run the camp? Together?"

"No. We're all going to live here." He smiled. "Together."

Launching herself at Luke across the center console wasn't planned, but in her exuberance, the hug felt natural. "Congratulations!" she squealed as his strong arms wrapped around her shoulders, her face buried in his neck, his aftershave making her heady.

"If I knew I'd get hugs like this for buying property, I'd start a real estate company."

Kylie began to pull back, but his arms were too tight.

And their mouths were so close.

The buzz from Luke's phone made him groan. The spell was broken, giving Kylie the chance to pull away and get her wits back.

Not that she wouldn't have preferred a kiss.

Scrambling out of the car, she willed her libido to stop flashing a big red pulsing light on Luke and calm itself down.

Number 14, Part A.

No matter what.

Luke was out of the car, too, staring intently at her.

"Let's go down to the pier," he said. Already on her way there, she smiled as he held out his hand. The *zing* of contact made her inner mantra–*Number 14, Part A*–grow weaker and weaker. Finally, she just chanted *14A, 14A, 14A*.

As if that did one bit of good.

A path led them down to the shore, the wooden pier intact, a thick layer of bird tracks and likely fox prints dotting the surface of the snow. The beach was the same, the little wooden boathouse locked up tight, small windows showing the neatly racked canoes and kayaks inside. Camp Wannacanhopa was never a huge facility, but at peak there'd been over a hundred campers, and there were always plenty of watercraft for everyone.

"No sitting on the edge dipping our feet in," she joked, but when she made eye contact, Luke's gaze was serious.

"I brought you here for a reason."

"You did?"

"Do you remember the last time we were here together?"

"Of course. How could I forget? It was the last time I was truly happy." She swallowed, hard. "Until this Thanksgiving."

Luke pulled her into a hug, the warm embrace, the scent of him, the contact, the view, all blending into a pool of bliss.

"That kiss on the pier is the reason I have Harriet."

Kylie laughed. "Do you need a little lesson on how reproduction works, Luke? Because that's *not* how babies are made."

Hot breath warmed her ear, making her shiver. "Trust me, Kylie. I know exactly how babies are made."

All thought rushed out of her, need filling the void.

And then he kissed the top of her head. That wasn't what she wanted next, but it would do for now.

"Amber saw me kiss you that day. Then you disappeared. A week or so later, she told me she liked me. Then, she confessed she'd been too shy to tell me how she felt, but seeing me kiss you made her realize she had to take the chance. And when you ghosted on me–"

"*Ghosted?* On *you?*"

He chuckled, the sound wry and a little sad. "I still don't understand why you cut me off."

Kylie's legs went numb.

"*What?*"

"It's fine," he said quickly. "It's all in the past, and I don't want to make this awkward. But we do need to talk about it."

"We definitely do!"

He tilted his head, studying her. "You disappeared. Unfriended me on social media. Stopped answering my emails. Stopping writing me letters."

"*You* did all that to *me*, Luke! Not the other way around!"

"No, I didn't! I woke up one day and tried to message you and you'd disappeared. Literally. You blocked me."

"I didn't block you! I would never, ever have blocked you!"

"You stopped answering my emails, Kylie."

"I got bouncebacks! Your email system said your address was undeliverable!"

"It's the same personal email address I use now."

They stared at each other, dumbfounded.

And each reached for their phone.

Kylie was livid that he would think she'd have ghosted on him like that. "I can't," she said between angry jabs at her phone, "believe you would ever think that I would be so cruel to you! I would never ghost you!"

"But you did."

"You ghosted *me*!"

"Only because you made it abundantly clear you didn't want to talk to me. The silence was deafening, Kylie."

He held up his email account on his phone.

He was right. Same address.

Baffled, Kylie went into her social media account and did a search for him. Nothing came up. She showed him.

"See? You blocked me. Go into your security settings and look." She pulled hers up and showed him. "I don't have you blocked. I swear."

Shaking his head, Luke did as asked, and then pulled his head back in shock at what he saw. She leaned over his arm and read.

Kylie Hood was on his blocked list.

"What the *hell?*" he rumbled, voice low and tight. "I never did that."

"Your account says otherwise."

"No, Kylie. I mean it. I never did that."

"We were kids. Teens do stupid things."

"Kylie Hood, so help me God, I never blocked you." He tapped his phone, hitting Unblock.

Kylie looked at hers, doing a search for his name.

Voila! There he was, for the first time in years.

"And there you are," he whispered softly, clearly doing the same thing she was.

He tapped his phone, going back to his email account.

A sound, small and pained, came out of him. "No. No way."

"What are you doing?"

"I have an idea about what may have happened." He sounded sick.

Positively *sick*.

"What're you doing?"

"Going back fifteen years to old Sent emails."

"Huh? What will that prove?"

He did a search for her in his account. Kylie watching his nimble fingers type it in as if he had it memorized.

Did he? All these years?

"Oh, no. No, no, no. Amber, *no*."

"Amber? What does *Amber* have to do with this?"

Luke turned his phone toward her.

"I just searched for your email, Kylie. And I found this."

It was the familiar "bounce" email, the kind an automated system sends when an email address is invalid.

Except it was in his Sent folder. Manually created.

It looked very much like the kind you get when the email address is no longer in service.

It was the exact email Kylie received fifteen years ago.

The last kind of email she ever got from Luke before she gave up trying.

Chapter Twenty-Six

Luke

"I don't understand," Kylie said, but her tone made it clear she was catching on.

Fast.

"It looks like Amber created a fake email and sent it from my account to make you think my email wasn't working. And if I blocked you on social media, it wasn't me–she did it."

"Why would Amber do all that?"

"We can't ask her now, can we?" he snapped, hating his tone, repulsed by what he and Kylie were uncovering.

Had his late wife really gone to such extremes?

"Hold on, hold on," Kylie said softly. "If she did this, she did it when she was *fifteen*, Luke. You disappeared on social media shortly after I moved. So it happened way back then."

"And your point is?"

"She was fifteen, Luke. A teenager. A baby. We all were, back then. She–she must have been jealous. And maybe insecure."

"Maybe?"

"Okay." Kylie ran her hand up and down her arm, what they were experiencing a bit spooky. "Obviously, I'm shocked, too, but doesn't it fill in the blanks for you? It does for me. I spent all those years more troubled by how your behavior didn't make sense than by the rejection."

"ME, TOO!" he shouted, relieved to hear his emotions put into words.

She jumped, startled. Before he could say something, anything, about all the years they'd lost, all the anger he had at Amber, the crunch of tires on dirt made them both turn.

His stomach lurched.

His parents, with Harriet.

Never one to handle too many emotions at once very well–unless they were other people's emotions–Luke closed his eyes and took a deep breath.

Suddenly, Kylie's hand held his.

"It's okay. We can process this later. Together."

Together.

He'd longed for *together* for so long. That's what he'd had with his late wife. A sense of togetherness. Someone had his emotional back. A partner, a lover, a co-parent–for sure.

And what he had with Amber was more than that. Never lonely with her, he felt seen.

Finding that email, Kylie's name on his blocked list–that was different. *Hard.* Add in his growing feelings for Kylie and Luke didn't know what to do.

A gentle hand squeeze from her brought him back to the present.

Quickly, she released him. His mom, Deanna, and his dad, Dean, were shutting the truck doors, Harriet's blur of dark hair running toward him.

"Luke!" his mom called out, his dad wrapping his arm around her shoulders, the two looking so happy and relaxed. The European vacation was a big one, a cornerstone of a life as they aged. A pang made his chest hurt a little.

His parents were graying. Wrinkling a bit, too. Old enough to take a "trip of a lifetime" and mean it.

How many more good years did they have left?

Dean had fallen a few times, forty years of climbing trees finally catching up to him, time a cruel mistress. Kell took on the bigger climbing jobs now, and they had a young apprentice, Allen. Luke helped sometimes with really big jobs, but wasn't as sure in the trees as Kell. His brother was part squirrel, part Spider-Man, able to climb like he had sticky fingers.

Their mom had put her foot down when their dad had fallen five and a half years ago, breaking too many bones in a free fall that his harness caught, late enough to trigger damage. It wasn't about the business any more.

It was about keeping her husband around long enough for her to enjoy him.

And what about Luke? The thought of spending the rest of his life without someone special was unbearable.

No. That wasn't quite right.

It was the thought of spending it without Kylie that made him ache.

Before he could think the next thought, his mom buried him in a hug, Harriet on his dad's shoulders now. Kylie introduced herself and made small talk with his dad while Harriet chattered excitedly about fairy muffins, scrambling down off his dad.

"I loved seeing Dennis and Europe, but I missed you. Missed this," his mom whispered in his ear. As Luke pulled away, she held him tighter and added, "Kylie Hood, huh? You look a lot like your dad."

She touched her blonde hair. "I hear that a lot."

"He was famous, too." Deanna gave a sad smile. "Or infamous."

"Famous?" Kylie squeaked. "Too? Why would I be famous? Rachel said the same thing!"

Deanna gave her a side glance. "Don't pretend. Everyone in town is talking about you two."

"Don't embarrass me, Mom," Luke said in a tone of warning.

"Why on earth would I do that?"

He laughed, his mom joining in. But then she leaned even closer, smelling like her Elizabeth Arden Red Door perfume, the only scent he ever remembered her wearing.

"But if you get together, can you wait until January 12th? Because–"

"You, too?" His voice cracked with betrayal. "You were in Europe!"

"Colleen texted and offered us a buy-in for the betting pool."

"I can't believe this."

"It's Love You, Maine, Lukey," she said, using his childhood nickname with impunity. "People can't help but gossip about love."

"We're not in love. And don't call me Lukey."

"Of course not. I see what you're *really* in."

"Huh?"

"You're in denial, my dear."

"Denial about what?" his dad called out. Kylie turned to look at him. If Luke were the blushing type, he'd be as red as a Main Street decoration in February.

And the tips of Kylie's ears looked dipped in red paint.

"About who gets the old office building," he tossed out, rescuing himself from his mom's teasing. "We're all going to fight over it."

"Why?" Kylie asked. Harriet casually reached for her hand, so easily that Luke's heart squeezed a little. His daughter did, in fact, love Kylie.

Did he?

"It's—well, let's go look at it and *you* tell *me* why," he said, gesturing for her to walk ahead of him, his parents following as Harriet and Kylie took the lead. The camp had the main lodge, the office building, the old director's house, the first aid cabin, and a few other small cabins spread around.

The lodge had an enormous commercial kitchen and dining hall attached to it, which Luke planned to turn into an extraordinary recreation room, complete with a pool table, darts, ping-pong, and if he got lucky, some vintage video games and pinball machines.

Build a home that no one ever wanted to leave.

His eyes cut over to Kylie at the thought.

Speaking of leaving... he had ten weeks left with her. At most. If she got a job in New York, maybe less. Attachment swung from one extreme to the other as he worried over the situation:

Let himself feel what he really felt for her, or keep the wall up, knowing she would disappear from their lives again? Harriet had no hesitation over becoming attached, even though they'd repeatedly explained that Kylie wasn't here for much longer.

Kids were like that, attaching with their whole hearts, both feet in, every fiber of their being open to the world.

Luke had changed.

"I'm so glad to hear how wonderful you've been for Luke and Harriet," he overheard his mother saying to Kylie as they reached the old office, the glass storm door covered with faded, peeling stickers. "Sounds like you've settled into a nice routine, the three of you."

If she weren't his mom, he'd kick her ankle. His mother was so far beyond obvious, she should need an astronaut suit to breathe. Always matchmaking for her kids, he knew how her mind worked. Kell and Rachel were together now in no small part due to Deanna Luview's intervention.

One down, three to go. If she could get Luke and Kylie together, Colleen would be next.

His dad just gave him a big old grin.

Great. This was about to go from bad to worse if even his dad was chiming in.

"Your mom is laying it on thick. That means she likes her," was all Dean muttered as Deanna opened the office door and the building swallowed her, Kylie, and Harriet.

"This is just as amazing as I remembered it!" Kylie gasped when he walked in, her eyes drawn immediately to the sky-climbing, open-air loft that made up half the office. Built back in a time when timber frames were popular and labor was cheap, the office had cathedral ceilings pushing two and a half stories on one side of the building, and galleries on three levels.

"This would be perfect for fairy shows," Kylie muttered to herself, eyeing the old stage, which was down on the first floor. Years of "No Talent" shows from bygone times flashed through Luke's memory, the Bathrobe Band that he, Kell, Brewer, and Moore formed making him groan internally. They thought they were so cool, wearing bathrobes and swimsuits, banging on "drums" made of five-gallon buckets and playing the out-of-tune piano.

The very same one that was still on stage, though now covered with an inch of dust.

Note to self: Call Tommy the Tuner and get the piano fixed. Yet another item on the never-ending list of money-pit projects.

But he grinned at the thought.

"Do you still play?" he called out to Kylie, who froze on the spot.

"That?" She pointed to the piano. "I haven't played in years."

"You probably just need a little practice," his mom said, giving him an impish look. "Only way to know is to find out. Luke'll have it tuned and you can come and play anytime, Kylie."

She wasn't just laying it on thick. She was smothering them in it.

"What about you?" Kylie asked Luke. "Remember the Bathrobe Band? You, Kell, Moore and Brewer?"

"I haven't pretended to play a five-gallon bucket in fourteen years."

"Pity," Kylie shot back. "You missed your shot at a recording contract. Could have been huge in Poughkeepsie."

They all laughed.

"Where are Brewer and Moore?" she asked, a sheen of nostalgia in her eyes.

"Moore's here. Runs the family jewelry store. Brewer's long gone, living in Texas."

"Texas?"

"He hit it big. Billionaire."

"NO!"

"Yep."

"He was always bumming money off me in school to buy ice cream on Fridays."

"Add in compound interest and ask him for fifty grand," his dad cracked.

"Kylie! Come here!" Harriet shouted, her voice tinny and distant. As Luke followed Kylie, he realized where his daughter was.

The attached greenhouse. Dull, filthy windows were framed by rotting wood with peeling paint, pots on their sides on the cracked concrete floor. Two windows were broken, but the bones were there. It was clear that being empty for a few years had led to parts of the camp going into disrepair, and the greenhouse was one of them.

"The fairies can live in here!" Harriet gushed, eyes jumping from his face to Kylie's. "You said they like to be warm in the sun, but it's winter, so there aren't many outside now. This could be their home!"

One hand on Harriet's curly hair, Kylie gave her a wistful smile. "You have some really wonderful ideas, Harriet."

The change in her countenance caught him off-guard. Why the sudden distance?

Then it hit him.

She was job searching in New York. She was leaving in two months.

Kylie was drawing boundaries.

Physical pain hit his chest, the wall forming around her one he had to scale, climb over, fight against. Losing her could not happen, must not happen.

Would not happen.

A hand on his arm, together with the familiar scent of her perfume, made him turn, his face close to hers, though he had to look down, as always.

"Did you invite Kylie to Christmas?" his mom whispered. His dad had joined in chatter with Harriet about wood sprites and garden gnomes.

"What? No. Of course not."

"Why 'of course not'?" She seemed offended. "Poor woman, all alone in her own hometown, no one to be with. It's just being neighborly to offer."

"Mom."

"Don't look at me like that, Luke! Kylie is part of Luview. It's my job to make her feel it."

"Mom," he said again, in a voice of warning.

That earned him a stuck-out tongue as his mother released his arm, turned to Kylie, and said loudly, "Kylie! What are you doing for Christmas?"

Harriet's face lit up like a, well...

Christmas tree.

"Christmas?" Kylie peeped, looking straight at Luke, who didn't know what to say or do.

So he shrugged.

"You know. A nice little holiday? Falls on December 25?" Dean joked. "Involves a bearded guy who was kind to the poor and–"

"Ha ha," Deanna interrupted. "Yes, *Christmas*. We'd love to have you. I hear you make a mean fairy muffin. Why don't you make some and come along around seven? We start eating then, and it would be lovely to have you for Christmas dinner. Unless you'd like to come earlier and join the gift exchange?"

"Mom," Luke said tightly, moving toward Kylie, his protective instincts on overdrive. "You're overwhelming her."

Kylie's throat bobbed as she swallowed, hard. He saw the tension in her, trying to read his signals, trying to understand the subtext.

And make no mistake, there was one.

More than one.

Because Luke desperately wanted her to come to Christmas. Stay for New Year's. Be here every day.

Every single day.

Forever.

But Kylie Hood had plans that didn't include being in Luview, Maine, forever, and that–that was the part he couldn't tease out. The part that made falling in love with her so hard.

The part that made him radiate too many conflicting emotions.

Emotions she picked up on with supersonic empathy radar.

"No," Kylie said firmly to Luke, eyes holding his in a steady gaze that didn't waver, heat rising between the two of them until he damn near took her in his arms and kissed the ambiguity out of both of them. "I'm not overwhelmed. I feel very welcomed, and yes, Deanna. I would love to come for Christmas dinner. You said seven?"

Deanna was bursting with victory. He was never going to hear the end of this.

"Yes. Seven. You know where we live?" She waved her hand and laughed. "Luke can give you directions, I'm sure."

Dean's phone went nuts.

"That's Kell. Work emergency."

Luke frowned, but before he could speak up, his dad added, "Not *that* kind of emergency! Nothing dangerous. Just needs me for an estimate."

Shoulders relaxing, Luke let his guard down.

Sort of.

Deanna grabbed Kylie for a big hug, not reaching for Luke, which was some professional-grade shade.

"This is exciting! I hope you like board games. We play a very competitive round of Apples to Apples and Telestrations."

"Competitive Apples to Apples?"

Luke leaned in and whispered to Kylie, "Blood is sometimes drawn. Bring triple antibiotic cream."

His parents laughed as Dean tugged Deanna out the door, both waving as Harriet popped up on the second floor of the building, waving from the balcony.

"Bye!"

Luke stared at his disappearing parents in a daze.

Not only had his mother outplayed him, badly, she'd left without giving him a hug.

Between realizing what Amber had done fifteen years ago, registering Kylie's glee about the office and fairy camp, managing an overexcited six-year-old, and digesting his mother's assertive invitation for Kylie to join the family, Luke was in sore need of a break.

Instead, he got one heck of an intense stare down from Kylie before she asked:

"What *are* you planning to do with this building?"

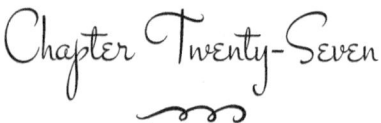

Chapter Twenty-Seven

Kylie

Amber cut Luke out of Kylie's life all those years ago.

Amber.

It was *Amber*.

The entire time Luke's parents were here, she'd run Amber's name through her mind in an endless loop, a tornado with her name in it, airborne by the force of the emotion generated by learning the truth.

Swept away by all of the feelings–shock, anger, disgust, betrayal, silliness, regret–Kylie found that one overrode all of that.

Love.

Heaven help her, she was really, truly falling in love with Luke.

"What I'm going to do with the building isn't important, Kylie. We have other things to talk about."

"Like Christmas? Because if you don't want me there, I understand. Your mom put us on the spot when she asked like that."

"No. Not Christmas. Amber."

"What about Mommy?" Harriet called out from her perch on the second-story balcony.

The word *Mommy* made Kylie wince.

"We can talk about this later," she whispered, reaching for his arm. He slipped his hand in hers and squeezed, eyes sad, blinking hard as he clearly processed the same swirl of emotions she was feeling.

"We absolutely will. I'm so–"

"Conflicted?"

"I was going to say angry. And sad. And wistful. And–"

She couldn't help but laugh. "Right. Conflicted."

Luke's wry smile tugged at her heart, his warm touch grounding her so nicely.

"You're not mad at me?" he asked.

"No! Why would I be?"

"Because I should have figured this out long ago. Think about how different life might have been."

"Different? How? We were fifteen and seventeen, Luke. I left town and moved halfway across the country. Amber must have been jealous, and she did what an immature fifteen-year-old might think was a good idea. I can't be angry at you for something she did. I can't even be angry at her. We were young. I was in Indiana. Were we going to somehow magically hold onto a relationship based on a single kiss?"

A thump next to them made them both look. Harriet's sweet face looked up at Kylie, her mouth twisted in a gross look.

"Ewww. Don't kiss!"

Luke's hand went to his mouth to cover what she knew was a grin.

"We're not talking about kissing each other," Kylie lied.

"Good!" Harriet poked Kylie in the belly button. "Because kissing makes babies and we don't need any babies!"

Luke looked like someone poured ice water all over him.

Bending quickly, he tipped his chin down, eyes up, the interrogative expression making Kylie go sober.

"Who told you that?" he questioned Harriet.

"Jace Morgenstern."

The flutter of Luke's eyelashes revealed a deep irritation with the answer, as if he expected it.

"Kissing does not make babies," he said softly. "Please put that out of your head and don't repeat it."

"But Jace said–"

"Jace is wrong."

"Then how are babies made if you don't kiss?"

Luke's look of horror was followed by an inarticulate choking sound.

"Harriet!" Kylie interrupted, sensing this wasn't going in a productive direction. "Why don't we go outside and look for good places to put gnome homes?"

"Ooo! Okay!"

As Harriet scampered outside, Luke shot Kylie a grumpy look.

"She's six! I thought I had years before I had to worry about the birds and the bees."

"It troubles me that you're using 1950s terminology to describe sex and reproduction."

"You're deflecting."

"Yes."

"Great way to redirect her."

"Maybe she's not the one I'm redirecting."

His hand grabbed hers and yanked her into a hallway, her back against the wall, Luke's lips on hers before she could think another thought. The kiss was hot and sweet at the same time, everything she wanted in a passionate moment with him all rolled into one, the way his breath hitched making it clear he was barely holding himself back, the urgency of the kiss so intense.

Except it was too brief.

Gasping as he broke it off, she asked, "What was that for?"

"I have to have a reason to kiss you?"

"No."

"Good. Not that I don't have plenty."

Another kiss, this one deeper, longer, his hands wrapping around her waist, sliding up under her coat, the chill of his cool palms no match for the racing heat pumping into her.

What if she could have this every day?

What if she really could come home again?

What would it feel like to be accepted, embraced, brought into the town's fold and given a place in their world?

What if his tongue, so warm and urgent, could touch her like this forever, her hands threading in his hair, her little gasps turning to moans as his palms caressed her spine, moving to her ribs, floating down to firmly hold her butt, the grip a claim she liked.

Liked very much.

What if everything bad that had happened to her over the last few months was part of the journey that brought her here, to this moment, to this potential future with Luke?

So many what ifs.

"You smell so good," she whispered into his neck.

"You taste even better," he replied, licking her ear, making her shiver and melt into him.

"DADEEEEEEEE! WHERE ARE YOU?"

Luke's eyelids lowered shut, exasperation etched into his face. The smirk didn't help any, her mouth on his in an impulsive lunge before he breathlessly pulled away and whispered, "Jace Morgenstern might be right."

"Huh?"

"This kiss could lead us to do something that makes babies."

And with that he jogged away, Kylie following but pausing on the threshold. As he grabbed Harriet in his arms and lifted the squealing little girl up onto his shoulders, Kylie tried to find air for her lungs.

One longing look at the giant auditorium attached to the office and she shut the door, took a deep breath of cold air, and told herself there would be plenty of time to talk later.

Because Luke promised.

And he always kept his promises.

At least, the ones Amber hadn't subverted...

For the next hour, they wandered the camp, walking into each building, Kylie and Luke weighing out the practical versus the wish list for renovations. Harriet wandered outside, making snow angels, throwing snowballs, and generally keeping busy in the way a kid who spends a lot of time outdoors can.

She noticed he avoided the pier.

So did she.

No need to be tempted by more kissing.

By the time Luke's phone buzzed, they were thoroughly chilled and ready to leave.

Dusk was coming soon, too.

"Gotta stop in at the office," he said as they walked to the car.

"We need to let Jester go piddle, too, Daddy," Harriet solemnly reminded him.

They climbed into the Jeep, Harriet expertly clicking herself into her car seat, the three of them setting off for downtown as if they were already a little family.

The memory of Luke's kiss, the Jace Morgenstern comments—babies!—made Kylie flush all over.

One of Harriet's favorite songs came on the radio and they bopped to it, her infectious giggles even getting Luke in on the fun, his goofiness a welcome change from his otherwise serious demeanor. What Kylie loved more than anything about whatever this was that brewed between them was the gradual unveiling of more and more facets of Luke Luview.

She found him endlessly interesting.

Endlessly attractive, too.

By the time he pulled into the parking lot at the police station, Kylie was overcome by a wave of sadness.

Her small, empty apartment suddenly felt lonely.

"Tomorrow?" he asked, giving her a smoldering look as they climbed out of his car and she looked down the street, spotting hers. The parking lot held a pink cruiser, a few pick-up trucks, plenty of older compact cars, and Kell's poison ivy truck, with his company logo and tagline:

Pulling for You, Inc.

We touch it so you don't have to.

Snow piled in giant white icebergs in the corners of most of the parking lots. Early enough in the season to escape the gross, slushy gray of late winter, the piles looked like fun. When they were kids, those giant mountains were instant kid magnets for easy sledding and fort building.

As Christmas loomed, though, they were untouched.

"Tomorrow's my day off."

"I know. I mean, I'd like to take you out."

"Out? What about Number 14, Part A?"

"We'll call it a business dinner."

"What about waiting until January 12?"

"Huh?"

"The betting pool. Your mother told me we had to wait until January 12."

"Oh, geez. She did not."

"She most certainly did. And Dotty Chen asked me to wait until December 31."

"I don't care what they want. I care about what you want, Kylie. What do you want?"

"I want to go out to dinner with you."

"Good. Pick you up at six. Wear something nice."

"Like what? It'll be covered in a ski parka no matter what."

"I'm taking you to a place with cloth napkins and no kids' menu."

Harriet must have overheard because she pouted. "What will I eat, then?"

"Chicken nuggets and fries and apple slices with Aunt Colleen."

"*Pfft.*" When she made the noise, a curl on her forehead flew straight up. "That's better than any rest'rant food."

Kylie gave her a quick hug, then turned to Luke, who opened his arms wide, pulling her in for a heated embrace that sent shivers of arousal through her.

The station curtains parted.

Rusty's face appeared in the window, followed by some guy Kylie didn't know, though he wore a red police uniform.

"We're being watched," she whispered in his ear. "Who's that?"

"Jude. Fellow officer."

"Ah."

"Let them watch." But he didn't kiss her.

Just shot her a wicked grin.

And with that, she walked to her car as Luke and Harriet entered the station, feeling like it was all a dream.

The best dream.

The kind you don't want to wake up from.

New reality slowly seeping in, she grinned like a mad fool, mouth still tingling from his kiss, heart shining like sunbeams. The streets of downtown were filled with shoppers, Love You Flowers hopping and full of poinsettias, Love You Books busy with so many customers, there was a line snaking across the display window.

Kylie paused, taking it all in with deep breaths. Christmas songs were being piped over the town's public address system, local radio station WLUV playing holiday music. The station normally played only love songs, but weren't Christmas songs all about love, at the core?

This was what she wanted, her soul incredulous, her mind racing to process it all. Goodness and decency radiated off of Luke, and Harriet was the absolute sweetest. Kylie almost needed to pinch herself to be convinced this wasn't a dream.

Her phone buzzed with a text from Wendy.

How's it going? she asked. *I'm up late with Estelle. She got food poisoning and is puking. The fun side of my job.*

Way to take the shine off Kylie's afternoon.

I'm better off than you, Kylie texted back. *Welcome to nannying. It isn't all hot German dudes named Johann. Just spent time with Luke and Harriet.*

You're working, too?

No, she typed, hesitating. Desperate for someone to talk to, she spilled her guts. *Luke and I kissed.*

CONGRATS!!! Has he proposed yet?

Kylie sputtered, looking around as if people could read her sister's crazy words.

Uh, one kiss isn't grounds for engagement, she replied.

In some countries, it is. But Kylie! YAY! You snagged Hot Cop.

I don't know about snagged, but he asked me out on a date tomorrow.

Date! This is serious!

It's... nice.

Kylie's getting laid!

A purple eggplant appeared. Wendy was a walking cliché when it came to sex emojis.

We'll see.

Does this mean you're staying? Calling off the job search?

Finger hovering over her screen, she let Wendy's question percolate.

I don't know, she said honestly. *So far, no bites from New York.*

I know it's your dream, Ky, but maybe your new dream could be staying in Luview? Or having a Luview in you?;)

You are sick.

I am right.

I need advice, not a bunch of vulgar jokes.

You want my advice? Keep your options open. No one's locked down here. If you get an interview, go for it. You don't have to make any decisions until you have a job offer in hand. Until then, explore.

When did you become so insightful?

People in Europe just are flat out smarter than Americans.

You're not European!

No, but I had one in me...

LOL! Kylie wrote back, literally laughing out loud. Her sister was right, though. About all of it.

Options were good.

TTYL, Wendy typed. *Estelle's calling for me.*

The conversation was over.

By the time she reached the driver's side door to her car, the downtown streetlights were on, giving the shopping district a warm glow that matched her internal state.

Her phone buzzed with a notification, and she looked. An email.

An email from one of the jobs she'd applied for.

Dear Ms. Hood,

Thank you for applying for the production coordinator position with KidzdocTV. We're impressed by your credentials, especially

*your experience with on-site children's programming, and would
like to invite you to an online interview on...*

The letter's words turned into gibberish as her eyes raced across
the page, barely able to absorb meaning. She got a Zoom
interview?

She got the interview.

KidzdocTV was the premiere children's programming
station for high-quality documentaries and reality TV for kids. If
she got a job there, she'd be set for life.

Or, at least, set for a couple of years. Nothing was permanent
in the corporate world, but this would be a huge steppingstone.

In New York City.

Looking down the street, she stared at the police station.

Looked down at her phone.

Police station.

Phone.

The glow of the afternoon spent with Luke, Harriet, and his
parents faded as if an ill wind blew it away, chilling Kylie to the
bone suddenly as two worlds clashed.

Still reeling from what they'd learned about Amber, and
excited by the camp's possibilities, she'd let herself live in a future
where she became part of Luview, in every way possible.

Part of the town.

Part of a family.

Part of Luke's heart.

And now she faced a fork in the road, where the need to
choose between two possible futures had to finally resolve itself.
She was either setting down roots, or she was spreading her
wings.

No. Hold on.

Nothing said she had the New York job. This was just an
interview, right? And it was just a Zoom interview, which wasn't
a big deal. Just like the kisses with Luke weren't technically
violating Number 14, Part A, accepting an online interview for a
job wasn't about making a commitment.

It was about exploring a possibility.

Fifteen years ago, Kylie was wrenched from one world to another without a choice. Without input. Without consideration for what *she* wanted.

And now?

What *did* she want?

The right thing for her heart was to turn down the interview, get in her car, drive to Luke's house and tell him how she felt. Pour it all out and take a deep breath, hoping he felt the same way. Take a big leap and be vulnerable. Open. Honest.

Real.

The right thing for her pride was to prove that Perry hadn't ruined her. To go back to New York and resume the career she'd always wanted. To shape what children saw in the media and to make a difference in the world.

To be independent, her mother's voice hissed in her head. *To protect yourself.*

Heart and pride were in conflict.

And Kylie hated conflict.

"'When in doubt, don't,'" she muttered aloud, her mother's words coming easily to the tip of her tongue. They rang hollow, though, a product of fear.

Kylie didn't want to live in fear.

She wanted to live in abundance.

Wendy told her to keep her options open.

Without further hesitation, she replied to the email, accepting the online interview. It was just a screening, a weeder interview. Chances were good nothing would come of it, and it would be good practice. Maintaining more than one option was smart.

Options were always good, right?

Right?

Chapter Twenty-Eight

Luke

He couldn't stop thinking about Kylie's face when she walked into the office at the camp yesterday.

And not just because she was so gorgeous.

The attached auditorium and greenhouse were unique features, the kind of structures you just didn't find anywhere else, and Kylie had the vision to see how special it could be. Those very same features made the camp a white elephant of sorts on the real estate market, leading buyers who lacked imagination to say no to the place.

Earlier in the year, the giant chocolate corporation Markstone's had nearly bought the camp, but their goal was to raze it and put in a theme park and condominiums. Rachel, Kell's now-girlfriend, had worked for Markstone's, and she was sent here to convince Lucinda Armistead to sell her small company, Love You Chocolate, to the behemoth.

Rachel knew that the Luview family was also trying to buy it, and when she learned about the plans for the old camp, she lost her job by warning Deanna about the deal. Luke had been grateful to Rachel for sacrificing so much for their town and family, but the real reason she'd done it hadn't been simple kindness.

Love had made her do it. She loved Kell, but she also loved the town.

Kylie loved this camp even more than Rachel had loved Love You, Maine.

Leave it to Kylie to find the treasure in something others cast aside.

Tonight was date night. Six days before Christmas.

And Luke was running errands, mad at himself for being so late mailing their gift to Amber's parents in Florida. The lines at the post office on Main Street would be long by their small-town standards.

Which meant five people deep.

By New York City standards, that was slow, he knew, but this wasn't a bustling city.

Not by a longshot.

And the town liked it that way, thank you very much.

But the Love You postmark was the only one in the country that wasn't a simple circle. It was, of course, a heart, and Love stamps postmarked Love You, Maine, were in high demand worldwide. Accordingly, every tourist wanted to send postcards from the town, and that meant a lot of extra customers.

Especially in mid-February. Visitors swelled the numbers everywhere in town then, of course. You couldn't move an inch without seeing red foil-wrapped chocolate somewhere in the town of Love You during the whole Valentine's Day month. Red and white holiday lights peppered every surface then, with the Love Games, the Valentine's Day festival, and so much more every February. Add in all the couples deciding to get married at Love You Forever, the town's 24/7 drive-thru wedding site, and the town exploded.

But now, on December 19, it was just New England small-town holiday cheer, and when he reached the post office, he did a double take.

Not because the line was longer than expected.

But because a dog riding a skateboard whizzed past him. *Smiling.*

It was a little French bulldog, ugly as sin, using its right two legs to propel itself on the skateboard, deftly navigating small curves, pitching its weight left and right to keep up with physics.

Mel jogged slowly behind it, shouting. "Yes! Pierre! Good dog!"

Oh, brother.

While the little bugger didn't have long fur, he somehow looked windblown as he sped through downtown, pedestrians dodging the surprise torpedo as he made his way through the shopping district, many whipping out phones to video the spectacle. Holiday customers rushed out of shops to gawk.

"Hey, Luke!" Mel waved as she ran past, people chuckling and whispering as the post office line moved him indoors.

"You coming to Tuba Christmas?" Moore Mottin asked, nudging him with one elbow, his arms full of a stack of pre-packaged boxes. Moore and Luke had been friends since infancy, born three days apart in the same hospital, but Moore's job took him on the road a lot. Heir to Love You Jewelers, he was a busy man, the town's only jewelry store kept hopping with steady sales of engagement rings, wedding bands, and heart-shaped pendants.

"Listen to forty big horns oompah-pah their way through Jingle Bells?" Luke snorted.

"You're coming," Moore, a tuba player, shot back. "Harriet won't let you miss it."

"Right. It's tomorrow?"

"Yep."

"I'm on duty. Mom or Colleen must be bringing her."

"Even better. Get paid to hear a good bass line."

Luke snorted. "Sounds more like a dying moose colliding with Santa's sleigh."

"Says the cocky quarterback from high school. You never had the satisfaction of playing 'Star-Spangled Banner' at halftime."

"Nope. Too busy nursing my sore shoulder."

Moore's eyes narrowed. Dressed in a suit, he looked a little too mature for Luke's tastes, their normal garb leaning toward flannels and jeans, though Moore always dressed up for work. Both were on the other side of thirty, a transition no one handled well, but something about the difference between Luke's police uniform and Moore's tailored wool suit set his teeth on edge.

Maybe that promotion to chief wasn't such a bad idea after all.

"How's Kylie?" Moore asked, voice low.

"Not you, too? Which date did you grab in the betting pool?"

"Date? I've been gone all week doing wholesale buys. What date?"

Moore wasn't fooling anyone.

"Oh, come on. Don't play dumb. I'm sure someone bought you in."

His buddy gave up the charade. "Kell did. Just don't do anything until December 29, okay?"

"Your store does just fine. You don't need the winnings."

"Since when did betting have anything to do with *needing* the money?"

The line moved closer, three people ahead of Luke now. He knew two of them, Mitch Crawczyk from the auto body shop, and Sydney Ikoff, who worked as a CNA at the big nursing home on the edge of town, toward Fryeburg. Both had boxes from online retailers they'd repurposed for sending Christmas gifts, a stark contrast from Moore's neatly packed and branded merchandise from the jewelry store.

And a larger box on the bottom.

"Why are you here? You're the boss. Shouldn't you send Joey to do this?" Joey was Moore's nephew, twenty-two, fresh out of college, and a true townie. He'd made it through four years down at University of Southern Maine, coming home every weekend, and moved back to Luview the day he graduated.

"Joey went to Boston to pick up charms from this artisanal co-op we found on Etsy that takes heirloom silverware sets and turns them into fine jewelry. Really great stuff. Dirt cheap in volume, too. It's where we're getting most of our Love You charms now."

"That sounds so... Love You."

The two snickered like schoolboys.

"Hey. Pays the mortgage, right? At least I don't walk around looking like a red lollipop for my job."

"Not always. Sometimes I shake it up and look like a bottle of calamine lotion, when we wear pink."

"Ooo, you rebel, you."

"Mailing Christmas gifts to Jordy?" Jordy was Moore's fourteen-year-old son from his first marriage. When they were high school seniors, Moore and his then-girlfriend, Cammie Forsythe, accidentally got themselves pregnant. By the time they both graduated high school, they were married, and Cammie gave birth a week later. Luke admired his friend, though he secretly ribbed him, too.

Because the marriage fell apart when Jordy was five, and Moore went on to remarry three years later, to a banking executive who cheated on him with the wedding reception DJ.

At the reception.

Right here in Love You.

Their divorce was quick, which left Moore twice married and twice divorced at twenty-seven.

AKA, cursed.

"Jordy wants cash. I got him something better," Moore said, uncertainty filling his eyes. Cammie had disappeared with Jordy nine years ago, running off to California to meet some dude she got to know on the Internet. For nearly a year, she kept Moore away from his own kid, a year of nothing but suffering and pain. Luke and Amber had just finished college and settled into their new jobs in Luview, while Moore lost his mind, using every legal maneuver, plenty of help from his parents, and lots of donations from townsfolk to get visitation rights and partial custody of Jordy.

He won.

Then, Cammie met some other dude, moved to Minnesota a few years ago, and spat out another kid with a new guy. Now, Moore got Jordy on alternating holidays and school breaks, and three weeks in the summer.

But Jordy had begun to blame Moore for "disappearing" for that year, and their relationship was strained. Unlike Moore, Cammie didn't honor his "don't bash the other parent" request, though Moore did. Too young to remember the truth, Jordy was living through puberty, Moore an easy target.

"Let me guess," Luke said, noticing the Red Sox label in the box. "A signed jersey."

"Yup."

"You don't have to compete with Mike." Cammie's current partner and father of Jordy's half-sister was a minor league baseball player.

"I absolutely do," Moore said tightly. "You know how much Jordy loves baseball."

"And Colleen."

"And Colleen," Moore agreed, suddenly cheerful at the mention of her name. "She's the best." Colleen had helped Moore and Cammie with babysitting from the time Jordy was born until Cammie took off with him. These days, Jordy was blunt: he came to Luview to see Colleen and his grandparents.

His dad? Not so much.

"Most of the time," Luke agreed. "She's still my sister. I remember all her sins."

"Colleen's only sin is nearly killing off every guy she sees on the third date."

"We all have our private curses, don't we?" Luke muttered.

The line moved up, Mitch giving Moore and Luke a wave as he left, Sydney hefting what looked like five well-taped shoe boxes onto the counter. Tim Kurdan, the postmaster, was pitching in at the front desk.

"There's Joey," Moore commented. Luke turned around to see Moore's nephew parking in front of the jewelry shop just as Ashley Mitteracht, Wolf's oldest daughter and Marni's sister, walked out of Love You Coffee with a to-go cup in one hand and three shopping bags in the other. It was apparent that Ashley was Christmas shopping, and one other fact was equally apparent:

Joey was head-over-heels in love with Ashley.

Who may or may not have noticed.

"Ashley!" he called out. "Just got back from Boston!" The way Joey said *Boston* made it clear he was trying to impress her.

Moore snorted.

"He's not supposed to park in front of the store. I've told him a million times. Takes up a customer spot."

Tim hollered, "NEXT!" as Sydney finished at the counter, and then it was Luke's turn.

"Make your move, kid," Moore muttered as he watched Joey, triggering more laughter from Luke.

"Sending stuff to Tally and Marilyn, I see." Nothing got past Tim. *Nothing.* You bought a fruitcake from a mail order place instead of Greta's? Tim knew.

Got a special computer for your teenager?

Tim knew.

Bought something a bit lascivious?

Yep. Tim knew *everything*.

"Presents are presents, right?" Luke said, noncommittal but friendly.

"Going to see them in February?"

"Yep."

"Good man. Even if you finally move on, good to make sure they still see Harriet."

Great. He was getting advice on dating from Tim now.

Luke just grunted and pulled out his debit card.

"How's that going, by the way?"

"How's *what* going?"

"You and the Hood girl."

Only someone in his late sixties in Luview could get away with calling Kylie "the Hood girl."

But it set Luke's teeth on edge anyhow.

"Not talking about it, Tim."

"Oh, ho ho! Hit a nerve." Like most old yankees, Tim was normally the type to mind his own business, taciturn and a little grumpy, but always ready to help a neighbor out. For him to persist in prying meant only one thing.

A long-suffering sigh escaped Luke as he asked, "What date did you pick?"

"January 26. No need to rush it. Good things in life are best savored."

"Good grief."

"I'm not wrong," Tim said as he punched in the zip code, pulled the postage sticker out of the machine, and carefully affixed it to the corner of the box. "Done. This'll arrive in two to three days."

"Great."

"And by February, your sweet Harriet will have plenty to tell her grandparents about that Kylie."

"Tim."

"Be courtly, Luke. Give it time."

"Stop."

"My snow blower needs a new timing belt. That jackpot could cover it and more."

"Bye, Tim."

Disgusted by the conversation and taunted by Moore's laughter, Luke stormed outside and nearly ran into Joey, who was now nervously chatting up Ashley.

Who seemed remarkably interested in Joey's story about artisanal co-ops, maker spaces, and craftspeople in Boston.

Huh. Maybe this was budding love after all. Why didn't the town have betting squares on *them?*

As Luke wondered about that, the little French bulldog, Pierre, made a sudden reappearance, Mel trailing behind him, shouting, "Watch out!"

As if in slow motion, the following happened in seconds:

1. Pierre's skateboard hit a crack in the sidewalk and pitched forward, turning him into a projectile, like something launched from a trebuchet.

2. Joey looked up and realized Pierre was about to flatten poor Ashley.

3. In a valiant act of chivalry, likely motivated purely by hormones, Joey inserted himself between Pierre and Ashley,

taking the full force of the parabolic trajectory of a small but very dense dog.

In other words, Joey ended up flattened by an eighteen-pound bag of steel bones and resting bulldog face.

"Oh. My. Goodness!" Ashley squealed as Joey, on the ground with a dog licking his face, slowly came to. "That little thing was about to hit me! You saved us both!"

Breathless, Mel Chassi ran up, scooping Pierre off Joey's chest. "Good catch."

"Uh, thanks," Joey groaned, hand going to his elbow. "Felt like a direct hit from Thor's hammer."

Ashley bent down, a long strand of honey-brown hair sweeping across Joey's cheek. She touched his shoulders, then chest, finally resting her hands on one knee and one forearm.

Joey turned a furious shade of red that matched every foil-wrapped heart in town.

"Thank you!" she gasped. "Let me help you up!" As Joey sat up, Mel gave him an appreciative grin.

"You saved Pierre here."

A honk made them all look over toward the sound. The skateboard had flipped into the street and was lazily making its way diagonally across the two lanes.

"He would have been thrown into traffic!" Ashley squealed, Joey now upright and brushing himself off. Without warning, Ashley threw her arms around him in a huge hug, breathlessly adding, "You're a hero!"

"Kid's head is going to swell bigger than the crush he has on her," Moore muttered in Luke's ear, arms empty after finishing up in the post office.

"That bad?"

"Isn't it obvious?"

"Can I get you a coffee?" Ashley asked Joey. Mel gave Moore and Luke an amused look and winked.

"What?" Joey's voice broke across three octaves.

"I want to thank you somehow! Let's go get a coffee!"

Moore cleared his throat. "How about Joey takes you out to Greta's?"

Joey's eyes widened so far, they were about to join the back of his scalp.

"You'd do that?" he squeaked at Ashley, and Luke's gut tightened with a suppressed laugh. For a college graduate, the kid had zero game.

Then again, Luke was the last person to be commenting on *that*.

"I'd love to!" Ashley said, picking up her shopping bags and her coffee. "I already have this, but an apple fritter sounds great. And we can talk. You said you just got back from Boston?"

Joey looked at the part of his body where she was touching him.

Moore walked over and whispered something in his ear. Joey immediately offered to take Ashley's shopping bags for her.

And with that, they wandered toward Greta's, Joey twisting back to look at the dog in Mel's arms, mouthing, *Thank you*.

"I need a stiff drink after watching that," Moore declared. "Join me?" he asked Luke, then Mel.

"Can't," Mel begged off. "Capybara needs her meds."

"First time I've been stood up for a capybara. They're rodents, aren't they?"

She patted his shoulder. "Knowing you, I'm sure it won't be the last."

Bilbee's Tavern was one of the few places in town that didn't have the words Love You in the name. An old traveler's tavern that predated the founding of Luview by Luke's ancestors, it had been owned by the same family for eleven generations now. By comparison, the Luviews were newcomers.

The Bilbees and the Luviews got along just fine, but that didn't mean there hadn't been a few prickly moments over the last century and a half.

Starting with the Bilbees refusing to call their establishment the Love You Tavern.

Luke knew the legends from the late 1800s, how Jedidiah Bilbee thought it was nothing but lust and sin to shape the town around love.

Rider Bilbee was the current owner, with more heart tattoos than skin. Given his reputation as "Ride Her" Bilbee, he didn't seem to hold the same opinions about love—or its derivatives—that his ancestors once held.

Forced by the Love Committee, a town meeting subcommittee devoted to keeping everything in town love-themed, to add a heart to the tavern's sign, Rider's first version had a grizzled old goat eating a blood-gushing heart.

The head of the Love Committee at the time was Nadine, who had personally stolen the sign one early morning, hiding it at the police station. Luke had heard that Chief Anderssen had consumed an entire bottle of Pepto-Bismol that day, wondering aloud what it would taste like with vodka added.

In a compromise, Rider finally settled for the goat standing on the heart. But he'd added the tavern's tagline:

If we don't have it, you shouldn't be drinking it.

Rider's brother, Mikah, was behind the counter. A quick "hey" and a handwave were all Moore and Luke got as they walked in, Mikah quickly grabbing their favorite beers. This time of day was perfect, between lunch and dinner rushes. The place was half full, most tables filled with groups of two or four, all with shopping bags at their feet.

Two cold ones and a small table later, Moore and Luke had drained half their beers in silence, then let out twin sighs, provoking good-natured laughter. If they hadn't been born to different sets of parents, they'd have been twins.

Luke pulled out his phone. Two-forty. He had an hour before he had to get Harriet off the bus. Today there had been an all-school field trip to the Nordicbeth resort, where Harriet would take ski lessons for eight weeks this winter. He welcomed the rare day off, but had to stick to one beer.

Besides, he had a date tonight. Six p.m. His mom was coming over at five-thirty and he had to pace himself. A wide grin stretched across his face as he thought about going out to dinner, talking without Harriet around, being normal.

Normal.

Dinner dates were normal. Sweet kisses that turned hotter were normal. The buttery softness of a woman's hip resting under your palm was normal.

He craved normal.

He craved Kylie.

Speaking of whom, he typed out a quick text to her:

Miss you.

Without hesitation, he sent it, starting a cascade he couldn't undo.

It felt good.

Maybe that was the beer talking, though he didn't think so.

"Texting her?" Moore asked, the question rhetorical.

"Yep."

"Good."

Then Kell walked in.

"Look at you two slackers," he called out, bellying up to the bar. Mikah popped the top off a red sour ale, handed it over, and Kell joined Luke and Moore, dragging a metal chair over to their table. "The cop and the jeweler during the holiday rush, getting wasted."

"You nailed it, Kell. Great judge of character," Moore said with an eye roll.

Kell took a sip, then laughed. "That's why I pull poison ivy and do tree work for a living, bro. Don't deal with many people, and plants don't complain."

"Why don't you marry a ficus tree, then?"

"If you found one that kisses worth a damn, I'd be in. But I think Rachel would have something to say about *that*." Kell shot them a grin, then took another sip. "You two talking about Kylie?"

Luke gawked at him.

"Of course," Moore snickered.

"What do you think he should do?" Kell asked Moore as Luke ignored them both and finished his beer, setting the bottle on the table. How fast could he get away from this conversation?

"Go for it." Moore was peeling the label off his bottle, leaving a tiny pile of red foil on top of his coaster. He turned to Luke. "You had the biggest crush on her that summer, before she moved."

"She's my nanny, and as Darren says–"

"Don't bang the nanny," Kell and Moore intoned in unison,

earning a curious look from Janis McMurty, sipping an old fashioned with her husband, Seamus.

"Go ahead and bang her," Seamus called out. "Just wait until December 26. We want that $450!"

"You would sell your soul to the devil for $450," Janis groused at him.

"If I thought he'd pay me that much, damn right I would, woman!"

Kell lasered his gaze on his brother. "I don't get the hesitation. Harriet loves her. Kylie's friendly and fun and not hard to look at–"

"Kell," Luke warned.

"Mom invited her to Christmas–"

Moore's eyebrows shot up. "She did?"

Kell nodded, elbow nudging Luke. "Mom's in heaven. Kylie *and* Rachel for Christmas? She'll practically glow all night. So go for it. Why draw this out?"

Luke picked up on something in that last comment. "Maybe drawing it out, nice and slow, is the best approach."

Kell's face fell.

"You, too?" Luke shook his head in disgust, raising his voice. "Has anyone in this town *not* made a bet on me and Kylie?"

"No time like the present. Like... today. A hot and heavy quickie is a great start to a new relationship."

Moore tossed a balled-up piece of foil at Kell. It caught in his beard.

Luke's phone buzzed. Work. Nothing from Kylie.

It's not that she should be texting back instantly. Plenty of times she'd gone a day or two without replying, always about work.

This was different.

This was about them.

Whatever *them* meant.

"You keep looking at your phone like you expect it to sprout four legs and start walking," Kell said to him as he picked the foil out of his dark strands. "Kylie ghosting on you?"

"No."

"What'd you get her for Christmas?"

Luke's skin tingled with dread. He said a curse under his breath.

Kell and Moore started hooting.

And Luke got out of there.

Because he had some last-minute shopping to do.

And he wasn't about to do it in Love You, Maine.

Chapter Twenty-Nine

Kylie

Five people stared back at Kylie on the video conference call, all of them morphing into the same face, an imaginary frowning emoji.

They were pleasant, so it wasn't an adversarial environment. Kylie just couldn't focus.

The position: children's television production coordinator.

Location: New York City. The downtown studios of KidzdocTV.

And if she could get an offer for an on-site interview, flight and hotel and meals paid for, she could *become* one of those faces.

In due time.

Her eyes drifted to the new photo on her desk, the only thing she'd added to her apartment since Wendy had left.

A framed picture Luke had taken of her playing with Harriet, both of them dressed as fairies. Harriet's cheek was equal parts glitter and cupcake frosting, and they were grinning at each other, noses touching.

How could she give that up?

How could she leave Love You for the Big Apple?

Focus, she told herself. *This is just practice. Be yourself. They're interviewing a hundred people. Just have fun with it.*

Eyes skittering to the picture again, she laughed slightly, her smile making others on the screen grin.

Manu Jalics, the biggest name in children's programming, cleared his throat, dark eyes narrowing. "Ms. Hood?" He was impeccably groomed, with hair that was short on the sides, a shock of dark wave floating over one thick eyebrow. When he smiled, he looked like a model.

When he frowned, he looked like her failure.

"Sorry." She smiled nervously, seconds ticking by as pieces of her fought with each other inside her brain and heart. The longer she delayed giving these faces an answer, the weirder this got–and the less likely she was to be accepted. Recognized. Respected and considered worthy of their job.

Important enough to join their club.

"No problem. We were asking you about your work at Nordicbeth Resorts. Could you go into further detail about how that ties in with children's television programming?"

"Happy to explain. Let me tell you about the winter fairy camp program I created, and how it increased revenues for Nordicbeth Resorts. The concept was used as a marketing vehicle to increase family reservations," she said with a burst of confidence that made her relax. Aha. There she was. That piece of herself that went into a flow state when it came to children's media and working with kids.

Thinking about how to reach a kid while maintaining the adult perspective.

Meeting children where they needed connection and enriching their lives.

Like she did every day with Harriet now.

As she spoke, several bored interviewers began looking up from their papers at the screen, the slow migration of people on the panel from boredom to interest fueling Kylie's self-assurance.

Ah, there you *are*, she thought to herself. *Underestimated me, didn't you?*

Big mistake.

Few parts of her life generated this kind of confidence, but anything related to children was a slam dunk. By the time she finished her explanation, every member of the panel was leaning forward, completely engaged.

"It's not just about entertaining them, or even about educating them. Good children's programming seeks to do both. Great children's programming also makes children feel understood and connected to something larger than themselves," she concluded.

Everyone nodded. Something in Manu's face made her see she'd hooked him.

Her heart began to speed up.

This was everything she ever wanted.

Right?

Right?

"I like your take on it," he said. "Can you hold for a moment? Roberta will put you in a waiting room while the team has a moment alone."

"Of course," she said, the end of her reply cut off by instant change on her computer monitor as she stared back at herself, alone in the virtual "room."

They were conferencing about her future.

They were debating her as a pro or a con.

They were deciding her fate.

As each heartbeat pushed blood through her, she fought for clarity, wondering if she should just walk away, half hoping they didn't ask her to come for an in-person interview.

That would be easier, wouldn't it? No dilemma. No tension between falling for Luke and disappointing Harriet versus the vast potential New York offered.

She could say she tried and life made the choice for her.

Failure would be a welcome outcome right now.

Bzzzz

Her phone made her jolt, her face reflecting her struggle as she watched herself on the monitor. That was probably Luke again. For the last eighteen and a half hours (but who was counting?) she'd ignored his texts.

This one she indulged in reading, quickly.

Miss you, it said.

Her throat seized with emotion.

At six sharp, she knew, he'd be at her door. The date made her heart flutter, her body flush, and her mind turn to stardust. She was going on a date with Luke Luview, Number 14, Part A be damned.

Tonight was just dinner, but she knew they were leading up to more.

She *wanted* more.

"Kylie?"

She barely held back a scream as Roberta, the KidzdocTV admin, came on screen.

"Yes?" She flung her phone on the floor like it was a live spider.

"They're ready for you." The kind woman with purple hair, who looked to be about fourteen, gave her a sweet smile. "Good luck!"

"Thanks."

And then back to the panel.

Manu was smiling, too.

Kylie's heart soared.

But her gut clenched.

"Thank you so much, Kylie. We're still interviewing candidates, but we'll be in touch if you make it to the next round." He licked his lower lip, then tapped a pen on a pad of paper in front of him. "I must say, the fairy camp idea is intriguing."

"Really?" she squeaked.

"Fairies test well with kids, especially young girls. Lots of merchandising tie-ins, too."

"Right." She felt like an idiot not saying more, but this wasn't the kind of interview back-and-forth she was expecting.

He gave her the kind of polite smile busy executives flash when they're done with you. "Roberta will be in touch. Have a nice day."

And... the Zoom call ended.

Whoa.

That wasn't a yes, wasn't a no, and as she took a few deep breaths and processed it all, she felt like she'd taken a huge risk and been right.

Exactly right.

How often did that happen to her these days?

Out of an abundance of caution, she hadn't told Luke about the interview. Why borrow trouble and complexity? Now she'd had a little practice and knew she needed to work on not being nervous, but she'd made a strong pitch for her skills. She also knew the chance she'd make it to the next round was infinitesimal.

Whew.

She could breathe again.

"Plus," she said aloud, "you did it. You got an interview! Resume and cover letter can't be bad. You'll find a job eventually."

You have a job, she thought instantly.

Then her mother's voice said, *Another job that relies on the man you're dating.*

As if she'd been struck, Kylie's whole body jerked. Oh, no. She hadn't thought of it that way, but yes—just like Perry. She'd loved him and moved here, her job dependent on his family.

She was doing it again with Luke, wasn't she?

"What am I doing?" she groaned, wondering if she should have tried harder in the interview, wishing she could get these worries out of her head and just think with more clarity.

Every moment she spent with Luke was more thrilling than the last. As their time together deepened their connection, something grew between them. He was opening up to her more and more, and she was falling for him.

Was this just her pattern? Was she blindly repeating a mistake?

This was a situation that called for reaching out to Wendy, and some good takeout.

You there? she texted Wendy, then moved over to the app for Mountain Dragon for a quick lunch. Some toasted sesame oil and red bean paste wouldn't solve her problems, but mixed with rice, a nice fried egg, vegetables, and beef, it sure could help.

The drive to Mountain Dragon would be long enough that she might as well leave now, so she did, driving along roads with snow piled knee deep. As winter trudged on, the long January,

February, and March of New England still ahead, those piles would grow to her height, and in some years, far above.

Ski season was in full swing. A pang of sadness hit her. Until a few months ago, she assumed she'd be at Nordicbeth, enjoying the slopes, taking time on her days off to use the free lift ticket that came with her old job.

Skiing with the kids, directing photographers and videographers, coming up with fun programming for a high-end family resort was a blast.

Now? Now skiing was something she might do one day with Harriet, after she'd finished her lessons.

But it wasn't the same.

"No," she said aloud as she pulled into the parking lot at the Asian restaurant. "It's better."

You can't ski in New York City, a voice in her head reminded her.

It sounded like her mother.

Her stomach fluttered at the thought of actually getting the job. That was about as likely as...

Getting stuck in a charity donation bin.

Ugh.

If KidzdocTV offered her the job, she'd have to make a decision. Until that moment, though, she could keep this to herself.

Why did it feel like lying?

Their date tonight suddenly seemed different. Still eager, still wanting, she felt a sick, twisty sensation in her gut.

Hopefully, the take-out lunch would kill it.

As she got out of the car, she had to laugh, the sound coming out of her making the object of her giggles turn and look.

Colleen Luview.

"Great minds think alike!" Kylie called out as she jogged across the cleared parking lot, catching up to Luke's sister. "We have to stop meeting like this."

"No, we don't. We should meet here more often!" Colleen countered as she rushed inside to escape the bitter cold, the two entering an empty foyer.

"Colleen!" the woman at the hostess stand said, giving her a wave.

"Hey, Eun-ah! Quiet day?"

"Everyone's in town for Tuba Christmas. They'll all come in soon."

Kylie frowned. Oh. Right. Tuba Christmas. She knew Harriet had begged Luke to take her. Normally, she'd go, too, hoping to run into Luke, but right now she felt sleazy. Slimy.

Unworthy.

Stuffing her face with bi bim bap was her punishment.

"Do you know Kylie?" Colleen asked Eun-ah, who gave her a suspicious look, eyebrow cocked.

"Sure. New to town. Don't sleep with her brother yet," she added, pointing to Colleen. "Wait until February 2."

"Excuse me?"

Colleen and Eun-ah burst into laughter, and Kylie got the point. The betting pool Luke mentioned.

It was so widespread, it had reached Mountain Dragon?

Kylie gave her a wan smile as she took her bag of food. "I don't know what to say to that."

"Your blushing face says it all," Eun-ah added, patting the back of her hand before disappearing into the kitchen, leaving Colleen chuckling.

But the laughter faded fast as Colleen went quiet.

"Luke asked you out tonight. Six, right?"

"Does everyone in this town know everything about everyone else's business?" The question out of Kylie's mouth was unequivocally rhetorical.

"He asked me to babysit. Can't. Working."

"Oh. Right. He said your mom was watching Harriet tonight."

"I guess that whole 'don't bang your nanny' thing is out the window."

"Hey!"

They laughed, a comfortable feeling that quickly turned tense, making Kylie's head spin.

"I wanted to ask you something," Colleen said, her voice slow with meaning.

Assuming this was about Christmas, Kylie smiled and leaned against the wall of the foyer, close to the outside door.

"Sure."

"Are you really leaving Maine when your lease is up?"

Uh oh.

A lump formed in Kylie's throat, swift and full.

"I–"

"Because you need to understand how tender-hearted they both are."

"I, well..."

"My brother has made Harriet the center of his world. Which is how it should be. No little girl deserves to lose their mommy. And not the way we lost Amber and–" Colleen choked up.

"I'm so sorry."

Colleen sighed, long and sad, the sound one of bonding more than frustration. Lifting her eyes, she locked her gaze with Kylie's.

"Luke may have a messy house, and wash his reds with his whites and end up with pink underwear, and his shirts may get half-ironed and dinner around there is take-out or PB&J, but he also never misses a Daisy Scouts meeting. The guys at the station make sure he has time for every conference, every concert, every field trip. Luke coaches T-ball for Harriet's team, and soccer, too. He learned how to braid her hair from me and YouTube videos, and has back-up bottles of nail polish remover because Harriet loves to paint his nails."

"He's a wonderful father."

"He is." Colleen looked away. "But he's lost sight of what it means to be something other than a father. You know?"

"I guess?"

"I'll lay it all out there, because I'm not good at being subtle, Kylie: Luke likes you. It's obvious. Harriet adores you. But you're leaving soon. He told me. Two more months on your lease, and you're job hunting in New York. That's great. Really. You do you and all that. But I have to say my piece. And my piece is this: Don't jerk my little brother's heart around."

"I'm not! I would never."

"Maybe not on purpose. But you're falling for him, too. The whole town knows you two are a great match. You're both just too stupid to go for it. And I'm telling you, you either need to go for it, or walk away–but walk away before you hurt Luke and Harriet."

"I would never hurt them!"

When Kylie was younger and lived here, Colleen was the older, smarter girl who had more common sense than charisma, and who seemed to know who she was long before any of Kylie's friends had a clue about life. Three years older than Luke, she was off to college the year The Divorce ruined everything Kylie loved most.

And took her away from the boy she loved even more.

She softened.

"Do you want to stay?"

"This is a lot, Colleen."

"I see. That's your answer."

"I didn't say yes or no."

"You did. Just not in those words."

"For someone who doesn't know me, you make some huge assumptions."

"I don't need to know you. I know Luke and Harriet. I knew Amber," she said fiercely, pain in her eyes. "I can't watch my brother and niece lose someone they're attached to like that again. It would break them. No one's allowed to break people I love. A cruel accident did it once. I can't let you do it again."

"I–"

Colleen's head reared back, as if from shock, then her steely features softened, her palm going up in a gesture that said, *Wait*.

As she took a deep breath, Kylie's whole body tensed, head beginning to pound.

Conflicted eyes met hers, half apologetic, half fierce. "That comment was out of bounds. I'm being presumptuous. I'm also overprotective."

"For good reason."

A dip of the head acknowledged her words. "Thank you for that. You're being gracious. I came on too strong." The skin between her eyes folded into wrinkles at the bridge of her nose as she visibly wrestled with too many emotions.

"It's okay."

"I just love them so much."

"I see that."

"And when they hurt, I hurt."

"I understand."

"Do you?" Colleen tilted her head, studying Kylie. "Do you really? Because it seems like you want it both ways."

"I do want it both ways," Kylie admitted. "But I'm grown up enough to know that's not how this works."

"Mom said she invited you to Christmas and you accepted."

"I did."

"In our family, that means something. You're not just a guest she's inviting to be polite."

"Is this an audition?" Kylie joked.

Colleen laughed. "No. Not like that. But... if you join us, it's not casual, you know?"

"I know."

"And you're still coming?"

"Yes."

"And you're still job hunting in New York?"

If silence had a sound, it would sound like her heart screaming.

Disappointment made the outer corners of Colleen's eyes turn down even more. She chewed on the inside of her lip, taking a deep breath before walking away.

As she opened the door, a blast of icy wind made Kylie gasp.

And breathe in cold steel.

Chapter Thirty

Luke

Dinner reservations? Done.

Business casual pants and a jacket? Yep.

Wallet with cash, credit cards, and... a condom?

Indeed.

And probably overkill.

Sleeping with Kylie on the first date wasn't what he planned, but he'd been a Boy Scout. Eagle Scout, even.

And that meant being prepared.

"Daddy, you smell really good!" Harriet lifted her arms for him to pick her up. She was getting big for this, but he did. She sniffed his neck. "Why do you smell so good?"

"It's called cologne."

"Why don't you wear clone all the time?"

His mother's laughter from the kitchen didn't help matters.

Ignoring his daughter's question, Luke set her down and shot his mom a look, not that it did him any good.

"Why's Gamma laughing so hard?"

"Because she's a wee bit wicked."

"I wanna be wicked!"

"Here." His mom held out a sparkly fairy muffin from Kylie's most recent batch, baked with Harriet. "Go crazy being wicked with some sugar."

Before Luke could object, Harriet's face was smeared with edible glitter and delicious buttercream frosting.

"Gamma, when I'm a grown-up, I'm getting wicked hitched at Love You Forever!" The town's 24/7 drive-thru wedding chapel had a slogan:

We got wicked hitched in Love You, Maine!

The bumper sticker was wildly popular.

"You're the one who has to spend time with her all sugared up," he said to his mother as his child disappeared under smears of sweetness.

His mom smiled. "But you're the one who has to take over when you're done with your date. Gamma gets to spoil her."

"You were so strict with us when we were kids! You've fed Harriet more sugar in her little life than we four kids got, combined, the whole time you raised us."

In response, his mother grabbed another muffin and took an enormous bite out of it, licking frosting off her fingers.

Wuff!

Jester's muffled bark made them both turn, just as someone knocked on the door. Luke crossed the room to answer it.

Annabeth Khouri.

Carrying a cookie container.

"Hi," he said, unable to hold back his surprise.

Instead of a similar greeting, he got a slow crawl of her eyes, from the ends of the hair on his head down to the tips of his shined dress shoes.

With a few pauses in between.

"Don't you look amazing. Why so dressed up?" Arm outstretched, she pressed the container into his midsection before he could easily grab it.

"I–"

"Who's at the door, Luke?" his mom called out, appearing around the corner with a dish towel, wiping wet hands. Her mouth formed an O of surprise.

"Annabeth!" Her eyes cut to the container in Luke's hands. "What a surprise!"

"I hope I wasn't interrupting anything?" The way her voice rose made it clear she wanted every detail, in triplicate, and that she was beginning to get an idea that didn't align with her claim on Luke.

A claim she had no right to.

Inwardly, he sighed. On the outside, though, he took command.

"I was just about to leave," he said directly to Annabeth. "What's up?"

"Going anywhere interesting?"

What was up were his mom's eyebrows. Didn't anyone in Love You, Maine, have anything better to do than watch his love life–or lack thereof–unfold before their eyes?

Didn't people have Netflix or Prime Video to watch? Who decided *The Luke Love Chronicles* were part of your regularly scheduled programming?

Oh. Right.

Once he became Poor Luke, he was town property.

"I am. What's this?" he asked, tapping the top.

"I heard Harriet likes edible glitter. Thought I'd make some fun chocolate heart cookies for her."

As she spoke the words *chocolate* and *cookies*, Harriet magically appeared, grabbing the container. "Thank you, Ms. Khouri!" she squealed, before plopping down in front of the television.

His mom took the container away, laughing.

His phone buzzed.

A glance showed the text was a reminder about his dinner reservation.

"Thank you," he said sincerely to Annabeth. "That's really sweet."

"I heard you like lemon bars. I put some in there, too."

Ah.

Now he understood.

This wasn't a normal "Annabeth tries to get Luke interested" social visit.

This was about territory. Annabeth viewed Kylie as competition.

Which she wasn't.

Because he wasn't a prize someone won.

He was a man who had already made a choice.

"I do like them." He smiled, then looked over her head as he reached for his wool dress coat. "Now, if you'll excuse me, I–"

"Your cologne is lovely."

"It's just aftershave."

"And your dress coat! I don't think I've ever seen you looking so sophisticated."

"Mmm." He grabbed his keys. She was blocking him. His mom was now openly watching them, munching on what looked like one of Annabeth's cookies.

Harriet wasn't the only Luview getting sugared up tonight.

Annabeth laughed. "It's almost as if you're going on a date, Luke."

He blinked.

"Good catch, Annabeth. Because I am. I really appreciate the cookies, but I'll be late if I don't leave now." Touching her elbow, he tried to gently give her the signal to move.

She flinched, face twisting with emotion. "I was joking!"

"I'm not," he said kindly.

"Who–what–who are you going out with? Not that nanny of yours!"

Her outraged tone had a tinge of disgust in it that made him see red.

"Goodbye, Annabeth."

As he walked out the door, he realized his mom would have to deal with the mess.

Served her right for mocking him.

Backing out of the driveway, he saw them talking inside, his mom offering her a seat at the dining table. If anyone could soothe hurt feelings, it was Deanna Luview.

And if anyone could milk a conflict for attention, it was Annabeth.

On the drive to Kylie's, he let himself rant internally, his mind going to other ways he could have responded, and projecting ahead to when he would see Annabeth's mother, Nadine, at work.

Fortunately, Nadine was a consummate professional. Never, ever had she said a word about Annabeth coming over to his house before church, or suggested they date.

Didn't make it any less complicated, though.

By the time he pulled into Kylie's driveway, the residue from the weird interaction had worn off. Excitement at seeing Kylie dominated now. A lightness he hadn't felt in years soaked into him, the scent of his own cologne making him grin.

He cleaned up nice.

Who knew?

Kylie was at the door before he could ring the bell, dressed in a simple black, high-neck dress that hugged every curve.

And made his hands itch to touch her.

"Come in. It's freezing!" she said, ushering him over the threshold. As he walked in, she turned her back to him, and holy smokes.

The neckline in the back dipped way down, with a red silk accent along the dip. Her shoes were fire-engine red, and matched her lips.

At home, he'd wondered if the suit jacket and shined shoes were too formal, but Kylie matched him perfectly. They were on the same page.

This was a real date. A grown-up date.

And while dates were supposed to end with a kiss, why not start with one, too?

Before he could reach for her, she turned, eyes going wide, giving him a look over that he enjoyed far, far more than the one Annabeth had inflicted on him.

"Wow! You look—*wow.* That coat. Your cologne." She inhaled deeply, then gave him a flirty smile. "It's almost like we're mature adults being sophisticated."

Luke made his move, closing the gap between them, his hand sliding to the bare expanse of skin on her back.

"Almost," he murmured as their lips touched, her hands looping around his neck, the embrace tightening as they kissed.

And kissed.

And *kissed*.

Maybe being a well-prepared Boy Scout wasn't such a bad idea, after all.

Bzzzz

"Your pants are vibrating," she said.

"It's that obvious?"

Joyful laughter poured out of her. "I think that's your phone. If not, you're scaring me. Or exciting me. A little of both."

His turn to laugh. The buzz was another reminder about their dinner reservations.

"The Food Alchemist says we need to be on time or they'll give our table away."

"You got us a reservation there?"

"Is that a problem?"

"No! It's amazing! They're so booked out. I heard there's a three-month wait."

"I know someone who knows someone."

"In this town, Luke, when you're a Luview, the people you know are all blood related somehow."

"True."

"This is going to be so much fun."

"Already is." He kissed her temple softly, hand caressing her back. "You look extraordinary."

She pulled away, eyes serious. "Number 14, Part A."

"Stupid clause. Let's nullify it."

"How?"

He cleared his throat suggestively. "I can think of one way."

"Luke!" The blush on the tips of her ears told him what he needed to know. They were on the same page about sex, too.

Not yet.

Too soon.

But there was plenty of territory to explore between a kiss and a bed.

"We didn't plan for this, Kylie. When I had my lawyer draw up that employment contract, it was because I thought I'd have really young nannies I'd never dream of becoming involved with. Or because I wanted strict boundaries between us. No confusion."

"Confusion?"

Annabeth's appearance at his door half an hour ago was the very definition of confusion, but he didn't want to think about her right now.

Bzzzz

"We're going to be late," she whispered, moving to get her coat. The glimpse of the deep dive of fabric on the back of her dress took his breath away.

Reaching for her coat, he took it, opened it, and offered it to her. It was black wool with big buttons, not a ski parka after all. Her arms slid in with such grace. Kylie reached for a thick red scarf, carefully donned a red wool toque, and reached for black leather gloves.

And with that, they were out the door, down her apartment's stairs, and into his car, Luke opening her door for her, Kylie grinning as he did it.

Courtliness wasn't in his nature, but she sure did bring it out.

And make him want to offer her more.

As they drove to The Food Alchemist, a small farm-to-table place just on the edge of downtown Luview, out by the old hot springs, they listened to an old Ella Fitzgerald mp3 he thought might be perfect for the date. Something soft and smooth, comforting and pleasant, but cool, not staid.

"You've never been to this restaurant?"

"Are you kidding me?" Her eyes were shining. "No. Perry talked about it once–" She clapped her hand over her mouth, eyes wide with regret. "Sorry."

"For what?"

"Talking about him."

"Why can't you talk about him?" *Even though I think he's a jerk*, he thought but didn't say.

"Who talks about their ex on a date?"

"Fair enough." Luke cleared his throat, nose tickled by her perfume. It made him want to bury his nose in her hair.

And bury himself in her.

"But we can talk about Amber, of course."

He tensed. "Why would we?"

"Because, well–it's different. I didn't want you to feel like you couldn't. Just because I'm not talking about Perry and–oh! I did it again. I said his name. I'm sorry. I–"

With his free hand, he grabbed hers.

"Kylie. Breathe. It's okay."

She let out a huge puff of air. "I'm really bad at dating."

"That makes two of us."

"What? You're great! You smell so good. And you look so hot when you dress like that. I can't believe you asked me out."

"I can't believe you said yes."

"I feel like I'm fifteen again, Luke. This is crazy."

"We're not those kids anymore."

"I know. I think there are two Kylies in my head. The one on that pier, and the one in this car."

He squeezed her hand lightly before returning both of his to the steering wheel for safety. "I like them both."

Because the restaurant was on the side of town closer to Kylie's place, right on the edge of the hot springs, the drive was fairly short. Luke caught someone backing out of a parking spot just in time, scoring a place right in front of the main door. Parking wasn't usually a problem in late December in Luview, but The Food Alchemist had exactly twelve tables and only eight spots in their little parking area.

Once in a while, the timing was off.

Decorated for the season, the cottage looked like a Christmas wonderland. You couldn't tell in the dark night, but it was painted the palest pink with white trim, darker pink shutters and white rocking chairs finishing the country look. Strings of white incandescent bulbs stretched in long lines from lamp posts in the parking lot to the edge of the cottage's roof, lighting the walk from car to restaurant with an ethereal glow.

Luke took Kylie's hand in his as they entered the small restaurant. Bo Bilbee instantly greeted them. All of seventeen, he was like a male puppy: nothing but big hands, big feet, and super eager to please.

But awkward. So awkward.

"Oh! It's you!" he blurted out, eyes glued to Kylie.

Luke waited for it.

One.

Two.

Three.

A bright red blush covered Bo's face like a relief map being filled in.

"Luview. Reservation for two," Luke said in an authoritative voice that made Bo literally jump in place, startled, as if he'd only noticed Luke just now.

"Right. Of course. Welcome to The Food Alchemist," he said formally. "Have you folks been here before?"

Luke fixed him with a flat stare.

"Why are you acting like you don't know me, Bo? You know I was here for my dad's birthday two months ago. You served the bread."

"Uh," he said, glancing at Kylie, who gave a polite smile. "Training. We're trained to say that. We can't assume we know someone's been here, so we ask everyone."

"LUKE!" Sheila Bilbee, Bo's mother, called out his name, waving slightly. "We have your table, right on the water. Come on back."

Clapping Bo on the back exactly once, Luke left him at the hostess stand, careful to put his hand on the small of Kylie's back. The possessive gesture was unnecessary, but it sure felt good.

The table was perfect. Sheila and Blake Bilbee opened The Food Alchemist a good ten years ago, buying the old broken-down information booth that the town abandoned decades ago and turning it into a fine little restaurant. Unlike the taverns in town, which served pub food, or coffee shops and diners, The Food Alchemist had a scratch kitchen, and Blake was devoted to clean cooking. No preservatives, no chemicals, and as much local produce, meat, and dairy as possible.

Blake had trained at the Culinary Institute of America, and the place got rave reviews from Zagat's and the various food magazines and websites.

None of that mattered to Luke as he helped Kylie out of her coat, breathing in her scent. Sheila took both of their coats and Luke held his date's chair as she sat.

His hands shook a little.

What was wrong with him?

Bo appeared with water, a tray of lemon slices, and various kinds of bread. Pouring olive oil, he doctored it with ground pepper and something that looked like red flakes, then disappeared with a partial bow.

Kylie looked at Luke across the table, her smile softening, sinking deeper and deeper into an intimacy between them that made his heart simultaneously gallop and relax. She reached for a piece of bread and dipped it in the oil, her other hand cupped underneath it. As she bit into it, her face showed how much she enjoyed the flavor.

He loved watching her experience pleasure.

"Good?"

"Mmmm."

"I'll take that as a yes." Soon he joined her, and the quiet between them as they ate was a peaceful one.

Until Bo arrived to tell them the specials.

"For our fish this evening, we have wild-caught North Atlantic salmon in a reduced fig and salt licorice sauce, with grilled fennel and chipotle-lime, with a hint of maple. For our land meat, we have," he said, brow twisting as he clearly forgot his script. A tiny note tucked into his sleeve came to the rescue, cheat notes making Luke smother a grin.

"We have beef bourguignon in a rich red wine sauce, served with sauteed mushrooms, caramelized onion and pork belly lardons, and as always, Mom's prime rib with gratin dauphinois and roasted asparagus." Bo winced. "I mean, *the chef's* prime rib."

"That all sounds amazing," Kylie declared.

"You look amazing," Luke replied.

Bo skedaddled.

And Luke reached across the table for Kylie's hand.

Her eyes swept the room in an arc. "People will see us."

"Good. Let them."

"We're really doing this?"

His thumb found a soft spot between her knuckles. "Am I doing it wrong?"

"No!" Her chin dipped down, big eyes looking up at him, fingers tightening against his thumb. "Absolutely not."

"Good. Because I haven't been on a date in forever.

Wondered if I'd forgotten how."

"I think it's like riding a bike."

"That's so much easier!"

"Look at you two lovebirds," Blake Bilbee said, suddenly next to them, handing out menus. Blake was two years older than Dennis, so while they were cousins, Luke had never crossed paths with him in school. He and Sheila had gotten pregnant with Bo when they were still pretty young, but they'd stuck it out, carefully working their way to their shared goal: success in the restaurant world and the freedom of owning The Food Alchemist.

Didn't hurt that her dad was rolling in it after selling some land to developers just outside of Luview, and bankrolled the restaurant. But Luke knew Blake and Sheila hadn't had it easy, and were good people.

"Cut it out," Luke grumped at him, Kylie suppressing a smile.

"Hi! I'm Kylie," she said to Blake, who looked at the hand she was offering like it was a dead snake.

"I'd have to be comatose not to know who you are." He winked at her, then took her in just carefully enough to make Luke's hackles start to rise.

"Let me guess," Blake continued. "You're a salmon."

"I'm a... what?"

"A salmon. When you eat a fine meal, you always order salmon."

"How did you know?"

"It's a gift."

"He's right," she said to Luke. "What about him?"

"Luke? Luke's a prime rib guy. Every time."

Handing him the menu, Luke shook his head. "Why bother with these?" he said as Blake took Kylie's. "Why don't you just tell people what they want?"

"Life works that way? I can do that? Great." Blake shot Luke a mischievous grin. "Then don't officially get together until January 6. That $450 could pay for part of an espresso machine upgrade."

Before Luke could growl at him, the guy was gone, snickering.

An epic eye roll from Kylie made Luke burst into laughter he didn't know he could access so quickly.

"I think we need to find out the range of dates for this betting pool and pick one nobody took, no matter how long it takes."

"You sound like a sure thing." He took a sip of his water with the hand that wasn't currently enjoying caressing hers.

"What if we wait two years and show them all?"

A spit take on the first date was definitely not the best way to start a relationship.

"I think there has to be a better way we can all get what we need," he said carefully, her warm amusement making them both hold eye contact.

Teenage Luke and Kylie couldn't hold a candle to this.

A wave of emotion washed over him.

This was real.

This was happening.

And it felt better than he ever imagined.

For two years, he'd held his heart back, never wanting to let it out of the safe space he'd slowly carved out inside himself. Always mourning Amber, that first year had been torture. Focusing on Harriet was safe. Ignoring the women who came on to him was safe. Being a good police officer, a good neighbor, a good son, a good brother–it meant that he never took risks with his heart.

And then he found Kylie Hood trapped in a steel donation bin.

As it turned out, using those bolt cutters on the lock that night hadn't just been about releasing her from a prison she didn't mean to be in.

It was about unlocking his heart, too.

"Luke?"

"Mmm?" Her hand moved, fingers threading in his on the table.

"Thank you."

"For what?"

"Violating Number 14, Part A."

"Darren is going to give me so much flack for this."

"Because you're breaking the Don't Bang Your Nanny clause?" she asked, the tips of her ears blushing.

Just then, Bo appeared with their salads, his timing flawless, the phrase "bang your nanny" floating in the air like a devilish Cupid with a very naughty mind.

Red suited Bo's face. Good thing the kid was born in Love You, Maine. He fit right in.

Pretending she hadn't said a word, Kylie speared a piece of fennel and Parmesan, and began eating. Luke joined in. Bo disappeared.

And for five minutes, they ate in sweet harmony.

Twelve tables meant The Food Alchemist was a very small bistro, designed to be intimate and cozy, but the food–the food was anything but.

It was wild and free, uninhibited and yet carefully curated.

The way life should taste.

"Mmmmm," Kylie moaned, the sound pleasing him. "This is heaven. What's in the salad dressing?"

Licking his lower lip, he took a moment, then said, "Lemon. And something chive-like. Green shallots? The lemon is different, like the lemons we had in Amalfi, when I was studying in Italy."

"You have quite the palate, tasting different lemons that way!"

"I prefer plain old oil and vinegar on salad, though," he admitted.

"Nothing wrong with that. My favorite is ginger dressing, like the kind they use at Mountain Dragon."

"Want some wine? I could order a bottle. Or a glass, since you're having fish and I'm having beef. Red for me, white for you? Or a rosé?"

Her eyes narrowed, surprising him. "You know," she replied slowly, lifting her fork to her mouth but pausing before taking a bite, "I think I want a clear head for tonight. Wine another time?"

"Deal."

The rest of the salad course passed quietly, but the tables around them filled up, the other coveted spot overlooking the water taken by Tim, the postmaster, and his wife, June. They gave a wave, then huddled heads.

"I heard her say January 26," Kylie whispered

conspiratorially.

Luke just sighed and wished he had that glass of wine, after all.

Fortunately for him and Kylie, the other tables filled with out-of-towners, tourists shopping for the holidays in Love You. Places like The Food Alchemist drew a different crowd, something that made his brother's girlfriend, Rachel, very excited as she settled into her new role as director of business development for the town. New business meant expanded opportunities for the tiny town.

Luke, Kell, and their family liked the emphasis on *tiny*.

"I thought you'd spend Christmas with your mom," he said, venturing into a topic he'd been wondering about for a bit. "Not that you aren't welcome with us," he added hastily.

A genuine smile greeted him. "No offense taken. Mom isn't easy to be around when Wendy's not there."

"Ah. Right. Paris."

"Every young woman's dream."

"Is it yours? You ever been?"

"No. You?"

"Yes. Amber and I–" He cut himself off with a sharp inhale.

"It's fine. She's part of you, Luke. Part of who you are. I want to hear all about Paris. Amber included."

"After what we know now?"

"Why would that change anything? She was just a kid. We were kids. I don't hold it against her."

"Neither do I," he said, marveling at the woman across the table from him.

"Good. So tell me about Paris."

"It's one long blur of great wine, amazing fruit and cheese from the markets, and a shocking amount of bread."

"Your stomach is your memory bank for the trip?"

"Of course. Same with Rome. The pasta, the espresso with lemon peel, the–"

"Sounds delicious," Sheila interrupted, delivering Luke's plate with a flourish. "We do have great espresso for later, and I can twist lemon zest like no one's business if it'll make you feel more like you're in Italy, Luke." The wink made him laugh.

"I'm good. I like where I am." His eyes held Kylie's gaze for a beat.

Sheila's signature prime rib hit his olfactory nerve and he groaned as Kylie's salmon was set before her, perfectly cooked, making him jealous for a split second.

"This looks incredible," Kylie said, and Sheila beamed before she disappeared into the kitchen.

Good food. Great company. A promising future with Kylie.

What more could he want?

Horseradish sauce, actually. Sheila had set a ramekin next to his plate.

Life could not be more perfect.

"Oh, wow," Kylie moaned through a bite of her fish. "This is extraordinary. I haven't had salmon this good since I was in Seattle."

"Never been. I imagine it's nothing but coffee and the world's biggest store."

"And Pike Market! And the Cascades. I'd love to go back."

"I'd love to go with you."

The tilt of her head changed as she swallowed. Kylie reached for his hand.

"And you could show me Paris someday."

"I'm going to hold you to that, Kylie."

"Good. But we can't let these dinners get cold. That would be criminal. I'd have to perform a citizen's arrest on you, Officer Luview. Don't make me put handcuffs on you."

He cleared his throat and said, "That's my line, Kylie."

Fanning herself with her napkin, she laughed. "Is it getting hot in here?"

"Must be all the spice."

Digging into the cuisine, they stopped the flirting for a while, the rhythm of their time together finding its pace between them. Luke felt some piece of himself downshift, as if he'd been revving too high, taking too much out of him. The low, steady hum of goodness he felt from Kylie was directed at him now.

Not just his daughter.

Him.

A vision of a future together made his throat go tight with

emotion. Just watching her as she enjoyed dinner was a delight, in and of itself.

Could a heart really burst from too much happiness? The edges of his pressed hard against his ribs, finally unbound.

Finally ready to explore a whole new world.

"I am stuffed," Kylie declared as she ate her last bite.

"Member of the Clean Plate Club, I see."

"Hope you didn't want to share a dessert, Luke, because I can't." Leaning back in her chair, she patted her belly. The movement reminded him so much of his father at holiday dinners that he burst out laughing.

"What?"

"Unbuckle your belt and you're basically my dad, every Christmas and Easter."

"I have never been on a date before where the guy compared me to his *dad*."

"I told you I'm bad at this."

Bo quietly removed their empty plates and disappeared as Luke took a deep breath and assessed the scene. The other tables were filled with people eating, smiling, or engaged in deep conversation.

"Are you sure you don't want dessert?" he asked her.

"You're a sadist. A food sadist."

"Normally, people only call me a sadist when I'm issuing them a speeding ticket."

"Let me guess. They're always from New York."

"Nope, lots of Bostonians, or someone from Montreal. That's how I learned to curse in French."

Just then, Blake appeared, hands on his hips. "Dessert?"

"Too full," Luke replied.

"Coffee?"

Kylie shook her head. "Not this late. I'm good, actually."

She was more than good.

Blake's chin jutted up. "Gotcha. Hope the meal was as outstanding as I know it was?"

"You're humble." Luke took a sip of his water and cocked an eyebrow at Blake.

"Am I wrong?"

"No," Luke conceded. "That's why I brought Kylie here. Best restaurant in town–best restaurant in Maine, actually."

Magic words like that cracked Blake's face open in a genuine smile.

With a flourish, he presented the check and walked away. Luke reached for it, his hand colliding with Kylie's.

Electricity coursed through his fingers, and not just from her touch.

From actual shock.

"What are you doing?" he asked as he peeled the check out of her hands.

"I'm–"

"No."

"Hey!"

Reaching for his wallet, Luke took care of the bill with cash. "First of all, I asked you out, so I'm paying."

"But–"

"Second of all, if word got back to Deanna Luview that one of her sons let their date pay, she'd turn into a nuclear reactor. I don't need that kind of radioactive fallout in my life."

"That's sexist. Does the same rule apply to Colleen?"

Surprised by her words, and trying not to concede the point, Luke stood, walked around to the back of her chair, and leaned down to whisper, "Let's not have our first fight in public."

Amused, throaty sounds from Kylie made him smile, and he was happy to have a moment to take a deep inhale of her neck. Perfume, yes, but something more. A warm, vanilla, home-baked, delightful scent.

He could smell her forever.

"Thank you, Luke, for a lovely dinner," she said as he pulled her chair out for her, earning nods of approval from Tim and June. Within twenty minutes, everyone in Luview would know every sip, every touch, every bite they'd taken.

Spies. Small towns were nothing but spy academies.

And Luke knew very well that his mom and dad would eat up every last morsel of gossip.

They said their goodbyes to Bo and Sheila, wrapped up carefully for the weather, then stood in the cold night, sharp air piercing their lungs. Luke took her gloved hand in his and said, "Go for a walk?"

"Sounds great. I need to burn off some of the calories."

"You don't need to burn off anything, Kylie." He took the chance to wrap his arm around her waist. It was a waist covered in layers of fabric, but he felt the gentle swell of her hip, and she leaned into him.

Heading out of the parking lot, they took a right, toward the smattering of shops and restaurants leading to the famous hot springs. People walked along the sidewalk in twos and fours. One couple was headed toward them, the man tall and imperious, the woman dressed in a real fur coat, holding his arm.

"Oh, no! Come here." She grabbed Luke's arm and yanked him into a small area with benches.

"What's wrong?"

"That couple ahead of us? They're Perry's parents."

"Tommy and Kris? I know them. What's—oh. Right." His brow tightened as his brain caught up to Kylie's reaction. "You're afraid of them?"

"No, just... it's uncomfortable. After Perry dumped me, they laid me off from my job at Nordicbeth. I think they did it because they didn't want the complication."

"You mean they did it because Perry told them to."

She shrugged.

Anger swelled in him. "Kylie?

"Yeah?"

"Take my arm."

"What?"

Moving her gloved hand, he placed it in the crook of his elbow, and walked them both back to the sidewalk, jaw tight, eyes fixed ahead on the approaching couple.

"Take my arm. You have nothing to be ashamed of. We're going to continue our walk, Perry's parents be damned. No way I'm letting anyone make you feel lesser, Kylie. Never."

And with that, they marched forward, Kylie's shoulders squaring, nodding firmly as she said:

"Right. Never."

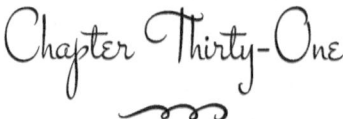

Chapter Thirty-One

Kylie

Every time Perry had taken Kylie to dinner with Tommy and Kris, back when they were together, she'd come away from the event with a head full of comments that could be interpreted two different ways: neutrally, or with bite.

Over time, she realized that there were lots of teeth in Perry's family.

Lots.

And boy, did they know how to sink them, deeply, into your weakest spot.

"Tommy!" Luke called out, his voice confident, with a deep timbre that instantly made Kylie feel safer.

"Luke? That you? How's it go... ing?" The change in Tommy's voice came as he looked at Kylie, his wife gripping his arm as Tommy leaned toward Luke, the two men shaking hands.

"Kylie?" Kris said with a light laugh, eyes cunning. "How are you?"

Luke moved an inch closer to her, the nonverbal cue clear: She was just fine.

"I'm good. And you?"

"We just had a wonderful meal at Bilbee's. Who ever says that?" she chortled. "They have a guest chef from New York visiting for the holiday brunch, and the food was divine. Gastro-pub—a special, invitation-only event."

Kylie just smiled and nodded.

And waited.

"Didn't expect to run into you here, and certainly not with a police officer," Tommy said, addressing Kylie, eyes on Luke. "You arresting her for doing something wrong?"

"I'm thoroughly enjoying her delightful company," Luke said, unblinking.

"I thought you moved," Kris said. "Back to Iowa? Indiana? Wherever your mom lives."

"Kylie's one of our own," Luke answered, her own words stuck in her throat, crouched behind a fortified wall of fear she didn't understand. It was just there.

"One of what?"

"I lived here until I was fifteen. Born at the local hospital," she finally managed, tilting her head in contemplation as Kris shot her a carefully cultivated look of boredom.

"I had no idea!"

"Of course you did. I told you the first time we met," Kylie replied with a sweet-as-pie smile, finding her backbone.

Kris's eyes turned cold.

"I can't be bothered to remember all the details of Perry's dates," Kris replied.

Luke opened his mouth to say something, but Kylie squeezed once to signal to him, *I've got this.*

Never the type to say the exact right thing at the exact right moment, Kylie typically fumbled, then spent the next few hours after a conflict beating herself up, thinking of all the retorts she could have come back with. Luke's steady defense made a difference.

Or maybe she just didn't care anymore what Perry's parents thought.

"I was with him for seven years."

Kris just gave a single-shoulder shrug.

"I understand, Kris," Kylie said, leaning closer to pat the

woman's hand, the gesture warm but also a power move. "Remembering that anyone but you exists is hard."

Tommy cleared his throat.

"How dare you–"

Luke pulled Kylie forward, past them, as he said, "Goodnight, Tommy and Kris."

Heart slamming in her throat, Kylie stopped, turned around, and said, "By the way, Perry's blowing through his trust fund. Maybe you wouldn't bother to notice that, either. Not that I care, but you might want to know."

Luke leaned down and whispered, "Ouch."

Shaking, she didn't say a word until they made the right turn toward the famous hot springs. Then she slumped against him, pure fury pumping through her.

"Those jerks! They can't even be civil to me in public!"

He brushed her hair off her face. "You dished it right back."

"Then why do I feel simultaneously triumphant and awful?"

"That's what standing up for yourself feels like."

"I know how to stand up for myself and not feel this way, though. What is it about them that makes me shake and stammer and feel so afraid?"

"Everyone has strange triggers they don't understand."

"You don't."

"Sure do."

"Like what?"

"My kid walking on the side of the road where there's no sidewalk."

"You have a reason for that, Luke. A very sad, good reason I understand now."

"And I'll bet Perry's parents–and Perry, from the sound of it–kept you on edge so they could feel better about themselves. Enough time spent in that kind of environment re-wired you a little differently."

Reaching around her waist, he pulled her close, the hug forcing her to release a long breath she didn't realize she was holding.

"That was weird," she muttered, instead of thanking him, which was what she meant to say.

"Eh. They're full of themselves. Folks like that consider themselves above the town, but they sure do love the money Love You brings to the ski resorts."

"You're 100 percent right. They mock Love You."

"Everyone around us does."

"And it doesn't bother you?"

"That's on them, not us. Not me. If someone doesn't like how this town works, they can just drive on by."

"And they didn't like me."

"Ah. Is that what it's about? You never felt accepted by them?"

"Yes."

"Then I'm sorry they rejected you. Fired you, even, when Perry broke it off with you. But you know what? I'm grateful to them."

Surprise made Kylie pull back.

"What?"

He slipped his arm around her shoulders and began guiding her toward the steamy water. "If Perry hadn't met—what do you call her?"

"Systina the Wonder... well, you don't want to know the rest. Starts with F."

"Systina the Wonderfart?"

She giggled. "Let's go with that."

"If he hadn't been so shallow, and hadn't met her, and hadn't broken up with you, and had done the right thing and come for his stuff, you wouldn't have been dumping it in that donation bin, and you never would have gotten stuck."

"That's a huge gratitude stretch."

"I'm going with it. And if his parents hadn't been assholes and fired you, I could never have hired you to be Harriet's nanny." His voice softened as they approached the water's edge, the air magical. Luke paused and looked down at her. "And we wouldn't have this."

"This?"

"*This.*"

Bending at the knees, he crouched, took off his glove, and dragged his fingertips along the water's surface.

Sheer amusement made her nearly guffaw.

"Come on, Kylie. Touch the water, too."

Joining him, she did as asked, always surprised by the water's warmth, even in the dead of winter.

"This is such a cliché," she whispered, though why she kept her voice down was a mystery, even to her. Not another soul was anywhere nearby.

"Clichés exist for a reason."

"That's a clichéed response, too."

"How about I kiss you now and just become a stereotype?"

And then he did, their ungloved hands freezing cold, only the fingertips warmed by the hot springs. Both of them were carefully balanced as they crouched, his lips soft, his hot breath a mist that warmed her nose.

Every kiss they'd shared had been better than the last, but this one–oh, it was so much more.

Until practicality hit them both.

"We're going to freeze or fall in if we keep this up. I prefer to respond to emergencies, not be one," Luke said as he stood without effort, still holding her around the waist with his free arm, body balanced with an athleticism she admired.

And needed right now, because she was wearing high heels, after all, on the edge of a body of water, in late December, in Maine.

What were they thinking?

Step by step, they moved to a safer spot. Kylie's body was glowing from the inside out, although even so, she couldn't defy nature. Her fingers felt like icicles and, against her better judgment, she shoved her hand into her glove, the wetness a problem if they stayed outside for too long.

Mist wafted up between them, the steam rising enough to make her feel enveloped by warmth and love, the stark contrast of the icy cold with the water's magic so surreal.

Surreal and beautiful.

"You came back, Kylie," Luke said, his hand still ungloved but dry, cold fingers brushing her hair away from her neck. A shiver shot through her, body full of too many emotions to contain.

"I did. Not quite the way I always imagined."

"You imagined coming back to Luview?"

"Are you kidding me? It's all I thought about for years. I dreamed about this place. Cried myself to sleep every night for a year. Wondered why you ghosted on me..." Her voice faded in recognition of what they'd learned earlier about Amber's role in that.

"I didn't know Luview meant so much to you."

"It's the only place where I ever felt like I belonged. Until everything happened with my father."

"What do you mean?"

"My mom left for a reason."

"You said it was because she was embarrassed."

"She was."

"Why would what your dad did have an impact on you? People here aren't that small minded. No one would ever reject you because your dad had an affair."

"Mom always said she could handle the cheating, but she couldn't handle being pitied by every single person in town."

He reared back. "I deeply understand that feeling. Half the time, I think my full name is Poor Luke."

"Right. So I know that what my dad did wouldn't affect me here–at least, I know it intellectually. But..."

"I want you to know it here." Luke's palm pressed flat over her heart, and she reached up to cover his hand. Breathing together, they made their own mist, each exhale a cloud that lifted and dispersed, as if taking the pain of lost chances and moving joy and potential into the now.

Now, they were together.

Now, she was part of Luview.

Now.

Kylie's jaw began to twitch, her teeth starting to chatter. Luke gave her a quick kiss on the lips, then turned them both back toward the street.

"You're cold. Let's get you home."

No argument here.

The walk back to The Food Alchemist was expeditious, no meandering allowed. Luke's car was ice cold but he turned the heat on full blast. As they pulled out of the parking lot and turned toward her place, it hit her.

What was next?

They weren't fifteen and seventeen years old.

He'd been to her apartment and they'd shared hot kisses. She'd spent enough time with him to feel every drop of chemistry—so much chemistry, they might as well be a discovery lab—and so now the question loomed.

Would they make love?

The night was perfect. She didn't want it to end. Inviting him in to have a drink made sense, and was what she wanted, but the commitment of sex was a new level.

And then there was that pesky interview in New York she wasn't talking about.

Sleeping with Luke was an act she didn't take lightly. Crossing that bridge meant committing to him, even if they didn't say it with words.

Sharing her body with him carried meaning. Emotional depth.

A promise.

And she couldn't make that kind of promise if she were living in two worlds.

New York?

Luview?

Being on two paths at the same time made sense until tonight.

"Cat got your tongue?" Luke asked as he glanced at her, then immediately set his eyes back on the road.

"Just thinking."

"About what?"

"You."

That wasn't a lie.

"Me? What about me?"

"Everything about you."

He cleared his throat suggestively. "Everything?"

"I've seen you wearing only a towel, mister. It didn't leave much to the imagination."

"I'm not sure whether that's a compliment or not."

"It absolutely, positively is."

Silence blanketed them again, their banter light and without tension. It felt good to be with a man she could talk to like this. Nothing about Luke was pretense.

He was who he was, liked what he liked, loved who he loved.

And Kylie felt like she could be herself.

Whoever that was.

With him, she knew who she could be. The future would be laid out and clear.

In New York, she knew who she had the potential to be.

Here in town, she would be entwined with him—her job, her life, everything.

In New York, she would be wholly independent, but disconnected.

Luke turned on music, the same pleasant jazz and blues he'd played earlier in the car. It hearkened back to an earlier time, a simpler, quieter pace of life.

One she found in Luview.

As Luke steered the car down roads he'd memorized long ago, Kylie let herself live in the moment, her limbs relaxing in the warming air, the glow of the night seeping into her.

Happy.

She was so happy.

Could a person feel so much joy? She didn't know it was possible.

Luke's phone buzzed.

"That's my personal line." Frowning, he looked at it, then made a face just as they reached Kylie's driveway, her inner calm disappearing as anticipation washed over her.

Invite him in?

Give him a kiss at the door and draw a boundary?

What should she do?

"Oh, good grief," he muttered as he turned his phone over.

"What?"

"Colleen. Reminding me that Nadine has today in the betting pool, and I'll never hear the end of it if she wins."

A snort Kylie didn't know she could make came out of her. Luke parked, cut the engine, and turned to her.

"Let's talk about this."

"The bet?"

"All of it."

"Okay. Want to come in for a drink?"

"I do. Very much."

Impulse made her invite him.

What else would impulse make her do tonight?

Without waiting for him to walk around, Kylie climbed out of the car and walked up the steep set of stairs to her apartment, Luke pressing the small of her back with a firm, guiding hand. Once they were inside her blissfully warm apartment, she relaxed.

And then didn't.

Because the bedroom was right there.

Luke made himself at home without being overbearing, hanging his coat and hat, setting gloves on a small table by the door, and rubbing his hands together to warm up. Kylie took off her outerwear, then stood before him.

"Beer? Spiked seltzer? Coffee?"

A small smile, topped by eyes that showed how much he wanted her, was her answer.

A few beats of silence passed, not uncomfortably, before he said, "I think I'll stick to coffee."

"You sure?"

"I need to drive home in an hour."

"An *hour*?"

"My mom is babysitting, plus I have to work in the morning. Remember?"

"Oh! Right!"

"And so do you."

"Of course! At eight-thirty. I'll have coffee, too. Decaf? Or I have apple juice, milk, some soda."

"Kylie?"

"Yes?"

"I'm not ready to sleep with you just yet."

"Oh! You really *do* want to talk about it.'"

"Mm hmm." Crossing the space between them, he put his hands on her hips, a light touch that made her want more. "It doesn't have to be tonight. And I only have an hour. No way I want to rush."

Reminding herself that she could say anything–including how she really felt–she replied with, "Me, too. I'm not ready. Not that I'm not ready–I mean, I am. I just... I'd rather wait, too."

"Don't take it the wrong way."

"What do you mean?"

"I want you. Desperately. Insanely. I spend all day at work thinking about you. All day at home thinking about you. And nights... nights are hard." He pulled her tighter toward him.

She felt how hard.

"Nothing's stopping us. We're adults, which means we choose. We decide. No one else's expectation–and certainly no damn betting pool–is going to influence us."

"No." Reaching up, she ran her fingers through his hair above one ear. It curled a bit, and she realized she'd been in town long enough to watch his short hair grow out to this point. It had been less than a month, but felt like a lifetime.

"But there's a big range between kisses and making love," he whispered as his lips found her neck, the touch transporting her, his hands around her waist, pressing her to him.

No need for a drink, or even caffeine.

Bzzz

The text alert had a different tone, one Kylie recognized instantly as Luke groaned.

That was his work phone.

"I'm ignoring that," he said. "Can't believe I didn't turn it off."

"You know you can't ignore it."

"Watch me."

"You wouldn't have brought it if it wasn't important. And you're too responsible to blow off a text that might involve public safety."

"You know me well, don't you?" His sigh spoke volumes as he walked over to his coat, pulled out the phone, and made a face.

"Damn. Chief needs me at work at six, not nine."

Kylie's wall clock said it was just past eleven.

"I can be at your house at half past five. Don't worry about Harriet."

Smoldering eyes met hers. "Wish I could invite you back and you could spend the night."

"I can sleep on the couch. I've done it before."

"Only when I was working an overnight."

"How is that different?"

"Kylie, if you came back to my house and were there overnight, I'm not sure I could wait. And I don't want a quickie."

"I'm getting pretty close to compromising."

The startled laugh that boomed out of him made her laugh, too.

And then they were kissing, deep and hot, a kiss that promised more later.

Which was all they really could ask for.

And it was enough.

More than enough.

"Kylie," he said in a hushed tone, one filled with heat and carrying a wish she shared with him for time, space, and intimacy. "I know you're still job hunting in New York, and I want to say this: I would never want to stop you from pursuing your dream."

"Luke, I–"

"But please reconsider. I don't know exactly where this is going, but it definitely is headed in the right direction."

"It is," she agreed.

"And I know it's only been a few weeks, but oh, Kylie," he said cradling her face, "you fit in so easily. It's like you were meant to step in. Harriet adores you. I'm falling for you. Everyone knows you, even if you've been gone all these years. You understand the town. You understand *me*. That's so rare. It's hard to put into words how invisible I've felt these last two years. Invisible by choice. I needed to hide all my feelings that weren't about Harriet and pretend they weren't there. Pretend I didn't matter."

Listening intently, her mind was a swirl, his vulnerability piercing her.

"You matter."

"You make me feel like I matter. Like all those feelings I hated having to carry are manageable. When I'm with you, they're not burdens, or millstones around my neck. They're just part of me. I can have them. You give me space to grieve. To let the hollow parts of me fill in again. You show me how I can feel joy and pleasure again because I *deserve* to feel joy and pleasure."

"Of course you do."

"That 'of course' isn't obvious to me, Kylie. When you look at me, all the empty spaces in my heart stop echoing. Your smile fills me. Your kisses drive the pain away and make room for what needs to be in me: a partner. But not just any partner. *You.*"

Their mouths met in a tender kiss that turned hotter as time passed, Kylie's emotions taking flight inside her chest, buzzing like bees, sending tingles everywhere through her as she let herself get swept away by Luke's very open words.

As his tongue pressed against her lips, parting them, she moved closer, her thigh between his, his hands on the small of her back, cupping her ass.

It would be so easy to change their minds, have him come to bed, be very tired tomorrow, but sated.

She didn't want satiety.

She wanted *certainty.*

Bzzz

This time, it was her phone.

"The only person that could be is Wendy. But it's like four a.m. in Paris."

Sure enough, it was.

Kylie? You up? I need someone to talk to.

The bridge of her nose practically folded in half as she frowned.

"Something bad?" Luke asked.

"My sister. She needs a call now. Probably man troubles."

"Men are trouble," he agreed, pulling her in for an embrace. "But some of us are worth it."

"You are."

"I'll see you tomorrow. We'll talk about our next date."

"Next date? Christmas is coming."

"That's not a date. That's an interrogation."

"Hah!"

He gave her a sweet, quick kiss, the kind you give someone you're close to for the long run. "Thank you, Kylie."

"Thank you. Tonight was magical."

"Did you see fairies when you kissed me?"

"No. But I did see a future."

"Good. So did I."

As he left, she shook her head quickly, sighing as she texted Wendy back.

I'm here.

The phone lit up almost instantly, the FaceTime call a surprise.

Wendy was sobbing. The glow from her perfect date with Luke was dimmed a bit, but she had to re-center herself and support her poor sister.

"What happened? Are you safe? Hurt? Wendy?"

Shaking her head fast, her hair rumpled, Kylie's sister choked out the words, "Johann dumped me."

"Oh, no!"

"He–he–he did it by text! Then he ghosted me. And I stupidly slept with him–I never sleep with guys that fast!"

"Honey, I'm sorry." Distance made Kylie's only comfort-giving ability a verbal one, the words feeling empty and futile, but she said them anyway.

"I don't know why I'm crying so hard. We were barely together. I just can't. Can't. Stop. Crying."

"It's probably culture shock, sweetie. Remember how the au pair coordinator said that could happen? Three to four weeks in, right?"

"Yeah?"

"You're there. You made a cross-Atlantic flight. You jumped immediately into working with two strange-to-you kids, forty hours a week. You live in someone else's home and have a job you can't leave. Then you met a hot German and of course you slept with him fast. You wanted a connection. Adventure. Fun! And you're also just depleted, so you're crying."

"You mean I'm not an insecure weirdo who is being melo-dramatic?"

If Wendy were back home, Kylie would have made a joke, but she could see how fragile her baby sister was.

"Absolutely not. You're a strong, independent woman who is tasting life in every way possible. Johann is the one who screwed up, dumping you. He was lucky to sleep with you."

Wendy sniffed. "Right."

"I mean it! When did he dump you?"

"An hour ago. We were at a nightclub. He asked me to go into a back room with him and have an orgy. I said no. He disappeared, then I got the text."

"WHAT A JERK!!"

"I know. He's worse than Perry. But at least I still have a job."

"Huh?"

"When Perry dumped you, you lost your job, too. You know all that crap Mom says about always being independent, and never depending on a man for anything, not money, not a social life—nothing? I used to think she was so bitter." A sour laugh came out of Wendy. "Now I understand better."

Ouch.

Trying hard not to personalize this, Kylie just said, "I'm so sorry. You did the right thing if being in an orgy wasn't what you wanted."

Wendy laughed through her nose, then quickly grabbed a tissue, honking hard as she blew into it. "No judgment for people who are into it, but that was definitely not my thing. I thought he was joking at first. Then he got mad at me."

"Mad? Mad!" Kylie's outrage meter ticked up a bit.

"Yeah. Yelled at me. Said I was repressed."

"Whatever. There are other guys out there. He was obviously not for you."

"Nope. The sex was amazing, but the lack of respect is a deal-breaker."

"No kidding. You deserve someone who delivers huge doses of both, Wendy."

"I know. Thanks." She squared her shoulders. "It's late. I'm surprised you're up. Don't you normally go to bed earlier?"

"I was on a date with Luke." She cringed. "Sorry."

"For what?"

"Mentioning my fabulous date when you're suffering."

"I love that you went on a date with Luke! Did you sleep with him?"

"Not yet."

"Ooooh! So there's a future here?"

"Well..."

"What's up?"

"I had an interview with KidzdocTV."

"SERIOUSLY?"

"Yeah."

"In New York?"

"No. Not yet. I mean, it was a Zoom interview. A weeder interview. You know. They said they'll tell me soon if I get an in-person interview as a finalist."

"What does 'soon' mean?"

"Like... I don't know. Haven't checked email since around four."

"Are you going to take it if you get a job offer? Sounds like things are getting deeper with Luke."

"I don't know! I realize I screwed up here. Luke is my boss. My job and my relationship are intertwined!"

"Oh," Wendy groaned. "I never thought of it that way. Damn, Kylie. That's deep."

"Deep?"

"You did it again. With Perry, and now with Luke."

"They are nothing alike!"

"I mean the situation. You're right. Whoa."

"I know! And if I stay here, there are no jobs in children's programming. Nordicbeth is the closest thing. I might be able to dust off my teaching credentials and go back to the classroom, or work seasonally at a camp, but western Maine isn't exactly a hotbed of creative media content development for kids."

"Hah. No." Wendy sniffed, then stuffed what looked like a chunk of chocolate in her mouth. "You'd be better off starting a fairy camp from scratch."

"With what money?"

"If you wish hard enough, a fairy can give you some!" Wendy said, laughing.

"Funny."

"I think you need to keep your options open," Wendy said slowly. "Like Mom always says. After what just happened to me with Johann, I am not trusting anyone easily. I'm sure Luke's great and all, but... go slowly. This has all happened really fast. Like me and Johann."

"No offense, Wendy, but Luke's nothing like him."

"No. He's not. But you are the one who needs to look out for you. What *you* want. What *you* need. And most important, what makes you safe. Independent. Secure."

"What happened to Wild Wendy, going out in the world to take a big bite out of life?"

"She got a mouthful of rejection."

"Oh, honey."

"Look at us, Ky. Aren't we a pair?" Wendy yawned. "It's four in the morning. The shock of my night is wearing off. I have to work at eight. I love you, Kylie. Thanks for talking me down."

"Any time. Love you, too."

The call ended.

Kylie's mind was a cloud of glitter on fire.

As she set the phone down, she saw she had three new emails. Tapping the glass, she opened the app to find an email from Roberta at KidzdocTV.

Heart slamming hard, she opened it, halfway hoping for a standard rejection letter.

But no...

Dear Kylie, the email began. *Congratulations! You're one of four finalists we'd like to invite to our New York office for an interview on December 28...*

December 28? That was just over a week away.

Her calendar, embedded in her email program, said it was one of her days off.

Details about travel logistics were a blur as she read the email, overwhelmed.

At the end, it said, *Please reply ASAP, as our timeline is condensed. We want to finalize our hiring before Q4 ends.*

Oh, boy.

Now she was in a pickle.

Celebrating her successes was always a bit hard; she knew she should be cheering for herself, but instead, she just felt the agony of being pulled in two directions.

With Luke's taste still on her tongue.

Go to New York, or stay?

The career she always wanted, or the sweet boy she kissed on a pier, who turned into a man she admired and–

Loved?

With both faces in her mind, boy and man, she took the easy way out.

At least, it felt that way in the moment.

"Dear Roberta," she wrote, nerves getting the better of her. *"Thank you so much. I would be delighted to..."*

And besides, she was still exploring. This was about being open to possibility. No commitment was needed. This wasn't about picking a path.

She hadn't gotten the job.

Yet.

Guilt filled her, the fact that she hadn't said a word about the Zoom interview to Luke now an indictment of sorts. When he found out about the in-person interview, he would be crushed.

He would also, she knew, try to convince her to stay.

Colleen warned her, back at Mountain Dragon, not to toy with Luke's affections. Firm in her belief that she wasn't, Kylie nevertheless knew that this balancing act had her on a very shaky wire.

With no safety net.

"Haven't fallen yet. Haven't decided on a direction, either," she reminded herself as she slowly undressed, hanging the elegant garment in the closet, a whiff of Luke's aftershave wafting up from the neckline.

Luke, or New York?

Interdependence, or Independence?

Possible love, or possible career success?

As she climbed into sweats, a text came in.

Luke.

Tonight was wonderful. Our next date will be longer, more private, and dinner will be followed by breakfast in bed.

A shiver ran through her as she grabbed a pillow and threw it across the room.

Why did all the good stuff have to come at once? And put her in a double bind?

As she wandered into the bathroom and began scrubbing off her makeup, she remembered Wendy's mascara-streaked face, and her words:

"You did it again. With Perry, and now with Luke."

Accepting the interview still wasn't a commitment.

Sleeping with Luke, though? That would be.

Time was what she needed most.

Time, sleep, and some magic fairy intervention that would make all this easier.

Chapter Thirty-Two

Kylie

Walking into Bilbee's Tavern was like turning back time.

As she walked in, the floorboards groaned like she was inconveniencing them with her presence. Mismatched wooden chairs were pulled up to scarred-wood tables, nothing matching. An enormous bar gleamed in the low light, a wall of spirits begging to be tasted. Each bottle seemed to have its own history, Kylie nearly swooning as she took in the enormity of it all.

Two wood stoves pumped out plenty of heat, but as she took more steps inside, she realized it was erratic. One spot was blazing, the next – frigid.

Nothing was consistent, which suited her state of mind just fine.

For the last two days, she'd wrestled with her conscience, prepared for her December 28 interview, and put the finishing touches on Christmas plans. Texts and the larger family Zoom call seemed to suffice, Kylie's surprise at her mother's lack of a request for a private phone call filling her with mixed emotions.

Now here she was, Luke's surprise invitation a few hours ago making her happy.

Come join me and the gang at Bilbee's, his text had said. *Mom is watching Harriet for me. Let's have fun.*

Fun. Remember fun, Kylie? she told herself. *You had it before Perry.*

You can have it again.

Kylie took a deep inhale through her nose, the familiar scent of woodsmoke and sour beer surprising her. Deep in her memory somewhere, the scent was imprinted in her. Years of coming here with her parents, and especially her father, were all still stored away in memory.

Not much had changed, other than the electronics, big, flat screen televisions perched high over the bar, an array of five of them on different sports channels, the volume turned low but captions on.

Bilbee's was old, the tavern created in 1788, though the building was even older, the porch a bit crooked, the whole place drafty but warmed by wood stoves that were always on in winter.

"Kylie?" Rider Bilbee looked like an older, balder, more tattooed version of his teen self, but she recognized him instantly.

"Rider! How are you?" Christmas music floated through the bar, an instrumental she'd heard a thousand times but couldn't name.

His eyes jumped to a spot over her shoulder, face changing slightly, suddenly on guard. "I'm good. How about you?"

Instinct made her want to look behind her, but something in her said she didn't need to.

Yet.

"Back in my hometown, you know? Nothing's changed here, except for the wall of televisions."

He chuckled through his nose. "Plenty's changed, but plenty's stayed the same. Heard you moved to New York City and came back here because you were with Prissy."

"Prissy?"

"That's what we call Perry Nordicbeth."

Kylie nearly choked on her surprise, laughing so hard she had to grab the back of a chair. "*Prissy?*"

"He's a jerk. Luke's better. And speaking of," Rider said, eyes scanning the room, clearly watching for some kind of danger

Kylie didn't see. "Luke and the rest of 'em are back by the pool table."

"The rest of them?"

"You'll see. Quite a crowd. Before you go back, what can I get you?"

"A Shirley Tem – " The words died out in her mouth as Rider caught her eye and smiled, instantly going from grumpy biker to friendly bartender as the old familiar drink from her childhood came out of her from muscle memory.

"You're over twenty-one, you know. You can drink the devil's juice now," he mock whispered.

That made her laugh even harder. "How about a lemon drop martini?"

"Not a beer drinker?"

"I'll drink it if I'm in the mood. Tonight I want something sweeter."

"So does Luke."

As Rider said the words, Kylie felt a hand on her hip, possessive and stark.

"Hey there," Luke murmured in her ear, the affectionate gesture earning looks from everyone in the room.

Kylie imagined them all calculating their dates in the betting pool.

"We're about to get teased," she whispered back.

"It wouldn't be our hometown if we didn't."

Our hometown.

Kylie hadn't felt at home like this in... fifteen years. She was, of course, *literally* home right now, but this was more than location.

This was belonging.

Rider's easy talk with her. The familiarity of the tavern. How people gave her quick nods of recognition, or smiles and waves. It was all so easy.

And with Luke's arms around her, it was even easier.

"We're really doing this?" she said softly.

"Doing what?"

"Being open in public?"

As she turned to look at him, their eyes locked, Kylie

suddenly awash in emotion. Every part of Bilbee's receded, the woodsmoke scent fading, the creak of floorboards as people walked muting, the shouts of joy around the dart board turning to a simple hum as Luke took her hands in his and grinned.

"We are," he said as Rider appeared with her drink, holding it aloft.

His mouth twisted with disapproval.

"Not yet. Hold out for a while," he replied as Kylie took the drink from him, the first sip delicious.

Luke sighed, then gave Kylie a quick kiss on the lips as she carefully held the cocktail, half her mind focused on not spilling, the rest of her enjoying the kiss.

"So much for the Don't Bang Your Nanny clause," said a gravelly voice from behind them, though the tone was playful.

"Darren," Luke said in a tone of warning.

Kylie raced to pattern match the face and the name. The man standing behind them was about ten years older than Luke, with a long chin and a mouth that didn't seem to smile often, though keen, sharp eyes spoke to intelligence.

"I'm Darren Chassi," he said directly to Kylie, weathered hand extended. "You probably don't remember me. I was off at college and veterinary school when you lived here."

"I feel like I've heard of you. Mel was my horse riding instructor at camp."

"Yep. My wife – er, ex-wife."

Luke's eyebrow shot up at the mistake.

"Yes! Mel. Nice to meet you, Darren. Or, meet you again." She giggled like a little girl. "It's very disconcerting to be here," she confessed. "I used to come in here with my dad. I feel like I'm frozen in time."

"You're not," Luke said, eyeing her appreciatively. "But I can understand the feeling."

"Can you? You stayed here."

"Just because I haven't experienced something doesn't mean I can't empathize with it."

Luke motioned for her to follow him, Darren staying at the counter to chat with Rider. Winding between tables, Luke greeted by every single person, though she noticed he did a double take to the right. A big guy in a t-shirt that stretched across impossibly-large biceps was playing pool in a corner, tattoos covering both arms, his head shaved bald. Leaning over a pool table, he was taking a shot, one eye closed, the expression on his face distilled down to a single word:

Mean.

Kylie had to look away, because her drink would slosh, so she took a sip instead, watching Luke's back.

And backside.

It was a far better view.

A lively group was Luke's target, Kylie instantly recognizing Colleen, Kell, Rachel, and –

"Is that Moore Mottin?" she gasped.

"It is."

"He looks so mature!"

"You mean old? You realize we're three days apart," he groused.

"No, I mean... is he wearing a suit?"

"Yep. He runs the jewelry store, remember? Took over from his dad a few years ago."

"Right."

"Got off work and came straight here."

"And that's Jake! From the handyman family."

"Jake Forsythe. Yep."

"Does his family still run Love You Handy Jobs?"

"Sure do."

Kylie started snickering. Luke stopped in his tracks and turned around, eyebrows up, as if he knew exactly what she was about to ask.

"And do kids still prank them by stealing the Y off the sign?"

"Not only do they still do it, now there's a secret teen ritual where they have to steal it and take a picture for social media. Most of them post on Snapchat now so they don't get caught."

"Why on earth don't the Forsythes change the name of the company? I'd imagine the Love Committee goes nuts every time there's a picture of that sign floating around."

"Why do people resist change, Kylie? If I could figure out the answer to that, I wouldn't be a cop."

"What would you be if you weren't a police officer?"

"That's a very philosophical conversation for a fun night out at a tavern. Let me get more drinks in me before tackling it." He kissed her forehead and turned around.

Darren had joined them, and Jake was standing, a puzzled look on his face as he peered at Kylie.

"I know you."

"You probably bet on her," Luke growled.

"No, I mean... didn't you babysit me?" Jake was about five years younger than the rest of them. A flood of surprise shot through her, but then she realized he was right.

"Yes! Your mom had me watch you while she sang in the community choir! I forgot about that."

Jake let out a low whistle as he sized her up, Kylie starting to get embarrassed in the moment. "I didn't. You were my first crush, Kylie."

Jake Forsythe was built like Kell, big and broad, with muscle that came from working with his body for a living. A natural redhead, his hair had deepened to a rich auburn, his neatly-trimmed beard a shade darker. Hair long and around his collar, he looked like he could easily live in an artist's colony in a gentrifying warehouse district in New York or Boston, or work as a lumberjack in the woods.

"I'm sure I wasn't your last," Kylie said diplomatically, as Luke wrapped his arm around her waist and gave Jake a very clear signal to back off.

A single nod from Jake to Luke was enough to clarify matters.

Platters of appetizers scattered around the big table, it was clear everyone had been here a while. Rachel scooted over to make room for her.

"Sit!" she urged, Kylie finding a spot, Luke creating a second one by giving Kell a nudge. Soon, they were seated at the table, Kylie sipping her drink, taking it all in.

It was like everyone from her childhood grew up and decided to have a reunion, except this was daily life.

Weird.

Weird, and so good.

Jake and Darren drank half their beers, then headed for a darts board. Kell and Rachel were talking about a squirrel's nest he'd found in a tree. Colleen reached across Moore and took a handful of sweet potato fries, settling back in her seat as he sipped on his beer and gave Kylie a nod. Something that looked like knitting was resting on the table next to Colleen, until Kylie spotted a crochet hook. Looked like a granny square in its infancy.

As she looked around the table, she smiled, knowing every single person here. She flashed back to her years in New York, where avoiding eye contact was an art form. If she had stayed in Luview, would this have been her life? Hanging out with the same people she went to preschool, elementary, middle, and high school with? Her entire life like a vine that starts with small shoots and climbs slowly, twisting with other vines as it blooms?

How different would she be as a person if she hadn't been forced to leave?

"Hey! Moore! You remember Kylie, right?" Colleen said, the casual way she interacted with Moore making it clear they were good friends, but Kylie wondered if there was something deeper there.

"Of course," he said with a smile, looking around the table. "All we need are Layla and Brewer and we're one big camp reunion."

"Luke said Brewer's in Texas? And rich?" Kylie asked before sipping her drink again, Luke's thigh snug against her own as he leaned forward on the table, reaching for some peppered fries from a basket.

"Yep. He swings by every few years," Moore replied.

"Too good for us now," Colleen sniffed.

"Just because someone leaves doesn't mean anything like that," Kylie said, regretting the words as they came out.

Colleen shot Luke a glance Kylie definitely noticed.

"That's true," Luke said softly. "Except Brewer *told us* he was too good for Luview."

"What?" Kylie gasped. "No one's 'too good' for this town!"

"I'll drink to that," Luke said, raising his glass, everyone else scrambling to join in the toast.

"To being good enough for Luview!" Colleen called out

before Luke could say a word, the group bursting into laughter. Rachel caught Kylie's eye and gave her a sympathetic nod.

That sense of comfort had diminished. Brewer had left. Kylie had left. Now they were talking about him.

What had they said about her? Her dad? Her family? Maybe her mom was right. Maybe leaving town before being the topic of gossip and living with prying eyes and shame hadn't been so wrong after all.

Then again, she never said she was too good for Luview, Maine.

"What about Layla?" she asked as everyone filled their mouths with their drinks. She had to wait until they swallowed, all eyes on her.

"She moved to Boston," Kell said. "Got her law degree. Her parents are still here, running the insurance agency."

"It's hard to think of these people I remember as teenagers being out in the world, living grown-up lives," Kylie said as she looked around. "I always wanted to come back."

"Why didn't you? Until a month ago? Luke said you were living near Fixby Hills," Kell asked.

"It's embarrassing."

"No," Luke said firmly. "Embarrassing is having the entire town do a betting grid on when we're going to sleep together."

"That's not embarrassing," Colleen scoffed. "That's entertainment."

A low growl from the pool table made Luke half-stand in his chair, the sound entering Kylie's awareness seconds after Luke began to react. A sharp sound, like a very hard hand slapping against wood, came from that huge, muscular guy clearly venting some anger.

"Sit down, Luke," Kell said. "You're off duty. Not your job."

"Not your problem," Moore joined in.

"Lyle Morgenstern's not my job, but he's *definitely* my problem."

"We've got your back," Kell said softly, earning an incredulous look from Luke, who wrapped his arm around Kylie's shoulders, but his body was tense as a board.

"You think I want a bunch of guys brawling in Bilbee's, Kell?

Last thing I need is a group of friends taking someone like Lyle from bad to worse."

"If he takes a swing at you, I'm not standing by and watching," Kell said menacingly, earning a wide-eyed stare from Rachel.

"Brawl? What are you talking about?" she hissed in his ear. "You sound like a caveman!"

"No," Kell said in a low, controlled voice. "Lyle's the caveman. I'm just saying if he starts trouble here with Luke, Moore and I will help finish it."

Colleen gave Moore an appreciative look.

"Why would he start trouble with Luke?" Kylie asked, heart racing with a spike of fear.

"Because Luke caught him breaking into Kendrill's Market a year ago. Literally caught him red-handed stealing inventory out the back, plus nearly a grand in cash was missing. Luke arrested him, and Lyle did time. Just got out this week," Colleen explained.

The drink in Kylie's stomach started to churn.

"Oh."

"He's a mean old jerk, but he's not stupid," Moore said quietly. "Lyle might bark but he won't bite."

"You bumped me!" Lyle shouted to the guy he was playing pool with, someone Kylie didn't recognize. "No fair! I get a redo." The man's words were slurred, and as he took a step around the pool table, he stumbled slightly, grabbing the hanging lamp over the middle of the table.

Light swung in strange, sinister arcs in that corner, making Kylie turn to her city instincts.

See nothing.

Pretend it's not happening.

Be boring.

Don't make eye contact.

Safety in numbers.

"Maybe we should go," she said to Luke, whose jaw tightened in response.

"Hell, no. Lyle Morgenstern doesn't scare me. And he certainly doesn't get to force us to run off. We're here to have fun. If he causes a disturbance, I'll get him out of here."

"You'd arrest him again?"

"I'll do everything I can to avoid it. The guy's had a hard life. But if he breaks the law, yes."

Darren and Jake returned, questions in their eyes as they glanced at Lyle, then Luke.

"I know," he said to them both. "I hear him. Drunk, right?"

"I went to the bathroom and walked past. It's clear he was three sheets to the wind before he came in, and he's kept Rider busy."

"Rider'll cut him off when it's time," Luke said. "He took his keys."

"How do you know?" Kylie asked. "He didn't ask for mine."

"If you ask Rider to run a tab, which Lyle does, he wants your keys. It's a smokescreen, though. He just wants the keys of anyone he thinks can't drive home safely."

"Did you have to hand over your keys?" she asked.

The table erupted into laughter.

"Luke doesn't go anywhere," Jake said with a grin. "Haven't seen you hang with us in..."

"A while," Luke snapped, clearly unhappy at being ribbed.

Colleen's smile lit up the room as she looked at her brother. "It's good to have you back. The handful of times you've come out, you looked so mopey."

Luke squeezed Kylie's knee. "No reason to be mopey anymore."

"I SAID," shouted Lyle from the bar, "GIVE ME MY DAMN KEYS!"

"Uh oh," Luke muttered, shooting to his feet, Kell, Jake, and Moore standing as well, Darren watching carefully from his seat.

"Lyle," Rider said, hands on his bar, splayed wide, his stance one that said *Don't mess with me*, but also said, *I'm giving you an out here.*

"KEYS!"

"You're too drunk. I already called Tabby."

"You called my woman?" Lyle's face turned red from anger. "She's busy working. You better not cost her her shift. Just give me my damn keys. I'm fine, you little piece of – "

"Hey, hey, now," Luke said as Kylie watched helplessly from

the table, Darren putting his hand on her forearm as she started to rise.

"Stay out of it," Darren whispered in her ear. "If anyone can diffuse this, it's Luke." Darren looked up at Kell, Jake, and Moore, raising his voice. "And sit your asses down. You look like a flank of bouncers, and it'll only anger Lyle more. You can jump in and help when it's really needed. Luke knows what he's doing."

"Lyle's been in jail or prison for most of the last year, Darren," Kell countered, clearly worried. "He bulked up."

"Let the sworn law officer handle it, Kell. He'll call for help when he needs it. Trust your brother."

A string of profanities poured out of Lyle, all of it aimed at Luke.

" – and get out of my face. You're the one who put me in prison!"

"I've got no problem with you, man," Luke said, standing a few steps behind Lyle, the bar a barrier between Lyle and Rider. Luke had no such luxury, and it terrified Kylie. She knew that one well-placed blow could seriously injure Luke.

Not that he wasn't able to fight, if needed. His body was a study in control and power, feet wide enough apart to stabilize himself, but close enough together to pivot if needed.

Training had clearly made him ready for anything.

But Lyle was big, drunk, and mean. That combination was dangerous.

"I got a problem with you, though," Lyle said menacingly, scowling at Luke, muttering more obscenities, one of them making Luke's nostrils flare, but he didn't escalate.

Kylie noticed Kell wrapping his arm around Rachel, eyes on the exits.

Luke said nothing.

"More of a problem with him, though," he said, turning to Rider, who was in the same position, hands on the bar, leaning forward. A cook in the kitchen stood in the doorway, white apron smeared with food, watching the front carefully, phone in hand. He looked like Mark Faroni, a guy in Kylie's grade, with a big head of curly brown hair and wide eyeglasses slipped halfway down his nose.

Now wasn't the time for a quick catch up.

"I'll drive you home if you need a ride," Rider said. "Mikah's on his way here. If Tabby can't take time off, we can swing it."

"I. Want. My. Keys."

Lyle's position was clear.

"No."

Rider's single syllable answer set the next five seconds in motion, Kylie leaping to her feet on instinct as Lyle's elbow shot back, his arm like a thick piece of split firewood. Luke moved with lightning fast reflexes and nearly broke his nose on Lyle's elbow as the bigger man cocked back his arm, aiming to punch Rider.

Who dodged back fast –

– leaving Luke holding Lyle in a chokehold, his arms shaking but body resolute. Lyle thrashed in Luke's grip, trying to head-butt, the alcohol that soaked Lyle's bloodstream making the match more even as his reflexes were slower

"Stop it, Lyle," Luke said, panting hard. "Think about your kid."

Lyle jolted. "My what?"

"Jace. Your son, Jace. Can't play ball with your kid in jail, man."

"Why are you talking about my *kid*?" The question came out more like a whine than a real inquiry.

"Because he needs his dad. Our kids need their dads. I don't want my little girl being told Jace Morgenstern's daddy beat hers up, and you sure as hell don't want Tabby to have to explain to Jace where his daddy went after a bar fight. So if you won't stop this for yourself or Tabby, do it for your kid."

Luke's words echoed through the tavern, the place so quiet you could practically hear the sour sweat on Lyle's brow plunking onto the bar, drop by drop.

"You're the reason Tabby had to explain the first time, Luke," Lyle spat out as Kell appeared to hit his limit, walking over to Luke, standing five feet behind him in silent support, arms crossed over his huge chest.

"Don't let there be a second time, man," Luke said softly in his ear. "I could take you in just for this."

319

"Haven't hit anyone. Yet," Lyle hissed.

"Let's keep it that way."

Before anyone could take the next step, the front door to Bilbee's Tavern was flung open by a woman Kylie hadn't seen in fifteen years, but would recognize anywhere.

Tabby.

Tabitha Bilbee.

Rider and Mikah's *sister*.

Wait. *Wait*.

Lyle Morgenstern was dating Tabitha Bilbee, and Jace was their *son*? Kylie's mind raced to piece it all together, her mental map of "Who's Who" starting to fray at the edges, turning into ashes that blew off on the winds of change.

Back when she lived here, Tabby had worked at Love You Chocolate the one and only year Kylie had worked there, too. Tabby was short on sense but full on heart, the kind of person who rescued kittens from bushes and nursed abandoned baby bunnies. A fixture at the local humane society, she spent more time petting strays and making homemade bandanas for dogs to wear on adoption day than she did on her studies.

Clearly, that tender heart wasn't doing her any favors in the human relationship department.

"Tabby!" Rider shouted. "Come collect him."

"Shut up!" she screeched, coming to a dead halt in front of Luke. "What're *you* touching him for?" she said, her whole demeanor changing, cowering a bit in deference. "He's not under arrest, is he?"

"I'm trying to keep him from punching your brother and going back to prison."

"Gawd, Lyle! Honey, come home. Let me take care of you the way you deserve."

Rider and half the men in the tavern all snorted. Kylie noticed no one from their table did, though she suspected Darren was close.

"Lyle," Tabby said, her voice going syrupy-sweet. "Luke's going to let you go, and we'll go home so I can – " She stood on tiptoe and whispered something in his ear that made the man's eyebrows shoot up, one corner of his mouth curling into a leer.

"Gross," Rider groaned. "I can hear you, Tabby."

"Then move away!" she snapped.

From the look on Luke's face, as he slowly let Lyle go and moved back one step, he heard it, too.

"And get me two bacon cheeseburgers, no tomato, Sriracha on one. And a kids' burger with fries the way Jace likes it."

At the mention of Jace, who must be Rider's nephew, his face softened, what looked like a brewing objection instantly diffused. Rider stormed back to the kitchen and told the guy who looked like Mark Faroni what to make.

Then Rider stomped back to the counter and pointed at his sister.

"Get him out of here, and from now on," he said, pointedly snagging Lyle's keys off the hook behind him and shoving them in his front jeans pocket, "I'll let him swing. Won't hit me, but it'll give Luke a reason to bring him in."

"Never," Lyle said in a low, spine-tingling voice, throwing his arm across Tabby's shoulders, cupping her breast with a vulgar grab. "Never going back."

"Then think of your little boy," Luke said, hands on his hips, eyes scanning the room then settling back on Lyle. Not backing down, he wasn't escalating, either. Another man would have let Lyle make the hit, and welcomed the chance to put the guy away.

Luke didn't.

And that took a different kind of strength.

Still nervous, Kylie felt her worry draining, Luke's steady command of the situation triggering a deep calm in her. How did he know exactly what to say? What made him so brave? Lyle was big and drunk, angry at Luke, and Luke knew the right combination of words and actions to get the best possible outcome.

No one got hurt, and Lyle stayed out of police custody.

"C'mon, baby." Tabby shot Luke a glare. "Don't give him another fake reason to take you in."

"Tabby," Luke said in a firm voice. Whatever he meant by it, the way he said it made her shut up.

Fast.

"I'm not leavin'," Lyle declared. "He's the one who should go."

"Jace is in the car, freezing, baby," Tabby crooned. "Let's go home and be a family. Rider'll pay for dinner. Least he can do. You know how you love the bacon cheeseburgers here. We can chow down and watch a fun movie."

Kylie's throat tightened at the thought of a little kid sitting outside a bar, waiting for his mother to pick up his drunk dad, fresh out of jail. Tears threatened to choke her. That poor little boy.

"Listen to Tabby," Luke said to Lyle, who was so drunk his eyes couldn't even focus on Luke.

"Hmph," she said, pulling on Lyle, the big guy finally headed toward the door, half the tavern's population letting out their breath in relief. "I'll meet you at the back door for those burgers, Rider!"

The door slammed shut as they left.

Kylie went straight to Luke and touched his arm, finding him steady, her own hands shaking, though. "That was amazing."

"That was stupid," Luke spat out. "Dumb Lyle. Trying to take a swing at his own brother-in-law?"

"My fault," Rider said with a sick look. "Didn't realize how drunk he already was when he came in. Should have cut him off a long time ago."

"Sorry you had to see that," Luke said softly to Kylie, worry in his eyes as he took a step closer to her, his tense protectiveness making her feel safer. "That doesn't happen often."

"But it does happen."

"Sure. I'm a likable guy, but not for people I arrest." He let out a sour laugh through his nose. "Or ticket. Or put in jail."

"You have enemies."

He made a face. "Lyle's a rare one. Most people accept that they have to follow the law."

"Lyle, not so much?"

"Lyle's on a collision course with the law because of the bottle. He's got an addiction and it's been sad all around to watch him decline." Running his hand through his hair, he walked her back to the big table, where Moore and Colleen broke out in polite golf claps.

"Bravo, bro," Kell said. "You were like a bomb squad expert."

"Huh?"

"Defusing an explosive."

"Tabby did that, Kell."

"I can't believe Tabitha Bilbee and Lyle Morgenstern have a child!" Kylie gasped.

Everyone looked at her like she was crazy.

"A child who is telling Harriet a bunch of lies about how babies are made," Luke muttered before draining the rest of his beer.

"A child who is waiting in a car in the dead of winter outside his uncle's bar, while his p-p-poor mom collects his drunk dad by pleading and begging," Kylie said softly, fighting tears, feeling profound sadness and sympathy for that small child.

Everyone went quiet as she took in a deep breath and got her emotions under control.

"If it's any consolation," Colleen said, reaching across the table to hold her hand, "social services is aware of everything. Tabby's getting lots of support. Jace is in school. He's fed, his grandma helps out, and people are stepping up. It's not ideal, but...."

A shaky inhale made Kylie nod. "I don't even know him, but I feel so bad for little Jace."

"Of course you do. Because you're a caring person," Luke said as Edina, one of the servers, came on over with a fresh drink for everyone at the table, and a huge tray of nachos.

"What's this?" Moore asked, moving empty plates into a stack to make room.

"This is your mess, Moore!" Colleen snarked. "You always order too much food. Now there's no room for this new stuff."

"Exhibit A, Colleen," he replied, holding up empty dishes. "It's not too much food if everyone eats it."

She just rolled her eyes. "And you cover the check too often, you softy."

That last comment just made him grin.

"Rider had me bring it over," Edina explained to the table. "His way of saying thanks," she announced, all grins and winks. "Lyle's been an ass the past couple of days, Luke. Thanks for that."

"I can't guarantee he won't be back."

"I can guarantee he will," Kell said in a voice dripping with distaste.

"I know." Edina patted his cheek gently. Older than the group by at least a generation, she was someone Kylie didn't remember. "But this time, he'll think twice."

Luke and Darren made sounds of disagreement.

Edina took the dirty glasses and dishes away, leaving them all to stare at the newfound bounty.

"Whew," Darren said with a long sigh. "Not my idea of a relaxing evening with friends!"

"Not mine, either," Luke said, reaching for the fresh beer, Kylie mirroring him as she took in most of the rest of her drink, her heartbeat slowing down, the tension fading as Rider welcomed a large group of people, none of whom she recognized.

Their happy chatter was a welcome change, and soon, she was done with her drink, Luke's hand on her knee, the nachos tasting better than she expected. Maybe the close call with Lyle made the flavor stand out, or perhaps it was the good company, but as Kylie ate her way through the enormous pile in front of them, cruets of sour cream, guacamole, and salsa adding to the yum, she felt a glow from within moving out all the fear.

"Too bad there's no peanut butter for you, Moore," Colleen said, elbowing him. He smacked her upper arm, mouth full of nachos.

"Peanut butter?" Kylie asked, the entire table groaning at her words.

Moore held up one finger in a gesture that asked her to wait, the guy chewing fast.

"Moore is a freak," Colleen announced. "He eats peanut butter on his burgers."

Kylie tilted her head and frowned. "That's not freakish. It's a thing in New York."

Moore swallowed, spreading his hands out toward Kylie, looking pointedly at his mocking friends. "See? I told you all it's a sign of a sophisticated palate."

"I wouldn't go that far," Kylie replied. "It's just a menu item."

Colleen laughed at Moore. "Just a menu item."

"Does Rider put the peanut butter in the ground beef, or just on the finished burger?" Kylie asked as everyone's face, minus Moore, twisted in disgust.

"Put the peanut butter in the beef?" Luke asked, incredulous. "That's disgusting."

"It's no more disgusting than putting it on," she argued.

"None of it is disgusting! It's personal preference," Moore countered. "Kell likes mint jelly on his roasted lamb. Why can't I enjoy peanut butter on a burger?"

"Because mint jelly and lamb go together. Next thing you're going to tell us you like grape jelly in your omelettes," Colleen snapped back.

"Hoo!" Jake said, holding his mouth open, waving his hand in front of it. "Anyone got an unused water? I just chewed through a big piece of jalapeno!"

Moore slid his unused water on over as Jake gave him a grateful look and chugged.

"There are delis that put grape jelly in omelettes in New York, actually," Kylie said to Colleen, earning a few dropped chins, including Luke's.

"That's a crime against humanity," Darren declared. "Who would do that?"

"Sometimes they layer cream cheese inside, then add the jelly," Kylie explained.

"Have you tried it?" Colleen asked.

"No." Kylie shivered. "I like to taste new things like anyone else, but I have my limits."

Luke squeezed her knees, leaned in, and whispered, "No need for limits with me."

"I HEARD THAT! I am right here!" Colleen said, adding gagging sounds.

Luke shrugged. "Then move."

The first sip of her second drink had a soundtrack of laughter, the whole table a moving feast of friendliness, comfort, and community. Kylie reached for Luke's hand and held it, fingers threading, as he smiled at her, she smiled back, and the world clicked into place a little bit more.

Every piece fitting better.

Her included.

Perry never would have acted the way Luke did with Lyle, protective of his friends, yet trying to help Lyle. Kylie didn't know what her ex would have done – likely egged Lyle on, or escaped as fast as possible, then made nothing but snide comments about the Luview "inbreds," like he had before.

Knowing full well she was from the town.

What Kylie hadn't explained to anyone was the real reason she'd stayed away, though she'd lived nearby for much of the last year: Perry. Shame, sure, but Perry. He'd convinced her that being from Luview was a disadvantage. A stumbling block. Something to hide.

And that what her father had done was even more reason to stay away.

As another man held her hand right now, the glow of good food, good drink, and even better company filling her with happiness, Kylie could look at her past and see how Perry had – much like Lyle – decided that whatever he wanted was what everyone else should let him have. Perry wanted a girlfriend who would agree with him. Who would be dependent on him. Who would let him feel superior by making her feel like less.

And she'd let him.

For no reason other than his stupid opinion, Kylie had deprived herself of *this*. People who knew her. Welcomed her. Included her.

Luke was just the icing on the cake.

Fairy glitter icing, sweeter than heaven.

On impulse, she leaned close to him, and gave his cheek a kiss. Everyone at the table picked up utensils and began gently banging the edges of forks and spoons on glasses.

"Kiss! Kiss!" Rachel said, clapping and laughing, but it was Colleen's reaction that struck Kylie before Luke pulled her in for a soft, perfect kiss.

Eyes narrowed, hands empty of utensils, Luke's sister just watched them.

While Moore watched Colleen.

"Tomorrow's the big Christmas parade," Rachel said. "Brings

a ton of customers into town. Are you planning to go?" she asked Kylie, who was still breathless from the kiss.

"What?"

"She's a little distracted," Kell chided Rachel. "Give her a minute to find her brain."

"Hah. As if a kiss could make you lose your mind," Rachel snarked back.

Apparently, Kell took that as a challenge, because he dipped her back in her chair and proceeded to kiss her to deeply, so intensely, that even Kylie and Luke had to look away.

When he finally relinquished Rachel, she sat there, struck dumb, Kell triumphant.

"See?"

"Wow," Rachel whispered, reaching for her drink. "You were right."

Luke cleared his throat and glared at Kell. "Show off."

"Anyhow," Kylie said pointedly, "I can't go to the parade. We're having a family video call right at the same time. With my mom, grandparents, and sister in different time zones, we settled on the same two hour stretch as the parade."

"Next year," Luke reassured her, his fingers caressing the inside of her arm.

Next year, she thought to herself.

Would there be a next year?

Chapter Thirty-Three

Luke

Convincing his mom to hold Christmas at the camp was easier than he thought.

His brother, sister, and dad, on the other hand…

"This isn't as comfortable as my chair back home," Dean groused as he shifted his butt, leaning on each hip, wiggling his thighs, and crossing his knees.

"When we all move in, you can bring *your* chair," Deanna reminded him, her tone making it clear this wasn't the first time they'd had this conversation.

And her sigh showed she knew it wouldn't be the last.

"It's Christmas! Can't blame a man for wanting to be comfortable."

"Since when are you comfortable on Christmas? You eat so much, you unbuckle your belt and moan and groan in your chair half the night about your stomach exploding."

"Two words, Deanna: 'your chair.' I have a right to roll around in pain in *my* chair. The one in *my* home."

"You're impossible."

"And you're standing under the mistletoe."

Watching his dad turn into an alpha male and kiss his mother silly filled Luke with a weird blend of amusement and disgust.

Mostly disgust.

"Get a room!" Colleen called out, throwing a tiny candy cane at their dad's head, which he caught blind, while kissing their mother.

He didn't flinch, the kiss meandering, his hand sliding down Mom's waist to her–

"Dean!" she gasped, batting at his hand. "Not in front of the kids!"

"It's not as if they don't know how we brought them into this world, Deanna."

Colleen threw a cracker.

Again he didn't flinch, catching it easily.

"Keep it coming, little girl," he said to her. "I'd love a beer next."

That finally got Deanna to smack him, the show over.

Thank goodness.

The Luview family Christmas was going to be small this year, with Dennis in Germany. Once a year, in the summer, the entire extended family got together. Every Luview, Bilbee, Forsythe, and Labrecque–all descended, one way or another, from Abram Luview and Jedidiah Bilbee–gathered at a small campground about an hour away. Other holidays, until Amber died on Thanksgiving, had always been a bit of a blend, but this year, Luke had wanted Christmas to be small.

Intimate, even.

And late. It was seven p.m. and dinner wasn't ready yet. Colleen had worked a holiday shift at the hospital, done at five, and they'd all adjusted their schedules.

The plan: mingle, eat, and go to bed. They'd brought old camping equipment to the lodge, with a real bed for his parents. Rachel found it all quaint and called it "camping," while Kell had teased her mercilessly and threatened to take her on a real back-country camping trip. In the end, everyone had some kind of bed, and the Luview family would spend their very first night here at their new home.

Everyone except Dennis.

And Kylie. This year, at least. Next year would be a whole different matter, if he had anything to say about it.

Nothing fancy, but it worked.

Kylie walked into the room holding a mug of hot cocoa with a dollop of Fluff floating in it, Kell behind her, mischief in his eyes.

"Where's Rachel?" Luke asked.

He nodded toward one of the bedrooms. "At the wrapping station. She found a gift she forgot about in the car just now for Harriet."

"You know we ran into her the other day in town?"

"Oh, yes. Heard all about it. Rachel introduced Kylie to the Love Bomb."

"Does she seriously think Reef will go for that?"

"You know Rachel. She won't give up easily."

"I'm so glad you guys are here."

Kell grinned. "Wouldn't miss it for the world."

Luke took inventory: Mom and Dad; Kell and Rachel; Luke, Kylie, and Harriet; Colleen.

Small, but rich with love. Dennis was sorely missed. Luke wished he'd retire from the military and come join them. He'd helped out with the camp, putting in a share and telling them to give him a small cabin or else he'd build his own, but Luke wanted him *here*, woven into their lives, wanting selfishly for Harriet to know him better.

"You look happy," Kylie said, her arm sliding around his waist, an act not unnoticed by his mom, who winked at him. Kylie's touch made him feel something he hadn't experienced in a long time: comfort.

And passion, but not in front of his parents.

Just then, Rachel walked into the room, holding a stack of shiny presents, the wrapping paper different from everyone else's. Not a spot of red, pink, or white was on the paper. It was all silver, gold, blue, and green.

"I thought you found *one* present!" Kell said, taking the three boxes from her.

Rachel's chin jutted up. "There were two more. I can't come close to competing with Kylie's fairy cape, but I have to try!"

Kell kissed her as he took the presents and walked toward the enormous tree.

"I see someone's not a fan of Love You's colors," Kylie said out of the corner of her mouth, *sotto voce*, her mannerisms making Luke chuckle.

"In town, she conforms. Everywhere else, no. She's a force to be reckoned with. A little like you."

"Me?" She pinched his waist.

"That's a compliment. City girl who came here for an acquisitions assignment that would elevate Love You's chocolate company into an international brand. Ran into Kell. Fell in love. You know the story." He gave her a squeeze.

Kylie smiled up at him. "City girl?"

"Uh, city *woman*."

Kylie laughed. "I meant I'm not from the city."

"No, you're not, but it's where you've been." He frowned. "And where you might still go."

"Hi!" Rachel interrupted them, smoothing her green cashmere sweater before coming in for a hug. "My Love Bomb buddy!"

Luke snorted, looking to his baby brother, who clearly wanted to join in and snicker but knew he'd pay for it dearly later with his beloved.

He just froze with a fake smile on his face.

Kell shot Rachel an amused glance. Luke knew his brother was crazy for her, and everyone in town expected a proposal soon.

Their mom was practically drooling over the prospect of more grandkids.

Rachel was from L.A., and a city person through and through. But falling in love with Kell made her stay.

Were Kylie's feelings for him strong enough for the same outcome?

"Daddy?" He looked down to find Harriet's face covered in shiny red smears. "Can I have a candy cane?"

Using his thumb, he swiped the corner of her mouth, showing her the sticky streak. "Looks like you already had one."

Innocent eyes met his. "How did you know?"

He tapped his temple. "I'm psychic."

"What's *sidekick* mean?"

As Kylie and Rachel made plans to meet for coffee in the next few days, Luke turned into a marshmallow and let Harriet have more candy. She'd be buzzing half the night, but that's what holidays were for, right?

Not gloom and doom and mourning.

A smile took over his face as he watched Kylie and Rachel talking. Kylie was using her hands animatedly, Rachel's touchy-feely gestures connecting the two women as much as their experiences living in New York and L.A. seemed to, if the snippets of conversation he overheard were any measure.

Calamine, Kell's enormous Maine coon cat, made her way into the room, slinking over to the fireplace and curling up on a small braided rug. Kylie did a double take at the animal, then said something to Rachel, who gave her a sympathetic look.

A few weeks ago, Kylie had mentioned she was allergic. Good thing dogs weren't an issue. Once she settled in with him, Jester wouldn't be an obstacle.

Whoa, boy, he thought to himself. *You're really a goner.*

The thought made him grin.

Mom walked over to him, her ginger beer half gone. She held up her bottle and tapped his glass.

"To new beginnings," she said with a wink.

Instead of groaning, he just smiled.

Mischief filled her eyes. "To new beginnings in *eighteen days*."

"You're impossible, Mom."

"Where do you think you inherited it from?"

Dean clapped his hands loudly for attention.

"Let's eat!" He pointed to the table. Eight chairs were set around the big square table Luke had improvised from four smaller tables, covered with a green linen tablecloth. Tall white candles in silver candlesticks, brought from home, stood in the center, with fresh holly laid between them.

Dean and Deanna were on one side.

Kell and Rachel next.

Colleen and Harriet after them.

And, finally... Luke and Kylie.

Dennis's absence was duly noted, and Colleen hadn't had a long-term boyfriend in forever because of her dating curse. They'd invited Moore, but he'd decided last-minute to fly out to Minnesota to watch his son, Jordy, perform in a local A Christmas Carol production.

It was eight for Christmas.

Kylie took her place next to him, sitting nervously, her butt half in the chair.

"I should help," she whispered. "Your mom must need some help in the kitchen, right? I don't want them to think I'm a slacker."

He was confused. "Why would they think that?" His hand went to her hip, encouraging her to sit. She looked around, the tips of her ears blushing red.

Her sweet embarrassment made him remember to be a gentleman again.

"Sit," he urged her. "No need to help. Remember? If you insist, help me with dishes." He squeezed her hand. She held his tightly.

"Okay."

Dinner was his mother's traditional Christmas feast. Deanna Luview had married into the famous local family and had four children. While she enjoyed large gatherings, the Luview kids also knew one truth about their mother: she enjoyed cooking alone.

Everything *her* way.

Woe be unto anyone who walked into the kitchen when she was multitasking. Deanna was calm, cool, and always collected, with two exceptions: when someone she loved was hurting, and while managing a big holiday dinner.

Offer to take something off a burner and you'd get a glare, a snappy comeback, or worse: a "Don't mess up my system. Shoo!"

Push too hard and she simply snapped, "Get out."

His mom was loving, but she was also ready to blow if someone inserted themselves into her mental plan of how the whole dinner worked.

Rachel, fortunately, wasn't the type to intrude, and Luke had warned Kylie, who hadn't liked the idea of not helping, but who was willing to wait and do cleanup.

Deanna Luview may have been a dictator during the cooking stage, but she gladly handed off the aftermath to everyone else.

His parents walked from the lodge's big commercial kitchen out to the large table, the two deftly handling the ham, mashed potatoes, baked yams, green beans, salad, and grilled focaccia. Luke's stomach felt full before he took a single bite, just from looking at the food.

"Kylie made special Christmas fairy cupcakes, too!" Harriet crowed.

Kell shoved a poker into the fire he'd built in the giant stone fireplace, moving around the hanging stockings. He wore a green wool sweater that matched Rachel's perfectly. Everyone dressed in shades of green and red, leaning heavily on green. In a town like Love You, Maine, any chance to wear something other than red, pink, or white was warmly welcomed.

"Say grace?" His mom asked his dad as they sat down, his somber nod enough. Everyone reached for each other's hand and Kylie shot him a nervous, inquiring look. He just smiled back.

His dad cleared his throat and said, "This food is good, my kids are not, thank you Lord for what we've got."

"DEAN!" his mom shouted, throwing her napkin at him.

"You said to say grace! I did!"

"Not like *that!*"

Kell reached across the table for the bread, half standing to grab the edge of the basket.

"Kell! Manners!"

Kell winked at her. "But Dad says we're bad. Don't have to have good manners if we're bad."

"Don't listen to your father!"

"Hey!" His dad smacked his mom on the butt. "Don't undermine my authority."

Luke, Colleen, and Kell burst into uncontrollable laughter.

"Authority," Colleen said, wiping a tear from the corner of her eye.

Luke saw Kylie and Rachel share shrugs.

"Let's eat!" Harriet declared, proving that children have infinitely more common sense than adults.

Sometimes.

For fifteen blissful minutes, Luke's family ate in silence, other than compliments to the chef, which his mom accepted happily. Although his hands were too busy to put one on Kylie's knee, they still sat close enough that he could smell her perfume, a light, lemony cologne overlaid on her own vanilla and sugar scent.

It was almost like touching her.

Kylie often smelled like freshly baked goodness.

Earlier in the week, his mom had made the tactful decision to have the family exchange Christmas gifts before Kylie came over, so she didn't feel like she had to bring something for people she didn't really know yet. Yesterday, Kylie had given Harriet her present, the fairy cape she'd had made at Labreque's, his little girl wearing it now.

In fact, she'd slept in it.

Luke had a special gift for Kylie in his back pocket, in a tiny box. No, it wasn't an engagement ring.

It was better.

You always knew when dinner was over, because Dad pushed his chair back, let out an enormous groan, and said, "Deanna, I don't know how you do it. Thirty-nine years of holiday meals and each one is better than the last."

"You said that last year, Dean."

"Meant it then, too."

Colleen gave Kylie a peculiar look that set Luke's senses on edge, but he didn't know why.

"And Dad'll say it next year, too," his sister called out. She winked at Kylie. "You'll hear it again if–when, I mean *when*– you're here."

If? *IF*? He wanted to throttle her. What was going on?

Kylie went pale and blushed at the same time, which Luke didn't know was possible. She just smiled at Colleen, but drank quite a bit of her glass of wine after.

Kell, Luke, and Colleen stood, Kell saying to their father, "Come on. Our turn to work."

Lumbering up, his tall, teddy bear of a father made a pouty face. "But I don't wanna."

His mom poured herself a nice, full glass of pinot grigio. "That's what I said when I got up at six a.m. to start cooking this morning!"

And with that, the Luview kids and their dad began clearing the table.

Rachel and Kylie both stood to help, but Mom waved them back into their seats. "Let them do it. This'll give me a chance to chat with you two." She winked at Rachel, then grinned at Kylie. "Two city girls finding their way home." Deanna reached for Kylie's hand as Luke hovered, torn between being useful and watching the conversation.

Kell's nudge did the trick. Kitchen it was.

"She's great," Dad said as he scraped dishes and began stacking them on one side of the industrial kitchen sink. Dinner for eight looked like a dollhouse set of dishes in this commercial kitchen attached to the lodge. A flash of a future where they rented the place out for weddings hit Luke between the eyes.

Weddings.

Kylie. Wedding. Bride.

Love swelled in his chest at the thought.

"Earth to Luke! You look lovestruck," Dad said with a hearty laugh. "Get to work with that sprayer and let's get this over with."

"Kylie's wonderful. Why wouldn't Luke be lovesick?"

"I said love*struck*, not lovesick."

"Same thing as far as Luke and Kylie are concerned."

That got Kell a quick squirt in the stomach. He howled in protest just as Colleen came in and dodged the spray. She quickly began putting away leftover sweet potatoes, shaking her head but laughing.

Luke sidled up to her. "What's going on with you and Kylie?" he whispered.

She stiffened. "What do you mean?"

As Kell and Dad began dueling with separate sprayers, Colleen and Luke played a word tango he didn't like one bit.

"I saw you giving her a funny look."

She snorted. "So now I can't look at her?"

"I thought you liked her."

"I did! I do." Her eyes narrowed. "Why are you so paranoid?"

"I'm a cop. It's in my blood."

"Not about people you love." Eyes dropping, Colleen sighed. "And you do. You love her."

He patted the box in his back pocket, pulling it out to show her. "Yes."

"Oh my! You're *proposing?*"

At her words, Dad dropped a big china platter. It shattered, silencing the room in an instant. Luke hurriedly shoved the box back in his pocket.

Kell called out, "I get to go first, bro."

Luke wondered how this all sounded to the three women at the dining table.

Then he heard Harriet shout, "I want Daddy to propose! Gamma, what does propose mean?"

A defensive shield formed around his skin, the kind he used throughout his days at work, separating himself from the world so he could do his job right.

Propose.

Propose?

He wasn't ready. Neither was she.

But it was coming.

Soon enough. He knew it deep in his bones.

And deeper in his heart.

His mom's head poked in, eyes going from brightly curious to deeply disappointed when she looked down and saw the shattered dish. "My grandmother's serving platter!"

"I'm so sorry, Deanna," Dean said, contrite. "It slipped."

"It slipped just when I heard the word *propose*. Who's proposing?" she asked eagerly, eyes jumping from Kell to Luke.

"Don't look at me," Colleen muttered. "I haven't had a date in so long, my leg hair could be donated to Locks of Love."

"No one. Yet," Kell said in a prickly tone. "But Luke has a box in his back pocket."

Deanna's eyes dropped to his butt. "What's in there?"

Kell and his dad started snickering.

He pulled out the present. "It's a charm necklace. Moore made a silver charm for me." Luke didn't mention he'd spent a useless afternoon in Portland trying to find the right present, and had realized–head smack and all–while in his fifth store, that he could have asked Moore for the custom design. His friend had pulled in some favors with a silversmith.

Cost him a pretty penny, but it was worth it.

"Awwwwww," his mom said, touching his shoulder. "Kylie has something special for you, too."

"She does?"

"Just told us. I can't wait for you two to exchange presents." She yawned.

"How about now?" Kell said, thumbing toward the door just as Kylie appeared at the threshold.

"Everything okay in here?" she asked, avoiding eye contact with Luke.

Ah. She'd *definitely* heard the proposal comments.

Taking her hand, he led her out of the kitchen, grabbing their coats as his mom called out, "Careful! Snow's thick! Might want to make it an early night or," she said with a wink, "have Kylie spend the night."

Luke was definitely ignoring that comment.

"What are you doing?" Kylie hissed as they lurched toward the door.

"I want to give you your present in private."

"Oh!" She pulled back, fished around in her tote bag, and pulled out a flat box about the size of a book. "Yours is here. Perfect."

Cool air and thick, fat flakes greeted them as they went outside, the moonglow lending the night some Christmas magic.

Both looked up at the stars as Luke walked her toward the lake.

"Where are we going?"

"Somewhere special."

The path to the pier was one he knew well now, drawn to it nearly every day, the water a kind of elixir stronger than even the hot springs in Luview. While he knew about Cupid's power, Lake Wannacanhopa was his potion.

His super power.

As their boots pounded the dock, the pier bound by ice, he pulled her close, wrapping his arms around her, offering her a deep, lovely kiss she gave right back.

Then, determined to make the night perfect, he put some space between them and pulled out the wrapped box.

Kylie gasped.

"It's not–it's not a ring. I haven't gone that far. But it's very special."

Pulling off her gloves, she quickly unwrapped the package and gave a sound of delight.

"Oh, Luke."

"You like it?"

"It's *so* perfect. Thank you."

Moore had commissioned the charm exactly as Luke had described. It was a little pier.

Just like the one they were standing on.

The chain was long enough to go over her head; he knew she didn't like tight choker necklaces. She fingered the charm for a moment, then practicality seeped in.

It was too cold not to wear gloves.

"Here," she said, offering her gift to him.

As he opened it, the moon caught the silver charm on Kylie's neck, and a sense of peace–deep and total peace–filled him.

Life was good.

He was healing.

Love was part of his world again.

And then he realized what Kylie had given him.

"The scarf? The one Amber made for me?" He couldn't keep the incredulity out of his voice.

Kylie's shy smile showed him how nervous she was. "I found it in the poncho pocket, that night I was stuck in the donation bin. It's cashmere, and it was falling apart."

He nodded. "She made it for me when I turned eighteen. Then moths got it."

"I mended it. Did my best, but about half of it is new."

"So it's half Kylie, half Amber."

Closing the gap, she pressed her hand over his chest. "Yes. Like your heart. Room for both of us."

"What's inside it?" he asked, grinning as he unwrapped the layers, laughing hard at the sight of the little carved giraffe.

"It's a silly little present. Found it at the antiques shop when you ran into me in town."

"Crooked neck, just like poor Needle."

"I took it as a sign."

"You found an adorable, meaningful carving at Love You Again. I found an ivory breast shield. I'm way outclassed by you, Kylie."

"Love You Again," she whispered. "I forgot that's the name of the store."

He turned the carving over in his hands. "It's wonderful. Just like you."

Like the night, their kiss was its own perfection, suspended through years, ending in seconds, every sweet sensation etching itself in him. With clarity, he saw his future spread out before him, Kylie and Harriet, more children, a settled life with his wife and children in the place he loved the most.

With the people he loved even more.

It was perfect.

Too perfect.

Breaking away, he looked down at her, cupping her jaw in both of his hands, kissing away a flake that fell on her nose.

"I can't believe you came back. All these years."

"I know."

"And here I am, with a kid."

"She's a great kid."

"If you'd stayed, she might have been your kid."

"That doesn't make sense, Luke."

"You know what I mean." He stared at her, reading her, surveying the emotional landscape and searching to find the weakness. It was built into him, a major part of who he was and why he was so good at law enforcement.

"I do. Life could have been different. Imagine if Amber had lived? None of this," she said, gesturing between them, "would be happening."

"But Amber did die. And I'm raising Harriet alone."

The word *alone* hung in the air.

He frowned. "I have to be everything for her, Kylie. *Everything*."

"That doesn't leave any room for you."

"I'll have plenty of room when she's eighteen."

"It's not like that, Luke. Your heart needs space, too. You can't put it in a box for the next twelve years and expect it to be healthy and whole when you finally spring it loose."

"For years, it felt like I didn't have a choice. Until now."

"It doesn't have to be either/or. What if you can have what you need *and* give Harriet everything she needs to thrive?"

He stepped forward, caressing the side of her face, fingers playing lightly with her earlobe. The touch made her shiver.

"What if what I need and what she needs are the same person? You."

Where he should have seen attraction, love, hope, joy—instead he saw nothing but guilt. Shame.

Sadness in Kylie's eyes.

Why?

"Luke."

"Mmm?" His mouth moved toward hers.

Bracing herself, Kylie stopped him with a palm flat against his chest, his heart beating steadily, calmly, under her touch.

"I need to tell you something."

"I need to tell you something, too," he said in a deep, emotion-filled voice. It was time.

Time to say those three little words.

"You go first."

"No, you."

The light laughter from both was self-conscious, funny, but also recognized as part of some nervous tension between the two that Luke wished he could wave away.

"I love you," he said, slowly, savoring every word.

"I have an interview in New York," she said at the same time, the words coming out as if disconnected, each one a skewed puzzle piece that didn't quite fit.

New York.

I have.

Interview.

"You *what?*" they both gasped in sync, the only time they seemed to be, a truth that caused a pain deep inside him, like his heart being seared over a flame.

No.

Not this.

Not now.

Not *her*.

He was the one who broke away, broke eye contact, broke all contact, because he was broken.

Broken heart.

Broken spirit.

Snapped right in two.

Again.

"New York? You got a job there?"

"An interview. Not an offer."

"When?"

"December 28."

"When were you going to tell me?"

"I *am* telling you."

"That's not what I meant and you know it!" He exploded, knowing his voice would carry, hating himself for it, reeling it in only because he didn't want to upset Harriet.

"Luke, I–"

"When did you know about this? When did someone ask you for an interview?"

"I had an online screening interview. Thought I bombed it. Then they asked me to come in person."

"WHEN?"

"Last week."

And there it was.

"You lied to me? You lied for a *week?*"

"I didn't technically lie for a week. The interview was on the eighteenth, and the offer came in–"

"Don't *technically* me, Kylie! A lie of omission is as bad as any other."

"I didn't know how to tell you! It's with KidzdocTV, the biggest channel in children's programming, and–"

"So you really are leaving." His head pitched down in defeat, jaw turning to granite. "What a fool I've been. I thought if I made it good enough here, you'd–" Disgusted with his own foolish fantasy, he realized he was just like his little girl.

Caught up in a dream world where playing pretend games was just that.

Pretend.

Kylie's love was nothing but a story he told himself, fiction, as real as the tooth fairy.

"I'm not automatically leaving! You did make it good, Luke. Life *is* good. Great, even. I love Harriet so much, and she's so sweet. And you, well... I'm torn. I'm so torn. It's not like this hasn't been hard. I'm falling for you and I feel split between two worlds."

"Split."

"Yes. Between what I thought I wanted and what I really want."

"Which one am I, Kylie?"

Who knew that a tiny sliver of a second could carry so much meaning? That's all it took–her hesitation–for his own to disappear.

He knew what needed to happen next.

It was simple, and it was horrible, but it was also *right*.

"Consider this your two-week notice," he said calmly, still holding her hand, eyes on her, going into protective law enforcement officer mode, folding his emotions in, going flat. He had a job to do–deliver bad news–and he was going to do it while he built a wall around his heart.

"My... what?"

"I'm firing you as Harriet's nanny, Kylie," he said softly.

"*Firing?*"

"Yes. That's the term for it. Letting you go. Terminating your employment. You'll finish up with her over the next two weeks." An acrid taste filled his mouth. "Taking December 28th off for your interview, of course."

"Luke, please."

"The two weeks are so there's a transition for both of you, and–"

She snatched her hand away. "You can't do this!"

"I *am* doing this. It's for the best."

"You're firing me because you're hurt that I want options in my life?"

"This has nothing to do with us."

"Liar."

The word hung in the air like a fireball in the falling snow.

"Excuse me?"

"I said *liar*. You're lying, Luke. This isn't about Harriet. You know I'd never do anything to hurt her."

"Sneaking around, having interviews in New York you don't mention is the opposite of not hurting her, Kylie." The coldness in the air filled his voice.

"You knew I was applying for jobs! You're upset I'm not turning down the New York interview. You're upset I'm not throwing myself into your arms without ever exploring a chance at a job I've wanted my whole career. You're asking me to give up everything and follow you into your life. How fair is that? Everything I thought I knew about life changed for me in August, and then again in November when you found me in that charity bin. It's been a month! One month, and you expect me to pivot and let go of what I've wanted in my career for years! And when I hesitate, you fire me."

Every word she said made sense. It did. In his mind, at least.

Heart? Heart was screaming and couldn't hear a word she said.

"It's for the best."

"Says who?"

"Says the man in charge of protecting a little girl who's already had her heart broken when someone she loved just disappeared."

"You're using Harriet as a shield. Own your feelings, Luke. Look me in the eye and tell me you don't love me. You just said the words, and we haven't even talked about *that* yet!"

The dare made him stare at her, awash in emotions he shoved down as hard as possible.

Instead of saying another word, he turned around and walked back into the lodge, knowing he'd face a wall of family with questions, mind too full to deal with them.

Because Kylie had been right.

He loved her. Deeply. Desperately.

Hopelessly.

Which was why he had to leave her first.

Chapter Thirty-Four

Kylie

"I just–just..." Words failed her as she sobbed during the FaceTime with Wendy, who was drinking out of a tiny espresso cup and eating tiny pieces of cheese with hand gestures that looked so sophisticated.

Kylie, on the other hand, looked like snot had moved into her head and paid half the rent.

"He dumped you on Christmas? Dumped you *and* fired you? That jerk!"

"He's not a jerk. *I'm* the jerk!" Kylie grabbed a spoon, a new pint of ice cream, and gave up on all decorum.

"How are you the jerk, Kylie? He didn't even give you a chance to talk about it."

"And I'm not even sure I'm dumped. We weren't technically together. We had one date." The first scoop of ice cream was a pleasant torture that made her palate ache.

It was a pain she could define, so that was a step up.

"He invited you to spend Christmas with his family! You kissed repeatedly! You talked about having sex! *He told you he loved you!* Duh, Kylie. You were together."

Were.

Oh, how final that single word sounded.

Were.

As if it would never happen again.

Which Luke had made abundantly clear.

"I know we were together," she conceded. "I know. I think my brain is just trying to untangle it all. I was so humiliated, I followed him back to the lodge, pretended I was sick, and left as fast as I could. How could life go from being wondrous and beautiful to destroying me in a single short conversation?"

"I think that's called adulthood," Wendy said bitterly.

"I wish I could jump on a plane and hang out in Berlin with you!" A chunk of frozen peanut butter, shaped like a scythe, threatened to stab her. With the edge of the spoon, she broke it up and took a bite.

"You can! He just fired you. You have no job now."

"THAT IS NOT HELPING, WENDY!"

"Just pointing out the obvious. Your lease runs out soon. You have no job. No romantic partner. You have a big interview in New York. You don't have to feel conflicted about that now."

"I don't? What do you mean?"

"Luke just made it easy for you. He dumped you and fired you. You don't have to choose between two options. You only have one now."

The sob began deep in her stunned heart, Wendy's simple, direct words shattering every organ inside her. Kylie went soft, crumpling into a ball on her couch, the sweet chocolate ice cream in her mouth turning to something sour.

The taste of failure.

"Um, sorry. Did I say the wrong thing?"

"No. You just said the truth."

"It feels like I did something wrong."

"You didn't. I'm just emotional."

"Be your emotional self, Kylie. Go on ahead. I wish we could be together. You've really had the worst year."

The worst year.

Until this moment, Kylie would have said that fifteen years ago was her worst year, but Wendy was right.

347

This was worse.

Way worse.

What started out as Perry's fault had somehow morphed into her fault.

Hers, and only hers.

Because if she'd just made the right choice...

But what was the right choice?

Luke?

New York?

"I don't want to lose Harriet," Kylie said, throat seizing with a sadness that ran through every cell in her body, bones heavier, muscles aching with grief. Caring for children was always a calling for Kylie, and her relationship with Luke's daughter had been so sweet, separate yet intertwined with her growing connection to Luke.

Losing one meant losing the other, and while she pined for him, she was also devastated to realize she was done being Harriet's nanny.

Tomorrow, when she wasn't a mess and had a little more than a handful of hours of distance from the confrontation with Luke, she would text him and ask to see Harriet. Even an angry Luke would agree to that.

He put his daughter's emotional needs first, above all else.

That's why he'd fired her.

Plus, she still had two weeks of work left. Plenty of time to transition the little girl with as little pain as possible.

"What would you do, Wendy? I want to fix this."

"You've asked me that a bazillion times. I refuse to answer."

"I won't hold it against you if I take your advice."

"I might not do the same thing you'd do, Kylie."

"I hate this."

"Hate..."

"Feeling paralyzed. Stupid. Like I threw away the best thing that ever happened to me."

"You have two best things, Kylie. Most people never even get one. I think it's the choice that's driving you crazy. Not the options." Wendy took a sip of her coffee. "Actually, scratch that. You don't have two choices now. You're down to one."

One.

"Unless you think you can go back and try to mend things with Luke?"

"No matter what, I want to. What if it's too late, though? The way he looked at me—so full of pain."

"I get it. Poor guy told you he loved you, and you didn't say it back."

"I didn't realize he was saying it!"

"Maybe you should find him and say it back. Unless you *don't* love him."

Love.

Love, so soon? It had been a month. Luke Luview was absolutely, positively not the kind of guy who lived life with his heart on his sleeve. Closed off and reserved, he was like that even as a teen. Pleasant and polite, sure.

Not an emotional kind of guy.

The part of himself he showed her over these last weeks, though, revealed a softer side. Deep caring was evident in the way he raised Harriet, but Kylie always knew there was more inside him, too.

Even at fifteen, she'd known.

Did she love him, now?

Yes.

Had she loved him all those years ago?

Yes.

Here she was, in love with him.

Again.

"I do."

"You do."

"I do."

"I can't wait to hear you say those words to a minister when you two get married."

"Hold on! Just a minute ago, you said he was out of my life and New York was my only option!"

"A minute ago, you hadn't said you love him!"

Wendy's grin made Kylie shake her head. "This isn't funny."

"I know. I'm sorry. Look, go to New York. Let Luke simmer

down. See what happens with KidzdocTV. If they make you an offer, then..."

"Then what?"

"*Then* you have to choose between living your awesome future life in New York and telling Luke how you feel."

"That's still a crappy set of options. Why can't I have both? Luke *and* the cool job?"

"Remember that pesky adulting thing? Yeah. That's why you can't have both."

Melted chocolate ice cream pooled a bit in her pint. Kylie stopped talking for a bit, eating her way through until the pint was half empty. The sisters sat in companionate silence, thousands of miles and an ocean apart, until Wendy cleared her throat and said:

"I never liked Perry. Neither did Mom."

"I know. You told me when he dumped me and you came to Maine."

"I haven't met Luke, but–"

"You met him when we lived here."

"I was eight, Kylie. Eight. Doesn't count. Can I finish?"

"Sure."

"My point is, I can already tell he lights your inner world on fire, and not like Perry firebombed you and did an uncontrolled burn. Luke is warm and steady, rock-solid and loyal. He's also not hard to look at, has a ton of local friends, and is absolutely the perfect brother-in-law to call when you need help moving."

"Brother-in-law?"

"I'm going to tell you my advice again: Go to New York. See what happens there. Then go back to Luview and do what you know you want Luke to do to you."

"Do to me?"

"Yeah." Wendy smirked. "Love you."

Chapter Thirty-Five

Luke

His mom had shown up tonight and practically shoved him out the door.

Summarily evicted him from his own house.

It was December 27, two days after Christmas, and two days after his heart cracked in half.

Unlike the last time that happened, two years ago, this time he was entirely responsible. His choice, his initiative.

So why did he feel so damn awful?

Maybe because he had shown Kylie his wet, unprotected, slobbering heart and told her he'd loved her, and instead of saying those same tender words back, she'd told him she had an interview.

In New York.

"Go be with your friends at Bilbee's." His mom had arrived with Harriet's favorite kid's meal from a fast food place twenty minutes away, and Harriet was ignoring them both, munching on French fries as she played dolls with Jester.

"I don't want to go to Bilbee's and drink, Mom. I've got plenty of beer here."

"Plenty of misery, too. You need to go hang out with your buddies."

"If I go to Bilbee's, I'll just be hounded endlessly by people who are disappointed the betting pool is off."

"Paused."

"Excuse me?"

"It's not off. Just paused. And there's a side bet running three to one that you'll end up together."

"This town," he muttered. "Maybe I should just move away and have a *private* life."

His mom's eyes had narrowed. "I've never heard you say that before."

"Complain about the town? Of course you have, unless you don't listen to any of us."

"No, Luke. Talk about moving away from Luview. *Ever*."

A shrug was all he could offer.

But it spoke volumes.

"You're thinking about moving to New York to be with Kylie."

"No."

"Luke." The way she drew out his name made his hackles rise. His middle name was next, wasn't it?

Suddenly, he felt like he was eleven and crashed the front picture window playing softball in the living room.

"I'm not talking about this."

"That's right. You're going to Bilbee's and your friends can talk some sense into you."

"My friends? Have you met my friends? Moore is the last person to give relationship advice."

"No kidding," his mom muttered. "I wish he and Colleen would just admit how they feel about each other and stop this friendship nonsense."

Luke went wide-eyed, eyebrows climbing. "What? My best friend and my sister? No. Absolutely not."

"Oh, please. As if we all can't see it. They're made for each other."

"You are a bored pseudo-Cupid who sees love where there is none. Moore was married and divorced twice before he was thirty, and Colleen lives under a curse where she can't get past the third date with a guy who doesn't end up in her ER. You think they should be in a *relationship?*" Laughter, cold and hard, came out of him like a jailbreak.

"I'll accept the Cupid title, but nothing is pseudo about me. I know when two people belong together." Hard stares from Deanna Luview were nothing new to him, but this one took the cake.

"I told you everything's over and done with Kylie."

She snorted. "And I told you you're delusional if you think you can just shut your feelings for her off like a light switch."

"Not up for discussion, Mom."

"You have to talk to someone. Have you reached out to Maura?" A change in her tone, from playfully firm to wounded worry, made him jolt and stare at her.

Worried eyes met his.

"Maura Kirkendaal? Why would I reach out to her?"

"She helped you and Harriet so much after Amber died."

"I know. Still sees Harriet for check-ins. Do you think Harriet needs her because of this mess with Kylie?"

"I think maybe *you* need to see Maura."

"For *what*?" Flabbergasted didn't begin to explain how he felt at this turn of the conversation.

"I remember how you were after Amber. I know how deeply you feel, Luke. You're not one for light connections to people. Kylie Hood made her way into your heart for a reason."

"It's not that I don't love her. I do. I'm man enough to own that. We just want different things. And I don't need a therapist to see that."

"You need to talk about this with Kylie, then. Not fire her and leave the poor girl in shock on Christmas."

"That's not quite how it went, Mom."

"That's exactly how it went."

"I drew a boundary."

"No, kiddo. You cut her out. You're this close to shunning her. That's extreme."

"I have to protect Harriet."

"Kylie's not a threat to Harriet. But I think you're overreacting and can't see it."

"Kylie hid the truth from me."

"Honey. She was open all along that she was job hunting."

Then why am I not enough?

The words slammed through his head, so sharp and full, a loud shout he was sure his mom could hear.

He growled. "You know what? Your plan is working." Walking to the closet, he snagged his coat and shoved his arms in it.

"Plan?"

"If you want to drive me out of my own house, this conversation is doing it."

She smirked. "Then I'm right on schedule."

Luke called out to his daughter. "Harriet!"

A half-hearted wave from his cheeseburger-drunk kid was all he got. Jester thumped his tail.

Twice.

He stormed out of the house and headed toward his Jeep, more than ready for a drink, after all.

Hand on the door, he paused, changing his mind.

A good, solid walk would help clear his head.

And make it easier to get home safely if he had more than one drink.

Crisp nights like this were less common than you'd think, as January loomed and heavy snow was on the horizon. While the cold pierced his nose and mouth every time he inhaled, it felt good. Exactly right, as it should be.

A thin wool cap in his pocket made it easier, the cold tickling the tips of his ears, but the rest of him was warm enough.

The walk past Mrs. Petrinelli's house was dicey. Never knew when the old woman would come out on her porch and want a chat.

Or to grill him for gossip.

Last thing he needed right now.

Legs moving quickly, he relished the silence, the sound of his breath against the cold winter's night more than enough company. It's not that his mom was wrong.

She wasn't.

It's that he didn't much like being told what to do.

Never had.

If she hadn't barged in tonight and taken over, he would have done exactly what he did last night: sulk in an easy chair in front of the television and try to stop stewing in his own sense of failure.

Failure to guard his heart.

Failure to protect Harriet from abandonment.

Failure to be more reasonable.

Yeah. He knew he was being unreasonable. Problem was, he didn't know how *not* to be. And he sure didn't want to talk it through with the very woman who just hurt him more than she seemed to understand.

Easier to watch the classic sports channel and let Jester get away with sleeping on the couch.

As he turned the corner onto Main Street and walked past the library, he smiled. Last week, Harriet had told him all about a snowflake project, and he noticed the cute sprinkling of paper cut-outs all over the windows, some hanging like mobiles in the library's foyer.

"Mine had glitter, Daddy! Fairy snowflakes!"

He was sure Kylie was behind the glitter.

And his little girl's enormous, joyful grin.

Harriet loved Kylie.

And so did he, damn it.

Which was why this hurt so much.

Opening the door to Bilbee's was second nature, the heavy oak door bringing forth a blast of warm, yeasty air.

"Look what the cat dragged in!" Moore called out.

"More like, look who Deanna kicked out."

The entire bar snickered as if they were one organism.

The crack came from Ollie Nolan, one of the facilities and maintenance guys who worked for the town. Big teddy bear with a few gray strands in his ZZ Top beard, and eyes that floated a little in his head, Ollie was clearly deep into his festivities for the night.

Luke made a mental note not to play darts with the guy. Didn't need puncture wounds right now.

His heart had been stabbed through enough already.

Rider Bilbee grabbed a pint glass and held it aloft, eyebrows raised. Luke nodded.

Guinness it was.

"Hey!" His sister's shout wasn't a surprise, but his reaction was.

Gratitude. Relief. Comfort.

He felt them all.

Clustered around a big eight-top table, his friends were clearly hours into hanging out, stacks of quarters next to coasters soaked by condensation. A basket of wings, half eaten, and some kind of nacho monstrosity sat in the center of the table, among other appetizers.

Good to see that they were eating some of their dinner instead of drinking it all.

The view of the table made his heart pang a little, remembering being here just last week with Kylie. While the incident with Lyle had been tricky, the time after had been an hours-long fest of good food, shooting pool, conversation, and fun.

Fun he wouldn't have again with her.

"Hey, yourself. What's going on?"

Colleen stared at him. "We're waiting for you. Mom ordered us all to show up and hang out so she could make it seem like we're just naturally here for my heartbroken brother."

Rider appeared, setting the pint glass before Luke.

"Man. Wish I'd thought of betting on you two breaking up. Outlier bet. Could have used that $450."

"Shut up, Rider."

"No problem, Luke."

Every Luview was related to every Bilbee in town, going back to Abram Luview and Adelaide Bilbee. Being teased by a Bilbee was like being teased by any other cousin, but Luke didn't have much tolerance in him.

Maybe a little liquid acceptance was in order.

Moore whispered something to Colleen, who looked at Luke

and laughed, then smacked Moore's hand as he went for the last remaining mozzarella triangle.

"What'd you do that for?" Moore barked.

"It's mine!"

"We can order more."

And he did just that, waving the empty basket at Rider as Colleen ate her victory snack, smiling smugly at Luke.

The first sip of his beer turned into a long, slow guzzle, the warm sound of classic rock floating through the air. His butt had never liked the chairs here, which was why he normally played pool or darts, but he wasn't here to play, was he?

He was here for some kind of love intervention.

Palm up, he looked at Colleen and Moore just as Kell and Rachel wandered over from the pool table area, holding hands. They took empty seats he now understood weren't so empty.

"Listen. Whatever Mom thinks she's up to, I want none of it. I am here to have a beer and play some pool. That's it. Don't need a bunch of you yahoos trying to therapize me."

"Therapize?" Rachel laughed.

"Yahoos?" Kell seemed offended.

Luke drank more and kept his mouth shut. He'd said what he'd said.

"Is therapize even a real word?" Rachel asked Kell, who shrugged.

Watching his little brother and his girlfriend holding hands at the table as they sipped their drinks made something in Luke twist a little, the pain almost physical.

Kylie should be here with him, his hand on her knee, hanging out, playing pool.

Just being together.

Instead, he drank more beer.

"Mom was right," Colleen said.

"Them's fightin' words," Luke said in a fake drawl, but he growled a little at the end.

"How much beer did you drink before you came here?" Moore asked, giving Colleen a conspirator's look.

"None. I'm just sick of other people telling me how to live my life."

"Who, aside from Mom, is doing that?" Kell asked.

"Everyone. Kylie decides she's just going off to New York, and doesn't bother telling me–"

"That's not quite what's happening," Rachel tried to respond, but Kell wisely shook his head at her.

"You talked to her, didn't you?" he barked at Rachel, who shot Kell a look that asked, *How much do I say?*

"They're friends, Luke," Kell intervened.

Great. Rachel and Kylie were talking behind his back, and Rachel was feeding it all to Kell, which meant his mom was in on whatever they were sharing.

"Mom's pushing me to come here. The chief wants me to be chief when he retires–"

"He does?" Colleen squealed. "That's great! Why didn't you tell me?"

"–and Anne Petrinelli thinks I should paint my front door red instead of the blue I painted it last year, because it 'pops' more and blends in with the town. Annabeth keeps coming over with baked goods like she's Kylie's rival, and you two," he added, pointing to Kell and Rachel, "are the epitome of Love You, Maine, and all the lovey-dovey b.s. the town represents."

"Uh oh. He's ranting," Kell murmured in Rachel's ear.

"Is that a Luke thing?" she asked him.

"You should know all about ranting, Ms. Hot Microphone," Luke said sharply, earning a blush from Rachel and a glare from Kell. Back in February, right before the Valentine's Day festival, Rachel had been caught on a live microphone at the gazebo stage, going on and on about all the flaws she saw in the town.

Luke was pretty close to finding his own hot mic and giving the people he'd known his entire life a big old piece of his mind.

One shaped like the heart Kylie had just broken.

"Why not take Annabeth up on her offers?" Moore asked with an impish grin, knowing it would just provoke Luke.

"Shut up."

"I think," Kell said pointedly, standing, "it's time for another round of pool. Moore, come join us."

"I'll be the odd one. Can't play with three."

"You can keep score. Or we can ask Ollie to play with us."

"Ollie's so drunk, I don't want to be bent over anywhere near him when he has a pool cue."

"Moore." Kell gave him a flat look that made it clear he needed to come.

"Why don't you two play?" Colleen said to the men. "Rachel and I will sit here and let Luke be grumpy with us."

"Why would Rachel want that kind of abuse?" Kell asked genuinely.

Colleen shot him a look.

"Fine. Okay." He kissed Rachel's cheek. "Be back soon."

"After I wipe his ass," Moore challenged.

"Hah. You wish. Last time we played, I killed you," Kell replied as they walked away, voices fading.

"This isn't going to work," Luke told his sister, though the beer was loosening him up.

"I want to talk to you. And I want Rachel here because she has some unique insight into what you're going through."

"I do?" Rachel squeaked.

"You're a city girl who fell in love with my stupid lumberjack brother and uprooted your life and dreams to stay here. Which either means you're one brick shy of a load or you're deeply in love."

"It might be a little of both," Rachel joked. She turned to Luke. "I think you and Kylie need to go swim in the hot springs and let the water do its magic." The smirk she shot him made it clear she was joking, but it just made him more depressed.

And instantly serious.

"I didn't need a dip in the hot springs with her. That's for people who want love but haven't found it. I found love, damn it. I just..."

Colleen touched his arm. "You just what?"

"I can't believe she'd rather live in New York City by herself and work there than be here in Luview with me and Harriet."

"Maybe she's thinking she can't believe you broke up with her and fired her just because she wants to try something you don't."

"There's no way I'm living in New York. Do you have any

idea what crime is like there? Rural Maine is a paradise compared to that."

"Did she say she's definitely moving?"

"She wouldn't go there for a job interview if she weren't serious."

"Luke." Colleen's reproachful tone made him sigh. "She can want to try something and also want to stay here."

"That's not how real life works. People have to prioritize. I didn't rise up high enough on her priority list."

"You make it all seem so simple. So black and white."

"Must be a Luview family trait," Rachel muttered, until Colleen's sharp glare made her quickly add, "Male trait. *Male*."

Colleen turned the glare back on Luke. "Maybe Kylie wanted your support as she job searched in New York *and* she wanted to stay in Luview."

Rachel nodded. "Colleen has a good point."

"*You* stayed, though," he said to Rachel, his voice filled with more raw pain than he wanted. Couldn't help it. It was leaking out.

"Me?"

"Yes, you. You came here, all career oriented, bulldozing your way through a work thing. Trying to save your job and go back to L.A. and be some corporate hotshot. But you changed your mind and stayed."

"I did."

"Then why won't..."

...*Kylie do the same*, he almost said.

"Because I chose. I had two good choices, Luke. Kell didn't tell me I *had* to choose him, because that's not a choice. That's an edict. Free will means being free to exert your will. Once I knew I loved him and loved being here more than my life in L.A., I knew this was what I had to do."

A heavy weight settled in his stomach, pinning him to earth.

Colleen pressed her fingers against her mouth, looking down, blinking. The silence between the three of them felt like he was being sentenced before a judge.

And rightly so.

For a crime he *did* commit.

The crime of not giving Kylie the benefit of the doubt.

"Is that why she didn't tell me about the interview?" he asked Rachel, their eyes meeting, hers full of kindness and caring. She'd only been in town for less than a year, but he knew she and Kell were together forever. In his mind, she was already his sister-in-law.

"Maybe. Maybe she was afraid you'd freak out, and she needed time. Maybe she didn't want to say anything in case she didn't get offered the job."

"But I want her to trust me. She didn't have to hide that kind of news."

"She did, though," Colleen interjected. "Sounds like she was afraid to upset you. Carrying that kind of secret must have been hard."

It hadn't occurred to him to think about how Kylie must have felt about her secret. That maybe she couldn't trust him.

Didn't feel safe sharing her truth.

"Damn it," he muttered. "I'm the person in her world she's supposed to trust the most. Supposed to be safest with—always. I want her to feel free to share, even when it's something that hurts me, because I want to know everything about her. Share everything. Be everything for her. And I—oh, geez."

Leaning forward on the table, elbows resting on wet coasters, he shoved his fingers in his hair, gripping his scalp.

"I blew it."

When neither woman rushed in to argue, his stomach sank even further.

Out of the corner of his eye, he saw Colleen tap Rachel's hand and motion for her to leave. Very soon they were alone, Luke focused as much as possible on his own breathing as he beat himself up for being such an ass.

A soft, breathy sound from his sister made Luke look up.

"I said something to her, too."

He frowned. "To Kylie?"

"Yes. At Mountain Dragon. We were both there picking up takeout before Christmas and I... well..."

"What did you say?" he demanded, voice turning to iron.

"I told her not to hurt you or Harriet. That she had to make sure she was serious if she kept going with you."

"You *what?*"

"I was trying to protect you!"

"You invaded my life! Did you threaten her?"

"With what? The fried egg on top of her bi bim bap? Of course I didn't threaten her, Luke! But I warned her. Warned her that you're a serious guy and she needed to make sure she was serious, too, if she was going to fall for you."

"No wonder she hid her New York stuff from me. I made it so she didn't trust me, and you just added to it."

"I'm not sorry, Luke. I said what I said because I care. And she took it just fine."

He snorted. "Just fine. Between what you said to her, and me firing her and ending the relationship on Christmas, we turn out to be one hell of a 'loving' family." His finger quotes made Colleen flinch.

"It's not too late to fix this."

"How? How, Colleen? How do I fix this?"

"Go to her."

"To New York?"

"Yep. Go there. Tell her how you feel. Do this thing they call talking. You know, talking?"

"Oh, you seem to know plenty about talking, Colleen. You talked plenty to Kylie."

"And you can, too. Go. Listen. Keep your mouth shut and let her be herself and tell you what she's thinking. What she's feeling. What she wants out of life."

"Then what?"

"Then do whatever comes next. You're a smart guy. You can figure it out. Just don't shut her out like you did. You two can find your way through this together if it's meant to be."

"You are the most aggravating big sister ever."

"Just doing my job right."

Luke stood, knowing Rider put the beer on his tab, and grabbed his outerwear as Kell shouted, "Where you going?"

"To fix my mistakes."

"See you in ten years!" Moore joked, but Kell elbowed him hard enough for Moore to fold over a little, giving Luke a wave.

The chill of being outside cleared his mind just enough to stop, hands on hips, and think.

Colleen was a meddling busybody, but she wasn't wrong.

Go find Kylie. Listen to her. See if he could salvage things.

New York, huh?

Grabbing his phone, he dialed his mom's number. It would be easier to do this by phone than face to face.

And he'd need the walk home alone to brace himself.

"Hello? Luke? Everything all right?"

At the sound of her voice, he grinned, heart lifting.

"Yeah, Mom. Everything's great. But I need you to do me a big favor."

Chapter Thirty-Six

Kylie

New York was loud, rude, smelly, busy–and just like her ex, Perry.

Exhausting.

Sitting to the right of Manu at the large oval conference table here in the executive suite gave Kylie a turbocharge, her mind sharpening every second she was in such close proximity to him. The man was a legend in children's television programming, and she had a seat at his table, literally.

Finally.

Victory was hers if she could convince them that she was the right person for the job.

There was just one problem:

She wasn't sure she wanted the job.

Three days ago, her world fell apart, shattered like a dropped snow globe. What had been perfect and pure, picturesque and soothing, suddenly became shards of glass, all poking her heart, the world as she knew it impossible to put back together.

For a fleeting month, she had come so close to a life she wanted.

And now, two lives. Two incompatible lives that forced her to pick one.

One.

Only one.

"Nordicbeth involved television programming and commercials, right?" Elsa Foxx asked her again, the question feeling increasingly demeaning. She'd asked the same question during Kylie's initial interview, and now Kylie's stomach twisted.

Elsa wasn't a fan, clearly.

"Yes."

"That just means you understand New England ski audiences. How does that understanding apply to an international children's market? We translate our offering into..." The words came out of her mouth, but Kylie was paying more attention to her emotional tenor, and it didn't feel right. Second in command at KidzdocTV, Elsa needed to be won over if Kylie had any hope of getting this job.

And it wasn't looking good.

Opening her mouth, Kylie replied easily, almost too easily, her inner world shedding worries as each sentence emerged. In real time, without thinking, she felt gears inside going *click-click-click*, some piece of her separating from worrying about the outcome of this in-person interview.

Either she got the job, or she didn't.

The end result wasn't worth ruining her life over.

Luke.

His name ricocheted through her head a thousand times.

Christmas night had been horrible after he fired her. Not that it wasn't bad enough being summarily dismissed, but the worst had happened after.

She couldn't think about that right now.

"–and New England holds charm for people, not just in terms of outdoor activities like skiing. For instance, I live near Love You, Maine, the town where love isn't just a feeling, it's a way of life."

Snorts and snickers filled the room.

Kylie soldiered on.

"And there's a camp near Luview, a camp I attended as a

child." Nostalgia gripped her, a need to be open and vulnerable. Why not? Why not be genuine?

When you had nothing to lose, it was so freeing.

"For a long time, I've thought about designing a fairy camp, much like the winter fae camp I designed for Nordicbeth. But a big one, in the woods. Gnome villages, fairies in the trees, that sort of thing. And I thought it would work in Luview."

"You have a plan for this?" Elsa's voice revealed her boredom, and something else Kylie couldn't put her finger on, but Manu leaned in.

"Hold on. Hold on," he said suddenly, giving Kylie an appreciative look. "This camp is near Love You, Maine?"

"Yes."

"Who did you say owns it?"

"I didn't. But it's Luke Luview. And his family."

"*The* Luviews? The people who own the town?"

"They don't actually own the town, but yes."

"Love You, Maine? That crappy tourist trap where every day is Valentine's Day?"

Kylie just stared at the woman who asked that question.

A guy snorted. "What's next? The cheesy section of Niagara Falls where suckers buy tickets to Ripley's Believe It Or Not?"

Manu just watched them, eyes narrowing. The room was charged with a strange tension she couldn't name.

As the New Yorkers all laughed and sneered, Kylie felt her growing anger change to something very unique and unfamiliar.

Standing slowly, she splayed her palms on the table, bending forward in a power stance, chin up, eyes wide and strong as she looked at the interviewing team.

"Let me give you some market research on Luview, Maine, folks. I'm a local there. Born and mostly raised. But I'm also well aware of what life is really like in the town where 'every day is Valentine's Day.' It's not some local-yokel-filled New England hillbilly small town. Oh, no. It's all business."

Eyebrows cocked, but people shut up.

"The town's new director of business development and planning, Rachel Hart, did an analysis of Love You Chocolate last year, trying to help the multinational Markstone's Chocolatier fold it into their brand. You know what happened with that deal, I assume," she said, not asking with a lift in her voice, but instead tapping into the fearless part of her, the part that knew that she was right. That she was powerful.

That she was in command.

"I–I don't know," Elsa confessed.

"The deal fell through, in part because the small-town owners decided Markstone's didn't offer enough."

"So they didn't have enough money?"

"Not money. The right branding. Revenue is up thirty-six percent for Love You Chocolate. All because of Rachel, and because people in Love You, Maine, know how to market the town. The feelings. The emotion of the place itself. And that's how fairy camp works, too. How fairies work, period. It's pure emotion. You don't have to be anything to enjoy fairies. You don't have to be productive, or smart, or rich, or pretty. You just have to like them. Kids *love* them. And fairy camp gets kids outdoors, gives them a social opportunity, and they find acceptance. Who doesn't want that? Imagine a series for kids where they get to escape into something so simple and easy?"

"Like Bronies," Elsa said under her breath to murmurs of assent.

Manu gave Kylie a searching look, one that said he'd underestimated her.

Then he turned to Elsa and said, "You know we've been trying to get in there for years."

Elsa squirmed in her seat.

"What do you mean?" Kylie asked, all the self-consciousness draining out of her. She wasn't getting this job. Why be nervous? She was done. Time to go home and–

Home.

She had no home.

No job. No partner. No–

Nothing.

Just.... nothing.

Manu explained, "I know who Rachel Hart is. Smart woman. Settled in Luview last year. We've been wanting to do some sort of branded show with the town, but the locals have pushed back.

Hard. The town manager has his own vision of how to market Luview, and our television shows haven't cut it. Can't get permits to film there. That reality show with Portia Starman a few years ago never took off, but the place seems tailor-made for children's programming."

"Really?" She was being polite. Kylie didn't know about KidzdocTV being blocked by the town manager, but she could see people like Kell Luview fighting tooth and nail against the overcommercialization.

"Make you a deal, Kylie. You get us the fairy camp and the Luview family to star in the show, and we'll hire you to manage the pilot. If it goes well–"

"Me?" she peeped.

"You're not an experienced showrunner, so I can't put you in charge, but I can make you assistant, and add you as an associate producer to the credits. That's *if* the pilot does well. You said you're a local in Love You. Use your connections. Pull strings. Cash in favors. Get the Luview family to agree to our crew filming the creation of this fairy camp, and you've got a job with us."

"A job?"

"A *contingent* job offer. You'd spend most of your time on-site, in Maine. If this takes off, you'll need to be here in New York for post-production. You have an eye for marketing, so..."

His words turned into blabber, thoughts racing. The job was contingent on getting LUKE to agree to let her film a FAIRY CAMP reality show for kids at his family's camp.

Their former childhood camp.

What had she done?

What

Had

She

Done?

The next ten minutes mostly involved people looking at their phones as Manu and Elsa nattered on about the details, Kylie's head turning into a giant gong being struck every second. By the time she was shaking their hands and leaving, her face hurt from smiling, the muscles in the back of her neck tight and screaming.

She wanted a drink.

She wanted a massage.

She needed a hot tub to soak in.

But what she couldn't have was the one thing she needed most, personally and, now, professionally.

Luke.

Stumbling down the hall, she pressed the elevator button like she was borrowing someone else's hand, heart racing, finger like clay. When the doors opened, she was relieved to find no one else in the car.

As the elevator made its descent, she held her breath.

Streets in New York smell like old oil, gasoline, and urine, but it was December 28, so add melting piles of old snow to the mix. A deep breath of fresh air made her gag.

This was not home.

Home wasn't the city anymore.

Her hotel was, fortunately, only a few blocks away, her luck at finding a place close on KidzdocTV's dime a relief. By the time she made it to her hotel room, she barely had the energy to plop down on the bed, let her mind race until it slowed down enough to cry, and breathe.

Not in that order.

The skin under her eyes felt like burlap by the time she was done, her tongue stuck to the roof of her mouth, suit horribly wrinkled by laying there, staring into space and crying.

She did it.

She got her chance.

And it relied on Luke.

The man who had just rejected her with breathtaking clarity.

How could she ask him for this? How could she go to him and pitch a television series based at his camp? Luke was deeply private. Overprotective. Defensive of Harriet, he'd never, ever let a crew invade his new compound to film Kylie's series.

The universe was sending her a big, flashing, red neon sign.

This is not your path.

The thought made her sob harder.

"What do I *want?*" she moaned, knowing the answer because an image of Luke hit her hard, fingers going to the charm around her neck, the one she'd stared at in the mirror for three days straight.

He'd given her a handmade symbol of their past.

She'd given him a handmade symbol of his heart.

A heart she had no claim to now.

Now that she'd gone and blown it.

"Why did I come here?" she moaned into the pillow, the big, fluffy, cushy pillow that reminded her why she adored hotels. No pillow at home felt like this. Hotel room decorators had some magic she didn't possess when she was shopping in the housewares department.

"Why did I hide it from him? He told me he loves me. Loved me. What am I doing?" Her last words had a gritty feel to them, her throat raw.

I love you, he'd said.

And her reply? She might as well have kneecapped him.

She'd stumbled back to her car on Christmas night, alone, and texted Deanna and Luke her thanks for a wonderful evening, trying not to make the words sound snarky to Luke.

The next day, he'd texted her back, telling her the hours for Harriet as she transitioned out of her work. From now on, she'd pick Harriet up at Colleen's house and take her back to Luke's, and someone from his family would come at the end of her shift to take over.

He was shutting her out. Even doing a hand-off of Harriet was too much contact for him. She felt abruptly cut out of his life.

Just like Perry.

That night at Mountain Dragon, when she'd run into Colleen, loomed large in her memory. His sister was right.

Kylie had hurt Luke.

And it hurt her so much to know she'd done that.

Her phone buzzed.

It was probably Wendy. She'd sent an SOS text to her, but it was three a.m. in France, so...

But no.

It was her landlord.

Hi Kylie. Perry never sent his half of the rent for December, so

I'll need you to pay that and the remaining months in full going forward. I contacted him and his phone number is someone else's now. FYI.

"You have GOT to be kidding me!" she screamed. Life piled on, didn't it? No job, no Luke, and now... this?

Perry was the gift that just kept on giving.

Giving her nothing but grief.

Another text buzzed.

"What's next? Someone stole my debit card and cleaned out my bank account? Lightning struck my apartment building and burned it down?" she muttered as she looked at her phone screen.

It was Rachel.

How was the interview? she asked.

Instead of texting back, Kylie impulsively hit Audio on her phone, initiating a phone call.

"Kylie?" Rachel must have her as a contact. "What's going on?"

Kylie sobbed before she could form words.

"Kylie!" Rachel shouted into the phone. "Do you need 911?"

"No!" she choked out. "I need a friend."

"Oh, honey. Of course. I'm here. What can I do?"

"Just–just–just–" Kylie didn't know what to say. All she could do was cry.

"Let me guess. You spent the last month living in two different worlds, too afraid to believe that what you have with Luke is true and good and real, still scared after being dumped by Perry, and now the job of your dreams is being dangled in front of you but all you really want to do is come back to Luview and be with Luke."

Kylie stared at the phone like it was a talking walrus.

"Hello? Kylie? You there?"

"How did you crawl into my head?"

A knowing chuckle filled the phone. "Because I was in a similar place last year. You know the story. I had the big acquisition project here in Luview, for the chocolate company."

"I do. I mentioned you in my interview."

"Me? Why? I have nothing to do with children's television!"

"Long story." Sniffles interrupted her crying. "So you get it."

"I do. It's not exactly the same, though—I didn't grow up here, like you did."

"I was there until I was fifteen. I didn't want to leave! My mom made me. Life could have been so different if we hadn't moved!"

"Sure. But you did. And Luke married Amber, and Amber died." Rachel's words were firm. Clear. Like someone took a box cutter and sliced them in clean, straight lines. "Luke has a past. You have a past. You both have pain from that past. And you have goals."

"Yes."

"Goals that Perry screwed up."

"YES!"

"But Luke isn't Perry, Kylie. And you're not the same person who left the city and moved up here with him nearly a year ago."

"No. I'm not. You're right."

"I'm not telling you what to do. I swear, even though I'd love to have a smart, funny friend up here. Someone in the family."

"For someone trying not to be biased, you're failing horribly."

More laughter, this time low, with meaning.

"I adore Kell. It wasn't always that way."

"I heard you got attached to him immediately," she cracked.

"Hah!" She took a beat, then two, before replying. "In your shoes, with an offer on the table for your big break..."

"That's just it, Rachel. It's worse than an offer. They want me to be assistant producer and coordinator for a reality TV show about a fairy camp in Love You, Maine."

Silence.

Dead silence.

"They *what?*" Rachel croaked. "How did *that* happen?"

"It's another long story."

"I'll bet. You must have some creative acumen to pull *that* off in a job interview! Wow—you're in a double predicament. You need the very guy who dumped you—"

"He didn't just dump me! He *fired* me!"

Heart speeding up, she felt the room tilt, felt the blood in her legs pumping around bone, a feeling of doom washing over her.

No.

Oh, no.

Kylie hadn't had a panic attack since that night in the donation bin, and there was no one here to rescue her.

The thought made her freeze.

"Kylie?" Rachel's voice sounded like she was talking through an empty cardboard tube. "What's wrong?"

"Panic."

"Panic?"

A deep, hot flush took over both arms from elbows to fingertips.

There was a knock on the hotel room door.

Kylie shouted, "I don't need housekeeping!"

Tap tap tap

"I'm having a panic attack, Rachel. Please don't hang up. Stay on the line."

"Of course! How can I help?"

"I need to breathe."

"Okay, Kylie. Breathe. Just breathe. You're fine. You're going to be fine."

BANG! BANG! BANG!

"Hang on, Rachel. There's a maid at the door." Words were hard, like she was juggling a mouthful of coins around her tongue.

"Okay."

Kylie walked to the door, flipped the bolt, opened it–

And quickly realized the maid was none other than Luke Luview.

Here.

In New York City.

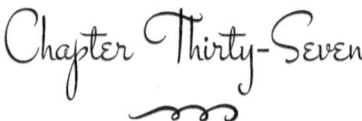

Chapter Thirty-Seven

Luke

"Luke!" she gasped, holding her phone to her ear, mouth dropping open. The skin around her eyes was red and puffy, melted mascara along the bottom lids.

She'd been crying.

He was sure it was all his fault.

"Hi."

Something was off, though, worse than just crying. Those green eyes looked too dark. Her pupils were dilated and she kept licking her lips, blinking rapidly.

"What's wrong, Kylie?"

"Um... everything. Luke?"

The squeak at the end of her words, followed by a breathlessness that tapped into something primeval in him, made him move, stepping into the room without being invited.

Because she was in *distress*.

"Kylie? Why are you saying Luke's name?" said someone from the phone in her hand.

"Uh," Kylie said, staring at the phone like it was a poisonous snake.

Taking command of the situation, he slipped the phone from her grip, looked at the contact information, and said into it, "This is Luke. I'm here now. I'll take care of her. Bye, Rachel."

Hitting End, he tossed the phone on the bed behind her, then leaned against the door jamb, crossing his arms over his chest. Being defensive wasn't going to help anyone, but if he didn't contain his hands, he was going to touch her. Hold her. Hug her. Kiss her.

And there were words to say first.

"You're having a panic attack."

She nodded.

"Breathe, Kylie. Breathe."

The rules were different now, after what he'd done on Christmas. Grabbing her hands, looking her in the eye, talking her through this, wouldn't work if she hated him.

And she had every right to hate him.

The panic attack started before he arrived, though. Why? What had happened to her?

The lines of her throat moved as she swallowed, then he watched as she gulped air. Face twisting in sadness, she began to cry. That's when he broke his own code.

And pulled her into his arms.

Sobbing, she buried her face in his chest and gulped air, his hand on her back tracing circles, presence the only way to soothe her. All his stupidity came roaring through him as he flashed back on the time since he'd found her in that donation bin at Deke's Service Station.

All his missteps.

Slowly, laboriously, her crying wound down, muscles softening, chest rising and falling in a steadier rhythm.

"That's more like it," he whispered into her hair, loose around her ears. She smelled so good. So warm and lush.

So perfect.

And then she pulled away.

"What are you doing here? Here? *Here!* Here in Manhattan!" she demanded, eyes red and puffy, voice shaking but determined.

"Had a hankering for a foot-long hot dog from one of those stands in Times Square. Thought I'd drop by while I was here."

"LUKE!"

Charming her wasn't going to work. Got it. Time to be direct.

And own his mistake.

"I'm here because I'm a dumbass. Colleen says so, but I knew it before she lectured me."

"Colleen *what?*"

"Not that she ever misses a chance to call me a dumbass whenever possible, but this time she's right. Really right. I was wrong, Kylie. *Wrong.*"

"Wrong about what?"

"Everything."

"I don't understand."

"Neither do I, but I'm going to try to undo the damage I've done, if you'll hear me out."

"Hear you out?"

"May I come in?"

"Of course!" Stepping aside, she pressed her back against the wall, one hand holding her other arm in a nervous gesture that made her look so confused and lost, he wanted to sweep her into his arms and hold her forever.

Except that's not what would happen.

He couldn't just hold her and make this all better. If only.

And before he could even entertain the thought of more, he had some wrongs to right. It was all on him.

The room was tiny, like most New York City hotels, but there was the bed and a single desk chair. He took the chair, his thighs aching as he settled in. Driving straight from Maine to New York with only one pit stop had been hard on his legs, but harder on his heart.

Hours alone in the car with nothing but the radio or conscience to keep him busy meant he'd been hammered hard by his own inner critic. In the heat of the moment on Christmas, he'd put up an instant wall, reinforced by a layer of pain, and it had been deeply unfair to her. He saw that now.

If she rejected him, he wasn't sure how he'd survive.

So he had to make this *good*.

She sat down on the bed, anxious, eyes darting everywhere.

"Kylie, on Christmas, I–"

The sun caught the silver pendant around her neck, a lump forming in his throat, emotion all over the place, suddenly pouring through the space that his logical, moral mind had just dominated.

She was wearing his present.

There was plenty of room for hope.

"–I was hasty. I told you I loved you, and I meant it. I do. I love you. And then I hurt you."

"I hurt you too, Luke! I never meant to, but I did."

He stood, legs aching, and gently pressed his fingertips over her lips, sitting next to her on the bed, his weight shifting her toward him, the heat of her body making this harder.

Because he knew he had no right to expect her to forgive him.

"*Shhh*. Let me finish. When a man apologizes, he needs to do it in full, go through all the layers, and say his piece. I refuse to do this halfway, Kylie. It's all or nothing with me, and I'll give you nothing less than my all."

Something flickered in her eyes, a gravity that clicked into place, one that took him in on a deeper level.

"Go ahead."

"I was afraid. Terrified. It was three days ago, but it feels like ten years. When I said I love you and your response was about leaving, it felt like you jumped up and down on my heart in spiked shoes." One corner of his mouth crooked up. "Like the goat on the Bilbee's Tavern sign."

She didn't laugh.

"You didn't know I was going to tell you how I feel about you, and I didn't know how important this job offer was to you. *Is* to you," he stressed.

Kylie opened her mouth to say something, but shut it quickly.

"Do you have any idea how grateful I am for everything you've done for me and Harriet, Kylie? How much I admire you? Even if you decide you don't want me in your life, I'll always have that. You came out of nowhere, tucked away in that metal charity box, and changed my whole life. Smiling and nothing but sunshine at my door the next day, holding a basket full of muffins, walking into my house and giving it so much light. You brought happiness and smiles back into our lives. You make it easy to come home from a hard day at work. We talk about life, and not just responsibilities. I want to date you. Hang out at Bilbee's with you. Take you out, treat you to everything you want in life. Every moment I'm with you, I feel a sense of hope again. Do you have any idea how special you are to me?"

"That's just me being... me," she replied, shaking her head like she didn't understand.

"Exactly." His soft laugh made her smile as he stared at her. "I'm grateful for you, Kylie. Who you are. How you are. Every drop of your being. Because you make me remember what being whole is like."

She sighed. "Which means that when you told me you loved me, and I told you about this – " She gestured to the window, where neon lights looked like abstract art behind the sheer curtains, Manhattan's skyline diffuse but looming.

"I flipped out. You're right–I used Harriet as an excuse. Not that there isn't some truth to what I said–she absolutely has to have that pure little heart protected."

"Of course!" Tears filled her eyes. "I would never, *ever* hurt her," she whispered furiously.

His fingers interlaced with hers. "I know."

"Good." She stared deeply into his eyes and took a deep, determined breath. "You're a package deal. I know that."

"Yes, we are. It's not just me. You get that. If we're doing this, you have to accept my daughter, too."

"Accept? Have to? You make it sound like something I do reluctantly. I wholeheartedly embrace her! I love her! And you. I feel honored to have life give me so much, Luke. What did I do to deserve such an incredible man and a wonderful child? Why me?"

Her words, *why me*, hit like a gut punch. The idea of starting over with a new woman had always been complicated by Harriet, because he'd never, *ever* compromise when it came to his child. He'd rather live a lonely, sad life than have any woman he brought into his home treat her like a burden, a third wheel, a nuisance. His little girl deserved a mother-figure who would open up her whole, entire heart and let Harriet snuggle right on in.

And here was Kylie, saying everything he assumed he'd never hear.

But desperately hoped for.

"After Amber died, I wondered: Why me? Pity party, right? But who am I to escape bad events? Everyone has problems, some of them bigger than others. Why *not* me? Having my wife die in an accident like that was random bad luck. I know that now. But I went through an awfully long time wondering *why me*. And at one point, I convinced myself I must not be good enough."

"Good enough for what?"

Hand shaking, he raked his hair, wondering if it was safe to be this vulnerable, yet feeling like he had no choice. For two years, he'd locked a piece of himself away, walled it off, boxed himself in, thinking that was the best way to give Harriet what she needed and get through the day.

Finding Kylie trapped in a box had freed him from his own.

"Good enough to be happy. To be loved. To be–"

She cut him off with a kiss, her mouth on his with a softness, tears wet on her cheeks as he reached up to hold her closer, their salty taste so real, so authentic. Emotion filled their mouths, tongues moving with grace and hope, his blood racing, warming as her hands encircled his waist, turning toward each other for more.

He broke the kiss.

"I'll move here. I'll find a job. Harriet would love the excitement of the city."

"Luke, stop."

"I mean it, Kylie. It'll take time. Or we could do that long-distance relationship thing, where you come up on weekends and we spend summers and school breaks in the city. I don't know." He shoved his fingers, hard, into his hairline, rubbing his scalp like he was willing blood to flow to his brain, to give him some new idea he hadn't thought of.

"It's not that simple."

Hope rose, and hope plummeted.

"Can't it be? What's wrong with simple?"

"I can't have you move here."

Confused, he watched her for signals, the mixed message harder with each passing second. "What do you mean?"

"I mean–I do have a job offer. Sort of. That all depends on you."

"Me?"

"It's, uh... complicated. But basically, they want me to come on board and manage a new reality show for kids."

"You *did* get the job!"

"I–well, it depends on whether you're willing to have a TV crew come to Luview and film the creation of a fairy camp at your new home."

Without question, those were the last words he ever expected out of her mouth.

"Could–could you explain that again? I don't think I heard you right."

"Oh, you did. I mentioned that I'm from Luview, and somehow we started talking about fairies–"

"Somehow," he said dryly.

She swatted him. "And it went from there. They loved the idea of a documentary series about the creation of a fairy camp in rural Maine, one near Love You. And when they learned I knew the Luview family... If – if –" Nerves made her stutter. "If I could convince you to–"

"Yes."

"What?"

"Whatever you want, yes. Yes to everything."

"You don't even know what I was about to ask!"

"Doesn't matter. Don't care. Yes."

"They want me to help produce a reality TV show in Luview."

"Like, Portia Starman's show?"

"A children's show about a fairy camp in Love You, Maine, the love-liest town on Earth."

"If it means you'll forgive me and we can be together, they can film a monster truck rally with ferrets driving the trucks while Lucinda Armistead pours chocolate all over them, for all I care."

"Luke!" To his surprise, she pulled out of his arms and stood, walking to the far end of the tiny room, then turning back, facing him with steely determination. "I have something else to say."

"Okay."

Her throat jumped with emotion, nostrils widening as she took in a deep breath, looked him straight in the eye, and said, "I love you, too."

"Didn't have to say it from across the room."

"I had to say it, though. I've been kicking myself for not responding in kind on Christmas."

"You had your own words to tell me."

"I did. And I'm a dumbass, too. Nothing about that conversation went the way I wanted it to."

"And here we are, in New York City, telling each other we're in love."

"I'm in love with you again, Luke. Again, or still. I don't think I ever stopped loving you, since that day we kissed on the pier."

Four steps. That's all it took to kiss her again.

And this time, there was no way he was stopping at just kissing.

Perfect moments never seemed to come the way he expected. This was another one. The kiss was timeless, her mouth a sanctuary, their touch more than a promise.

It was a vow.

Chapter Thirty-Eight

Kylie

For so many years, she'd imagined this moment, wondering how it would feel to be undressed by Luke Luview, his fingers working her shirt buttons, his mouth on hers, his hands seeking her, touching her, exploring her.

Knowing her.

How many nights had her breathless younger self imagined Luke finding her in Rio, Indiana, proclaiming his love, and sweeping her off her feet, the two of them stealing away to an imaginary paradise where they would live together in bliss?

Her fifteen-year-old self had never gotten beyond that part, because back then, it had been enough.

And it had been too silly for words.

Except now, it wasn't, and the words *I love you* had been shared. Luke had come all the way from Maine to New York City. Had found her hotel, her room, her soul.

And here he was, claiming her, bare skin getting barer by the minute.

"You're here," she murmured as she kissed his collarbone, his hands pushing her shirt off her shoulders, his sigh deep and hushed.

"I am. Forever, this time. Whatever I have of forever is yours, Kylie. I still believe in forever, even if it doesn't always believe in me."

The painful reminder of Amber didn't bother her one bit. It was part of who he was, and she accepted it.

Looking up, she took his face in her hands, eyes locking on his. "I'm here, Luke. I am yours. I want forever with you, too. That's all we can hope for."

"That's more than I ever dreamed." He looked down at her, one hand caressing her along her ribs until she gasped, body turned electric by his touch. "Do you have any idea how much I've wanted you, Kylie, since the moment you came back? Maybe even before? I wrote off the idea that I would ever find love again. I didn't think it was fair to ask the universe to send me another soulmate. Who gets to have such extraordinary love twice?"

"You do, Luke. Because you have an enormous capacity for love. It's not finite. You have so much love in your life because you give so much love to others. You grow it inside you. You spread it like wildflower seeds. There is more beauty in the world because of how you love people."

"Then you are the most beautiful woman in the world, Kylie, because I love you so, so very much. Let me make love with you, right here, right now. Please be with me. You've given me so much. Somehow, you dug deep inside me, found all the broken pieces of my heart, and you glued them together with glitter-filled muffin frosting and it started beating again."

Kylie laughed softly, her eyes welling with happy tears.

"That's quite a vision."

He took her hand and placed it on his bare skin, right over his heart.

"Touch me, Kylie. Be with me. I want to be close to you. Want to make you feel as good as you make me feel."

His mouth found hers, hungry and wanting, and she stood on tiptoe to match his urgency. All their words had said what their minds needed to hear, but now it was the body, the heart, the soul that needed to know, and that could only come from touch. Kisses. Caresses.

Invitations to enter.

Entering Luke's life had been an accident, but entering his heart was fate.

Now, she would invite him inside her, too, as his tongue flicked the line of her teeth, his lips lush and warm against hers, his hand on her breast, the sharp inhale of pleasure making her body shift into a warm glow.

As they kissed, he moved his hands to her button and zipper, her clothes falling off her as if by magic, though she knew damn well it was a very human series of motions causing them to stand before each other in underclothes, Luke's erection hard and alluring as he pulled her closer, the length of him finding her in the right spot as friction made her gasp and tense, her core pulling up with pleasure.

"You are so beautiful," he murmured in her ear as he reached down and freed himself, his boxers flung to one side, her panties off in seconds, bra unclasped and turned into simple strings that Luke tossed onto a chair.

Completely naked, they found each other's warmth, her body shouting *yes, yes, yes!*

"Finally," she whispered as the city lights made a gauzy, unfocused color show behind him, the thin white curtains a screen.

"Yes," he said before kissing her again. "Finally."

They moved to the bed, Kylie more comfortable with him than she'd ever been with a man, the familiarity so visceral. Simple. It felt as if they'd been like this a thousand times before, though the novelty of their newness was there, too.

As he stretched out on the bed, his head propped up by one hand, the smile he gave her was so sexy, so perfect. Her skin tingled with anticipation and she needed him, body begging for him inside her.

But first things first.

"Luke," she said, holding back from his embrace, staring deep into his eyes. "I have something to say."

He nodded, face suddenly serious.

"Go ahead."

"I'm in this forever. For real. I will come back to Maine with you. But I can't come back and *depend* on you."

"You can always depend on me!"

"Not–not the way I mean. I can't be in a relationship with you and be employed by you."

"Oh."

"It's too much. I'll need to find my own place. A job outside of being Harriet's nanny. I'll always help out, of course. But–"

"I understand. You want to keep the roles separate."

"Yes." Relief washed over her as he stroked her arm, the smile returning to his face as she continued. "And I have a job offer in front of me."

"You said. And I told you I'd move here, Kylie. We'll figure it all out."

"Luview is your home. Harriet's home. And it's my home, too. All these years, I tried to act like it wasn't, but coming back has been so wonderful. No place else compares."

"Whatever you want, you've got it. As long as we're together. That's all that matters to me." His kiss silenced whatever she was going to say next, their bodies moving against each other with a tenderness that turned to a flame.

He smoothed his hands along her legs, drifting his fingers up her thighs and along her belly, the hard ridge of his erection pressing into her hip from where he lay next to her. A hot and slow tingle made her skin flush, her nipples harden, and the insides of her thighs tremble.

Her eyes captured his, her soul reflected in his gaze. She couldn't look away. Couldn't blink. Couldn't stop.

Wouldn't stop.

Kylie could lose herself in Luke so easily, precisely because he wouldn't let her. She'd never be lost with him.

Their love had found a way.

Luke's sandy blond hair felt like cornsilk between her fingers, his scent a mix of cologne and sweat, his skin salty as she kissed his shoulder, then buried her face in his neck, her hand moving down to boldly stroke the long line of his torso, ridged muscle strong and flat. No sound invaded their lovemaking save for the city noise, muted and simple, a reminder of society outside.

And of the sanctuary they created between the two of them. Her body was alive and hard and full, and the sensations were overwhelming.

Nothing existed outside the two of them. Not her past, not her future, not a single thought, except the exquisite pleasure of his hands and his mouth and his body.

He kissed her, and she knew she was alive.

He touched her, and she knew she was special.

His hands on her breasts were almost an out-of-body experience.

And when he stroked her between her legs, she forgot her own name.

"It's–it's been two years, Kylie," he said in a rough voice, one that spoke of loneliness. She jolted in surprise, her hand stopping.

"Two years?"

"Since... yes."

"You dated, right?"

"Damn it. I'm sorry. This is the worst possible time for this conversation. I'm an idiot. Gorgeous, naked woman I'm in love with in bed with me, and all I can do is interrupt with the least appropriate comment anyone could ever say. Forgive me." The vibration of his groan made her laugh, her hand on his ribs feeling his mix of emotions.

"Nothing to forgive, Luke. This is a safe space. Safe in every way. I want the real you. I want to be the real me with you. If you want to talk about parking tickets, go ahead. If I want to talk about how pineapple belongs on pizza, I can."

"Hold on now," he said in mock horror. "I think we found our deal breaker."

"Pineapple, banana peppers, and glitter."

"I would eat edible glitter on a pizza before I'd eat pineapple."

"I'm going to take you up on that."

"You said that to make me stop feeling like a fool, didn't you?"

"You're not a fool," she said softly, kissing one cheek, then the other, admiring his strong face in the shadows from the city lights. "You're a very self-contained man who finally has some space to unravel a little. Unclench. Reveal yourself. I'm honored to be the woman you've chosen to give that to."

"Give?"

"Yes—give. It's a gift to be trusted the way you're trusting me. I'm honored. I get to see aspects of you no one else does. It's a secret between us. Do you know how special that makes me feel?"

"You are special, Kylie. I've never met anyone like you. Probably why I was so drawn to you when we were young. You see the world through a happy lens. You see the good in people. You see the good in the world."

"So do you."

"I did. I do, in Harriet. I do, in my family. Not so much in my job," he said, stroking her hair. "And I certainly see it in you. I can't—I can't bear to lose you, Kylie. I'm taking a big chance with my heart here."

"I know."

"And here I go again, babbling."

"Stop. *Stop*," she urged him, his eyes conflicted as she pressed her hand against his abs. "Stop downplaying talking about your feelings. You're allowed to have them. Allowed to express them. Allowed to be whole." As she leaned in for a kiss, he moved on top of her, broad shoulders so strong under her touch, the weight of him breathtaking, making her pulse quicken.

"I'm whole with you," he murmured into her ear.

"Let's be whole together," she said as she rested her fingertips on his mouth, Luke pulling her index finger in, sucking on it until she gasped and pulled it away as he moved to kiss one shoulder, then the other, fifteen years folding in seconds, like their bodies together, his kisses brushing her nipples, Luke sucking one into his mouth, making her arch up.

"You have no idea what you do to me when you make that sound in your throat, Kylie. Knowing I made you make that sound is even better."

"Luke," she whimpered, surprised by her own reaction. "I want you in me."

"Already?"

"Can we? Now? We have all night, right? I can't explain it. There's just—" Her voice thickened with tears. "I need you."

"Of course. Thought you'd never ask."

"I'm on the pill," she whispered. "And it's been a while for me, too."

"Then come here, Kylie. Let me love you a new way. Let me love you all the ways I can."

As she parted her legs he surprised her, pulling her up over him, straddling his hot, strong body, his hands gripping her hips, eyes utterly focused on her, appreciative expression making her feel more sensual than ever before. A shift, a hip rotated just right, and then he was in her, hands moving to her breasts, her shoulders going back as her hands found his chest, the free fall sensation of giving herself fully one she'd never felt before.

"You mesmerize me," he said into the night as he began slow strokes upward, Kylie bending down for a kiss, the motion making him hit a spot deep inside that turned her body into a flashpoint.

"You make me feel so special. So welcomed. You are my place in the world, Luke. You. Not the town. *You*."

"Wherever we are, as long as we're together, we're in the right place," he whispered, gently pushing her long hair off her face, moving with deeper thrusts as he closed his eyes, tensing slightly, Kylie's body reacting to his with intensity.

Their lovemaking was brief, blinding, and oh, so good as they came together, their kiss fast and heated, their climaxes a surrender to a love that took too long to be found, but was there all along.

As they both went still, Kylie collapsed on top of him, his breath in her ear, and she floated in a sweet, warm abyss, ageless and timeless, held in his arms.

Nothing was finer.

"Hey," he murmured in her ear, kissing the top of her head. "You okay?"

"I think I'm in another dimension."

"If you see any fairies, follow them back to me."

"I'll look for the glitter trail."

His chest bounced with laughter. "Now there's an image."

"I'll never get lost when I'm with you. Remember?"

"I remember."

He took in a long, shaky breath. "I was wrong, earlier. About soulmates."

Kylie froze. "You were?"

"Yes. I - I feel a connection to you I've never felt with anyone, *ever*. You're my one. It's so strong, and so good, and so — "

Kylie stopped him with a kiss that she felt with her whole heart, Luke's hands on her back, telling her without words this time, at home with his touch.

She rolled off him and curled against his side, looking through the opaque curtains, red, yellow, and blue light orbs filling the scene.

His stomach gurgled, hers following seconds later.

"Food," he said. "This place have room service?"

"Yes."

"Good. Because we're going to need it for the next day or two."

"Day or two?" she gasped. "You plan to keep me in this hotel room for that long?"

"We have a lot of catching up to do."

As she laughed, her stomach made a noise of protest again.

"Let me see if they have pineapple pizza with glitter," he said, stretching his arm over her head, pretending to reach for the phone.

"Hah! You order with the television remote."

His eyes paused on her, staring, before he said, "This is real."

"Yes."

"Really real."

"Mm hmm."

"Kylie Hood, I love you so, so much."

"Luke Luview, I love you, too."

"I hate my last name at times like this."

"It's quite the tongue twister."

He grinned at her, then dove under the sheet. "You order food with the remote while I do some tongue twisting..."

He was right.

This was definitely real.

* * *

The warm, thick bicep pressed against her cheek was the first clue that she wasn't at home.

The deep, definitely male voice that said "*mmmmmm*" as his hand cupped her hip was the second clue.

But when Luke's mouth spread into a grin before he nuzzled her neck and whispered, "Good morning, darling," she knew she wasn't dreaming.

Last night had happened.

For real.

A quick peek at her naked body against his made a *zing* of excitement shoot through her, mind still caught between fifteen years ago and now.

She was in bed with a boy.

No.

Oh, no.

He was *alllll* man.

A man who kissed her cheek, slid out from under the covers, pulled on boxers and walked over to the small coffee maker. Without asking, he made two cups of coffee in the double-shot machine.

As they brewed, he grabbed something from the nightstand, then walked to the large picture window and pulled back the curtains.

Bright light pierced the morning air.

Enormous billboards and skyscrapers dominated the view.

Luke pressed his palms against the wide glass windows, body strong and muscled, the ripple of his back making Kylie look.

And look.

And *look*.

Then she couldn't hold herself back any longer. She had to *touch*.

As she climbed out of bed, she grabbed his Henley shirt, a warm burgundy cotton weave sitting in a puddle next to the bed. It smelled like Luke as she pulled it over her head, then came up behind him, wrapping her arms around his bare waist and snuggling in.

"The view is amazing," he said, turning just enough for her to see he was wearing glasses.

"Oh!" she peeped. "You look so different!"

Fingering one stem, he laughed. "I'm half-blind without my contacts, and I had to take them out last night. I'll put them in so I go back to being me," he joked.

"No," she said. "You're you. You're always you."

He took the glasses off and kissed her, full and with heart, a surge of desire making Kylie want to drag him back to bed.

Instead, he wrapped her in his arms and faced her toward the city.

"So many people," she murmured.

"So much crime," he pointed out, frowning as she looked back at him.

"Once a cop, always a cop?"

"Something like that."

Luke's phone buzzed. He picked it up.

"Colleen's texting me." He tapped the screen and initiated a call, putting it on speakerphone as Kylie slipped back into bed, pulling the covers up, sipping her delicious cup of coffee.

"Luke?" Colleen said, appearing onscreen from her couch, her cat, Sandwich, nosing the screen. A tuxedo kitten, the bitty girl had a pink nose with a tiny mark on it, and big eyes.

"Who else would answer?" She gently moved Sandwich away as he asked, "How's Harriet?"

"She's fine."

"What's up?"

"Umm..."

He let out a low growl. Kylie knew instantly why Colleen was texting, and burst out laughing.

"The entire town has gone crazy with speculation about you two. They all know Luke went to New York to chase you down, and people keep driving by your house, Luke, looking for your Jeep."

"Of course."

Silence.

"Oh, for goodness sake, Colleen, spit it out."

"Was it yesterday or today? Because if it was today, I get my tires."

"And if it was yesterday? Who wins?"

"Annabeth Khouri."

Kylie scrambled across the bed and covered Luke's mouth with her hand, imploring him with a wide-eyed appeal.

"It *was* yesterday," she hissed.

He looked at the clock by the bed. "True."

"I do not want Annabeth winning that bet!"

"Why not?"

"Because she shouldn't benefit from our–*you know...*"

"I know all about our *you know,* and I want more *you know...* you know."

"Luke?" Colleen's voice came through the phone. "Kylie? You two realize I'm hearing every word."

Kylie and Luke winced.

"And as much as I want that money, fair is fair. If you two waited to schtup until after midnight–"

"*Schtup*?" Luke choked out at the word.

"Then I win. But if it was yesterday, then Annabeth wins." Her voice turned sly. "It's going to grind her up, Kylie, to take the money. Nadine bought her the spot in the betting pool anyhow. She wanted Luke, you know."

"Oh, yes. I know," Kylie said, touching Luke's thigh with a possession she thoroughly enjoyed.

"That time she showed up at my house with a box from Greta's, wearing a trench coat, high heels, and nothing else might have been a clue," Luke added.

"She did *that*?" Kylie and Colleen said in identical voices of outrage.

Suddenly, Luke wasn't making eye contact.

"We need more ice," he muttered, reaching for the ice bin.

"You're in your underwear," she reminded him, taking a moment to enjoy the view.

"Ew. Gross," Colleen said. "I think it's time to end this call."

"It was time to end this call before it started," Luke shot back.

"Annabeth it is, then," Colleen declared. "I'll let the town know."

Luke and Kylie groaned in unison. "Do you have to? Our sex life is no one else's business."

Deeply amused giggles poured forth from the phone's speaker.

"The entire town just wagered nearly five hundred dollars on your sex life, guys. You're in major denial."

"Bet's over, right?" Luke said into the phone, kissing Kylie's earlobe. She shivered.

"Yep!"

"And what we do is our business again, and no one else's?" he persisted.

Colleen practically brayed through the phone. "That has never worked for any soul who lives in Luview, Maine. You know that. Why?"

"Then let the gossips move on to another topic, sis," he said as his kisses grew more urgent, Kylie's body heating up in response. "Kylie and I are busy with another bet."

He ended the call and flung the phone under the bed.

"Bet? What bet?"

"I'll bet you I can make you..."

She shrieked, then gasped, then moaned as he did exactly what he promised.

Because that's what a Luview does.

They love you.

Epilogue

KYLIE

Four Months Later

"Harriet! Stop! What are you doing with all that glitter?" Luke shouted from across the room, Kylie wondering why on earth he was so upset. His voice rang out in the enormous room, the high ceilings carrying sound.

Once the old dining hall had area carpets, a pool table, the two large sectional sofas Luke had on order, and the foosball and ping-pong tables Kell was fixing up, leftover from when the place was a camp, it wouldn't echo so much.

"Yay!" Harriet said, giving Kylie a look before turning to her dad. "Fairy paint!"

Dismay filled Luke's face as he looked down at the five-gallon bucket of white paint, the pile of glitter slowly sinking into the center, like a shoe in quicksand.

"That's a lot of paint to ruin with glitter!"

"I think what you meant to say was, that's a lot of paint to make awesome using all that glitter!" Kylie corrected him, reaching for a stirring stick, beginning to blend it all.

"Huh?"

"You said we could paint the long hallway to the greenhouse

and the rooms for the fairy camp with whatever colors we wanted.

"Colors. Not glitter! It'll be walls of nothing but glitter!"

"EXACTLY!" Kylie and Harriet said, descending into giggles as they fist bumped each other.

Luke looked at the bucket. Looked down the hallway. Looked back at the bucket. Shaking his head, he breathed out through his nose, contemplating the situation.

Finally, he shrugged. "It's your fairy camp."

"That's right, Daddy," Harriet said, reaching for one of the long stir sticks, plunking it in the thick liquid hard enough to make some glop out on her hand. "Shocky and Griffy and Beezie need a shiny home."

Invoking Harriet's secret fairy name was a stroke of genius, the other two just fairies the little girl had invented. Since Luke and his family had truly begun to move in, the renovations were endless, every day off and most evenings spent fixing up the old camp. Kell and Rachel had already moved in, and Kylie had taken over his apartment above Bilbee's Tavern. Luke had pushed to have her move in with him and Harriet, but they'd agreed that going slow made sense, too.

One year, he'd agreed to. Just one.

Moments like this made Kylie wish she lived at the camp already. One more month and Luke's house on Clannagh would close, he and Harriet moving to the camp, giving up the only home Harriet had ever known.

And the only place where she remembered living with Amber.

Fortunately, Moore's nephew, Joey, was the buyer, and had offered to let them visit any time.

"I've got ninety more minutes before my shift starts," Luke declared, touching Kylie's shoulder. "Can I talk to you for a minute?"

Kylie eyed Harriet warily. "Can she be left alone to stir five gallons of paint?"

"I've got her." Kell walked into the room carrying a big bucket of spackle. "No problem." He frowned. "If you wanted glitter paint, why didn't you ask them to add it in at the hardware store? The spin machine can do it easily."

Kylie cleared her throat as Luke put his arm around her shoulders. "Because I didn't know we were doing it until Griffy and Beezie decided they couldn't live in a house without shiny walls, silly," she joked, making Kell laugh.

Luke guided her down the hall, into a living room area they'd created, right next to the dining table.

"I have to be at the library in two and a half hours," she said, realizing it was getting late already. "I'm taking Harriet, right? And your mom will get her after craft time?"

"Yep."

A week after Luke had come to New York and they'd gotten back together, KidzdocTV had offered her the job, surprising Kylie before she'd even put together the materials Manu had asked for. After careful consideration, and plenty of assurances from Luke that he would be happy with whatever choice she made, Kylie had felt free to choose what she felt in her heart:

A big, fat no.

Because the day before that job offer came in, another had been handed to her: children's librarian at Luview Library. It was a part-time gig, and not even close to being enough money to pay Kylie's basic bills, but she'd been lured in by Dotty Chen's confession:

Mrs. Chen planned to retire soon, and wanted Kylie to take over.

Between her part-time job at the library, and plans to open an actual fairy camp in the summer, Kylie was getting by.

And Luke made it abundantly clear that soon, he would propose. An engagement, marriage, and moving in with the Luview family at the camp were all in her future.

A future full of love.

"Hey," he said softly, pulling her close, the feel of his arms around her waist still sending tingles through her. Their kiss was warm and nice, gaining heat by the second, his hands cupping her ass as she pressed harder against him, her back against the wall now as his tongue told her how much he wanted her.

"Hey back," she said as they came up for air.

"Spending the night at my place tonight?" he asked, eyes hooded, gaze dropping to her mouth.

Over the last month, they'd decided to ease Harriet into life with Kylie as a mother figure, one she'd embraced instantly, telling anyone and everyone that Santa brought her a new mommy a little late, but that was okay.

"It's Saturday, right? That's the deal." To keep life consistent for Harriet, they'd decided on a schedule, regardless of work shifts. Because the library closed at six, Kylie could always be there.

And if Luke had to work, she just stayed with Harriet, who loved their "girls only" nights.

Jester excepted.

Another hot kiss made Kylie want to pull Luke into a spare room, rip his clothes off, and –

"GET A ROOM!" Colleen and Moore were suddenly there, both in painting clothes, Moore drinking a soda while Colleen typed on her phone.

"What are you two doing?"

"As little as possible," Moore said drolly. "And did I see *glitter* in that huge bucket of paint Harriet and Kell are stirring?" he asked Luke, who rubbed his chin.

"Don't ask."

"You realize it'll look way better if you sprinkle it on wet paint, instead of mixing it in?" Moore said to Kylie. "It's going to settle in that huge can. Better to mix smaller amounts so it's evenly distributed."

"You sound like an expert," she replied. Colleen's eyebrows went up.

"He should be. Painted houses for what – six years? High school and college?"

Moore's face hardened. "Yes."

"I thought you worked in your father's jewelry business your whole life."

"Nope. Not until I'd graduated college."

"Really? Why? You like painting?"

Something protective came out in Colleen's tone as she jumped in and said, "Moore did whatever he needed to do to support his family when he and Cammie had Jordy," Colleen explained, Moore frowning and blinking hard as she spoke. "Mike Hostettler hired him to paint back then."

Kylie knew there was a subtext she didn't understand.

Moore seemed to notice, catching her eye.

"When Cammie and I got pregnant, my dad told me I had to step up and be a man. Be independent. I wasn't allowed to work in the family business until I had a bachelor's degree. He and Mom cut me off financially. We were allowed to live in the basement apartment at home for free, but we were on our own otherwise."

"Oh, wow."

He shrugged. Luke was watching him closely, and Kylie could feel the past creeping into the present, the weight of their shared experience.

"So I painted. Went to community college, then transferred to USM and commuted."

"That's two hours each way!"

"Sure is. I was gone a lot from Jordy." Moore touched Colleen's shoulder. "And you saved my ass."

"I loved babysitting Jordy. Still do. Speaking of him, I'm texting now. We're playing League of Legends tonight, and he says he's coming for his extended spring break next week?"

Moore sighed. "He talks to you more than he talks to me."

"That's because I am so awesome," Colleen crowed.

The look Moore gave her made Kylie do a double take. The guy was Luke's best friend. Colleen was his sister. There was no way they would...

Nah.

"AAAAIIIIEEEEEEE!" Harriet's shriek cut through the air, Luke halfway down the hall before the rest of them began to run, his reflexes razor sharp.

"IT'S OKAY!" Kell boomed, his voice carrying down the hallway. "HARRIET'S FINE, BUT GRAB JESTER!"

"Jester?" Kylie gasped, as suddenly, she was knocked off her feet, falling on Moore, who fell on Colleen, the three of them like bowling pins being toppled by a ball.

A wet, dog-shaped ball.

"DADDDDYYY! JESTER RUINED IT!"

As Kylie sat up, her legs streaked with wet glitter paint, her elbow aching from her fall, she found her leg on top of poor Moore's torso, Colleen smashed under him.

"Arf!"

Jester was at the end of the hall, nothing but two eyeballs poking out from under a glittery white coat of wet paint.

Kell appeared as Jester turned to the right.

"Oh, no. Don't go in that door, Jester!" he shouted. "We just painted and set up the office!"

But the dog didn't listen, walking toward the office as Kell made a run for it.

Dogs think people chasing them are nothing but a game, so of course, Jester took off just as Kell reached the door, but suddenly, he slipped between Kell's legs, running at full speed back down to the end of the hall where Kylie, Moore, and Colleen were in the process of standing.

He stopped.

He panted.

And then he did what came naturally.

He shook.

Slow motion never happened in real time, but it did for Kylie, the long strands of honey-gold hair on the dog now sopping wet with glitter-infused white paint. It dropped in long waves on his body, and as he shook, the waves lifted up, viscous drops flying through the air in impressive arcs as she heard people shout, the aerodynamic propulsion of the liquid, and the *thwack* of it falling on her skin.

Her clothes.

Her hair.

And...

"JESTER!" she screamed as wet paint filled her mouth one drop at a time, the taste as horrifying as the feel. Because she was closest, she bore the brunt of the golden retriever's no-holds-barred, full-body shake off.

As Luke ran back, Harriet on his heels, he came to a screeching halt, bent down to grab Jester's collar, and looked up.

"Oh, Kylie," he said in a low voice.

Then he snickered.

"What happened?" she asked Harriet, who looked up at her and clapped her hands.

"You look just like I imagine Beezie does!"

"Beezie is coated in white glitter paint?" Colleen asked through uncontrolled laughter.

"And looks really pissed off?" Moore added as he wiped a glop of paint off his forearm.

Thumping footsteps made Kylie turn to her left to find Kell there, fingers threaded in his hair in frustration, eyes a bit wild.

"How many mops do we have here, Luke? He got the floor, but stayed off the couches, thankfully."

His eyes landed on Kylie and Kell burst out laughing, a deep, braying sound that made her anger pique.

"It's not funny!"

Colleen took her phone, reversed the camera, and showed her. "I beg to differ."

Seeing herself on the glass screen made her gasp. White paint ran in thick lines down her face, like she was melting. Much like a dappled mare, she looked like an assemblage of pieces, different colors jammed together, but her lips were glittery white. Light reflected off the glitter in the paint, giving her a luminous quality, as if someone were pranking a fairy.

She looked like a reverse Jackson Pollack painting.

An outraged one.

"Jester! Bad boy, Jester!" she snapped, holding her hands out, arms akimbo, trying to figure out what to do next.

He whined, shoulders hunching, tail dropping.

"Is that what you sound like when you're mad, Kylie?" asked a tiny voice, as Harriet hid behind Luke, who was still dropped to the ground, holding Jester's collar.

Harriet's words made Kylie feel awful.

"It's what I sound like when I am covered in glitter paint, sweetie."

"You sound way nicer than I would if Jester did that to me," Harriet replied. "I would yell so hard! You look awful!"

Now all the adults gave up trying to hold back, giggles, chuckles, and outright snorts dominating the air.

And then Jester shook himself again, spraying Luke, Colleen, Moore, and Harriet, squeals and shouts erupting.

"Hah!" Kylie called out. "Serves you right!"

And then, surrounded by the people she cared about most, they all laughed about the mess.

Because they'd gotten into it together, and she knew how they'd get out of it, too.

The same exact way.

Bonus Epilogue

KYLIE

After living in Luview, Maine her first fifteen years, then coming back and re-establishing roots here this last year and a half, Kylie was amazed that she could tell where she was on any given road in the mountains surrounding the small town just by *feel*.

Eyes closed as Luke drove, she imagined the turn off Route 113, then the slow right onto Old Auger Road, streetlights disappearing as corners faded away. In the city, you had lights illuminating roads and walkways everywhere, but out in the country they were for intersections.

If that.

Jolting suddenly, she realized Luke was taking her somewhere she had no desire to be.

Especially on a lovely date with the most wonderful man in the world.

"What are we doing here?" Kylie gasped as Luke pulled into the parking lot at Deke's Service Station and Breakfast Diner, a shiver running through her as ghosts from Thanksgiving Past rippled through her.

"You'll see," Luke said cryptically, making her whole body start to tingle. For the last year and a half, she'd carefully avoided going anywhere near Deke's, though some folks in Luview believed Deke's breakfast counter had the best home fries in the area.

Too much green pepper for her taste.

Plus the whole humiliation recall about how she'd gotten stuck in the charity donation bin in the parking lot.

"Luke! This is the last place on earth I want to go on a date with you!" she whined, knowing it was hopeless. For the last year and a half, she'd thoroughly enjoyed being Luke's girlfriend, and getting to know him deeply was her greatest joy. Bonding with Harriett, being accepted in town, and the warm welcome Deanna and Dean had given her, along with Kell and even Colleen, who'd finally thawed, meant Kylie felt like she belonged somewhere.

Luview wasn't just her hometown.

It was her lifeline.

"You'll regret those words," he said mildly, parking in the same spot he'd parked in that night a year and a half ago, dusk creeping into dark as the seconds ticked by. It was early May, so quite late in the day, his parents still watching Harriett. Kylie and Luke both had the next day off, so they got to stay out as late as they wanted. Plus, Luke was spending the night at her place, which meant sleeping in as late as they wanted, too.

"Why would I regret them?"

"You'll see."

Resorting to violence, she punched his shoulder lightly. "Quit saying that!"

As he opened his car door, Luke flashed her a grin that made her toes curl. The man could still do that to her, every time they caught each other's eye. Every single time.

Would it be the same way in ten years? Twenty?

Fifty?

Given the relationship his parents had, and how deeply in love Dean and Deanna still were after forty years, Kylie knew it was possible.

And oh, how that made her heart sing.

Scrambling out of the car before Luke could open her door, she marched up to him and tipped her chin high staring him down.

"Deke's isn't open. You promised me a dinner date!"

"I did."

The parking lot was bare, save for the broken down 1978

Camaro that was always parked near the shop, and a late-model Volvo that looked like it had hit a deer.

Or maybe a moose.

Had anyone seen Randy lately?

Jangling a set of keys on a caribiner clip hanging from his jeans loop, Luke unclicked it, went to the side door on the charity donation box, and began opening the padlock.

"What on earth are you doing?"

"You'll see," he said as the dark swallowed him whole, Luke shutting the door behind him. Faintly, through the metal, she heard, "Wait for my signal!"

Signal?

Luke was steady as can be. Stable. A rock. Sure, he had a great sense of humor and he could be mischievous with the rest of them, but this was *waaaay* out of character for him.

"Signal?" she called out as a truck filled with hay bales drove by, stray pieces of grass flying behind it like a cloud of gnats. "What signal?"

The front hatch opened, the creaky metal sound making her jump.

"This signal. Knock three times on the door and I'll let you in!" Luke called out. The creaky sound repeated itself, the front hatch slamming shut, and Kylie found herself staring at the little door, ready to scream.

Was this some kind of sick joke?

Instead of following Luke's ridiculous rules, she marched to the door, opened it, dipped her head down to enter, and braced herself for the rotten scent and disarray that came from these metal charity boxes.

She should know.

She'd stupidly trapped herself in one a year and a half ago.

But when she caught sight of the space, she gasped, reeling from surprise.

And from the amazing, mouth-watering scent that greeted her.

Because there sat Luke at a small table with two chairs, her amazing boyfriend resting in one of them, candlelight turning the metal container into a romantic bistro.

A breadbasket was at the table's center, a circle of six candles glowing beautifully. Two wine glasses glistened in the soft light, Luke slowly pouring wine from a bottle into both. Plates with what appeared to be salads with hearts of palm across the beds of lettuce were in front of each seat, and the soft sounds of music caught her ear.

"Luke!" she gasped, her voice shaky with emotion. "What is all this?"

"For you, Kylie. It's all for you. Come sit. Have our date."

"Date? We're having a date in here?"

"We are. I had it power-washed and sanitized. Blake and Shiela lent me the table, the candle holders, and they made the meal. Kell's experimental takeout from The Food Alchemist for his first date with Rachel turns out to be my gain," he said with a chuckle. "Come. Sit. Have a glass."

"You're crazy!"

"Maybe," he conceded as he took the stem of his wine glass and took a sip. "But this felt right."

"Felt right? For our date?"

An extraordinary expression fell across his face, even in the dim light. Luke was a serious man, the kind who said what he meant and expected others to do the same. A terrible liar, he had a moral core that made him talk things through, no matter what.

And reveal his hand.

As he took in a deep breath, she saw something else in him that didn't make sense.

Was Luke... nervous?

"Sit."

"I – "

"*Sit.*"

The command made more than her heart zing, as he used his voice of authority. Never one to abuse it, he used it only when needed.

Why did he need it now?

"Is something wrong?"

"Wrong? No. No. Kylie, something is very, very right," he said with a laugh that touched her so much she had to listen to his order.

She sat.

As he handed her a glass of wine, she tasted fruity tones, something lush and woodsy, and a few mouthfuls centered her, giving her the headspace to look around. The box was mercifully empty, save for a footstool, their table and chairs, and an increasingly handsome Luke, who just watched her.

"You are an enigma, aren't you?" she finally said, their wine glasses half empty by the time she found the right words. He reached for her hand and she realized the music came from his phone, which sat on the edge of the footstool.

"I'm not. I'm a simple man, actually."

"This isn't simple!"

"In a way, it is."

"How?"

Licking his lips, Luke took a big gulp, finishing his wine, then gave her a half smile that made her fall deeper for the man. Hand shaking, he ran it through his hair, the locks just long enough to show some wave.

Soulful eyes met hers and he asked, "What do you want first?"

"First? You mean you want to have sex in here?"

Boisterous laughter echoed in the small space, sounding tinny and loud at the same time.

"That's not quite what I was thinking, though if that's an option..."

"Then what were you thinking?"

"I'm really screwing this up, aren't I?"

"If you won't tell me what you're doing, Luke, I can't judge whether you're screwing it up or doing it magnificently!"

Luke frowned. "That standard doesn't seem to apply in bed."

"You magnificently screw me in bed!"

"This is why I want to spend the rest of my life with you."

Every molecule of Kylie's being held its breath, all at once, each cell in suspended animation, his words sinking in as Luke sank to one knee before her, the dim glow in the charity metal box making it feel warmer than it was.

Or maybe that was just her blood warming at the slow dawning of why Luke had gone to all this quirky trouble.

Was he – did he –

The velvet box appeared in his hand, Luke's thumb sliding up, the box with Love You Jeweler's emblazened into the velvet in tastefully small letters making her think of Luke's best friend, Moore.

Of summers spent jumping off the dock.

Of no-talent talent shows, campfires, field day contests, hikes, and summer fun.

Of the last year and a half spent at festivals with Luke's family, their friends, all the nights at Bilbee's.

Of being part of something bigger than herself.

"Oh!" she said in hushed tones, power building in her chest, her heart swelling with all of the emotion she felt for this man who looked up at her with grace and kindness, love and promise, the vastness of a life spent together a series of reflections in his eyes.

Come with me, those eyes invited. Let's walk the rest of this journey together.

Hand in hand. Hearts aligned.

"Kylie," he said softly, with meaning. "I found you in this god-forsaken charity box on a night that was filled with nothing but grief and pain for me. It was a time of letting go, of moving on, of literally sending off the material past by handing it off into the abyss of this box. That night, I was a different man. A broken man. One who held it together because I had to."

"For Harriet," she whispered.

"And for me," he added, his throat going tight. Kylie watched Luke close his eyes, take in a deep breath, and continue, the gravitas of the moment too intense for her to do anything but listen with her whole heart.

"For you," she replied. "of course. Because you matter."

"I do matter. I didn't realize it then, but the universe had other plans. I thought I was reluctantly moving on, using a ritual that felt like a clean break, but instead I found you, the cutest raccoon *ever*."

Tears filled her eyes as she laughed, the contradictory emotions feeling right at home inside her. If you couldn't feel more than one emotion at the same time as a man you loved was proposing, when could you?

"What a coincidence," she said, wiping under her eyes carefully, working hard not to look like an actual raccoon this time.

But the man was making it difficult. So many wonderful emotions swirled inside her.

"I don't think it was," he said, as he shook his head. "Call it fate. Call it spiritual. Call it whatever higher power you believe in. Call it a coincidence, but it was too perfect. I lost Amber. I was letting her go. Then I found you. Again."

"Again."

He cleared his throat. "And so, Kylie, I don't want to lose you. I want you all for myself. All mine, forever. Second chances are rare, and this one is even rarer. Will you make me the happiest man on earth by marrying me and Harriet? We're a package deal."

"I know," she said, her voice shaking, the words hard to form even if the emotions were crystal clear. "And yes, I will marry you, Harriet, and Jester!"

All she wanted in that moment was to kiss him, but Luke's steady command meant first things first as he pulled the beautiful marquis diamond ring from the jewelry box and slid it on her left ring finger.

It fit perfectly, as if it were custom designed for her.

"Moore had that custom-made for you," he said as if reading her mind. "Dumb luck that my best friend happens to be a jeweler," he said with a laugh that made her nearly levitate.

Their eyes met, and Luke moved closer, Kylie still sitting, his hands sliding into her loose hair, their mouths connecting as she kissed him with every fiber of her being, the Yes looping in her head over and over, her sense that all was right with the world growing stronger as he held her, their tongues playing with each other, the kiss deepening to a connection she didn't know was possible.

If it felt this good to be engaged, how much better would it feel when they were wed?

"Mrs. Kylie Luview," he said softly as they broke the kiss, Kylie jolting at his words.

"I – wow. Haven't thought of that name since I was fifteen and wrote it nine thousand times all over my notebooks."

"What?"

Her turn to laugh. "You seriously didn't know that?"

"Hell, no, I didn't. I had no idea. We were seventeen and fifteen?"

"Maybe I just knew."

He squeezed her hand, his gaze piercing her even deeper. "Seems like you did."

"Kylie Luview. Wow. That's... a lot."

"You don't have to take my name."

"I want to! I certainly did when I was younger. Everyone who isn't a Luview in this town wants to be one!""

"You do?"

"I – I feel like it's meant to be." She looked around, laughing as they both stood, the embrace warm and full, Luke's chin on her head, her arms around his shoulders, their hug a lifeline.

"Like finding you in here." He stroked her hair, need rising up inside her, her arousal swift and sudden, giving her another kind of clarity.

"Do you know what I want?" she asked, moving her left hand up his thigh, the metal ring unfamiliar but thrilling.

"I can take a very good guess by the way you're touching me there," he said in a low, passionate voice.

"How about we have dinner after."

"After... what?"

She gestured around the small box.

"You know."

"You want to... in here?"

"Why not?"

"Kylie Hood! You want to have sex in a metal donation box!" he said with faux outrage as his hand cupped her breast and he did something delicious to her nipple.

"It's kind of perfect," she said, holding back a moan as he kissed her neck. "No cell phone signal gets in here. No one will interrupt."

"And no dog will break into the room and nose my naked hip," Luke said bitterly.

"That only happened once. And boy, did you scare poor Jester with all that yelling!"

"Good!" He kissed her deeply, one hand going up her back, unclasping her bra like a pro. "Damn dog."

"And the yelling made Harriet come running and nearly get an eyeful."

"Can we please stop talking about Harriet and Jester and focus on us."

"Us?"

"Are we really doing this?" he asked in an amused voice. "It's not too weird to have sex in a metal donation bin?"

"Is it any weirder than finding your future wife in one?"

"I guess not." He laughed softly. "Confession time: I brought a camping mat just in case."

"Just in case – oh! Just in case I magically wanted to have sex in this bizarre little tin can?"

"Yep."

"You're always prepared."

"It's not just my job, ma'am – it's my personal credo."

She groaned and laughed at the same time, loving him even more as he pulled away, found the small mat, and set it down on the floor with a flourish.

"There are no kids in here. No dogs. No unexpected trees falling across state highways. No power outages. No police emergencies," she murmured. "Why, Mr. Luview, it's as if you planned the perfect proposal."

"More like I planned the perfect place to get laid."

"Then quit talking and start doing."

And so he did.

THE END

THANK YOU so much for reading this special bonus epilogue for Love You Again, featuring Luke and Kylie. I hope you've enjoyed all of the Love You, Maine books, but if you've missed any, please go back to my website and start with Love You Wrong, my FREE prequel (in eBook).

And if you've read all the Love You, Maine books but haven't tried my other books, here's where you start. Go to http://www.jkentauthor.com and click on "Books."

I have a LOT of books. You have LOTS of laughter and love coming your way.

<3

Julia

What's Next?

Thank you so much for reading *Love You Again*, book 2 in my Love You, Maine series, set in a small town in the mountains, where every day is Valentine's Day.

If you haven't already read book 1, *Love You Right*, head on back to Amazon and click it! Kell and Rachel's tale is a deep dive in "enemies to lovers" romance, and their free prequel, *Love You Wrong*, explains how they go to the point of squaring off.

There's so much more coming to you in this world! The next in the series, *Love You More*, features Colleen Luview and Moore Mottin (see what I did there with the title... ;)).

When two longtime friends get trapped in a snowstorm, can they overcome all the reasons not to sleep together... or will temptation be too great?

"Third Date Colleen" and twice-divorced-by-thirty Moore face the classic best friend's sister and friends-to-lovers situations as they discover that maybe - just maybe - they're not as cursed in love as they thought.

But the journey to figuring that out is a wild ride. <3

About the Author

New York Times and *USA Today* bestselling author Julia Kent writes romantic comedy with an edge. Since 2013, she has sold more than 2 million books, with 4 New York Times bestsellers and more than 21 appearances on the USA Today bestseller list. Her books have been translated into French, Italian, and German, with more titles releasing in the future.

From billionaires to BBWs to new adult rock stars, Julia finds a sensual, goofy joy in every contemporary romance she writes. Unlike Shannon from *Shopping for a Billionaire*, she did not meet her husband after dropping her phone in a men's room toilet (and he isn't a billionaire in a rom com).

She lives in New England with her husband and children in a household where everyone but Julia lacks the gene to change empty toilet paper rolls.

Join her newsletter at http://www.jkentauthor.com

Also by Julia Kent

Love You Wrong

Love You Right

Love You Again

Love You More

Love You Now

Shopping for a Billionaire: The Collection (Parts 1-5 in one bundle, 500 pages!)

Shopping for a Billionaire 1

Shopping for a Billionaire 2

Shopping for a Billionaire 3

Shopping for a Billionaire 4

Christmas Shopping for a Billionaire

Shopping for a Billionaire's Fiancée

Shopping for a CEO

Shopping for a Billionaire's Wife

Shopping for a CEO's Fiancée

Shopping for an Heir

Shopping for a Billionaire's Honeymoon

Shopping for a CEO's Wife

Shopping for a Billionaire's Baby

Shopping for a CEO's Honeymoon

Shopping for a Baby's First Christmas

Shopping for a CEO's Baby

Shopping for a Yankee Swap

Shopping for a Turkey

Shopping for a Highlander